Under an Open Sky

Book 3 of the
Scions of the Aegean C series

A novel by

Terry L. Craig

Wild Flower Press, Inc.
Leland, NC

Under an Open Sky

Book 3 of the Scions of the Aegean C series
Published by Wild Flower Press, Inc.
P O Box 2532
Leland, NC 28451

www.wildflowerpress.biz

Scripture quotations marked NLT are taken from the Holy Bible, New Living Translation, copyright 1996, 2004, 2007 by Tyndale House Foundation. Used by permission of Tyndale House Publishers, Inc., Carol Stream, Illinois 60188. All rights reserved

This is a work of fiction. Both the story and the characters are fictional.

Images on the cover used under license from istock.com

Paperback Version:

ISBN: 978-1-946549-04-4

Library of Congress Control Number: 2020945503

DEDICATION

To my sister JoJo: my childhood enemy
who became my sister in the Lord
and my dear friend.
I still miss her.

To my beloved husband, William.

ACKNOWLEDGEMENT

Thanks to Tonya Brown, my friend, fellow author, and sister
in the Lord, who put on her editor's hat for me.

Backstory

The People

In 2044, people of the Genon race—a peaceful agricultural people with a specialized skill for turning inhospitable terrain into verdant gardens were tasked as terraformers to transform the off-world settlement of New Hope. They expected to carry out their mission with little, if any, input from the soldiers who were to deliver them, then depart. Others on the mission—technicians, biologists, doctors, and engineers—were to remain in the colony for several years to observe and document Genon procedures, then return to Earth and share the knowledge gained for use in future settlements.

The Crash

The spacecraft, a BX-9 christened the Aegean C, left Earth on the mission but suffered catastrophic damage shortly after leaving Earth's atmosphere. The flight deck officers were killed when the ship crash landed on a shelf in a mountain range, not far from the equator. Miraculously, most of the passengers survived, but in the first hours after the crash, something became a source of growing concern: There were no signs of other human life on the planet. There were no responding radio transmissions, no visible roads or trails, no lights in the distance, no satellites moving through the night sky. And the night sky was not the one they knew. This was neither the place they left nor where they intended to go—they'd catapulted through time or space into a place unknown to any of them. They were determined to make a life in this new world that was as wild and dangerous as it was bountiful.

The "Firstlanders," as the survivors came to be called in later generations, soon realized that they were extremely fortunate to have landed on a plateau where the land was suitable for growing crops and the climate was moderate year-round. Had they crashed into the icy slopes above the plateau, many would have quickly succumbed to exposure. Had they landed in the vast jungle below the plateau, they would have died in the steaming tangle of toxic plants, poisonous insects, and huge predatory creatures. The plateau, which they named

Aegea, could be transformed into an oasis where future generations could remain. In less than two generations the spacecraft was almost completely dismantled so the metals and other materials could be repurposed.

The Rebellion

After the crash, there was a need for protection from predatory creatures and an honest concern about the possibility of attacks from an unseen enemy whose weapon may have caused the crash of their spaceship. Even if they wanted to go back to the world they left, the soldiers, scientists, and technicians had no means to do so, and their hope of rescue faded. Within a generation, most of the threats originally faced by the Firstlanders were gone, but the military leadership found continuing reasons to "protect" all of the civilians. The Genon, despite the fact that their efforts made long-term survival possible, became a race of laborers.

During the Second Generation after the crash, a few of the Genon Firstlanders led a revolt, demanding equality in status, assets, and living conditions. All who participated in the rebellion were rounded up along with their immediate family members while a tribunal was held. After much debate and a divided vote, the General of all Aegea signed an order. Each of the rebels would be forever banished.

The Exiles

The guilty, some with their small children, were taken down the mountainside, deep into the endless jungle that the military called "the Poison Forest," and abandoned there with no weapons or tools. They were told that any of them who attempted to return to the plateau by any means would be killed on sight. The Exiles quickly vanished and no one was ever certain what happened to them, although scattered stories of them, somehow living on in the jungle, became legends repeated among the Genon on the plateau.

Following Generations

By the third generation, the spaceship was nowhere in sight, and some began to claim an alternate history for Aegea. Leaders promoted the idea that the people had *always* been in

Aegea and that the military had always been in charge. The eyewitness accounts of the Firstlanders were derided as the fantasies of aging minds. Families from each segment of society hoarded the knowledge of any useful skill in order to keep from slipping further down in a system increasingly skewed in favor of the military and the professionals. The ways and means of life for the people of Aegea became a mix of early industrial technology and secret recipes.

In Book 1—The fifth generation after the crash

The aging leader of Aegea dies after selecting Jubal McClaren as his replacement. On that same day, one of McClaren's servants, Shaye Penway tries to escape a cruel punishment. She climbs into a large wooden crate believing she will be taken across the plateau to town, in hopes she will find someone who can intervene.

Also on that day, McClaren's daughter, Jariel, is abducted. Sedated, she's thrown into the same crate where Shaye hid, and the box is secretly transported to the Poison Forest, far below the plateau. The men who carried the box to the forest are killed by a giant creature, leaving Shaye and Jariel to wake up deep in the forest with the creature still on the prowl nearby. Descendants of the original Exiles come upon the scene and, in the belief that they are *rescuing* the two Genon women from some terrible fate, they take them further into the forest, away from Aegea.

In Book 2--Two women lose all hope of returning to life as they knew it.

As an orphan girl growing up, Shaye fantasized an escape of her life as a servant to live as a free and "upright" woman of faith among her people (perhaps even among the legendary Exiles in a place her people call the Great Forest or "the land of cloud and leaf"). But in her fantasy, she hadn't done things she'd sworn to never do. In her dreams, she wasn't an unwed mother, running to escape criminal charges for striking her master's daughter. In her dream world, there was no need to concoct a lie to protect her enemy from being slain. Now, she's lost certainty in herself and in her faith, and she is staggered by the realization that her nemesis may become her permanent responsibility.

Even though the forest where Jariel was abandoned by her kidnappers is filled with dangers, its vast beauty stirs her beyond anything she's ever known. In the middle of all these new experiences, she must come to terms with several facts: It was *soldiers*, not Genon people, who carried out her kidnapping and it was the *Exiles* who saved her from being killed by a jungle creature, and her very life now depends upon the servant she's tormented for years. As Jariel hears the Exile's version of Aegea's history, she's left to wonder which account is true.

The two young women are led through the perils of the jungle to the breathtaking beauty of homeplace, a settlement founded by the original Exiles on the shore of an ocean—something no one in Aegea has ever seen. They prepare to face a new life in the homeplace of the Exiles, certain that those they left behind will believe they are dead and life on the Aegean Plateau will continue without them.

The search for the missing women

After Shaye and Jariel vanish, an unprecedented reward for information is offered—but even the masterminds of the kidnapping have no idea where the young women are. As both sides search for clues, General McClaren's trackers find a gravely ill Exile in the jungle and secretly transport him to Aegea. If the man survives, he *may* be the key to finding out what happened to Jariel and Shaye.

List of Main Characters

Basil—of the line of Tosh, grandson of Old Menoh

Ben—one of the Exiles who discovered Shaye and Jariel

Canaan—of the line of Imm, an Exile found in the Poison Forest and secretly brought to Aegea

Chessie—a gleaner (the lowest status) of Aegea

David—one of the Exiles who discovered Shaye and Jariel

Dell—assistant to the inventor, Sage Dooley

Duana McClaren—Jubal McClaren's wife

Fiona—Old Menoh's wife

Francis (Flint) Hunter—resident bad boy of homeplace

Garam Manash (Sgt. Shocky)—the first Genon soldier in Aegea

Gwen—the former general's oldest daughter

Jariel McClaren—the only daughter of Jubal and Duana McClaren

Jubal McClaren—the General (and leader) of Aegea

Kosh—Son of Old Menoh

Lemon—former houseman and servant for Jubal McClaren

Menoh—"Old Menoh," a patriarch from the line of Tosh and Elder of the Genon workers in Westland

Mosely—Colonel Grayson Mosely the chief rival of Jubal McClaren for rulership of Aegea

Mosha—a cook in the service of Jubal McClaren for thirty years, now working for former general's daughter.

Nathan—an elder of the Genon Exiles in homeplace

Pearl—of the Penway family, a Great Aunt to Shaye

Peony—Nathan's wife (homeplace)

Outpost Family: John and Lilly—the innkeepers have four sons and three daughters—all of them are distant cousins of Shaye (through the family of Zim)

Sage Dooley—Chief inventor of Aegea

Samuel—"Mule," a stonecutter and builder among the Exiles from the line of Hoste, one of the men who found Shaye and Jariel in the forest

Shaye—daughter of Cpt. Frank Penway and his wife, Elle (a Genon of the family of Zim)

Ty—Tyrone McClaren, the only son of Jubal and Duana McClaren

Willow—Nathan's sister in (homeplace)

Locations on the Aegean Plateau (Aegea)

Oldtown—the location of the first settlement, now falling into decay and mostly populated by Genon workers

Midtown—west of Oldtown with finer homes for officers and upper class citizens

Waypoint—a small military checkpoint between Midtown and the Outpost

The Outpost—a small settlement in the central part of the Aegean plateau that began as an equipment repair station and a stable for horses. Eventually, an Inn was built there for officers who were traveling out west.

Westland—a military post on the far western end of the plateau. The Great House of Westland (belonging to Jubal McClaren is here).

Outside Aegea

The Poison Forest—the name the military first gave to the jungle below the Aegean Plateau, but known to the Genon people as the **Great Forest** or the **Land of Cloud and Leaf**

Homeplace—the home village of the Exiles on the shore of a great ocean.

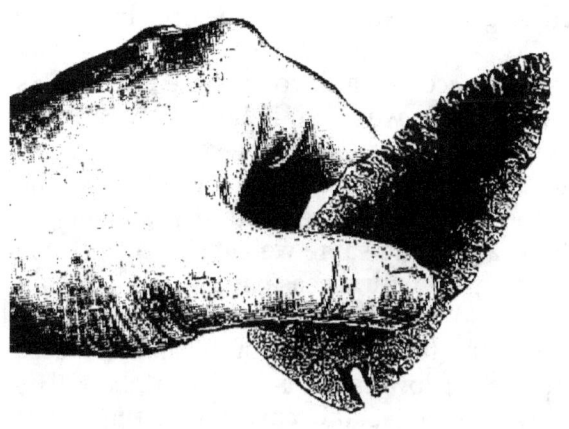

CHAPTER 1
The Evidence

The dark secrets we carry are like heavy stones. If we keep them, how can we hope to cross the deep water between here and eternity?—
A proverb of His own people

Never in the whole of his life could he have imagined being as cold as he's been here. Goosebumps harden on his legs, arms, chest, and neck. Shivering, he leans upon his caretaker—as much for warmth as for support.

He looks at the surrounding mountaintops and wonders, *One would think being so high up on the side of a mountain it would be hotter, because it's closer to the sun, isn't it? This makes no sense. At home, people would be seeking relief from the heat by this time of the day.*

When they first found him far below in the Great Forest, he was delirious from a raging fever. Realizing he was one of the Exiles they sought and knowing he would perish without skilled care, they sent word to the general who had him covertly transported thousands of feet above the steaming jungle to a secret location on the Aegean Plateau. Never had the general violated Aegea's laws like this before, but these were desperate times.

Two full moons have come and gone since the Exile's arrival. He still doesn't know when or if he will be able to escape and find his way back to the Great Forest.

He glances at the man helping him walk into the courtyard. Although the two of them are about the same height and would normally be about the same weight, his own feeble diet for the past year, coupled with disease, has made him thin and frail.

His dark, curly hair and baggy clothes flutter in the breeze and his teeth chatter as he lowers himself into a chair. His caretaker unfolds a wool blanket and covers him the way a mother might cover a child.

The blood of these people is surely different from mine— how else could they walk around in this cold air as if they were comfortable?

The other man hovers over him for a moment, then asks, "Do you need more blankets?"

After all this time, the only people he's met here are those who've watched over him throughout his illness and recovery: An old man by the name of Menoh, Basil (Menoh's grandson), and the man now watching over him. Menoh and his grandson are both Genon like him—but this man, Ty, has fair skin and strange, golden-red hair.

He shivers once more. "No. In a moment I will be fine."

"Then I will sit with you for a while."

It's still odd to hear Ty try to speak the Genon language. He has a stilted pronunciation and he's often at a loss to find the right words so he has to ask the old man or Basil for help.

Clearly, he won't give up. He will keep trying to get me to tell him. The Exile cautiously allows his focus to drift around the dark stone floor and walls of the courtyard. A stairway with an iron railing on the far side of the courtyard leads to the top of the wall. *If I could get to the stairs and climb them, could I get beyond the walls? What's on the other side?*

His companion coughs and Canaan looks at him again. Since the night he first regained consciousness, the sights, smells, and sounds here have often jolted his senses. The color of Ty's hair and the bright blueness of his eyes were just the first of many things here that seemed completely surreal. The worst part is when Ty and the other two talk to each other in the nonsensical language of the Aegeans—Command Dialect. It almost makes him dizzy to listen to it. Nothing here feels right.

After so much time alone in the jungle, even common comforts like being indoors, sleeping on a bed, and sitting on a chair feel strange. He closes his eyes. *Growing up, I could be surrounded by people and not even notice their presence. Now, after all this time . . . when the three of them stand near me, it's as if I might suffocate! If only I could go back to the forest. At least it's warm there. . . .* A thought that is both startling and grim occurs to him: *Perhaps I AM in the Great Forest. Perhaps I'm in the phantom realms of the fever. Perhaps this is all imagined and I've actually fallen into the river . . . with its cool waters carrying me away. . . . If my body washes ashore at homeplace, would they at least bury me among my people? Or would they cast me adrift in death the way they have in life?*

He grasps the arms of his chair and squeezes with all his might, fighting to keep from thinking about his trial before the Elders. For one terrible moment, words start ringing through his head, *"Some in our midst will never recover from the deep wounds we've suffered . . ."*

He opens his eyes to reassure himself. *No. I'm here, and as Old Menoh says, I will find my strength and my footing again. Even in this strange place, the Maker still sees me. I haven't drifted out of His sight. I must take courage. I must, somehow, learn how to be here.* The voice of his caretaker interrupts his thoughts.

"It's a clear day," Ty says. "You can see for miles."

Canaan looks above the walls of the courtyard to the bright white of the peaks that rise along one side of the Aegean plateau. For him, they have a surreal beauty—like one would find when seeing an unknown world for the first time. Menoh, told him the air on the peaks is many times colder and that the white substance on the mountain tops isn't salt or sand but "ice" and "snow," and that these things are frozen water. *What does "frozen" mean?*

The old man also told him that if a man walks upon the heights, it gets increasingly difficult to breathe, and when you exhale, small clouds will come out of your mouth. All his life, Canaan thought of himself as a man of the wilds, a fearless hunter and explorer but these ideas are too much to ponder. *Oh, Maker of my soul . . . help me find courage. . . .* He clears his throat and answers, "Yes. I can see all the mountains today."

His hosts still know next to nothing about him. So far, he's only revealed his name and his age: Canaan, twenty-six. His clothes, the weapons, and tools they found near him are all foreign, and he can only speak the ancient language of the Genon people, so pretending he isn't an Exile would be pointless. But he's offered no other information.

He's keenly aware of the fact that he hasn't seen a woman since his arrival. Nor has he seen any children. Menoh mentioned his wife . . . but that's the only reference to a female he's heard. *Is there a shortage of women here, too? If so, it might explain their desperation to know what I know about the women we found.*

Thus far, no one has restricted his movements but is that because he's free to move about or because they know he is too weak to escape their custody? Now that he's able to walk more than three or four steps at a time, they've let him come out into this courtyard . . . but it has high walls.

"We've had so much rain here lately," Ty offers. "It feels good to see the sun again."

"Just so," he answers. "It would be the rainy season in . . . in the forest now." He closes his eyes and leans his head back with the pretense of soaking in the sun's warmth. *They have been kind . . . but it's a ruse. Everyone in homeplace knows of the cruelty of Ageans.*

The silence becomes uncomfortable and he runs his fingers over the arms of the chair, polished smooth by the touch of countless hands over the years. He opens his eyes and asks, "Where do you go when you leave here? I haven't seen you for more than a week."

"I have work I must attend to. I oversee things for my father."

They both watch as Menoh, enters the courtyard carrying a pair of garden shears in his left hand. Despite his age, his short, wiry frame is still upright. His gait is a little stiff, and he doesn't swing the shears at the end of his arm the way a young man would, but he's still able to grip them in a gnarled hand that can do daily tasks. Seeing him at a distance like this, it dawns on Canaan that Menoh has been *allowed* to grow a beard. It's white, and very long—in fact, the wind is blowing the end of it over his shoulder as he walks. *How odd. We were always told the soldiers of Aegea forbade the traditional beards of Genon men and forced them to live with the shame of faces that were as hairless as that of a little boy. He has his beard, but his grandson is clean shaven . . . what does that mean?*

The old man makes his way to a leafy vine clinging to a nearby wall and begins trimming back all the loose branches that dangle more than a few inches from the surface. Canaan and Ty silently watch him until he's cut all the branches he can reach and placed them in a wooden bucket. Once he's finished, he turns and walks toward them, white beard still billowing in the breeze, but this time the whiskers blow like a windsock pointing the way ahead of him.

Canaan frowns with the weight of a growing list of mysteries as he watches Ty hop up and drag another chair into the grouping, then wait for Menoh to sit before seating himself again.

The Genon are supposed to be the slaves here and the others think they are the masters. Is this all a game to fool me?

Menoh sets the shears on the courtyard floor.

The people here have so much metal. And the blades on this instrument are sharp. *Could I reach it?* A hint of a bleak smile briefly lights his face. *I haven't got the strength to escape this courtyard, much less fight off the two of them. The old man alone could knock me down.*

Now that someone can help with any needed translation, he asks Ty, "You mention your father. What does your father do?"

"He is a soldier."

This is no surprise, but he did wonder if Ty would say it. "So . . . that means you are a soldier as well, does it not?"

"Yes."

"Is your mother still alive?"

Ty looks at Menoh as if he misunderstood the question. The old man looks a bit puzzled as well, but he nods.

"Yes, my mother is alive. But she mostly stays to herself these days. She is . . ." he says the last word as if it is a sentence in and of itself, "mourning."

"Who died?"

There is a brief exchange in the other language before Menoh spreads his hands, shrugs, and says in Genon, "Wisdom says, 'Today is always a good day to speak truth.'"

A gust of wind swirls Ty's hair around and he pushes it away from his eyes before responding, "She is mourning the loss of my sister."

"Did your sister die of a fever? Or in childbirth?"

"No. She may be dead or she may be alive. We don't know where she is or what happened to her. She was stolen from our home months ago."

Canaan grips his chair and stares into the distance. "Why would someone do such a thing?"

"To gain an advantage over my father." Ty glances at the old man before he continues. "I'm not certain if I should tell you this . . . but I have the hope that if I speak the truth, you will speak truth as well. The day my sister was taken was the day my father became the ruler of Aegea."

Canaan's mind flies back to the forest that day. *Jariel. She looked so fragile. I knew she wasn't Genon.* His thoughts begin to form around possible responses while Ty is talking.

"She isn't the only woman who disappeared that day. We believe the men who took the women fled to the forest, because they thought no one would look there. Perhaps they meant to bring the women back but something happened. We think a creature you call a *k'mosh* killed the men." He pauses, perhaps waiting for some sort of response, but there is none.

If Shaye hadn't spoken for her, Benjamin surely would have killed her or left her where she was. That girl was so sick.

"We believe you have seen them. We believe you might know what happened to the women . . . and we *hope* that you will tell us where they are."

The Exile musters the strength to lean forward and consider his two companions for a moment. "Missing women in the forest? Why would I know about them? When your trackers found me I was far away from the paths to Aegea and I was alone, was I not?"

"Neither of us," Menoh interjects, "thinks you *took* the women. We think perhaps you are a witness to what happened."

His face hardens into a scowl before he shrugs. "It all sounds very sad, but the forest is much bigger than you can imagine and it can swallow even the most experienced person. If the soldiers who did this crime were no match for the *k'mosh* why would you dare to hope the women survived? Neither a *k'mosh* nor the Great Forest would take pity on a couple of women." He looks at Ty before he says, "Your mother is right to mourn."

The response is swift. "I said 'women,' I never said there were *two* women. I never said soldiers took them. How do you know these things?"

The shock of his blunder sends Canaan's head back against his chair. He finally manages, "I just assumed it was soldiers. Who else would do such a thing?"

Ty gets up and walks out of the courtyard. *Is the conversation over?* Soon, however, he's back, holding a leather satchel in his hands. He sits down and pulls out an object out of the bag, then holds it out: an arrowhead with a small bit of a broken arrow shaft still attached.

Canaan tries to grasp the artifact but it slips through his fingers and plops onto the blanket in his lap. He stares at it. *How heavy it feels to me! How feeble I have become. Will I ever be strong again?*

Ty asks Menoh to translate his words then says, "We found it stuck high in a tree in the same place where some of the bones of the soldiers were found. It's where the *k'mosh* was, where all traces of the women disappear. The soldiers weren't killed by arrows, but other people were shooting arrows. What were they shooting at? The only logical conclusion is the *k'mosh*. I doubt they were fighting to rescue the soldiers . . . but they may have been trying to save a couple of women—one of whom was obviously Genon."

When the translation is finished, he grudgingly responds. "I'm not part of any 'others.' I was found alone. I have been alone for years. That is the truth."

The old man points to the artifact in his lap. "That arrowhead didn't come from Aegea. Neither did the wood of the shaft it was on. It didn't match the arrows we found with you but, somehow, you know details you shouldn't know unless you were there . . . or someone that *was* there told you."

His heart feels as if it's wobbling around in his rib cage as he slowly picks up the evidence and turns it over. He sees a small mark on the shaft and fights the urge to smirk. *Benjamin's father made this. If it was an arrow made by my father or my brother it would have found the k'mosh. Wouldn't you know that it would be Benjamin who gets me caught up in this?* He slowly hands it back to Ty before he says, "So?"

Ty pulls a piece of cloth from the bag. "This is a piece of the dress my sister was wearing the day they took her. My mother fainted when she saw it." Next, he unbuttons the top button of his shirt and pulls out a leather necklace with a small pouch tied to it. He carefully opens the bundle and extracts long, black hairs tied together with a string. "And these belonged to the other woman. A Genon woman."

Canaan doesn't touch either of the items. "Why would you keep hair from a Genon woman? Surely she was just a servant."

"She grew up as a servant in my father's house—but she is more than that to me. I would do anything to see her safe return, and that of my sister."

The Exile closes his eyes and shivers. "It's too cold out here for me and my strength is spent. I need to go back to my room."

Once the patient is back in his room, Ty and Menoh sit in the courtyard again and talk.

"I hope you are encouraged," the old Genon says. "I know he seems determined, but I think his mistakes today are a revelation of his heart. He *wants* to tell us. Give him time."

"Perhaps. It's just that every single day seems an eternity to me."

"Soon, Ty, soon."

"I must leave now. Tomorrow the trial will end and I must be there with my parents. I should be back in a few days."

The patient remains in his bed, but his eyes search the room as he tries to avoid thinking about his predicament. Despite the fact that he can hear a nearby waterfall, he has yet to look upon it. His windows and the patio where he sat earlier face away from the mountain, but the sound of the cascading water constantly echoes around the large room. The light gray walls are mostly mortar and stone, the high ceiling is made of wood slats held up with large wooden beams. In several places, the walls and ceiling are nearly black with soot from the fireplace and from the golden oil that continuously burns in lamps on two large tables. His bed and another for a continual caretaker are new additions to the décor, no doubt hastily brought in upon his arrival. A soft woven rug, under his bed helps keep out the cold of the stone floor. *What did they use this room for before I came? Did they gather here and eat? It's larger than some of the houses that people live in at home. Why can't I see any other dwellings from here? Why is this building so large?*

When the old man returns to the room he asks, "What is this place?"

"It is called a mill. The water flowing down the mountain turns a giant wheel," he says, holding out his hands and then allowing them to chase each other in a circle, "that wheel then turns other large wheels that grind grain. It can also turn wheels and belts that aid in cutting logs. Perhaps your people don't have such machinery, but it was something the Genon knew when they first came to Aegea. It has helped to feed many people and to build new homes. When you are stronger, would you like to see how it works?"

"Am I your prisoner? Could I leave if my body were able? Would the soldiers kill me if I tried?"

Menoh slowly sits on the bed nearby and rubs his hand around on an aching elbow. "When they found you, the fever had nearly finished you. You needed medicine and help beyond what they could give, so they carried you through the Great Forest and brought you up the mountain. Ty's father had you brought here, where you would be safe and we could care for you. For now you are hidden—as much for your own safety as anything else."

"So I am in danger here? Ty said his father was the leader, didn't he?"

His caretaker shrugs. "Well . . . technically, you're not one of the Exiles from the second generation, but the laws written back then did include 'family members'. Someone could claim you were a 'family member' of an Exile and kill you. The law will be set aside soon, but until then . . ."

The young man scratches the scalp under his short but wild mane of hair and Menoh watches his brows come together in a frown.

"If you are wondering," he says, "I'm the one who shaved off your hair when you first arrived because it was so full of insects and filth . . . but your beard wasn't as bad so I cleaned it and left it alone. I think the Exile men keep their beards, don't they?"

He gets no response, so he continues with a different line of reasoning. "As strange as this place must seem to you, at least you always knew there was a place in the mountains called Aegea and that there were people living there. But to most of those who live here, any story of the Exiles is a legend. Since they first arrived, Aegeans have been told that the Great Forest below us is a place so deadly that no one can live there for long. Believing that, soldiers in the Second Generation abandoned those they considered rebels in the forest thinking the jungle would perform the executions for them. Although there are soldiers—such as Ty's father—who've known it was *possible* to survive in the forest, it would be alarming to most people here to realize that the descendants of Exiles really *are* roaming around down there. It might be an easy leap for them to think that any Exile alive today must have harmful intentions against Aegea."

"That was an evil thing. They banished people who only wanted freedom from oppression. It's the soldiers' own consciences that would haunt them and make them afraid of us."

The old man leans forward and rests his forearms on his knees. "The time of the exile was a *terrible* time for all the people here, too—Genon and soldier alike. I was but a small boy during those days of passion, when all of our people were forced to choose whether they were willing to die . . . or live on and protect their families here. It was an agonizing decision for every Genon who was of age. My oldest brother was among those taken into the forest. Some of my cousins, an aunt, and an uncle were exiled as well.

"My father had friends among the soldiers and they kept my second oldest brother, Sol, from going with the Exiles because our father said he was too young to make the decision to stand with my brother. Sol saw this as a compromise of our faith and never forgave our father. It created a divide in our family that never healed."

Canaan sniffs. "Just so. Should our people have yielded to those who were faithless? And for what? To live as slaves? Our people were the ones who came to this place with the promise of the land and freedom. We were the ones who were supposed to stay. The soldiers and the others were supposed to go back on that ship to their own place."

"Yes. What you say is *true*. And I can't imagine the fear and the suffering of those who found themselves deep in the forest with nothing . . . but we can't judge those who actually faced the choice back then. I *can* tell you of the great sorrows and the hard times for our people who remained here in Aegea. Several years of scarcity and disease came, and if the Maker hadn't been merciful, *everyone* on this plateau could have perished. Of a truth, my own father never smiled again and only lived for three years after the exile. My mother went home to the Maker just a year after that. But you and I *cannot* go back in time to make a stand for your family or mine. We cannot go back in time to punish those who did this wicked thing. What we *can* do is live out what we know to be right. Here and now. Things are being made right, but it is a process."

"All I know, is that soldiers are devils who wear matching clothes."

"Ah." He strokes his long, white beard. "And you can tell me that the Exiles are all righteous people? All of them live according to the ways of the Maker? They all live in harmony? They all keep the faith, all care for one another . . . all help one another, all forgive one another?"

The color drains from Canaan's face.

"Are you feeling ill?"

"I am fine. Just cold." He shivers. "Just cold."

Aging eyes squint to study him for a moment. "It is said in the Sacred Tell of our people, 'Whenever we attempt to marry faith to tradition or race, it is a match that will not result in virtue. The substance of faith isn't in our collective habits or our common flesh, it exists in our shared *hope*.' If the inward man doesn't choose faith, there is no real advantage to being born into a family of Genon." He sighs. "I cannot speak for the Genon people who are in Exile, but here, we fall short. There are some of us who are devout, and some who have fallen from the Way. Most of us are somewhere in between, so we must remind each other of our hope and press on together. Similarly, there are soldiers who are good men and some who are scoundrels, and many in between who are just trying to find their way. Believe it or not, some of them *have* found the Way."

"These are not my concerns."

Menoh slowly shakes his head. "Have you ever come to a place where something terrible has happened . . . but, alone, you cannot make it right? Have you been to a place in your life when—even if you could throw yourself down into the breach—you couldn't make it right?"

Canaan's eyelids flutter as the words spoken two years ago stalk him once more.

> "Some in our midst will *never* recover from the deep wounds we've suffered," Jared says to the council. "It says in the Sacred Tell that 'justice allows a community to heal, to live on, after a great tragedy.' It also says, 'Where there is no justice, evil things will grow.' The Maker knows our

heavy hearts—and His provision is *justice*. Canaan may feel deep regret for what happened, but our community will not feel any sort of resolution unless he suffers in some way proportionate to *our* suffering. I don't demand that his life be taken, but I cannot forgive him. I say that Canaan, too, should know the unending sorrow of never seeing his family again. . . ."

A hand placed on his chest jolts him back to the present. "Listen to me, son."

His eyes focus on the man who has tenderly cared for him.

"Bad things have happened here and *terrible* things could flourish again. No one person can overturn them, but each of us must do what we can. The men who took Ty's sister blamed the Genon girl who disappeared the same day—they said it was a Genon plot. Although these men will soon stand for judgement—they've also managed to raise suspicions in the minds of others. If it became known that Exiles were there in the forest that day, those suspicions would grow."

"So I could be used as proof of their worst fears," he concludes. "Perhaps you should just take me back to the Great Forest and leave me there." He exhales heavily, as if the idea is a relief to him.

"No. We both know the heat and damp of the forest are where the fever thrives. You are so weak right now, it would swallow you up."

The young man looks away. "Perhaps you should just let it."

The old man's eyes glisten with sorrow. "This I cannot do. Too much has been lost already. For the sake of the people of Aegea *and* the Exiles I am holding onto hope that the women are yet alive, that they will be able to return to our people."

"Do not hold onto hope because of me. Even if I knew something, it would be a betrayal to tell it."

"I don't think you've fully considered this. Think of it. As you heard today, Ty and his father have already pieced together much of what happened. They already *know* the Exiles are living somewhere on the other side of the forest. They already *know* that Exiles were right there in the forest the day the *k'mosh* killed the kidnappers. *And* they have found an old map that will lead soldiers to where they believe the Exiles went: down a river that empties into the great water—the ocean."

A look of surprise momentary flashes across Canaan's face.

Encouraged, the old man continues to press his case. "Yes, the general has learned about the ocean. Even if you don't care about the people here in Aegea, you must care what happens to the rest of your people. Soon, the general *will* send men across the forest. Eventually, they *will* find your people—with or without your help. You cannot prevent the encounter. All you can do is teach the Aegeans how to approach the Exiles so there is the best chance of a peaceful meeting. Otherwise, what will happen when men from Aegea suddenly appear where the Exiles live? What if both sides are fearful and ready to fight? I'm certain your people are skilled with spears and arrows in the forest . . . but the soldiers have weapons your people have never dreamed of. False assumptions could lead to bloodshed. The fate of the Exiles may very well rest in your hands."

A sarcastic laugh shoots out of Canaan's mouth before he can quench it. "It seems I cannot escape being a villain."

It's a riddle he can't unravel, so Menoh becomes quiet.

The young man suddenly turns toward the wall and shivers. "Please, do not ask this of me, Nathan."

Gnarled hands unfold another blanket and pull it over him. "Who is Nathan?"

CHAPTER 2
Justice for All

Anno, the ancient king, stood on the top of the hill outside the ancient city and laughed as he said, "We have defiled your people and your lands! You are defeated in every way! We have raped your women, stolen your children, and plundered your lands. No more shall you sing of your blessings, for they are all mine now. No more shall you praise your 'Maker' for he is not mightier than I!" Anno said all this, not knowing that destruction waited for him—a destruction more terrible than all he'd wrought in a lifetime of treachery. For he had placed his hands upon the Beloved of the Maker—His own people—and no earthly treasure could deliver him from the terror that would eventually overtake him.—*From the Sacred Sayings in the Tell.*

For the first time in many years, there is a trial. For the first time in several generations, the accused are soldiers. The room is packed with people who represent every segment of Aegean society. General Jubal McClaren, his wife Duana, and his son Tyrone are seated in the first row of the spectator section, just to the right of the center aisle. Nearly every officer above the rank of lieutenant is in the room along with many men and women who represent the Genon clans. Even the small gallery above the ground floor is standing room only.

Six men are seated behind a railing on the left side of the room. Five of them are wearing wrist restraints and leg shackles. The sixth man is their representative before the court.

The clerk calls for silence before saying, "Grayson Mosley, Raymond Litton, and Charles Beaumont will now stand for the reading of the verdict."

Three men rise to their feet.

Senior Judge Advocate Whitworth, a man well into his seventies, looks out into the packed courtroom. "For too long this place has stood empty. For the first time in many years, I feel I have the opportunity to sit here and actually dispense justice. It has been a long time coming, but today is the day." He clears his throat and reads from a paper in his hand. "Grayson Mosley, Raymond Litton, and Charles Beaumont—in the matter of charges for the murders of Jariel McClaren and Shaye Penway, you have been found *not* guilty due to insufficient evidence."

A cocky smile slowly appears on Col. Mosely's face as a low rumble of comments rises from the spectators. The general's wife sags forward in her seat and he puts his arm around her.

The clerk commands silence before the judge continues reading.

"Regarding the charge of the murder of George Hayworthy, guilty. In the charge of the kidnapping Jariel McClaren and Shaye Penway, guilty. In the charge of mutiny against the duly selected General of Aegea, guilty. Regarding the charges of planning and ordering a crime in which Spec. 5 John Grimes was murdered, guilty. In the charges of conspiracy to foment civil unrest, attempts to circumvent prosecution, guilty. In the charges of soliciting false testimony against Shaye Penway, guilty. In the charges of perjury before the Tribunal, ordering subordinates to commit other illegal acts, and of circumventing a ban you are also found guilty. You are hereby stripped of all ranks, discharged from the military. As of this moment you are stripped of all privileges and benefits, and your houses are forfeit . . ."

One of the defendants, Raymond Litton, falls back into his chair and begins to sob.

The judge continues, " . . . You will be taken directly to the fort where you will have twenty-one days to set your other affairs in order, for on this day in three weeks, at 10:30 a.m., you shall all be taken to the public courtyard outside the fort and publicly hanged."

Exclamations of shock and grief are heard among the prisoner's friends and families. At the same time, outbursts of "Just so!" and cries of relief erupt among spectators.

"Your honor," the officers' representative pleads above the din, "I must protest this cruel and hasty sentence."

Everyone is silenced when the judge stands and addresses the now disgraced colonel. "Grayson Mosely, you are on record, on multiple occasions, saying that the punishment given to those who participated in the uprising in the second generation was 'more than fair because they attempted an overthrow of a legal regime.' You've also publicly stated that if it was in your power you 'would gladly do the same to any Genon who resisted governmental authority.' Are you prepared to exchange your punishment for the one meted out to those in the second generation? Would you consent to having each of your family members brought up before this court and given the choice to publicly disown you or be taken along with you, deep into the Poison Forest, and left there with no weapons, tools, or provisions, never return to Aegea under penalty of instant death? I am prepared to make it so. Would you prefer it?"

Mosely stares contemptuously at the judge and gives no answer.

"Very well, the gallows in twenty-one days it is. Officers of the court, take these three men to the fort."

As Litton is hauled out of his chair, he resists. "No! I only did what I was ordered to do!"

The sounds of his protest are heard until the large doors of the room close behind him.

Judge Whitworth sits and looks out at the spectators. "Let this serve to refresh every soldier's memory: When he knows he is committing serious crimes against the lives of others—no soldier can use as his defense that he was 'just following orders.' Let this sad day serve as a marking post for *all* in Aegea. Yes. It is a sad day, but it is also a good day—for justice *will* be carried out."

Cries of, "Just so!" echo around the room.

The remaining two defendants are visibly shaken.

The judge resumes. "Now it is time to read the other verdicts. Gregory Potts and Owen Anson will now stand for the reading of the verdicts."

Both men rise, but neither of them looks up at the spectators or the judge.

"On the charges of participating in the kidnappings of Jariel McClaren and Shaye Penway, you are found guilty. Regarding the charges of participating in a conspiracy that resulted in the murder of Spec. 5 John Grimes and the deaths of other coconspirators, you are found guilty. Because a third conspirator corroborated your stories from his deathbed, and you also provided evidence which allowed this case to be brought to trial, you will not be hanged. Both of you are hereby stripped of rank and discharged from military service. Both of you will be taken to the fort where you will each begin serving sentences of twenty years—working on hard-labor projects wherever needed."

CHAPTER 3
At the Outpost

It's late afternoon as Ty McClaren approaches the outpost. He, doesn't need to give much guidance to the chestnut mare as she trots up to the familiar hitching post and stops, ready for some oats and some rest.

He dismounts and a clean-shaven Genon man sprints up to take the reins, saying, "I'll make sure she's fed." The horse knows the attendant and nudges him in the direction of the barn. He smiles but stands his ground long enough to ask her owner, "Are you staying or just stopping over? Do you need anything?"

Ty stretches before responding. "I'm just stopping over. Do you know where I could find Chessie?"

"I think," he says, pointing beyond the Inn, "she was helping my sister get the cows in from the pasture."

"Thanks. I'll probably be ready to leave in an hour or so." As he walks toward the pasture, he can hear the man chiding the horse.

"Stop pushing me. It's a good thing I like you. You need to remember you're a horse . . ."

A cool, steady breeze is still blowing so he shakes his arms, then rubs them to stave off a chill. Halfway across the green pasture, he can see two young women waving their hats, herding several cows in the general direction of the milking stalls. From a distance, the women look about the same. Both are wearing traditional Genon garb for females working outdoors; long dresses, aprons, and headscarves. When they recognize him, they wave, then pick up their pace.

With throats mooing and heavy udders swaying, the cows lope toward the stalls where they will be fed, washed and milked.

Now he recognizes the dark bangs sticking out of Chessie's scarf. Her short mane is now the only obvious sign of a brutal initiation into the clan of "wild women" who lived in a tangle of ancient hardwoods in the center of the plateau.

"Good day! How are you?" he calls out to the young women.

"I am well," Abby replies.

"I am well also," her companion echoes.

The two lean together and confer before Abby continues walking with the cattle and Chessie walks directly toward Ty. Her stride has changed. It's no longer the swaying, sensuous walk of the woman in search of an alliance with any man. Now she has the busy stride of one who doesn't waste motion.

"Did you want to speak to me?" she asks.

Months ago, when he found her washing clothes in a muddy river, she was so covered with welts, cuts, and bruises that he didn't recognize her. Since then, her face has healed, but it will take a year or more for her hair to grow back to a length acceptable to most Genon. It's uncertain whether she will fully recover from her abuse at the hands of the clan of criminals who camped in the woods.

He rests both of his arms on the top rail of the fence and one boot on the bottom rail. "I was on my way to Westland and I thought I would stop by."

She nods and continues her approach.

"Is it well with you?" he asks. "How are you faring here?"

"Have you spoken to the missus?" she asks, referring to the innkeeper's wife. "What does she say?"

He shakes his head. "I just arrived. I was planning on eating before I left, though, so I'll probably see her in a few minutes."

When she's about ten feet away from him, she stops walking. "I'm trying to learn. I work hard." She nervously adjusts her scarf, then straightens her apron. "I . . . would like to stay. If I'm allowed."

"That's up to John and Lilly."

She looks down and answers a quick, "Okay." After turning to walk away, she turns to him again. "I heard . . . I heard that Lemon was dead."

He rests his chin on his arms. "Bad news travels quickly in Aegea."

"So it's true?" There's a tremor in her voice.

"Yes."

"Oh."

"You look upset. Are you okay?"

"I . . . I didn't mean for that to happen. I just told you what I saw. I didn't mean for Lemon to die."

As he straightens his stance, his right hand brushes over a long splinter on the top rail of the fence and he starts to pick at it while he talks. "It's probably better if you allow people to tell whatever stories they want about Lemon. No one connects you with his troubles, so let it stay that way. The truth is, Lemon made many bad choices over a long period of time. You and I both know that he had a big mouth. Eventually, those who hired him would have feared he'd reveal something and taken his life." The splinter comes lose from the rail and he rolls it between his fingers before he meets her gaze again. "As it turned out, though, all his years of drinking took his body before any of his old friends could get to him. His choices were never your responsibility."

Her brow scrunches up. "My father was always drunk. He fell from the top of a tree and died when I was nine." Her posture relaxes again and she glances at him. "So no one killed Lemon?"

"In a sense, he killed himself. With drink." Stepping back from the fence, he tells her, "I'll speak with Lilly and John, and then talk to you again before I leave."

She turns back to her work and he makes his way toward the inn. His gaze sweeps over the cluster of buildings that make up the isolated settlement. A Genon couple, John and Lilly, have had oversight of this place for two decades. Located nearly in the center of the country, this is a waypoint in the open land between the largely populated eastern tip of Aegea and a small military post in Westland. Over the years, several Genon families have joined the low-key enterprises here—running the small inn that serves the military and tradesmen on their way from one end to the other, raising plants and livestock, cooking meals for guests, hitching up wagons, feeding horses, making leather goods, and providing blacksmith services.

When his father, Jubal McClaren, achieved the rank of major, the road to the far end of Aegea was little more than a thready trail for people on foot or horses. But under his persistent guidance, miles of wilderness in the western half of the country were transformed into orchards and fields that fed the growing population. When he volunteered to establish a post at the western end of the plateau, many of his peers saw it as professional suicide.

As the other officers jostled for position in the capitol, Ty's father, oversaw the taming of the land, directed the construction of a large mill at the base of Aegea's largest waterfall, then managed the construction of an aqueduct system that irrigated the land. As the countryside flourished, so did the career of Jubal McClaren. Within eight years he'd achieved the rank of Colonel and built a home that would be known as the Great House of Westland.

Lilly the innkeeper comes out to greet him. Her dark hair is streaked with gray now, and her face shows signs of aging, but her constant smile softens the impression. "Good afternoon, Lieutenant McClaren."

"Good afternoon, Miss Lilly. Please . . . call me Ty. I'm on leave from active duty in the military right now."

Her eyes ask a question before she says it. "How are you faring, Mr. Ty?"

He smiles at her insistence of formality, and shrugs. "I was on my way to Westland and I thought I would stop by to check on Chessie's progress."

Lilly opens the door to the inn and stands aside. "Come in. Would you like something to eat?"

"Yes, thank you, I would."

"I sent for John and he'll be here shortly."

She walks him through the dining hall on the ground floor then back to the staircase that leads to the private dining room. Each of the wooden stairs creaks in turn as they ascend into the warmer air of the second floor. She stops at the top to grab an oil lamp from a small table and light it.

After they enter the rectangular, wood-paneled room, she asks, "Do you want the windows open?" She points to the line of windows on the long wall across from them. "All of these face west, so the sun will be full into them by now. Or, we can light lamps if you wish."

"Just open the two at either end to freshen the air and leave the rest closed. I'll only be here long enough to eat and to talk about Chessie's status."

Soon, Lilly's husband, John, joins them and the two men shake hands.

"It's good to see you Lieutenant."

"Ty. Just call me Ty. I'm on leave . . . I'm no longer on active duty."

"Sure," the innkeeper says before moving onto another topic. "The trial is over, yes? What was decided?"

"Mosley and two other officers are to be hanged. The men of lower rank will do hard labor for twenty years."

The couple exchange a wide-eyed glance before they look back at their guest.

"I never thought *that* would happen," Lilly says. "To officers."

John just nods.

"No one should think they can do such evil with immunity. The courtroom has been empty for years because charges were so seldom brought. It's going to be different now. And I think the judge was trying to tell us all that the laws here will apply to *every*one."

One of the innkeepers' daughters, Joy, enters with a tray containing a bowl of stew and a small loaf of bread on a cutting board. Once Ty is seated, she lingers at the table with the pretense of placing his napkin and centering the spoon on it. When he looks up at her, she returns his gaze and he can see the pleading look in her eyes. Joy is not only a distant cousin to Shaye but her closest friend as well. Over the years, the two spent as many happy hours together as they were allowed.

She wants to know if I can tell her anything new. He looks away. "Thanks."

"That will be fine, Joy" her mother tells her. "Leave and let him eat his food."

She's in the hallway before Lilly adds, "And you can close the door before you go downstairs."

With a heavy sigh, the girl leans back into the room to pull the door shut.

They wait to hear the sound of her descent on the stairs before John asks, "I know you've come to talk about Chessie, but we wanted to know something—"

Lilly finishes the question. "Is Lemon dead?"

He looks at both of them before he answers. "Yes. Fiona and Old Menoh used all their skill to try and save him, but he'd made himself so sick drinking *meechi*, his insides were pickled and he couldn't keep down food or medicine."

"We heard . . . something different," John tells him.

Ty sets down his spoon and looks them both in the eye before he responds. "There's no doubt in anyone's mind that he was in trouble again, and I'm sure people have all sorts of theories and stories about what may have happened to him. But the one person—the only person—to blame for his death is Lemon."

Lilly shakes her head and sighs. "He was so young to die in such a bitter way."

"True," their guest sighs. "And, in the end, the one who took it the hardest was the one he'd given the most disappointment to: Menoh."

"Lu told us that Menoh hasn't been seen around Westland much lately. Is he alright?"

Ty takes a bite of his stew while he tries to formulate a truthful answer. "My father has asked him to oversee a project. I hope it will be a distraction from his grief. And you know Menoh. He needs something to do."

They nod.

He's ready to get back on topic. "Now. About Chessie. How is she doing? She told me she'd like to stay—but it really is up to you. Is it working out having her here?"

They exchange a look before Lilly answers. "That first time you checked up on her, she'd been pretty docile. After that, she caused some problems—mostly trying to pick arguments with our girls. Perhaps she was trying to work out where she fits in. The last time you were here, I was ready to have her hauled off but," she places a hand on top of her husband's, "John asked me to give it a while longer, so I held my tongue. Since then, actually, she's done pretty well. She does what she's asked to do, she's tried to learn the different tasks, and she's kept out of trouble. Unless that changes, I say she can stay."

"I think so, too," John says. "She was pretty rough—but she was raised in a rough manner. We're hoping she'll grow beyond that. So far, she seems to be doing that."

Thirty minutes later, Chessie stands in the doorway of the dining room where Ty sits alone, waiting to talk to her. It's the same room where she sat with him all those months ago after he'd rescued her from the camp of the wild women.

Just before coming upstairs, she took off her apron and shoes, then used a kerchief to wipe her face, but she knows her dress isn't entirely clean. Looking around the room, she asks, "You wish to talk to me?"

"Yes" he answers, pointing to a chair. "There isn't much to say, but you can sit down if you'd like."

Her bare feet pad across the shiny wood floor. In the silence, the scrape of the chair pulling away from the table seems loud. She seats herself with her hands in her lap.

He can tell she's nervous, so he gets right to it. "John and Lilly want you to stay."

A large smile lights her round face, but then a question springs to mind. "For how long?"

He smiles back. "As of today, I'm no longer in the picture here. You are free to work out the details with them."

Her next words come out like a sigh of relief. "Thank you."

"You are the one who worked for this," he says with a shrug. "This is your accomplishment, not mine. I only played a small part at the beginning." He rises from his seat and pushes it back into its place at the table. "I'm glad this has worked out for you and I hope you fare well here."

Before he reaches the door, she says, "Wait." When he turns, she hesitates, then blurts out, "There's something else."

"Yes?"

She looks down at her dusty hands while she musters up her courage, then says, "That first day when you found me . . ."

Anticipating another expression of gratitude, he feels embarrassed, but her next words catch him by surprise.

"I thought you only cared about finding your sister, not about me . . . or anybody else. I figured you already knew . . . or that you wouldn't care . . . about Shaye's trouble."

He moves swiftly back to the chair nearest to her, pulls it out, and sits down.

"What trouble?"

Her breathing speeds up, but she resumes talking. "After that, I started to think maybe you were different, maybe you *would* care. Then, when I feared Lilly and John would send me away, I thought about using the information to strike a bargain with you somehow, so I held onto it. Today, I'm thinking you will care, but it will trouble you, and I feel sorrow for that." She dares to look him in the eye for a moment. "You have been kind to me, so I don't wish to cause you pain . . . but I think I *should* tell you."

It's as if nothing else in the world exists but Chessie. He leans forward. "Tell me."

CHAPTER 4
Return to the Mill

The horse gallops down the road through the orchards and fields of Westland. He urges the animal to go faster. When he finally arrives at the mill, he quickly dismounts and ascends the stone steps two at a time. He's out of breath when he reaches the room where Canaan, Basil, and Menoh are sitting at a small table eating their evening meal, with a crackling fire in the fireplace to ward off the evening chill.

Menoh looks up at him. "You're here. I was going to send Basil to fetch you. Is something amiss?"

He walks directly to Canaan. "I can't wait any longer. While you were delirious, I heard you say that you 'watched over them', that you would make sure 'no harm came to them', you would make sure 'they' were safe. I am certain that you saw Shaye and Jariel. *Will you not help me?* Every day, I walk about in a place which has no meaning or hope for me. Surely, in being here you must feel this way as well. *Please, let me take you home so that you can see your family again* . . . and I can see mine."

After a moment of stunned silence, Menoh says, "Well . . . he's already agreed to help us."

Ty takes a shaky breath before he looks at the Exile and says. "Thank you. Although I don't think I can ever fully repay you, I will do whatever is in my power to help you."

The old man tells him, "Catch your breath, boy, for there is much to do and much to learn while we wait for Canaan to gain strength. This is more complicated than any of us imagined."

Ty squats down close to Canaan and says in Genon, "I want to hear all that you know about them."

With the help of Old Menoh's translation, Canaan tells him, "My people rescued them from certain death when the soldiers who brought them to the forest were killed by the *k'mosh*. Jariel nearly died from a spider bite, but she got well. The two women did not like each other and often argued.

"Jariel cried the first few days, then she seemed to accept what had happened. But Shaye grieved much. When they reached the river, I stayed and watched the trail behind for a time, to make sure no one followed." The Exile pauses and looks at the general's son. "The place where they live . . . it's a very far journey from here, but I can show you the way."

CHAPTER 5
Fresh Hope, With a Wrinkle

"**H**ope can breathe life into courage."—*From the Sacred Sayings in the Tell.*

Yesterday, when the general got a message from his son that contained the agreed upon phrase, "field production increase expected for harvest," all of the patience and restraint he'd acquired in a lifetime of practice barely kept him from mounting up and riding full speed to the mill in Westland. Ty's signal meant Canaan the Exile was cooperating with them. He'd hardly slept all night in anticipation of the news.

As soon as his son arrives they go to a courtyard on the roof to talk.

Ty gives him the abbreviated version first. "Both of them were alive the last time Canaan saw them and he believes they are still safe."

The weight of so many months of work and worry is revealed when Jubal closes his eyes and his son can clearly see how this ordeal has aged him. Finally, he looks at his son again and says, "Go on."

"He told us that he was the first one on the scene and watched from a treetop as soldiers opened the box and pulled out Jariel. She was unconscious so they put her on the ground. He said they briefly gathered around the box again to look into it with surprise. Since he couldn't understand what they said to one another, we can assume this was when they realized for the first time that Shaye was in the box as well. The rest of it is just like Ethan and Asher figured, a large beast, a *k'mosh*, chemosh soon appeared and attacked them. One of them died near Jariel, the others attempted to run away before they were killed. When the rest of the Exiles showed up, he kept watch over Jariel while they chased the beast. Canaan said that as soon as he saw her, he knew she wasn't Genon and he also knew that the Exiles would probably leave her to die if someone couldn't convince them to save her. That was when

Shaye crawled out of the box. At first she was weak and bewildered, and she was stunned when he showed her that Jariel was in the forest, too. He told her that, unless she could convince them to save her, the Exiles would probably leave Jariel to die. So when they returned after killing the beast, she told them Jariel was half Genon and served a rich family, making cloth for them. The men, believing the soldiers must have brought the women down into the forest with some foul purpose in mind, decided to rescue them both and take them home."

"And where is their home? Will he tell us where that is?"

"There are many dangers between here and there. Many of them are things we've never encountered. We will need a guide and Canaan says he will take us most of the way there."

"Why only *most* of the way there?"

"Apparently, he was banished from the Exiles for his part in a tragedy. He'd been living alone in the forest for nearly two years before we found him. He said Shaye was the first person who'd spoken to him since he'd been banished. It explains why he's so . . . odd."

"What did he do? Is he some sort of criminal?"

"What he told Menoh is that he was supposed to be guarding a group of women and children from his village while they washed clothes on the bank of a river—even though there hadn't been any signs of dangerous animals in that area for years. He got bored and went hunting. When he was a mile away, a sudden flood came and swept nearly all of the women and children away."

"Why should we trust a man who—"

"He admits what he did was terrible and he'd give anything to live that day over again. The memory of it and the punishment they gave him have left scars on his mind that will probably never heal. The reason he was so steadfast in not telling us about Jariel and Shaye is that his deepest desire is to do what he wishes he'd done two years ago: protect his people."

"Then why is he talking now?"

"He agreed to help us because Menoh told him that we knew about the river north of here that travels toward the Exile's land, and convinced him that we would eventually find them, with or without his help—but without knowledge of how to approach the Exiles and what to say . . . the first meeting could prove disastrous to everyone."

"I'm not sure I want to trust such a man."

"We must remember that it was his own great sorrow over being banished that drove him to convince Shaye that she would need to speak up for Jariel. In the final analysis, *he* saved Jariel. And, despite being banished from his people—he still wants to save *them* as well."

"Isn't he too weak to serve as a guide?"

"Menoh says he has recovered, that he will grow stronger now, and within two months or so, he could be fit enough to travel. He longs to be back in the forest."

Jubal looks out at Oldtown while he taps on the top of the waist-high wall with his fingers. "We can use the time to put together a team for a rescue mission."

Ty takes up a stance near him. "Yes. And I will go with them,"

The tapping stops. "That's out of the question. It's impossible."

His son stands straighter and asks, "Would you have said it was *impossible* for soldiers to come and kidnap Jariel right out of our house and get her into the jungle? Don't most people in Aegea think it's *impossible* for Exiles to continue to exist in the forest? Could we have ever imagined that we would actually *find* an Exile and bring him back here? An Exile who would agree to *show* us where the women are?" He gazes out over the city. "Is my hope for Shaye and me impossible? It's only as impossible as these other things."

Jubal takes in a slow breath and turns to face him. "I know this is real and it's raw to you. But, as hard as it may be to hear . . . stop and think about this logically. We should allow the men with skills in the forest to go. If you got sick or wounded or if you couldn't keep up, you'd be a drag on the whole mission, you would become a complication who required resources and strength—resources necessary to bring everyone home safely."

The young man shakes his head. "I'll do whatever I need to do, learn whatever I need to learn."

A sad expression crosses the general's face as he studies his son. "Now that you know Shaye is safe, perhaps this is for the best. She's among her own people. Perhaps she wouldn't even *want* to come back. Perhaps she no longer *wants* you in her life."

"I know. But as I see it, this may be my one and only chance to be certain of that."

Jubal holds up one hand and attempts to finish his thought. "The men on the mission can take whatever message you'd like and deliver it to her personally."

"No. Any man who chooses to speak of love or beg for forgiveness from a distance is either a liar or a coward. She needs to see my eyes and hear my voice. When the mission departs, I am going with it. As it is, by the time we arrive, I'll already have missed the most important event in our lives."

The general is ready to continue the debate but stops at the unexpected turn in the conversation. "What event?"

"The birth of our child." He studies his father's face for any trace of deception. "Did you know?"

As it sinks in, Jubal slumps forward. "*What?*"

"You can't say anything I haven't already said to myself. And now, she's living among those who walk as Genon—and she is pregnant, without a husband. When they first found her, she told the Exiles that she crawled into the box because she was running away, trying to get to town." He stops as he considers it yet again. "I know she was trying to get to me . . . wanting to tell me." Once again, he looks out at the jumble of homes and other buildings below. "You know, Canaan thought she was the most beautiful woman he'd ever seen—and the other Exiles were very happy to think she would be returning home with them. I can only hope that she has found favor among them. I pray that the Exiles have accepted her and Jariel."

"If you didn't know it before she was taken, how did you find out she was pregnant? Did the Exile know?"

"No. He still doesn't know. Chessie told me how she figured it out when she and Shaye shared that room. She told me that, at first, she was saving the information, hoping to gain an advantage over Shaye . . . and then perhaps to gain an advantage over us, but changed her mind after we helped her. I did tell Basil and Menoh. I have no secrets from them." He turns to look at his father. "Last night when I had time to think about it, everything Mother and Mosha said about Shaye's deep sorrow—it all made so much more sense. Do you understand now? I must go. I must find her."

The response is almost a whisper. "Even if your sister has survived, I could still lose her in this undertaking. You're asking me to risk losing *you* as well."

"Actually, I've been lost since the day it happened. It would have haunted me my whole life. But now I have the opportunity to say what I *should* have said and do what I *should* have done a year ago. I am not afraid. I can do this. . . . Very soon you will have a grandchild. *Your first grandchild.* Doesn't that *mean* anything to you?"

Jubal closes his eyes again, perhaps unable to find the words to express what he's feeling.

"Basil volunteered to go with me. We've always watched out for each other, and we're the ones that Canaan knows and trusts."

After a prolonged silence, the general makes a rare admission. "I don't know what to do. I need some time to think."

"I've already given it a lot of thought."

Ty watches as one of his father's eyebrows arches upward. It's a sign that he's skeptical, but willing to hear someone present an idea. "Go ahead."

"Canaan says that not all of the Exiles hate us, but some of them definitely do—and *none* of them believes they can trust us. None of them—not even Jariel or Shaye—knows *why* Jariel was kidnapped. So far as the Exiles know, their own presence in the world is still unknown. The day they found the women was the closest they've come to Aegea in a decade. They stopped coming this far when we no longer let Genon women gatherers go into the forest. And Menoh is right: to have people from Aegea suddenly show up where they felt they'd never be discovered will probably stun and frighten them. In order to have any real hope of success, we need to know exactly what to say and do at our first encounter." Although it's not part of the discussion, he can't help asking, "Was General Fairmont onto the fact that the Genon women were defecting to the Exiles? Was the story about 'greater danger to women gatherers' just a cover for the truth?"

Jubal shrugs and nods. "Fairmont *suspected* that the women weren't just perishing in the forest. As for myself, I'd heard some of the stories about Exiles years ago and I was pretty sure most of the women were disappearing rather than dying. Obviously, they were travelling farther out of range than any of us dared to go, and I didn't see any benefit in publicly speculating about something that was contrary to what everyone was being told. Once we stopped letting women go into the forest, the stories of Exiles dried up. No coincidence, that. . . . Did Canaan say *why* they came back after all this time?"

"Even before they lost so many women in that flood, they had a disproportionate number of men in their community. They were hoping, after all these years, we might be letting women back into the forest and that they could find some who wanted to join them. They believe finding Shaye and Jariel was a miracle—and so do I. But that also means they won't be happy to see them return to Aegea."

The general resumes tapping on the wall as he thinks.

His son offers another point for him to consider. "We'll need the most compelling evidence we can give the Exiles that our intent isn't to harm them, and that it could be to their benefit to have contact or trade with us. Safe arrival requires the help of Canaan and others who are skilled in the forest. But negotiating with the Exiles is another thing altogether. To send soldiers who would need translation is not a good idea. I am physically fit, I know Genon customs and language as few soldiers do, I have at least some knowledge of the wild, *and* I am the one who would best be able to communicate your wishes. This may be our *only* opportunity to present our case."

"If they knew who you were, they might be just as likely to seize or kill you."

"Everything is a risk, but I think the bigger risk is to send the men without me."

His brows come together as he closes his eyes. "I could never tell your mother I sent you into such peril. Jariel's disappearance was nearly the end of her."

"What do you think would happen if she found out you knew Jariel was alive someplace and we didn't do *whatever* it took to save her? My advice is not to tell her anything about it until it's over. The fewer people who know what we intend, the higher our chances of success. Mosely and some of his minions are out of the picture, but we can't be certain there aren't others who wanted to overthrow you, who might still strike at you if they had the chance. I'm already on a leave of absence from the Academy. While I train for the mission, I will visit town on and off, like I've visited Westland. When I leave, just let Mother and everyone else here assume I'm in Westland for an extended stay. In the same way, we can let the people in Westland assume I'm out doing something with Basil or here in town."

The general studies his son's face. All the dogged determination and thorough planning that marked his own life are sitting right there, looking back at him.

"Dad, I know you would go and get Jariel if you could . . . but you can't just disappear from Aegea for several months. I can. With Canaan as a guide through the forest and down the river, we don't need to search for the women, we will be *led* to them. We have at least a couple of months to prepare for the trip. During that time, Canaan can tell us what things the Exiles might need or want and you can formulate specific offers to them."

"And what if Shaye doesn't want to return with you? What if she has taken vows with someone else?"

Ty's somber expression says that this is something he's already considered. "Lots of things may have happened and still could happen. Some of them we cannot prepare for." He gazes at the horizon. "I understand what you're saying—and I realize why you might think it would be better for everyone if Shaye stayed with the Exiles. But regardless of what happens with her and me, the life of everyone in our whole family has *already* been permanently altered. Life in *Aegea* has been permanently altered. . . . Even if Jariel has survived thus far, do you think that someone as *fragile* as she is could live out a full life in the wilds with them? I know that if we do nothing, Mother will go to her grave, grief-stricken. Mosely and his cohorts may have been punished, but a lot of what he did still needs to be undone. The weeds of discord and suspicion he's planted all over Aegea need to be plucked up and burned—and the trial was only a first step. You were wise to agree that the charges of murdering the women be dropped. Now, when the women return there will be no room for people to rethink the verdicts. Jariel's account of what happened may bring some goodwill between the military and the Genon."

CHAPTER 6
Sgt. Shocky

"Integrity is when one thing has become so much a part of the other, they can no longer be separated."—*A proverb of His own people*

The general's aide looks up from the stack of paper on his desk to see a soldier standing before him.

"I was ordered to report here," the soldier says. "My name is Sergeant Manash."

"Yes. He's expecting you. Go right in."

"Thank you, sir." Stepping to the door, he raps on it once and opens it.

Jubal McClaren looks up from his desk. "Sergeant. Come in and close the door. Please be seated."

The soldier's quiet demeanor and small frame might give those who don't know him a false sense that he's timid. To the contrary, he is lightning, sinew, and resolve—all under his own control. He is capable of meeting nearly any challenge with surprising force. Removing his cap from where it was stowed under his left arm, he seats himself and places the hat upon his lap. Even while sitting, everything about his rigid posture says he's still at attention. "Thank you, sir."

The general lifts a silver pitcher off a tray and pours himself a cup of water. "Would you care for some?"

A blink is the only change of countenance. "No thank you, sir."

Jubal takes several swallows from the cup, then places it on a gray stone coaster before addressing the soldier by his famous nickname.

"Shocky, I've had my eye on you since you first applied for the games. I wasn't at all surprised that you won top honors and I was glad to see you become a draft pick. Certainly, only an exceptional man could make it as far as you have in the face of so much opposition."

"Thank you, sir."

Eight years ago, for the first time in the sixty year history of "the games," Genon men were permitted to compete. Shocky entered, won, and became a "first draft pick" (for entrance into the military). He was the first Genon man in the history of Aegea to be drafted. Since then, other Genon men have competed and three more have earned draft pick status.

When Jubal McClaren drafted Shocky into the signal corps, he became the first Genon to walk the halls at the Academy who wasn't a janitor or a stable boy. During his early years of service, he withstood all the insults and abuse that other soldiers could hurl his way and earned a certain amount of grudging respect, even among those who contested his place in the military. Two years ago, he achieved the rank of sergeant—another first.

Despite their consistently high level of performance, admittance of Genon men to the military is still a hotly debated issue throughout the land. Even among his own people, there are mixed sentiments about Shocky's success. Some see him as a hero who is breaking down barriers. Others think he's a traitor to the ways of his people. He is the most respected, feared, admired, and hated Genon in the world—but his customary calm expression gives no hint that he cares about the opinions of others. He has the rare gift of being at peace with himself.

"I'm aware of your attention to detail, your endurance, your sense of duty, your ability to act with honor under duress, and your ability to maintain secrecy. I have an assignment which will require all of these qualities."

"Yes sir?"

"The assignment will be long, dangerous, and will test the very limits of every man involved. There are no guarantees of a safe return. Are you willing to volunteer for such a mission?"

There's a gleam in his eye. "Yes sir."

"Everything we say in here today," McClaren tells him, "is classified. When you leave here, this conversation will only exist in your head and mine. Understood?"

"Understood, sir."

"The mission may take you away from the Academy for many months and no one, other than the mission team and myself, will know where you have gone. We will try to make your departure as discreet as possible but people may notice and questions might arise. Until your return, however, everyone—family, friends, fellow soldiers—*everyone* but the mission planners and myself must be allowed to think you are dead or that you have deserted your post."

"It is my honor to accept such a challenge, sir."

Jubal raises his cup as if he were about to make a toast. "You've never disappointed me, Shocky. If this mission is successful and you return, you *will* be rewarded."

CHAPTER 7
Jariel in Homeplace

All the windows in the shop open for the first time in more than a year so it isn't long before curious villagers begin peering in and word of her presence soon spreads throughout the neighborhood. Little conversations spring up everywhere.

"Caleb's shop is open! And one of the new women is working there! He says it's just a test, but I think he should do it."

"Well, he *is* very old . . . and without his sons to help, it was too much for him. Quality was going downhill."

"Which woman is there? Shaye? I heard she's a good worker."

"No. It's the other one."

"The skinny one? The poor thing, I hear they starved her in Aegea."

"Well, she's not so skinny anymore. She's quite the woman now. And she seems to know what she's doing on the looms."

"That's right. I remember now that someone said she made fine cloth back in Aegea and made great wealth for the family who kept her. How do you say her name again?"

"JAIR-ee-el."

"That Caleb is blessed! Perhaps she will marry one of his sons!"

"Perhaps she will marry one of *my* sons instead!"

Back in the shop, Jariel tilts her head to one side as she ponders the cloth Caleb handed her. All the stress she felt this morning is forgotten. She'd barely slept the night before, worrying about how the test would go. What if she couldn't figure out how to use his looms? What if the mechanisms were different from anything she'd seen in Aegea? What if he didn't like what she could produce? What if he decided he just didn't want to open his shop again? Even though Nathan told her not to worry and accompanied her to Caleb's shop, she was very nervous.

As soon as she saw the looms then samples of his work and the work of his competitors. her worries began to melt away. Although she might not be an expert in the Genon language or the ways of this people, she knows cloth—and the plant fiber that the people of homeplace use in making their cloth is the softest and most resilient that she has ever seen. What a joy it would be to be able to make fine things from it.

Caleb himself worked on looms for more than 40 years. The samples he showed her were not only sturdy, some of them were actually pretty. Best of all, Jariel knew she could not only produce similar quality work—in some instances, she was certain she could do better.

Once she started making the first sample and Nathan could see she was in her element, he departed. Genon culture didn't favor coddling, but rather challenging others to grow, to be allowed opportunities to do more. Without Nathan to translate or bargain, she was on her own. If Caleb hired her, they would eventually have to work out how they could communicate (and possibly work) with each other.

A continual stream of onlookers passes by the windows and some of them linger, leaning on the sills to watch. During the course of the day, at least ten people came inside to make inquiries. The first two times, Caleb just shrugged and gave a short reply. After that he shrugged and Jariel heard the Genon word for "maybe." By the last two inquiries, he just smiled.

Several hours pass quickly while she works on three different looms, making samples of different kinds of cloth. The only snag occurs when one of the old looms needs a repair before she can continue.

The agreement Caleb made with Nathan was that he would see if she could work on his looms, what she could produce, and how fast she might be able to produce it. After the test, Jariel would go home, allowing Caleb some time to evaluate her work and decide whether or not to reopen his shop. He would let Nathan know of his decision within a day or two.

The afternoon sun is bearing down through the west windows when he finally signals that she can go home. He says lots of things she can't understand but hopes that his nod and his broad smile mean she will have a job here.

When she's nearly ready to leave, someone familiar comes through the door. It's Samuel, known as "Mule," to his friends. He greets Caleb then turns to her.

She thought the day couldn't get any better, but it just did.

"Good afternoon," he says slowly in Genon. Then, he points to himself before moving two fingers on one hand to walk across the palm of his other hand. "I can walk you home?" He has a contagious smile.

She briefly looks into his warm brown eyes before answering with some of the Genon she has learned in recent weeks. "Yes. You honor me," before picking up her bag and slinging it over her shoulder.

Several men who'd waited outside the shop in hopes of offering to escort her home depart when they see Samuel will get the happy task.

Aware that her vocabulary is still very limited, he uses simple words. "It was a good day for you?"

She can feel her face lighting up with color. "Yes."

When she first woke up in the forest, she was so, pale, skinny, and frail, no one was certain she'd survive a venomous spider bite, much less the long trip through the many perils in the jungle. But even when she was at her most pathetic there were several times when Samuel looked at her and, possibly for the first time in her life, she felt like someone actually *saw* her. Not the colonel's daughter, not a potential heir to Westland, not the skinny insecure girl who'd never been kissed before her 17th birthday. He saw *her*. Was it what the Genon called her "sacred self" that he recognized? Both the way he looked at her and his behavior gave context to something she'd never truly considered before: There was more to her than her physical appearance, her status, her works, or things she could offer to people.

Since she first learned about this concept of sacred self a few weeks ago, she's spent time considering it. The thought that she's more than a collection of organs and bones wrapped up in skin somehow makes her glad. She wonders if the sacred self is the seat where things like joy, awe, sorrow, and love sit.

CHAPTER 8
A Day's Wages

"**D**eep sorrow is a thing that soaks into you—mind, muscle, and bone."—*A saying in the Sacred Tell*

Shaye's lungs burn with each ragged breath. The adrenalin that allowed her to bolt through the orchard and down the first half mile of the path has evaporated into shaky exhaustion. She gets to a switchback turn in the path and quickly glances up the ground she just traveled before she sighs with relief.

She chances another look away from her immediate path to view the hillside stretching out below her. *Still, I need to put more distance between them and me, and there's a long way to go.*

Loose strands of her long black hair whip across her face, tangle in her eyelashes, and tickle her nose, but she can do nothing about it. Both of her hands remain behind her back, holding up the bottom of the rough basket strapped over her shoulders. With such a large load of fruit in the basket, it's difficult to keep her balance. She blows on a wisp of hair only to have it fly back into her face.

The path grows a little steeper and she shortens her stride. *Isn't there a song with a quick rhythm to sing while I walk? A harvester's song perhaps . . .* She's so tired, nothing comes to mind. In the end she settles for quietly counting each measured step.

"One, two, three, four. One, two, three, four."

Soon, she navigates around another hairpin turn in the path. Grateful to now be moving against the wind, she shakes her head and all the loose hair blows away from her face. Tall grasses all along the path sway in the breeze with a gentle hissing sound. If she'd been here years ago, she would have run her fingers over the tops of the green blades as she sauntered down the hill or perhaps picked a spot to recline where she'd be enveloped in the gentle dance and listened to the sound. But today their whisper is drowned out by the sound of her heavy breathing and counting.

"One, two, three, four. One, two, three, four. One, two."

Wait. Isn't this what the soldiers of Aegea say as they march?

She stops counting but keeps walking. Without moving her hands from the basket, she tries to rotate each aching shoulder for even a single moment of relief. Eventually, she takes a chance and bounces the load just a little higher on her back. The higher the basket is, however, the more she must lean forward. Given the downward slope of the road and a growing baby in her belly, she can only lean forward so far without toppling over.

Just think about the wind drying out all the sweat in your dress. Feel every hair on your head, every fiber of your clothing getting lighter as the cool wind blows against it.

She arrives at the next switchback in the path and carefully steps through it. With the change in direction, the wind is now at her back again and wisps of hair return to torment her. A sudden gust pushes against the basket, forcing her to stop momentarily.

The monsoon season is nearly here and farmers are anxious to get in certain crops before daily torrential downpours begin. Harvesting is back-breaking labor so this is one of the few times they're glad to hire extra hands—but they pay with produce.

And to think, I was actually happy that I didn't have to bring Jariel today.

Jariel wasn't very adept at harvesting the one day she tried it. After the farmer doled out the shares for the workers, he told Shaye. "That girl won't get a full basket for her work. She's too weak to do a good day's work. You shouldn't have brought her to homeplace."

Sometimes she thought she'd scream if she heard the accusation one more time. No matter how many times or how firmly she said it, she hadn't managed to convince a single person that she *didn't* "bring" Jariel to homeplace. Not. One. Single. Person.

She huffs out a breath and says the name "Jariel" as if it's the name of some sickness. The girl was totally inept at outdoor work.

I must admit she tried harder to do the work than I would have imagined, and at least she let me put some of my fruit in her basket for the walk home.

Once again, her choice is weighed. *Would I rather have told the truth that day and be responsible for her death? Nathan would probably say I made the right choice, but hopefully no one will ever know.*

She keeps moving, but her steps become smaller. *Nathan. Just think about him instead of this nonsense. . . . He takes small strides and he just keeps going. Even though he's very old, he gets where he needs to be.*

She hears a single tap of something on the basket. *Was that a raindrop?* She can't straighten up and look up at the sky for fear of falling backwards with the basket. She could fall over and look like a giant, pregnant turtle—arms and legs flailing as she tried to find a way to get upright.

A tap on her head. Then another. The small, cool drops begin soaking into her hair and clothing. A quick glance tells her there are patches of sunshine and shadow all down the hillside, so she dares to hope it's just one small rain cloud, here one moment, gone the next. She groans as the tempo of the tapping increases.

Think of how refreshing it is. Pretend you're out here, dancing in a shower that the sky has provided.

Larger drops pelt her before the cloud moves on, leaving her in a mix of sunshine, the smell of damp soil, and a rising mist. *Remember that day Mother took us to get plants and see the cousins?*

She's at the Outpost of Aegea where her cousins live. It was one of the regular trips when Mama brought her, Jariel, and Ty in the wagon. The adults go inside when the rain starts but she and Jariel run with Joy and some of her other cousins through a field, laughing and dancing through the tall, sparkling stalks of corn . . . in a half-hearted attempt to hide from Ty.

They find a small lean-to where tools are often stored and hide under it when they hear footfalls nearby. "*Shhhhhhhhhhh!*" the girls tell each other and crouch down, with toes squishing into the warm, muddy soil.

She squeals as his wet face, framed with drenched, golden-red curls pops into view and he cries, "*Boo!* I got you! *I got you!*"

Lost in the memory she doesn't notice the patch of wet clay on the path. When her right foot hits it, she skids several feet before catching her balance.

That was a close call. She bumps the basket up on her back again and resumes walking, keeping a closer watch on the path, grunting with each step.

Have I ever felt this spent before? Even if I could stop and rest, how would I be able to get the basket up on my back again?

It's then that she notices a good-sized rock ahead, just before the next bend in the path. Was it there this morning? Glancing up the hill, she can see a fresh gash where the knee-high stone (probably set free by a passing shower) rolled down, crashing through hedges and grasses before it came to rest beside the bend in the path. She pulls in a deep breath and focuses all her will upon it.

I will sit upon it and rest . . . just for a few minutes.

By the time she's close to the stone she's nearly out of strength and staggers toward it. When she arrives, she has to place both hands upon it and push back in order to halt her forward progress. As she does so, several pieces of the yellow fruit roll out of the basket, pelt her head, then hit the ground. No longer caring how she will get the load back up on her back, she takes her arm out of one strap then leans sideways. The burden plops to the ground with a heavy thud, then starts to topple over. She manages to catch it, but not before nearly a third of the fruit scatters out onto the ground. Several pieces just keep rolling down the hill and she closes her eyes rather than watch them disappear into the grass.

I cannot chase them. I must sit down.

She props the basket against the rock and eases herself onto its muddy top, not caring about the stain the orange-red soil will leave on the back of her dress.

Perhaps I won't need to work in the orchard again.

Several of the men working the orchard with her would gladly have helped her carry the basket but the foul smelling farmer made her wait until all the other workers were long gone. As soon as she realized what he'd done, she feared he might harm her in some way but kept a brave face. When he approached her she tried to keep her distance.

"You know," he said, "you could be part of this family. We have fertile land here. If you remained a good worker," he paused while his eyes roamed her figure, "my son could overlook your transgressions of the past. He would be a good match for you since all of this will be his one day. If your child was a good worker, we would allow it a fair share here, too." With a pudgy finger, he wiped the sweat out of a fold in his neck and he stepped closer to her, but moved back when his son came into view. "Here he is now. Perhaps we could—"

She snatched up her basket. "Truly, it's late. I must be going!"

Somehow, she managed to hoist the basket on her back and hurry out of the orchard, scratching her face on a branch in her haste to get away. Now, all of the energy she expended in the escape is gone and she's not sure she can carry the basket another step, much less another mile down the path to homeplace.

With hands on the small of her back, she tries in vain to stretch out some of the aches. *Why is it so hard to breathe?*

She tries to distract herself by finding the scratch on her cheek. When her fingers trace over it, she realizes it's more than two inches long.

I cannot go back to that orchard. I can't.

The glimmers of hope she had when she first arrived in homeplace seem far in the distance, with each day becoming a long, painful ordeal, followed by a night where she often awakens, feeling abandoned and heartbroken, wondering if this is how overwhelmed her mother felt when her father died, leaving her to eke out a living and care for a small child.

Perhaps I will be so tired I will sleep tonight . . . but will my sleep be filled with dreams of being stalked by a creature, or seeing myself with the black line across my lips . . . or dreams of Ty taking vows with Linsey?

A slow exhale is accompanied by a long moan. She closes her mouth and pulls in a deep breath through her nose. Without wanting to, as she breathes out she moans again. This time it's louder and she shudders.

I can't go on like this.

She feels herself losing control but lacks the strength or the desire to restrain herself. At least in this solitude she doesn't have to bury her face in a pillow the way she does many nights while Jariel and Willow sleep nearby. She's alone and can make as much noise as she wants. As she opens her mouth, the moan turns into a wail and she suddenly pitches forward as the sound of all her accumulated grief boils out of her like a bad meal. At first, all she can do is howl, since there are no words to describe the anger and the sorrow. When language comes back to her, the only words she can say between sobs are, "I need help. Please help me."

At one point, she tries to rein it all in, but another wave sweeps over her. Finally, after the sounds have ceased, she wraps her arms around herself and just rocks back and forth.

Scurrying clouds move on, leaving the late-day sun to shine upon her. She's aware of the gentle breeze again, and she lets herself feel it.

Despite her fatigue, she knows she *must* get going, for the sun will set in less than an hour. After wiping her nose on her sleeve she tries to push herself off the boulder, but fails in her first attempt.

Her sore back and legs are forgotten when the sound of a man's voice comes to her ears. She looks up the path and there's an uptick in her heartbeat when she sees two men swiftly moving down the path in her direction.

A momentary rush of relief comes when she realizes that it *isn't* the farmer and his son—but concern grows again when she recognizes one of the men. She had an unpleasant encounter with him on her first day in homeplace.

Just before she set foot in the village, he strutted up to her with two companions who looked enough like him to be his brothers. He said his name was Flint and he eyed her as if she was naked before he made an indecent suggestion. She responded with all the scorn she could muster—which only made him laugh. He then made a similar suggestion to Jariel (who, fortunate for her, couldn't understand the language at the time). Then Nathan intervened and rebuked the young man, calling him by his real name, Francis, and told him to leave. The rude fellow turned and swaggered off with his entourage as if he didn't care. Even if he hadn't been so vulgar she would have remembered him because of his clean-shaven face. Genon tradition said men should let their beards grow, so in a whole settlement of whiskered men, his smooth face marked him as a rebel before he'd ever said a word. Since then, she'd only seen him from a distance, but every time he'd given her a mischievous grin and a wink.

And now, here he is to trouble me. I never asked for any of this.

She takes several quick breaths and makes another attempt to rise off of the boulder before Flint rushes forward and takes her arm. "We saw you from above," he says, nodding to a spot near the top of the hill.

Glancing into his eyes, she wonders, *Did he see me making a fool of myself?* She has no idea that her tears and snot have left trails through the dust on her face.

Without asking permission, he drops his bow and picks up her basket.

She's too exhausted to protest. She cannot bring herself to ask for the burden to be returned to her. She watches him slide his arms into the straps and realizes she's actually relieved. His companion also drops the items he was carrying so he can gather most of the scattered fruit, dusting each piece on his shirt before placing it back in the basket. She allows herself another glance at their faces. Flint has several days' worth of dark stubble on his face—a bit of a departure from the clean-shaven look he had when she first saw him. The other fellow, judging by his appearance, is perhaps in his mid-teens. Although there's a resemblance between the two of them, she hasn't seen this one before.

The young man fishes around in a pocket and pulls out a piece of cloth, then offers it to Shaye. When she's slow to accept it, he points to her face.

Flint tells her, "You have dirt on your face, and a cut on your cheek."

She takes the cloth and tells the owner, "Thank you."

The young man smiles as she rubs the rag across her face a couple of times and gives it back. He doesn't speak, but she's found that many of the males here in homeplace are either extremely bold or very shy in her presence.

"Are you one of Flint's brothers?" she asks.

He nods.

"He is the youngest of five brothers," Flint tells her. "His name is Seth."

With the breeze blowing over the two men she can smell the green scent of a walk among the trees on their clothes. They have bows, arrows, and the birds they've killed dangle from leather strings. Just like in Aegea, nearly every family in homeplace has a vocation that employs most of its members. Flint and his family must be hunters.

"I am Shaye," she says to the young man. They exchange a nod before Flint starts walking down the hill. She joins him and Seth falls in behind them, carrying the hunting gear and the birds. They get to the next bend in the path before anyone speaks again.

"Thank you for helping me."

"Sure."

No boasting, no strutting, no vile suggestions about what she might do to repay him. Instead, there is something almost kind in his manner.

Little by little, his long stride puts more and more distance between them. It's only when he reaches the next turn in the path that he realizes how far ahead he is. He stops and waits till she's near again before he says. "I'm used to walking fast. I wasn't thinking about you walking slower. Sorry."

They set off again at a slower pace, Flint walking side-by-side with her most of the time, and his brother trailing just behind. Finally, her curiosity gets the better of her. "Why were you behaving like such a villain when I first saw you? Why did you say those awful things to me?"

He shrugs. "We live in a place where there are plenty of men looking for courtship, a wife, a family. Many of them are good men and many of them lined the streets to see you and the other girl on that first day. How many of them did you notice? How many of them do you remember?"

She frowns. "I suppose none. But we were tired. We were afraid and overwhelmed."

He points a finger in the air. "Ah! But you *do* remember *me*, don't you?"

"Well, I suppose you're right about that . . . but still, why be noticed just to be disliked?"

He grins. "Some women are attracted to incorrigible men."

Ah! Here it comes, she tells herself. *Now he'll make a disgusting offer.*

When he sees she isn't amused, he clears his throat and says, "Well, some people are heroes who thrive on the admiration of others. But most are the invisible unknowns that make up a crowd. They don't make trouble, they just get pulled along with everyone else—sometimes they get pulled where they don't really want to go. Many work hard, survive, and have families before they die. *What's it all for?* And then there are villains. I've studied this, and frankly, being a villain gives you lots of space to move around with the least amount of work. The whole gift of it is that most people have no expectations for you to live up to and they leave you alone." He straightens his posture under the load of the basket. "Every community needs a villain to distract them once in a while . . . someone they can compare themselves to and feel better. . . . Well, that's me. They may not realize it, but I'm doing them a service, really. I've made my peace with it."

She cannot formulate any sort of response to this, so they continue the downward trek to town in silence for a while. When they reach a large, muddy hole in the road, the brothers take her hands as she circles the edge of it.

"So . . ." she finally says, hoping to start a more pleasant conversation, "are you the oldest of the five brothers?"

He nods.

"Any sisters?"

"No."

Her eyes widen. "No daughters and five sons! That must have been challenging for your mother. How did she survive with so many men under foot?"

He stares ahead. "Our mother went to be with the Maker the night Seth was born."

Mortified, she fixes her focus on the path before them, then finally offers a quiet, "I'm sorry that you lost her."

The sun is about to touch the far horizon when they round the last corner in the path and the tall grasses give way to a view of the village.

Flint stops walking and turns to her. Tucking his thumbs under the straps of the basket as if he's ready to take it off, he asks, "You want me to carry it further, or would you rather see if someone else wants to carry it for you?"

She considers the heavy load for a moment, then looks down the road toward the village. Several men are within earshot. If she called out, doubtless, at least one or two would jump at the chance to help her. Her gaze returns to Flint and Seth.

He finally says, "Well . . . ?"

"I . . ." she begins.

He leans his head to one side, awaiting an answer.

"You honor me. I would appreciate your help."

His eyebrows shoot up in surprise before he says, "Sure."

He hefts the basket higher onto his back and then moves his hand outward, inviting her to lead the way. As they approach, some of the villagers stop what they're doing to watch the trio. Many of them frown when they see Flint, but he returns their stares with a cocky smirk and keeps walking.

Shaye knows more about the village now; and many of the small streets are familiar to her. The rambling mix of stone buildings and wooden shacks with thatched roofs is beginning to feel more and more like home. After the first intersection, they pass by a shack that normally amuses her because the entire structure tilts to one side. Even the door and window openings to the dwelling have the same angle. The owner, either unwilling or unable to right the leaning structure, has resorted to ropes that loop over pegs to keep the door and shutters in place when they are opened and closed. She assumes that a great wind or some other calamity must have pushed upon the house in the past, but she doesn't really know why it is the way it is. Tonight, she's too tired to ponder the quirky little dwelling.

All she wants is to get home, to Willow's house. The widow took them in the first day they arrived and, although they probably could wheedle better accommodations now, they've both grown fond of the woman who seemed so formidable at first, but soon softened.

The citizens of homeplace are bustling about, using the last glow in the sky to find their way home, then prepare an evening meal and find a few hours of rest. The smells of burning charcoal, firewood, and various kinds of food fill the air. The scents seem to mingle with voices—bits of the day's news, people humming, laughter—as she passes by homes and shops along the way.

When they see her, people offer the customary greeting for that time of day, and she gives the polite response.

"Good evening."

"Good evening."

Neither Flint nor his brother speak, since it seems to be understood by everyone that no one is greeting the hunter brothers. A woman with a thick black line across her lips from her nose to her chin is walking the other direction. She passes them, saying nothing. Shaye recalls the first time she saw someone with this mark and asked what it was.

"It's the mark for speaking untruth," Willow told her. "When someone has told an untruth that hurts others, they can be brought before the council. If they are found guilty, the one who is harmed dips a stick in the juice made from inkberries and makes the mark across the person's lips.

"And they are marked like that forever? For telling an untruth?"

"No, the mark wears off in time. It's a vindication for the victim, a consequence for the one who lied, and a reminder to all not to speak untruth."

Shaye shudders and keeps walking down narrow streets that grow dimmer by the moment. People light candles or lamps inside their homes and the light shines out through open doors or windows, lending a little light to those walking by. Drawing on her last ounces of strength, Shaye tries to pick up the pace, but when they round a dark corner, she bumps into someone. For a moment she and the other person take hold of each other's arms in order to remain upright.

"Pardon me . . ." she says as they let go of the mutual grip.

When a woman steps out of a nearby doorway carrying a lamp, it allows Shaye to recognize the man's long, slender face and eyes almost as golden as her own.

"Good evening, Benjamin," she says.

A look of shock flashes across his face when he recognizes her, then hardens into full-blown scorn when he sees the hunter brothers behind her. His eyes nearly glow with anger as his focus zeros in on her stomach and slowly rises to her face again. He turns his head to spit toward Flint's feet before he walks away.

Completely stunned, she looks back at the brothers.

In an attempt to make light of it, Flint asks, "Do you suppose he was trying to insult me, or you, or all of us?" while drawing an imaginary circle between them with his finger. When it's obvious she's not amused, he clears his throat and pokes his chin at the retreating Benjamin. "Well anyway, that was very rude."

Her head slumps to her chest.

"You like that fellow?" he challenges. "His beard and his ways—are they *appealing* to you? Do you want him to pursue you?"

"No. I don't like him or his beard . . . or whatever," she exhales heavily. "And I never sought to have him like *me*, either. It's just that, during the trip to homeplace, he made all these assumptions about me . . . or about us—not that there was ever an 'us'. But once he realized . . ."

Flint waits for her to finish the sentence, then realizes she doesn't want to elaborate any further and he shrugs. "Benjamin considers himself a zealot for the 'pure' ways of our people, but that's disputable." Stepping closer to her, he peers into her eyes. "Someday you must ask yourself if he wanted you because he saw the true worth of your sacred self or merely because he saw you as a thing that would make him feel more significant. . . . If you had come here and you weren't carrying a child, would you have courted him?"

On the first day of the journey here, Ben kept his hand on his knife as he bombarded her with questions about Jariel—a girl who didn't look or dress like someone of Genon descent. She thought he might take the girl's life at any moment. During the entire trip, he aggressively guarded Shaye from the other men. She'd never forget how he whispered flatteries to her, and how his intensity made her skin crawl. Without consulting her, he'd assumed he had a right to some claim upon her. He assumed it until the moment they arrived here and a driving rain soaked her dress—revealing her baby bump. Shaye returns Flints gaze. "No. I wouldn't have courted him."

"Your downcast look is a confusion to me then. Are you sure you shouldn't go after him and do whatever it is you think he wants?"

Twilight has turned to darkness and Benjamin is gone from sight. She lets out a long sigh. "Nearly my whole life, I wanted to walk free among the Exiles I'd heard stories about. I wanted so much to walk as an upright woman among them. Now . . . it just hurts that people think I'm . . . not."

It's difficult to see Flint's face very well, but she can hear the seriousness in his voice. "Are any of *us* the people you imagined we'd be? Things rarely turn out the way we imagine they would. It's up to you to decide if you can be content with that or not. You'll have to let go of the life you imagined in order to live the one you have. You must choose between trying to be who people *imagine* you are and just being who you are."

Her pulse rises. "You're one to talk. Someone who chooses to portray himself as a scoundrel. Are you as rotten as you want people to believe you are?"

He steps back from her. "We should keep going."

Willow squints her eyes as she inspects the repair she just made to the fishing net suspended from a large hook in the ceiling. Her seat near the window gave her plenty of light until now. When a nearby lamp lights up, she looks away from her task.

"You honor me," she says.

Jariel steps around the piled netting and moves toward another lamp to be lit. She knows that "you honor me" is another way of saying "thank you" in the Genon culture and she's learned some of the proper responses, so she offers one in return.

"It's my honor to help."

Willow gives her an uncharacteristic smile and watches her light the other lamps in the front room of the house. When the girl first arrived, she was a skittish skeleton of a thing with dull brown hair. Her bony face, arms, and feet were covered with peeling, sun blistered skin. Any bit of clothing long enough for her to wear hung on her like a towel draped over a twig. But once she started eating, she devoured each meal as if she was hollow—and as weeks turned into months, her figure rounded out very nicely. The tropical sun has given her milky skin a bronzed glow and put golden streaks in her hair. Just as the outer woman has blossomed, so has the inner one. She's feasted on the hearty welcome of the people of homeplace. Growing in confidence, she's applied herself to learning the Genon language and culture. Not surprisingly, the line of men who would like to court her grows daily. The old woman shakes her head and goes back to mending the net.

Jariel's limited Genon vocabulary cannot express what she feels today so she opts for her native language. "I know you can't understand me, but I'm just so excited, I'm bursting to tell someone what a wonderful day I've had. I can hardly wait for Shaye to get here so she can translate for me. And I hope we can see Nathan tonight so we can tell him, too. I could tell that Caleb the Weaver was impressed with the sample cloths I made for him." She checks a pot over a small fire and switches to Genon again. "I get dishes for supper? Rice done, so I put her on the side for stay warm . . ."

There is an audible chuckle coming from the seat by the window.

Just down the street from Willow's home, Flint suddenly comes to a stop in the light of a doorway, "My brother and I need to leave you now."

"But the house is right there," Shaye says, pointing at it.

He ignores her statement and makes a gesture for her to turn around. When she does, the basket is carefully placed on her back, and the load is adjusted before she slowly turns to thank them for their help. When she does, she realizes they're already walking away. She starts to raise her voice and say something, but changes her mind.

When she arrives at home, the light inside the open door is welcoming. *Just a few more steps . . .* She takes several big breaths before climbing the last two stairs onto the porch. Once she crosses the threshold of the home, she leans against the wall near the door. Does she have the strength to shrug the basket off and not let it drop to the floor? No. The air smells of rice . . . and lamp oil . . . and something she wouldn't have recognized before she came to homeplace: seaweed. The scent of almost anything from the ocean made her queasy until a month ago, but it's not so bad now.

Willow pushes the net away from her feet and rises from her chair while Jariel rushes out of the kitchen with a flurry of unwelcome observations. "You look so dragged out and so *tired*. You're so *dirty*. And what happened to your face?"

In that moment, Shaye sees—really sees—her traveling companion for the first time in a long while. *No one in Aegea would recognize her.* And suddenly, she feels even more out of sorts. "I got scratched by a tree limb," she says in a grouchy tone.

Jariel helps her remove the basket as the old woman draws near. "My dear child, you look like you rolled in the mud." She reaches out and moves Shaye's chin to one side. "What happened to your face?"

This time, she answers the question in Genon—and more politely.

The old woman picks up a piece of the fruit from the basket. "I know a man, who can dry some of this fruit for us. And, perhaps he will offer us a trade for some of it. Once the rainy season is upon us, it will spoil pretty quickly."

The son of a neighbor appears in the doorway behind Shaye. He's carrying two wooden buckets, each filled nearly to the brim with water. "Here are the last two," he says, smiling at Jariel. "This should be more than enough." At fourteen, Isaac has a voice that alternates between that of a child and that of a man.

She nods and steps out of the pathway back to the bathroom before she offers another Genon expression of gratitude. "We are blessed."

His eyes shine as he nods at her and glides past with the pails. Within moments, he's dumped the water and standing before her like someone paying homage. "Let me know if you need anything else."

He backs out of the door with what looks like a little bow.

Shaye waits till he's out of earshot to speak. "Well, I'm so glad you have people to draw your water for you. You've probably had most of the afternoon to wash up, but now I suppose I'll have to wait for you to take one of your long baths!"

"How long I bathe is *none* of your concern, but—"

"I should have *known* you'd want to bathe first. Of *course* you would! The only person you ever worry about is yourself."

Jariel's mouth drops open. When she finds her voice she says, "The water is for *you*. I remembered how awful we felt after we worked in the orchard last time. I knew you'd be tired, so when Isaac asked if we needed anything, I asked him if he would bring the water in. For you."

It's the second time today she's embarrassed herself by jumping to a conclusion. "Oh."

"'*Oh*'? No apology, just '*Oh*'?" Jariel throws her hands up in exasperation. "That's right. How could I forget? The mighty Shaye *never* apologizes."

She nearly jumps back when her very pregnant adversary leans in, and in a voice barely above a whisper, says, "That's right. I'd almost forgotten that you weren't there the last time I tried to apologize for a conflict *you* started. You hid up in your room with your fine clothes and fancy pillows while it was decided that I'd be sold off like a sack of grain."

The old woman watches the exchange, not knowing what the two are saying. It's a scene she's seen played out often—a seemingly simple conversation suddenly turning ugly. The uproars between the two young women don't happen as often now, but there's an unmistakable intensity to their disagreements that goes beyond current offenses. Almost as if she's thinking aloud, she says, "You know . . . the two of you fight more like sisters." She stands at a distance eyeing the two of them as she continues pondering aloud. "It's . . . more like you grew up in the same house than that you were accidental travelling companions. Like there's a bad history that keeps springing up."

Shaye's manner suddenly changes. "I apologize."

Jariel's head snaps back in shock. "Is this like what you would call 'a miracle'? I must find out exactly what Willow said."

The response is slow and deliberate. "Take your victory and quit. Now."

"Fine. Apology accepted."

The flash of anger has given her a spurt of energy. She turns away and begins pulling the pins from her long, black mane. As it cascades down her back, she runs her fingers along her scalp lifting the weight of hair that's grown another four inches in the past few months. "I'll go and bathe now."

Before she can leave the room, they all hear a *tap, tap, tap* and a familiar voice with the standard Genon word that declares a desire to talk to someone in the house. "Inside. Inside."

It's Nathan, the old man who led the women through the Great Forest, down the long river, and to homeplace. He's standing there with his wife, Peony, smiling from the doorway. In his hands is a clay pot with a lid. It must be hot, for he's holding the handles with a cloth.

"We wanted to come and see you, and we brought something to share!" He says, holding out the pot.

His wife lifts the lid on it and the rising steam wafts into the room, bearing the scent of a perfectly cooked *sooshi* hen.

He looks at the women. "Did we interrupt something? Did we come at a bad time?"

Willow steps aside. "Come in. It's always good to see you both. And I'm sure the one of us who is pregnant will be *especially* glad, since she has endless cravings for *sooshi*." She leans toward her housemate and says, "So go quickly and bathe before dinner. I'm sure you will feel renewed once you're clean."

Shaye closes her eyes as she inhales the aroma. *Yes. Sooshi hen . . . and cool water to wash off the dirt of the day.* It's hard for her to imagine how one could yearn for something as much as she longs for roasted *sooshi*. Sometimes, she even dreams about it. Truth be told, she might even be willing to hug Jariel to eat that bird!

The tiny washroom in Willow's house has a wooden tub made from half of a barrel with a plug in the bottom. The plug is strategically placed over a clay pipe in the floor that runs under the wall and drains into a larger pipe behind the houses. When Shaye lights a lamp, she sees the tub is half-full with an extra two buckets of water for the final rinse after the tub drains. Jariel already placed a cloth and a little bar of soap on the shelf next to the tub. Fresh undergarments and a dress hang on pegs near the door.

The expression on her face softens as she looks at the clean dress. On the day they arrived in homeplace, Willow opened a cabinet containing shelves of clothes for them. Of all the dresses in the cupboard, the color of this one caught her eye first. Jariel noticed it, too. The color was the very reason, she resisted wearing it for the first week or so, but it seemed to call to her every time she looked in the cupboard so she finally gave in and wore it. After that, she couldn't resist wearing it whenever it was clean.

She runs her fingers along the fabric and wonders, *will I tell my child "this was the very color of your father's eyes"?*

She hears the chatter in the other room and remembers they are waiting for her to return before dinner is served.

###

The five of them huddle around the small table in the warm glow of oil lamps, basking in a contented moment. The bones of the *sooshi* and most of the dishes have been cleared away.

Nathan's wife, Peony, hasn't said much, but her eyes sparkle as if she's holding a delightful secret. Finally, she puts a tender hand on her husband's arm and says, "You'd better tell them before Shaye falls asleep right here at the table."

He rolls his eyes with feigned drama, before he relents. "Well daughters," he says, holding onto his long beard as he leans across the table, "we have good news! The Maker has answered our prayers for you and a provision has arrived."

Shaye, Willow, and Jariel all lean in closer.

"As you may have been told, Caleb the weaver, closed up his shop last year when he got too old to do it alone and his sons said they had no interest in weaving."

As Shaye translates, Jariel nods.

Not wanting to get to the good part of the story too soon, the old man feels the need to diverge a bit. "Instead, his sons joined their uncle who digs in the pits."

Shaye translates, but stops to ask a question of her own. "Digging in pits? What pits? What for? Charcoal? Or for metals like some do in the mountains?"

The old man shakes his head, "No. For pitch."

"For what? What is pitch?"

Anxious to hear about Caleb, Jariel gently taps her translator's arm—the established signal that she needs to know what is being said. Shaye complies and they watch the old man as he looks around the room—his mind must be searching for a way to describe pitch.

"It's almost like clay, but it's black . . ."

"And it's sticky," Peony adds with her nose scrunched up.

Willow scrunches up her nose as well. "And it smells bad."

As if they could smell it, the two young women mirror the unpleasant expression as Nathan continues, conceding the points of his wife and his sister. "Yes, it's sticky—stickier than honey, and strong smelling, and it is black like the darkest night. Workers gather it into gigantic clumps and cover it with cloth . . . and they skewer the clumps on long polls, then carry it back to homeplace. The pits where they dig it up are six-days walk from here—eight or ten days when they are walking back, heavy laden."

Shaye stops translating to ask another question. "What's it for?"

"Even though it is *nasty* to work with, it's very valuable. The pitch makes it possible for us to build large boats that can safely travel over the great waves of the ocean. It also gives us fuel for torches and lamps."

"You make boats from it?"

Nathan and Peony exchange an amused glance before he says, "No. But perhaps you have wondered how big boats can stay afloat on the water. How is it that the spaces between the pieces of wood don't let the water in?"

"Yes, Jariel and I worried about this on the river."

"Well, the pitch is sort of like this wax," he says, tipping the small candle at the center of the table. The hot liquid drips onto the table and he immediately swipes a rough finger across it, filling a small gap in the wood. "It fills the seams—but it is stronger than wax and water cannot wash it off."

Willow gives him a stern look and takes the candle off the table, so he quickly scratches most of the wax off the wood with his fingernail.

Both of the young women say, "*Ohhhhhhhhhh,*" before Jariel suddenly grabs Shaye's arm. "He doesn't think we can work digging it up, does he?"

Nathan understands her words and chuckles before he tells Peony, who taps his hand and says, "Stop teasing them and get to the point."

"No one expects either of you to work in the pits or with the pitch. As a matter of fact, Caleb was so impressed by Jariel's work today, he wasted no time in deliberations. He wants to open his shop again and to make her an offer."

As Jariel hears the translation, she jumps up from her seat and leans over to kiss Nathan on the cheek. "Oh thank you! Thank you!"

Willow grabs her hand and says "That's wonderful news!"

"Yes, yes," Nathan says. "It is good news, but I have more. Perhaps you didn't hear the runners tell the other bits of news today."

Jariel takes her seat again and they all lean in to hear it.

"As it turns out, the workers have had a good season in the pits and are coming home before the rainy season sets in. One of the oceangoing boats has returned and more will be returning soon, too. The men on the ships will spend much of the rainy season here, perhaps only venturing out for short trips. During that time," he pokes his chin in Willow's direction, "there will be many nets to repair, and the boats themselves will need repairs. Ren, the boat builder, told me he is even going to finish that boat he's been building for so long! What all this means is that a time of blessing, a time of plenty, may be upon us. It will spread all the way through the community as people buy, sell, trade, and give." Nathan stops for a moment to let Shaye's translation catch up with what he's said so far. When she looks at him again he smiles and says, "Since the two of you arrived, a feeling of hope has washed over many of the people in homeplace."

Even while she's translating, Shaye is thinking, *He must not have talked to Benjamin recently.*

"You know, Caleb closed his shop when his sons decided they wanted to strike out on their own and dig in the pits to make more money." Nathan continues, "Caleb was too old to work alone, but he told me this evening that his oldest son has sent word that digging pitch is not at all what he wants to do. Now that his son will rejoin him and with Jariel to work the looms, they can make a good go of it." He gives her a wink. "I'm also thinking that reports of fine looking young women coming to the village may have had *something* to do with his decision."

As he says this, he and his wife take Jariel's hands.

"We have prayed for you, daughter," he tells her, "and we know that the Maker is working on your behalf. You will be a blessing and you will be blessed."

While Jariel wipes away happy tears, Shaye stares down at the table.

When the room grows silent, Shaye looks up and sees the old man is now looking at her. He takes her hand. "We are praying for you, too. We see your difficulties, but many people have noted that you work hard, that you are honest, that you make sure to provide for Willow as well as your sister here. We all know you need easier work, and we've been looking for something that would bless you, too. It has happened. Now that the ships are returning, there is a lot of activity along the water's edge. You may have noticed some empty buildings there—but now they will be filled with activity and people again. A cousin of Peony whose name is Clay makes food for the workers there. We told him you know how to cook and he says you can work for him if you wish."

She should be happy, but all she feels is numbness . . . and exhaustion. She tries to smile as she says, "Truly, you honor me. I am grateful for all you have done."

Nathan raises his hands, then closes them as if he is grasping something. "Two years ago, a lingering darkness settled onto the Maker's own people. It took hold of us and we were walking away from our true selves—away from the part of us that knows Him, away from what He made us to be. We'd lost our hope. Then, I felt He was calling me to journey into the forest once again. From that time to this, I have known in my heart that the journey would change our course. I know you are weary, but don't lose heart, daughter, the Maker is at work." His face shines with delight as he says, "He is wakening us all—and who knows what He will do next?"

With the evening meal eaten, Willow and Peony busy themselves scraping off the dishes and setting things back in order, Shaye gravitates to the large chair in the corner that has a window on either side. With a cushioned back and seat, this seems to be the only piece of furniture in Willow's house that was made with comfort in mind.

As the village grows quiet, she can hear the ocean in the distance. In the soft light Shaye looks down at her belly and studies the blue of her dress for a moment before she turns her attention out into the night outside the window. The conversations in the room grow dim as she concentrates on the sound of the surf. Although the thought of letting waves touch her feet still frightens her, hearing their endless rhythm in the distance at night comforts her soul. It's a reminder that there are larger things than her problems and that the One who set the waves in continual motion can watch over her. Just as the cadenced creak of an old rocking chair helps lull a child to sleep, so the sound of the sea helps Shaye drift away. Willow drapes a thin blanket over her and quietly moves away.

The old women exchange the latest news—two hens softly clucking to each other out on the front porch, occasionally waving at people walking by. Nathan sits at the table teaching Jariel new words in Genon.

Eventually, Nathan and Peony go home, Willow and Jariel trudge off to bed, leaving Shaye by the open window where she dreams a dream she's had many times before.

> It's a moonlit night and she's standing on the roof of the Great House of Westland, looking at the sky. Someone else is there. She turns to face him and realizes it's Ty. A deep sorrow fills her heart and she says, "We have different paths set before us . . . and those paths lead in different directions."
>
> "I cannot accept that," he says, drawing close to her. "Stargazer Shaye . . . what a perplexity you are. You long to walk in heavenly realms . . . yet you choose this moment to insist on practicality." He leans forward so that his mouth is only an inch

from her ear. "Who is to say what changes we might see in this world? Don't say you won't see me anymore. I couldn't bear the thought."

The moonlight dims and a dark wind pushes him out of her presence. She cannot reach him, so she strains to keep his eyes in focus. Just as everything goes dark, she turns and sees her own reflection in the *ishi's* bright brass mirror. A black line appears over her lips and as she tries to wipe it off, the inky color starts to spread across her face and down her neck.

Something brushes by her face and she bolts awake, grateful to know it was only a dream. When she looks around, she realizes a breeze blew the long window curtain into the room and over her face. As the zephyr subsided, the curtain settled to one side, across her shoulder and lap. Outside, the moon must be setting for there is very little light.

When she pushes the curtain away, she suddenly realizes something is outside the window. It's a hazy figure of a man, like a dark vapor in the dim starlight. At first, she thinks she must still be dreaming, but she soon realizes there really *is* a man standing outside the window.

Startled, she asks, "*Who is that?*"

The silhouette takes a step closer and answers in a voice barely above a whisper. "It's me, Benjamin."

She pulls her blanket up below her chin and asks, "What are you doing here at this time of night? What do you want?"

"I must speak with you."

"Now?"

"I think—" he hesitates, then starts again. "You should take vows with me. I am willing to redeem you."

"What?"

"It's not that I want to, since I find your current state disgusting . . . but this is what the Maker wants, so we should be obedient."

Perhaps I am still in the nightmare. She blinks several times as she stares at the head of the shadowy figure. "So . . . you find me 'disgusting,' but think I should take vows with you?"

"The child needs someone's name. You need a husband who is upright who will teach you what is right."

She draws in a huge breath before she starts shouting, "If I *ever* take vows, it will not be with you! I would rather go to my grave in disgrace than marry a man such as you! How dare you *slink* up on me like this, in the dark of night—as if being seen talking to me would harm you in some way!"

It's as if he hasn't heard a word. "But marrying me would take away your shame."

Her head is almost spinning with rage. Despite sore muscles and a big belly, she shoots out of her chair with every intention of leaning out the window to strike him. "Why you rotten *goat!*"

The door to Willow's room flies open. "*Shaye, what's wrong?*"

She turns her head for an instant to say what is happening, "I woke up and—" then turns back to see he's gone. People along the street have heard the commotion and they're lighting lamps to investigate. Shaye grabs the lower shutters on the window then pulls them closed and locks them before she sits back in the chair, panting.

The old woman lights a candle on the table then pulls a kitchen chair over next to Shaye. "What's wrong child? Are you all right?"

"A man came to the window. It was Benjamin—the one who came through the forest with us." She shivers. "He crept up to the window and was watching me sleep. He insulted me. And *then* told me I should take vows with him."

Willow shakes her head and sighs before saying, "That sounds about like Benjamin. He's all fire and vinegar. That young man could just *walk* by a flower and it would wilt."

The baby kicks inside Shaye's womb and she places her hand on the spot where she feels her belly stretching out with the movement. "My heart hurts so much. How could I ever think of taking vows with *anyone,* especially a jot like him?"

A wrinkled hand gently sweeps the dark hair off her shoulder. "Get some rest. The things that worry us at night are easier to sort out in the daylight."

The light is blown out and she hears the creak of the bedroom door before she leans back into the chair again. Her heart is pounding so hard, she's unsure if she'll be able to get any more sleep. Soon, however, her pulse slows, her eyelids grow heavy, and exhaustion takes over.

In a dream she hears something her mother said to her years ago.

> "In our family, we love forever. It's a
> blessing and a curse. I loved your father with
> my whole heart . . . and I cannot stop.
> Forgive me."

It seems only a moment before she hears the sounds of a soft shuffle across the floor, but hours have passed. Willow is up and ready to start preparing the morning meal.

Shaye slowly rises from her chair feeling every muscle from the long day she spent in the orchards yesterday. She isn't anywhere near as nimble as she felt last night in full ire. Not quite ready to walk yet, she folds the blanket that was on her lap and sets it aside before saying, "Good morning. I'm sorry I woke you last night. Did you get any more sleep? Did Jariel wake up with all the commotion?"

"I'm an old woman. I rarely sleep well. As for Jariel," She chuckles as she lights the small candle and sets it on the counter, "I believe that girl could sleep through the end of the world. But how about you? I'm sorry I left the bottom shutters on the window open, but I couldn't get to them without waking you. I know how hot it is in our room, and you looked so comfortable there with the window open. I never considered that someone would bother you while you slept—much less Benjamin of all people. Did you get any more sleep?"

"Yes."

They already have a routine. Shaye gets the bowls out and brings in some water, Willow starts a small fire in the hearth and mixes up some meal in one of the bowls. The two of them cut up some fruit to have with their bread.

First, Shaye opens the shutters in the kitchen, then the ones on the living room windows. When she opens the last one, she leans out and looks up at the sky. One star stubbornly shines against the growing light of day in a cloudless morning but a brilliant blue will soon overtake the little glimmer.

More to herself than anyone else she says, "Thank the Maker, a clear day."

Straightening her stance again, she attempts to stretch while she draws in a deep breath, but a sharp spasm in her back abruptly stops the effort.

"Ouch *ouch!*"

The pain only lasts a moment but it's a portent of the not-too-distant future.

"Won't be long now." Willow says.

This brings to mind a serious question. "How long do you think?"

"Oh," she answers with a shrug, "you would be the better judge of that. I just know that for several weeks before my daughter was born, I would get twinges like that. It's normal."

Shaye knows next to nothing about having a baby. Growing up an orphan in the Great House of Westland in the nurture of a woman who never married or had children wasn't the typical upbringing for a Genon girl. Normally, one would have multiple siblings, even more cousins, aunts, uncles, and live in close connection with a tight-knit community. The details of living, loving, birthing, and dying were all in full view or generally broadcast. It was all part of the conversation in the shared fellowship of Genon people. But not so with Shaye, who lived on the bottom floor of the Great House of Westland. Although she never felt welcome inside the house, the fact that she lived there set her apart in the minds of the community. She was a child, it seemed, who belonged nowhere.

As an outsider, she never felt she could ask questions, so she just listened when the women talked at the lunch table. The sum of her knowledge about having a baby came from small bits of conversations she overheard among other women who chatted while they ate. And some of their descriptions of childbirth were horrible! She never had the nerve to ask questions back then, but her conversation with Flint yesterday shined a light on a terrible fear that's been stalking her for months now.

She sits down at the table and asks, "So this is not the labor?"

Willow puts her hand on top of Shaye's. "Oh my. No. The pains you feel right now are just little pinches. It's like your body is getting practice."

Shaye swallows hard. "Is the pain a lot worse when the labor comes? How do you know what to do?"

Willow sits across from her. "It's a little different for each woman, and for each baby . . . but it's a *natural* thing. For the most part, your body just takes over."

She looks down at her stomach. "Do many women here die in childbirth?"

"Look at me." Her voice has a serious tone. "You will be fine. The baby will be fine. I've been meaning to introduce you to the midwife I know. She's very good. Perhaps today would be a good day to see her."

The old woman gets up and goes back to kneading the mixture in the bowl, but continues to talk. "After breakfast, Nathan is coming by to get Jariel and take her to Caleb the weaver's place to discuss what he's going to offer her to work there. Once the two of them are gone, we'll go see if the midwife is busy. I'm sure she can put your mind at rest."

CHAPTER 9
The Room

"Each man has a storehouse in his mind. He can fill it with harvests of sweet joy or bitter sorrows, but he needs to consider what the meals will look like when he must eat from what he has saved."—*from the sayings in the Sacred Tell*

The time Shaye spent with the midwife was informative and helped to soothe her fears about giving birth. Even so, she's already thought of at least a dozen more questions she wants to ask when the midwife, Leah, visits her day after tomorrow. She says the baby might come in as little as a week from now. At the mere thought of it, Shaye needs to stop and breathe slowly to calm herself. There are so many things to consider. *Where will I give birth? In the living room with all the neighbors staring in through the windows? Once the baby is born, where will we sleep? There is barely space in the room when Jariel and I roll out our mats around Willow's bed. What if the baby cries a lot at night?* She stops walking and the voice of the midwife rings in her head.

"Remember; one thing at a time. Don't look for troubles that haven't reached you. The saying of our people is, 'A baby can't carry a bale of straw or bake a loaf of bread—but a baby is born with the Maker's provision.' The Maker will send what you need as you need it. Sometimes not a minute sooner—but He will provide."

Willow turns to look at her. "Are you all right?"

She exhales slowly and nods. "I need to walk and think for a while. May I go to the market for you?"

They part ways and Shaye meanders around in the market for a while. She's nearly finished selecting the vegetables for tonight's soup when she sees Flint looking around in a booth that sells coconuts, guavas, plantains, and bananas.

"Good afternoon," she says to him. "How do you know which of the coconuts are good?"

After looking around, he says. "Good afternoon."

"I didn't get the chance to thank you and your brother for helping me last night. You blessed me. Truly."

He glances at their surroundings again. "You shouldn't be seen talking to me again. Truly."

"Why? What is it, exactly, that—"

"Do you really not . . ." he lowers his voice, but is clearly annoyed. "Haven't we discussed this already?"

"What makes you want to—"

"Does it *matter*?"

"But you're not really a bad—"

"Not really a bad *what*?" The fierce look on his face frightens her. "You don't know me. Do yourself a favor and don't try to. It won't help me, and won't do *you* any good, either."

Her brow folds up in a confused frown. "But—"

"Every once in a while, someone gets to *choose* what role they will play here. You may be one of them. Don't throw away the opportunity." With that he suddenly shouts, "HA!" as if she just insulted him, then turns and walks swiftly out of the market.

Round-eyed, she watches his retreat, then looks around to see people scowling after him. She tells herself, *I must ask Willow about him when I get home.*

After half an hour in the market, she's tired and slowly makes her way home carrying the makings of the evening's soup. When she's at the steps, she sees the old woman through the window, rising from a chair, so she expects an offer of help with the bag or a greeting. But no one comes out the front door. She slowly mounts the stairs and enters the home to find Willow standing, almost frozen, in the middle of the room staring at a door that Shaye has never seen open. The mystery of Flint quickly fades from view in the light of a new concern. "What's wrong?"

"I've been thinking," she answers, still looking intently at the door. "I've known that you will need . . . more. I just never thought . . . " After taking several deep breaths, she straightens her posture and walks to the door she hasn't touched in nearly two years.

On the night they first arrived, Shaye noticed that not a single decoration or stick of furniture touched the wall that held this door. Her curiosity about it was great but the old widow who owned the home was so formidable during those first days, Shaye didn't dare ask what was behind the door. She'd even stayed awake for several nights wondering if some horrible thing happened in there. But after a friend told her about the death of Willow's daughter in the flood two years ago, it finally dawned on her that the room beyond the door must have belonged to Willow's daughter.

Now the old woman stands inches from it, staring down at the latch as if it's molten metal, her hand hovering just above it. Finally, she grasps the bolt, slides it over, then slowly pushes open the door. A strong, musty smell wafts out of the dark room as she disappears into it.

Shaye stands completely still. As the window shutters inside the room creak open, light fills the doorway. From her angle, though, she still can't see anything but the entrance. She waits. For the next minute, the only sounds she hears come from people walking by outside the house.

Finally, the old woman appears in the doorway, looking pale. She holds out a hand. "It's okay. Come, girl. Come inside."

Shaye inches toward the door and peers in. It's a small, neat space—very much like Willow's room, with a bed and two cupboards . . . but this room has a cradle in it.

"This can be your room now," Willow says in a barely audible voice. "If you want it, we'll need to scrub it down and replace all the bedding. . . ." She walks to the cupboards and lets out a groan when she opens the second one. "Well, I guess I should have cleaned this out before I shut the room. But we'll get to it later." As she exits the room she says, "I will put some water on to boil and we can have some tea."

Once the old woman is gone, stillness lingers there. Shaye slowly surveys the furniture. The bed looks sturdy. She decides not to sit on it, but gently touches the carved wood headboard. Next, she checks out the cradle. This was made by a craftsman—it's finely done. She runs her fingers over a delicate carving of a bird in flight and then gently rocks the little bed. When she looks in the first cupboard she sees baby clothes and blankets. In the other cupboard she sees great clumps of something dry and brown encrusting the shelves. It must be moss, which people here gather for women and babies. When it's fresh it's a luxurious green, quite soft and it's used on beds to capture moisture under both the baby and the mother. Shaye scrapes a fingernail across one of the brown, brittle lumps stuck to the edge of the shelf and recoils in disgust. In her haste to shut up the room, Willow must have forgotten the moss was here. The shelves will require quite a bit of scraping and scrubbing.

Diapers made of cloth were something that the wealthy people on the Aegean plateau used, but such things quickly smelled of ammonia and required constant laundering. The women of homeplace have no time for something that requires so much labor. So, until they are potty-trained, babies mostly wear only short shirts during the day, and are placed upon the moss at night. Soiled moss could be placed in buckets and carried off to be burned outside the village each day.

Willow reappears in the doorway but doesn't enter the room. "We can let it air out today and start cleaning it out tomorrow if you'd like. It's a good, safe place to give birth."

Never in the whole of her life has Shaye had a room with a window to herself—much less two windows. "I am overwhelmed. You have been so kind to me. I cannot repay you, but I'm very grateful."

"Come. We'll drink some tea and talk before Jariel comes home."

Once they are both out of the room, it's as if it didn't exist again. Shaye doesn't ask any questions and the two women make small talk while they sip tea, eating bits of bread with guava jam.

It's only after they've run out of inconsequential things to say that Willow stares down into her empty cup and begins the story.

"My daughter, Opal, was sweet, graceful, and funny. Her eyes were bright and her heart was pure . . . and she thought herself madly in love with a man by the name of Thomas—a handsome fellow whose smile could melt the heart of nearly any woman. She knew he was wild, but he sought her so earnestly, she thought she could tame him." She looks up from her cup and stares out the nearby window. "The day they married, my mother killed a bad spider in the house. She said it was a bad omen, but we thought that was nonsense." She sighs and becomes lost in thought for a while.

Although Willow has shared what must be her daughter's clothes with her houseguests, she's never said who owned the clothes, never spoken about her lost husband, daughter, grandchildren, or her son-in-law. Until today.

"He was a roof thatcher by trade and he did well enough by her in the beginning. But as time went by, he spent more time *inside* houses than working on roofs, taking up with women. Who knows how many." Her gaze comes back to Shaye. "You know, if you get more than a dozen people together here, between all of you, you'd know—or know someone who did know—nearly everyone in homeplace. It wasn't like these women didn't know he was married or couldn't have found out if they'd wanted to."

Her weathered hands tip the cup, and she watches the last drip of tea settle into one spot. "I suspected it at first, then I heard rumors, but by then my husband was dying and there was enough to worry about. I didn't tell her." She shrugs. "How can a mother tell her daughter that she married a worthless man? I think he tried to change a few times but eventually just gave up the effort. She gave birth to Eli, who was as handsome as his father, and two years later to Pansy," she says as her whole face momentarily softens at the thought. "Pansy had beautiful curls and amber eyes. . . ." Lost in remembrance, she gently rotates the cup to watch the drip slide around in the bottom. When she looks up, her face hardens again. "After Opal was pregnant with their third child, Thomas got entangled with a woman who wanted him for her own. She came to the market and told my daughter in front of everyone there that he didn't love her anymore. . . . After that, things rolled down the hill pretty quickly. Opal demanded that he stop seeing the woman, and people in the village started to shun him—so much so that he claimed to have broken off the relationship. But the lie was soon discovered. There was a terrible argument—and he told her that she and the children had ruined his life. He said he wished she were dead, that the children had never been born." Tears roll down deep lines on Willow's craggy face and gather under her chin before they drop down onto the table. She sobs as she says, "How could he say such an evil thing? I never . . . even got to know if the child she was still carrying was a boy or a girl."

Shaye reaches over to hold her hand, and bolstered by the empathy, she takes in a jagged breath and continues. "The next day, he agreed to be on a ship's crew and sailed away without a word—leaving her to scrape in order to survive. She came here to live with me . . . two months later, just when the baby was nearly due, the ships returned . . . and a few days later Opal and the children were washed away in the flood. He hadn't even tried to see them when he got back . . . but when they were suddenly gone—he was stricken with terrible guilt and grief."

"Where is he now?"

She wipes her eyes and pulls a small cloth from her sleeve before she pinches a drip from her nose into it. "Oh, he still lives in homeplace. He goes out on the ships or sometimes hires on to fix roofs, but when he's here he goes to a tap house just outside the village at night and drinks *meechi* until the owners cast him out." A look of grim satisfaction comes to her face. "He's aged poorly. And with the shortage of women now, his girlfriend found a younger, single man who didn't have a scandal attached to his name." She stares down into her cup again. "I hope the rest of his life will be completely empty of any companionship or joy."

After a few moments of silence, Shaye asks, "Willow, after your husband died . . . did *you* not think of remarriage? Was your love so deep for your husband that you couldn't look at another man?"

She's startled when the old woman snorts and then lets out a loud, "*Ha!*" before she shakes her head. "Not everyone has those great, sweeping loves like Nathan and Peony. Of a truth, I wasn't in love with Levi when I married him, but I knew he was a good man. Ours was a practical union and it suited us both well enough. We took care of one another, and over the years our affection grew. When he passed on . . . I didn't have the desire or the *energy* to start from scratch with a new man—going through the scrape of learning new wants and demands. No. I think that's for younger people to do. And after I lost Opal and the children . . . well I guess that is when my heart closed up tighter than Caleb the weaver's shop."

Shaye opens her mouth to say something but stops when they hear the creak of a step on the front porch. Jariel enters the home with a happy glow and doesn't wait for anyone to ask her how her day went.

"Oh, I'm so happy! I will begin working with Caleb day after tomorrow! He knows so much about cloth and weaving and has several good looms. I have a few ideas for improvements to one of the looms so if you can help me to tell him, Shaye, I could make a kind of cloth that would be unknown here." It's only then she notices Willow's red eyes and nose. "Did something happen?"

"Nothing is wrong," Shaye tells her. "I was just hearing a bit of history." Before Jariel can ask any more questions, Shaye translates the information about her job.

Willow nods. "That is good news. We were just having tea." She extends her hand to an empty chair. "Come and sit with us."

Jariel understands the gist of the invite and the gesture, so she seats herself and continues. "The reason I'm so excited, is that I'm certain I can do things that are beneficial to both his family and ours."

When she's told what was said, the old woman blows her nose on the cloth again. "Both of you, scoot closer, right here. Now let me take your hands." She peers at one girl, then the other. "I never expected a day like today." She looks down at the table. "I know what the people of homeplace call the women like me—the ones who had no one left after the flood. Already widows or soon to be . . . coupled with the loss of our children and grandchildren. We lived on, but there was nothing left to light our eyes. The people here started to call us 'shadow women.' There were six of us. We were like the dead, but still somehow waking up each day and walking around. Three gave up and went home to the Maker in that first year. This year, one more. I suspect that Nathan feared I would pass next." Her eyes fill with tears again. "So he brought two waifs to my door. I never expected a day like that day . . . or a day like this one." She squeezes their hands firmly. "Jariel, you just said, 'our family' . . . I never thought I'd know the joy of daughters, or babies in my home again. I am so blessed."

###

Few things in homeplace go unnoticed. Most will be commented upon. By the next day, word spreads throughout the neighborhood and beyond that Willow has opened the shutters on Opal's old room! It must mean the new woman, Shaye, and her baby will stay there. Also, Caleb will open his shop again with the other woman working the looms.

Many will say, "Perhaps this means that Willow is returning to her old self, perhaps she will walk in the light of the fellowship of homeplace again. Perhaps hope has truly returned to homeplace."

Nathan was right. So many good signs!

CHAPTER 10
Awake

"Real freedom always starts with truth."—*Nathan, a Gatherer and an elder of the people in homeplace.*

The smell of jasmine lingers in the still night air. Her sandals dangle from one hand as she walks down the road in her bare feet with the moon lighting her way. She never thought she'd love the feel of the earth beneath her feet, but the rainy season is over and the road is still radiating some of the heat of a day that ended hours ago.

Mother would be horrified if she could see me stepping about outside with no shoes. Her walk slows for a moment, then resumes its previous pace. *No. Don't spoil all this wonder with sad reminders from far away.*

She closes her eyes, lifting her arms up as if the beams of the moon are a delightful cascade and she can saturate her sacred self in the shower of their light.

"What is it, Jariel?" he asks. "What are you thinking?"

She keeps her eyes closed. "Oh how I wish I could tell you. I wish I had the words."

"Then I will be content to see the joy on your face."

"What?" Her eyes open.

Samuel smiles. "It is late. You should be home."

He's right. She starts moving again and they speak in the simple words she knows. They're both aware that people are probably listening and watching from nearby windows as they pass little homes lining the street that leads to Willow's house.

When they arrive, she quickly mounts the stairs without a sound, then tiptoes across the porch to the door and opens it with care, scrunching up her face when it creaks. She turns only long enough to wave at Samuel, then creep inside and gently close the door again.

Even though she and her housemates have spent two days cleaning and preparing the home's second bedroom, it still needs work, so Shaye can't sleep there yet. The living room chair is so much more comfortable than lying flat on a mat on the floor. It's also better than being in a hammock which, as it sags with the growing weight of her midsection, makes her feel as if she's being slowly folded in half and stuffed into a hole. Not to mention the difficulties involved in trying to crawl *out* of the hammock for an increasing number of trips to the bathroom each night. So she's perched in Willow's chair again, with the lower shutters on the window closed, but the upper ones open. The shafts of moonlight coming through the upper windows reflect all around the room, giving form to nearly every object.

Jariel's eyes adjust and she looks toward the big chair in the corner. The distinct shape of her housemate's belly is visible above the arm of the chair so she tries to silently drift across the floor to Willow's room.

She's not halfway there before she hears Shaye's voice. "Did you enjoy the meeting?"

Changing course, she walks toward the living room, then sits on the floor near the chair. In the beginning of their journey to homeplace, urgent need drove the two women to communicate despite their status as adversaries. Their interactions grew to include tolerance and—on the rare occasion—esteem. Now, when there is nothing to argue about, they can *almost* enjoy each other's company.

Only Jariel's upper torso and arms are directly lit but there's an unmistakable radiance on her face. Perhaps it's just a reflection of the light bouncing off her clothes.

"It was wonderful," she says in a quiet voice. "I've never experienced anything like it. Did people have meetings like this in Aegea?"

Shaye's hands roam around on her tummy before they find the perfect resting place. "Yes. I couldn't often go in the past couple of years, but they did have meetings."

"Did it stir you to be in them? Did it—how does Nathan say it—did it stir your heart? Did you believe what they told you?"

"Yes."

Jariel peers up at Shaye. "With no evidence?"

"I heard about the Maker from people whom I knew to be truth tellers. And, once my heart awakened, I could hear it whisper '*Yes*' to the evidence all around me. You know, my great aunt on my father's side was raised in a military family and lost everything for her faith, but she never blinked. She was the one who told me about the world that the Firstlanders lived in before they came here, about boats, and fish, and shell bones."

Jariel peers through the window to the sky. "The things I heard tonight weren't frightening like the things I heard the last night in the Great Forest when Nathan spoke about the other world and how equality with the Genon disappeared when the Firstlanders made a new life in Aegea. Or the day I found those shell bones in the ocean and showed them to you—and then you showed me the ones that your aunt gave you from the world of our ancestors. Those times, it was as if the ground had disappeared from under my feet. I felt like I was falling. To think so many things I'd been taught by my mother, things I believed, could be . . . false . . . well, it terrified me. Since then, I've had to consider everything I've known, and wonder if it's *real*. And I've seen that there is more to this world, more to *me* than I ever knew before."

She scoots near to the window, unlatches the lower shutters and pushes them open before she rests her arm on the sill. Her shadow on the floor looks like a blanket filling the space between them. "The world has stopped falling away from my feet and I'm looking up at the open sky now. I see its vast beauty, and it all makes sense. Tonight there was singing. It was sweet and *alive*—like it was part of a greater song . . . resonating all around us." She turns, resting her cheek upon her arm while she peers back at Shaye. "And different people had things to say. Iris was there so she translated for me. Samuel spoke about the stars and it made my heart melt. It was like a poem, but different somehow."

Shaye closes her eyes as she remembers it. "Before years or days or time were counted, before the first seed or root was planted in moist soil. Before a bird flew across the heavens or the first of our people drew breath, the Maker of all things existed. His voice rang out and light shined forth . . . the Maker separated the day and the night and He set the stars in the heavens—so when the cloak of darkness is pulled across the sky each night, there are yet lights that sing of His nature and power. . . . So all will be reminded—even when there is darkness—that He is over all things and His glory never dims.

We can look up and know that He is yet present and listening to those who seek Him."

"Yes," Jariel says in a breathless whisper. "That's it. How can people live their whole lives and not know this?"

Shaye recalls words she'd heard her Aunt Pearl say, and she echoes them. "Close your eyes and think. When you heard about the Maker and the stars . . . was it new to you . . . or was it a sudden grasp of something your heart has been whispering all along? Was this truly the first time you heard it . . . or was it that you finally *understood* some of the song that has echoed all around you all your life? The 'evidence' was always there, you just didn't have eyes to see it or ears to hear it."

Jariel thinks about it before she nods. "How wonderful it is . . . to finally perceive it."

"Just so."

They both sit in silence, staring up at the moon and the winking lights for a while before Jariel quietly latches the shutters, leaves the room, and goes to bed.

Shaye covers her face. *Oh, Maker of all that is . . . my heart should be happy for anyone who finally recognizes you, but I confess part of me feels like she is getting the life I always wanted, she is walking free among your people, able to come into your presence and commune with you. She's completely accepted into the fellowship I have wanted all my life. She's getting what I always longed for. Help me to reconcile the knowledge that you are just with the idea that one who gave me so much sorrow now prospers. Please . . . set things in motion that will help me to truly forgive . . . so I, too, can thrive under your open sky again.*

###

She awakens early with familiar sounds outside. It's the elderly man, Abel, who lives across the street with his wife, Ivy. Every morning, the same scene (with nearly the same dialog) is played out. Even though the lower shutters on the house are closed, she can picture it as if she was watching through the window.

The front door to Abel and Ivy's house is unlatched and opened. Next, there are various whistling and humming noises as Abel gets ready to leave the house and go to the docks where he will help the men who cast nets off the dock. He will clean all the little fish they've caught in preparation for catching bigger fish. Abel's only necessary tool is an old knife he's had nearly all his life.

The whistling gets louder—he's outside of his home now.

"Abel . . . Abel!" Ivy says from somewhere inside the house.

The whistling stops and he turns. "Yes, my love," he responds in a happy tone.

"Have you got your knife?"

"Yes, my fragrant flower," he says as he starts to shuffle away.

"Are you *sure* you have your knife?"

He halts, and this time his voice has lost a little of its perky tone. "Yes, dearest."

Setting off again, his random whistling and humming recedes and then suddenly stops . . . followed by a disgruntled mutter, then scuffling steps back toward his front door.

"Ivy! Have you seen my knife?"

"Of a truth," she scolds, "You'd let your feet wander off if they weren't attached to your legs."

Often, Shaye would hear this while she and Willow prepared breakfast. The first few times, she said nothing, but after a week of the same routine, she asked Willow, "Do they do this every morning?"

A soft laugh and nod. "Every single day that he goes to the dock."

Now that she's sleeping in the front room of the house she never misses the routine. Rather than it being an irritation, it's become a source of amusement to her as she anticipates each step. Ivy always nagging—in the way that some people show concern—and Abel's continued happy, absentminded ways.

This morning, it's no different. She covers her mouth so no one will hear her giggle when the repentant Abel stands in the doorway of his house and calls out, "Ivy? Have you seen my knife?"

Chapter 11
Goodbye to Westland

"**W**hen you are saying goodbye to a place you've known, you're either very sad or very glad as you look around and remind yourself of all the things about it that made you love it or hate it."—*A proverb of His people.*

Ty and another man dismount their horses. Each man takes a case off his horse before he walks to the front gate of the Great House of Westland. The general's son acknowledges the soldier who hauls open the gate as he and his guest walk through it and onto the grounds of the home. He waits while the gate closes behind them, then leads the way as Sage Dooley's chief assistant, Dell, follows him down the winding path to the house, both men carrying their cases. As a first time visitor, Dell is in awe.

Although he grew up here, Ty is suddenly aware of details that he gave so little thought to as a child. *The house is bigger than any other in Aegea . . . the grounds are beyond compare, the gardens are immaculate.* He shrugs as he gazes at Great House again. *The color has faded a little. If Mother were here, she'd make sure it was painted again. The trees are taller. . .*

His companion is startled when they hear a squawk and an odd voice saying, "Hello!"

Ty chuckles and says, "Not to worry, it's Topper," then points to a cage in a sunny corner of the garden. In it is one of several birds that caretakers bring outside on warm days. "Hello, Topper," he says as he walks over to the enclosure. The bird inside is nearly three feet in length with brilliant red, yellow, and blue plumage

The guest is entranced. "I've heard about birds like this, but I haven't seen one before."

"Believe it or not, he's older than I am and could live to be more than fifty years old. He was hatched in the jungle and brought to Aegea with a female bird. They were gifts for my great uncle."

"Exquisite. And it talks!"

The bird turns his head and looks at Ty with a knowing eye.

Not liking the look of the sharp beak, Dell stays more than a foot away from the cage.

"Hello," the bird says again.

"Yes, hello. I know it's been a while since you've seen me. How are you?"

The parrot preens several feathers, then moves closer to the bars of the cage.

The general's son looks into the metal cup fastened inside the enclosure. "Sorry, old fellow, I don't have any treats for you, but it looks like you have plenty to eat as it is."

One of the groundskeepers emerges from the nearby trees. "Good day, Mr. Ty. It's good to see you."

"Good day, Henry. How is your family?

"They are well, thank you for asking."

"And how is my old friend Topper doing these days?"

Henry glances at the man standing next to the general's son but knows not to ask questions about visitors. "He seemed lonely after Shirley died a few months ago. Since he's not friends with any of the other birds, I've been keeping him in my quarters at night and on days when the weather is bad. My wife and my daughters keep him company. They're spoiling him I think."

Ty looks at the parrot again. "It's too bad we cannot take you back to the forest and let you go, huh?"

The caretaker nods. "I hear your heart, Mr. Ty, but he knows little of the forest. He's lived in Aegea since he was old enough to fly. For him, *this* is home. He's gotten loose a few times, but he always comes back. Here," he says, handing a large seed to the young McClaren, "you can give this to him."

As soon as the parrot sees the seed he sticks his beak outside the bars. Ty offers the seed to his guest. "You want to give it to him?"

Dell shakes his head and takes another step back so Ty gives the seed to the bird.

The servant waves and heads back into the garden to finish his work.

Topper breaks open his prize and begins to eat it before the young man realizes he must move along as well. Ty taps the cage once and says, "See you," before he and Sage Dooley's assistant continue walking.

The *chunk, chunk, chunk* of someone hoeing up ground elsewhere in the garden reverberates through the trees along with the intermittent sounds of someone whistling. When they pass the pond in the middle of the garden, Ty can't help remembering the last night his whole family was home. It was Jariel's Planning Day party. His focus is drawn to a particular spot where the path from the house enters the garden and remembers her standing there.

It happens whenever he's at the Great House. Everything in this place is filled with memories of Shaye. In an effort to quiet his inner voice, he begins a sort of narrated tour for his guest, "The trees over there were here before the house. They are very old and my father thought they were too magnificent to cut down so he actually had the house built forty feet back from the location originally planned. These are the front steps to the house, but the entrance that we use for the tower is farther this way. . . ."

They make their way around to the side of the house where there is a single wooden door with dark iron hinges.

Since no one is manning the tower these days, the door is locked. He pulls a ring of keys out of his pocket and finds the one that opens the door. The shutters for the windows are all closed, so the small office at the bottom of the stairwell is dark. He quickly lights the lamps and carries one up the stairs, with Dell right behind him. They pass by the door that connects to the second story of the house, but it is also locked—from inside the house. They mount three more flights of stairs to enter an office and signal room at the top of the tower. They set their cases and the lamp on top of the large desk. He opens the shutters that face north, south, and east.

"The views from here are spectacular. How far can you see on a clear day?"

"You can easily see the signal light in the tower at Waypoint. On a clear night, you can sometimes see the light from Midtown."

Dell points to the closed shutters. "What can you see from the window on the other side here?"

"Oh. It mostly looks down on the roof of the house. . . . Is there anything else you need?"

"No. I'll run tests on the radios from here. As long as things go as planned, I should be ready to leave in about an hour.

"I should be back by then."

Leaving his guest in the tower, he travels back to the front of the house and uses the main entrance. Although all the familiar furniture and objects are here, regularly cleaned and polished, an uncomfortable stillness broods in this place. It's as if the owner died and nothing has been moved since.

He walks through the main floor and lights a lamp before heading down the stairs in the back—to the kitchen where so many of his early childhood memories still echo. This is where he feels the emptiness most keenly. The shutters, which were never closed in daylight hours during the entirety of his life, now hold the darkness in. Nothing here looks or smells the same as it did when the family cook, Mosha, was here.

He peers down at the spot where he stood the very first time he kissed Shaye, then holds up the lamp to allow the light to illuminate the hallway to the room where she slept since she was a child. There is the doorway where he stood the last time he saw her, too timid to declare his love for her in front of his father and Mosha.

He blows out the lamp and leaves it on a counter, departing through the back door of the home. He takes in a large breath of air as he walks across the courtyard behind the home and listens to the sound of his boots grinding dirt into the smooth stones. The smell of fresh bread and seasoned meat is in the air. Just beyond a short iron gate and to the right are rows of lines where the daily laundry hangs. Sheets, dresses, towels, shirts, and baby clothes are dangling and flapping in an intermittent breeze. He reaches the gate and swings it open before turning left toward the outdoor kitchen and dining room—a large, open area with a roof, where the workers gather to eat.

A new generation of Genon servants, grown to early adulthood, now sits in the dining hall—eating and extending fellowship to one another the way workers have since Westland was first built. And there is Basil's mother, Monique, presiding over the kitchen the way she has for the past ten years. A serious woman with little time for nonsense, she's the polar opposite of Mosha, who cooked the meals inside the Great House for Ty's whole life.

Nearly fifty people sit at the tables under the thatched roof, eating and quietly talking. Although the families of soldiers think of private meals as a privilege, most Genon consider common meals, taken together, as one of the joys of life. For them, a solitary meal is the result of punishment, or illness, or a display of grief. Since many of the people here work long hours at demanding tasks, this is where friendships form and common problems are discussed. To them, community is a living organism whose health and welfare often depend upon the relationships forged here.

After a quick scan, he sees Basil, sitting at the table where the single men generally sit—at the back where they can make a bit more mischief than Monique would like. Although everyone here has seen Ty and Basil growing up together it's still a bit odd to see the general's son in the dining area—so most of the people momentarily look up as he walks to the kitchen counter.

"Good day," he says to Monique.

"Good day, Mr. Ty. What would you like to eat?"

"Some of those," he says indicating the berries. "And I'll take some of the meat, and two of those. And an apple, please."

Using flatbread as a plate, she hands him his lunch. "It is good to see you."

"Thanks. It's good to see you as well."

After he seats himself at Basil's table, people return to their meals and conversations. Thus far, it's going according to plan. He was to meet up with Basil, who also comes here regularly. So does Menoh. The idea is for all three men to rotate in and out at random times so no one will suspect they are secretly doing something together at the mill. This way, when Basil and Ty finally go on the mission across the Great Forest, people will just assume they are somewhere around Westland or in town.

Basil gives him a nod. "Day."

The others at the table, ranging in age from sixteen to early twenties all look at each other. They're all too cool for the formal "Good day" of their parents, so "*day*" is the way they greet their close friends.

The general's son nods back. "Day."

Several of the older boys dare to chime in with their own "Day," and they're pleased when Ty nods and responds in kind. His presence means most of their conversations will stop, but they'll sit and try to look disinterested while they listen to whatever Basil and Ty say to each other—and this is also according to plan.

Already finished with his meal, Basil is stretched out in his chair, picking his teeth. He flicks the toothpick over to the corner of his mouth with his tongue. "I was wondering if you'd show up."

Ty shrugs. "Got hung up in town." He twists the stem off an apple and inspects the skin of the fruit before he bites into it. "I have a few things to do here before heading back. Too bad we won't have time to hunt this time."

"Yeah."

"How are Menoh and your grandmother?"

"They are well."

While the dialog between them is truthful and unrehearsed, they both know they need to appear casual and let everyone *assume* they haven't seen each other much in recent weeks.

"Well, if you see them before I do, please give them . . ." A movement across the room catches his eye before he can finish the sentence. ". . . a greeting from me."

Basil notes the change of expression on his friend's face and turns to see two people entering the dining room. One of them is Lou, a daughter of the innkeepers at the Outpost, the other is her husband, Ski. When Ty found out the couple wanted to marry he helped to make it happen in exchange for Shaye's former roommate, Chessie, being given a chance to work at the Outpost.

Ty watches as the couple stands in line for their lunch. Because they're in their first year of marriage, it's understood that they'll sit together. When she turns sideways to take her seat, he sees what first caught his attention: her baby bump. Within moments, she and Ski notice him and they give him happy smiles and a wave.

He returns the gesture, then realizes Basil is talking to him.

". . . will tell Grandfather, but you should stop by and see both of them soon. Grandmother told me that she was missing you the other day."

He nods. "I'll try." He looks down at his food before he adds, "I don't know why I got all this food. I'm actually not very hungry."

"I'll eat it," the guy to his left says.

He holds onto the apple and slides the rest over. "Enjoy."

CHAPTER 12
News of a Return

Word quickly spread among the soldiers at the military post at Westland and those who work for the McClaren family in and around the Great House. The general will return for a visit following an absence of many months. After reviewing the troops spending time with the officers, he'll stay at least two days in the home he began building two decades ago—when being General of Aegea was just a gleam in his eye.

The soldiers and Genon workers here speculate.

Could this mean he'll be returning more often again?

Could he decide to take up residence in Westland eventually and run the country from here?

What about the ishi, his wife? Will she ever return?

Behind the Great House two Genon women dressed in customary gray frocks place baskets filled with wet garments on the ground underneath the lines where they'll hang it to dry. The women, sisters who both live with their husbands in the servants' quarters, are anxious to share news and privately speculate while they hang up the morning's work.

The taller sister tucks a loose strand of hair back into the large bun on top of her head. "Who do you suppose will do the cooking, cleaning, and other chores inside the home since Mosha and Raymond are gone now?"

"Poor Mosha. Along with losing Shaye—to be pushed aside like that. "

"Did I tell you that Carmen told me she heard Mosha's situation in town was nice?"

"Yes . . . but still. It's a wonder she had the will to go on."

They nod at each other.

"And don't forget Lemon. Dead of . . . *who knows what*."

"*Eh eh!* Good riddance to that one," she says, shaking a shirt with a *snap* and pinning it up.

They pause the conversation long enough to nod and say, "Good day" to gardeners who walk by with a ladder and a tree saw. As soon as the men are out of earshot, the discussion resumes.

"Well Beth is still giving the inside of the house a polish every other week or so. She took care of the *ishi* and Miss Jariel well enough. Maybe they'll just have her work in the house while McClaren is here."

The smaller sibling takes a wooden clothespin out of her mouth to respond, "But I don't know as she could cook to suit the General's taste. Maybe he'll bring his new cook from town. I wonder what she's like?"

Her sister leans under the lines indicating she has an exclusive tidbit to share. When their heads are nearly touching, she says, "I heard it from Gerald who heard it from his cousin who works for Col. Kraton in town that the *ishi* told his wife that she wasn't *ever* coming back. Too many sad memories."

The response is a skeptical snort. "I always thought that woman had snow running through her veins. And her daughter wasn't far from that way, either. Only the Maker knows what Shaye and poor Mosha had to put up with."

"And Jariel didn't even have her mother's looks. Whoever would have married such a sickly spoiled creature?"

"Someone who wanted to be the next general maybe. But I guess we'll never know now."

There's a grunt of agreement. "Well one thing's for certain, young Ty isn't looking to be general. He's all but left the military. 'On leave,' they call it. He wanders in and out of here, looking for Basil half the time, as if he's got no purpose, no friends or family of his own. I remember when he was a boy he did seem to be a dreamer. Too much so to be a soldier I always said . . . playing up on the roof of that house all hours of the day and night, or running through the woods with Basil. Now he just looks lost. I feel sorry for him."

"Just so, sister, just so. Do you think they will ever give up and admit Jariel is dead? I knew it in my bones as soon as those two girls went missing that they'd not return."

"Oh what a terrible thing for the general, to lose a child like that."

"Just so. Even one such as Jariel."

"Maybe after some years have come and gone the family will be able to find peace with it."

CHAPTER 13
A Visit from Aunt Pearl

"Even a small gift can open a door."—*A proverb of His people*

His aide knocks once on the door and opens it. "Sir, one of the people on your list is here to speak with you. She says she won't keep you long."

The general looks up from his desk and closes a folder. His "list" (of people who had permission to speak to him at any time) had five names on it. The use of the word "she" narrowed it down to one person: Shaye's great aunt, Pearl Penway Curtis. Once he suspected the Exiles might have found and kept the women, he sent Ty and Basil to secretly visit Shaye's great aunt—an expert researcher in the Archives for many years before she was compelled to retire. When Ty interviewed her, she recalled documents and an early map which included a river. With her help, the General was able to locate documents that helped piece together initial ideas as to where the Exiles might be.

"Send her in."

A heavy-set elderly woman in a long dress shuffles into the office with a cane. The long strap to a large, brown leather bag is slung across her body.

He rises to meet her. "Mrs. Curtis, it's good to see you."

"I'm glad you would see me."

"Does your new housing situation meet with your approval?"

When Ty informed his father of the crumbling living quarters of Shaye's great aunt, the general made inquiries as to what could be done for her. She was deeply involved in community life in Oldtown, so she told him she wouldn't want to leave the aging ramble of buildings which housed the first generation of Aegea. He arranged for her to be quietly moved to an apartment there which, while still modest compared to newer homes elsewhere, was a vast improvement over her former home.

She's a little out of breath. "I am in your debt, General. Especially for the good shelving built in the back rooms for all my books. Thank you."

He waits till she is seated then pulls another chair close to hers. "What is it you wish to tell me?"

"After your son made his initial inquiry, it set me to thinking. I've heard no other news since then, so I'm assuming that anything you're doing with the information is," she looks back at the door to be sure it is closed, "still ongoing and confidential."

He only nods.

"Well, if I were going to use the information you have to find people, I would want to carry with me things of value to give as gifts to . . . anyone I encountered. If I found them. Given all my studies and my specialty in Genon culture and belief, I asked myself, 'What would Genon people find valuable? What is it they would treasure? What is it they probably lack that they would still want to have?'" She pauses.

"Did you think of anything specific?"

She lifts the leather strap to her purse over her head and sets the bag squarely on her lap. "Yes, I believe I did." She undoes the clasp on the flap of the purse. "Every Genon family among the Firstlanders brought at least one of these with them. Some were lost in the crash, many were damaged by the elements or fell into decay over the years. I know of two that were buried with people. Some are kept safe by family patriarchs and are considered so valuable that they are rarely handled. But I have two that I rescued from ruin at the Archives many years ago. This is one of them." She gently pulls a leather bound book from her bag and offers it to him. "It is a copy of the Sacred Tell. The inscription in the front says it belonged to the family line of Anab. I believe a number of this family were exiled before the family line here in Aegea ended—so if descendants of Anab are still alive among the Exiles, this would belong to them. Even if the family line ended among the Exiles as well, or even if those who survive can no longer read, this would be of great value to *any* group of Genon people. It's not only sacred, it's a tangible piece of their ancestry. There are probably fewer than two dozen of the original books left in existence."

"You said you had two of them. To whom does the other book belong? Has that line ended as well?"

Her face lights up with the smallest amount of hope. "It belonged to Shaye's grandfather. When she tried to move to town more than a year ago, she was going to live with me and she asked me to teach her to read. It would have been my joy to do so. I was saving the book for when she came of age, with the thought that she would be able to read and treasure it. When I see her again, I will give it to her."

The general meets her gaze but doesn't make any response to her remarks about Shaye or her assumptions about travel to find Exiles. He carefully receives the book from her and says, "I will take very good care of this and see that it finds a home. Thank you."

CHAPTER 14
Letter to the Exiles

The compound is abuzz with the news. For the first time since he became General of Aegea, Jubal McClaren has returned to the western end of the plateau. With him, came his cook and a guarded caravan of wagons laden with supplies for the soldiers at the military post and for his home, the Great House of Westland. After spending several hours with the officers on the post, he walked across the road to his home. When he came through the gate, he found most of the civilian staff standing on either side of the path, waiting to greet him.

Earlier in the day, several of the workers asked elders in the community if it would be appropriate to congratulate the general on his appointment to leadership. Since the day of his rise to office was also the same day his daughter was taken, they all agreed that a simple "Good day," or, "It is good to see you again," would be the most suitable remark to make to him.

Later in the evening, all five of the elders of the Genon community in Westland were invited to share a meal with the general inside the Great House. A formal meeting between a general and elders hadn't taken place since the early days of Aegea.

Jubal's cook made the dinner. The dessert, a traditional Genon dish, was supplied by Menoh's wife, Fiona, and their daughter-in-law, Monique. Would this event have taken place inside the general's home if his wife, the *ishi,* were there?

After the meal, Old Menoh was asked to stay and speak with McClaren. Alone. Perhaps, the workers told each other, this was so that the elder could privately convey the condolences of the community. It's no secret that the general has always held Menoh in high regard, and even, at times sought his advice.

The other guests are gone, the servants dismissed. The two men adjourn to the salon for the evening. It's a small private living room with dark wood panels and a large carpet that the general's wife purchased many years ago. A slow fire will keep the chill out of the damp night air. As per the general's orders, the sofa was moved against a wall to make room for a table with a dining chair on either side of it. A pot of hot *banji* and two man-sized mugs preside with a small plate of cut fruit on a tray at one side of the table.

Behind closed doors, the men will attempt to sketch out the details of what a letter, written to the Exiles should say. As one of the few people who is still able to read and write in the now forbidden language of Genon, the responsibility of transcribing the letter is Menoh's. It's a large weight, a solemn thing, to translate for the general and write this document—a treaty of sorts—to be offered to the descendants of people whom the military abandoned in the forest three generations ago. Much is at stake.

"I brought a lot of paper, pens, and ink," Jubal tells him. "We can burn old copies of the letter as we go."

Once the captured Exile, Canaan, started talking about life in the 'homeplace,' he told them that, unlike the Genon of Aegea, many of his people could read and write, and that most children are still taught these things in hopes of preserving the history, beliefs, and culture of their people. Knowing this, McClaren decided to write a letter to be carried through the forest and delivered by Ty and Basil.

It feels right to Menoh that the son of the General of Aegea and the grandson of an elder of the Genon, are the ones who will present the document.

Both men agree the letter should start with greetings and expressions of gratitude for safely delivering the women from certain death. Next, will be the request for the release of the women and for safe passage back to Aegea. With the letter, gifts of value should be given along with offers of future trade. Perhaps, examples of desirable goods could be sent.

Menoh wants to know, "What if they make requests of their own? What if they want you to guarantee that they will be left alone in the future? What would you say?"

"I couldn't promise that," Jubal says with a shake of his head. "I mean, I could, but it would be impossible to keep that promise. The existence of the Exiles has already passed from myth to fact. The revelation of their settlement cannot be hidden much longer. It's a pear that's already fallen off the tree. There's no putting it back. Once the existence of this place is confirmed . . . some within my ranks will want to keep an eye on them. Among your own people, wouldn't there be those who wanted to go and join them regardless of anything I promise?"

"True. But the safe return of the women and their testimony of being rescued and treated well should help to calm some fears among the military. As for the Genon . . . I think there are many on *both* sides who will want to reconnect with family." As he's speaking, the old Genon recalls the first conversation he had with Canaan when the man finally agreed to speak of the Exiles. There was something his own heart had burned to know for most of his life:

> "My oldest brother was David of the line of Tosh. Do you know of him? Does he have family that still live among your people?"
>
> "Only those who were small children among the first exiled still live—maybe three or four of them still live and I don't remember a man by the name of David among them. But there are many of the line of Tosh there. I have three cousins who married Tosh's people. Two are farmers, one is a fisherman."
>
> "A what?"
>
> Canaan nodded. "That's right, you have no fish here. Fish are animals that live in water. The one who catches them is a fisherman. People catch them mostly for food, but also for their bones and the oil that is in them."

Mingled with a fresh sense of sorrow over a lost brother was a kind of joy. *Even though David is probably no longer alive, he found a wife and they had children and grandchildren.* The memory of his brother consists of a few faded glimpses. There is no recollection of the sound of David's voice or his favorite songs or even if he was right-or left-handed. *But there are people among the Exiles who grew up knowing him. Would my heart rejoice to meet them, to know their names, to tell them more of the history of their family and to hear about their lives? Yes.*

The old Genon clears his throat. "I agree. Future contact is inevitable, but wisdom would tell us to let it unfold gradually. There are generations of mistrust and justifications for wrongdoing on both sides. Change is coming, but how much adjustment can each community accommodate all at once? Aegea would struggle if all the workers ran down into the forest. If what Canaan tells me is true, the Exiles couldn't feed a sudden multitude. They are doing better than surviving, but the losses they've had in recent years have put a strain on them. You can offer ways to improve and secure their lives."

"So . . . limited migration, mostly trade of goods?"

"Yes. But what of the laws concerning Exiles?"

"I am proposing that the council will officially declare a number of laws void next week. The law banning Exiles will be among them."

The old man nods. "Canaan says they have no similar laws regarding soldiers—but mostly because it hasn't occurred to them that soldiers would find them."

They both sip their *banji* for a moment while they consider other ideas.

"What about metal?" Menoh asks. "Could we offer them metal? He says they only have copper and its uses are limited. He was very impressed with the stronger metals we have here and he says the Exiles would desire it."

Jubal thinks about all the metal from the spaceship that has been steadily melted down and repurposed over the past century. Although small deposits of ores have been discovered nearby in the mountains, at this point, there is no longer a vast quantity of it. "Perhaps a limited amount. Our own supply is limited."

"I thought about cows, but I don't think we can get them through the forest."

"Precisely."

"Canaan has greatly enjoyed garlic, onions, and some of our peppers. He also says our rope is far superior to theirs.

"We will send some." Jubal takes another sip. "What else do you think we should offer?"

After more than an hour of discussion on what Aegea could offer in future trade with the Exiles, the conversation shifts to gifts that will go on this trip. What could the men on the first mission carry across the Great Forest that would be of value to the Genon there? The men can only carry so much.

Jubal leaves the room long enough to get his satchel. From it, he extracts the book that Shaye's Aunt Pearl gave him. "What about this?"

Menoh doesn't have to ask what it is. He slowly reaches across the table and wraps his hand around the binding of the book. He closes his eyes as if he were touching the hand of a long lost friend.

The general waits.

The old man finally opens his eyes and pulls the book close. "Where did you get this?"

"It was found in the Archives. Shaye's Aunt says it belonged to the family of Anab."

He nods as he remembers that the family line ended a couple of decades ago with no one in Aegea to carry on the name.

McClaren continues, "I've looked at the record of names of those who were exiled and there are five from that family listed on it. You might ask Canaan if any of the line of Anab are still alive. If so, this would make an excellent gift. Even if his line has died out over there as well, we would be honoring the family to pass it on to the Exiles."

Menoh opens it to carefully turn some of its pages. "Just so."

After hours of bouncing ideas back and forth, and burning several drafts of letters, they agree upon the final language. At last the general retires from the process, telling the elder that he could end the letter with words of his own to the Genons in exile. In the end, he composes less than a page of his own words, but he's satisfied with what he's written. He closes with the following words:

> I believe these offers to be sincere and the words to be true and I sign my name here,
>
> Menoh of the line of Tosh, an elder of His people on Aegea.

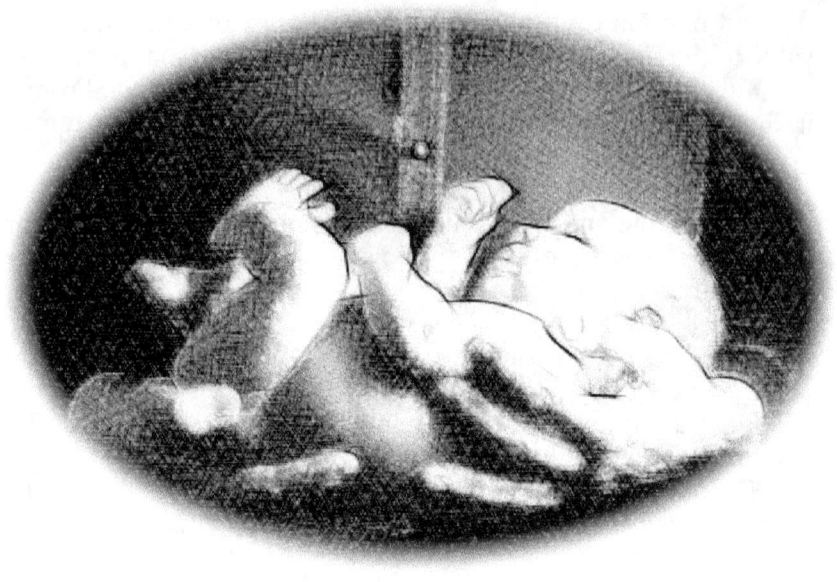

CHAPTER 15
A Child is Born

"A baby brings a revelation of what is in your heart."—*A proverb of His people*

Jariel looks so anxious that Leah the midwife asks her to leave the room. She's grateful for the excuse to make an exit. Her intent was to hold Shaye's hand, but she soon realized she wasn't ready to witness a child being born.

Nathan, Peony, and Willow's friend Iris are already sitting in the living room and will keep her company. Other than Shaye, Iris is one of the few people here that still speaks Command Dialect well. Although Jariel is learning Genon, her ability in the language is about at the level of a four-year-old so it isn't as if she can have a conversation of any depth with people in homeplace.

Since any open window in the village is a place where anyone can stand and watch or listen, only the upper shutters on the windows—well above eye level—are open in the birthing room. Most of the lamps from the house were taken into the room and lit. If a torrential downpour should come, they'll have to close all of the shutters against the rain.

She looks around. *There must be more than thirty people in or near the front windows and the door.* For Jariel, being in the constant presence of so many people is still an uncomfortable reality. Many press together on the walkway outside the windows while others pass by to hear or share the latest news. As the workday comes to a close, Samuel, Philip, Enoch, Tooth and most of the other men who traveled through the land of cloud and leaf with the two women join the gathering.

This will be the first baby born in the new year and many have begun to believe Nathan—who insists that this is but the beginning of better things for the Exiles.

The quiet conversations in the group become still whenever Shaye cries out. Another hush overtakes the crowd when Willow comes out of the birthing room looking worried. People lean in to hear what she says. Before Jariel gets the translation, the report is already filtering back through the gathering.

It's a market ritual that takes place at least once a week. Flint the hunter has game to sell to the meat vendor. The vendor opens the negotiations by offering a fraction of its worth. Flint counters with an amount the vendor will never pay and says what he's brought is fresh and of prime quality. They usually haggle for 15—30 minutes. During that time, each man will pretend to walk away, and each time the price will be altered slightly in favor of the other's price, and negotiations will resume again.

They've only been wrangling for five minutes when news that Shaye is about to give birth comes to the market. The vendor rolls his eyes and shrugs when he hears it then continues bartering.

"You are *killing* me, Francis. I won't make *anything* on this deal." He squints in his customary effort to look as if he's being squeezed by a giant, jungle snake. "I can possibly offer you two more, but that's all."

"Done."

The vendor was ready for a counteroffer, so he's not sure that he heard correctly. "What?"

"Done."

His eyes dart to the birds on the table. "Is there something wrong with them?"

"No. I'm in a hurry, so I will let you take advantage of me today."

Despite his suspicions he pays quickly before Flint changes his mind.

Inside the house, Nathan nods to Iris, who tries to explain it to Jariel. "The baby isn't in the right position yet. The midwife thinks she can move it around though."

She doesn't know how one would move a baby around inside a mother's womb, and she doesn't think she *wants* to know.

A loud moan comes from the room and Jariel suddenly feels lightheaded.

Iris takes her hand. "Here. Just sit here. We will call upon the Maker. I believe he will help Shaye."

A call for quiet pulses through the people. Everyone in the room and many of those outside lower their heads.

"Oh Maker of all that is," Iris begins, "you brought these women to us. I know you have good plans for them. I know you have plans for this life being entrusted to us tonight. We ask that you would speed the safe delivery of this little one and that you would protect Shaye. Give her strength and renewed hope. Renew *our* faith as well . . ."

Meanwhile, the report of a difficulty has reached the back of the crowd. *The baby might be breech.*

A man leaning against a porch pillar across the street hears the news before the aging owner of the home comes out to get the latest update on the birth and sees him standing there.

"*Eh eh!* Francis! Move your bad self from here!"

Heads turn. No one noticed him there until the old man's exclamations. Now that they do, they scowl and suck their teeth as he moves off the porch. When he takes up a stance at the back of the crowd, there is more tooth sucking, and grumbling before the group turns away from him and settles into listening mode again.

The people nearest the home can hear Shaye's loud groan. There is a finality to the sound. Silence spreads through the gathering. A collective breath is taken in . . . and they wait.

The little cry is soft at first, but it soon grows in strength.

Willow rushes out of the room and gives a joyful shout, "It's a GIRL! We have a GIRL and she is well! Mother and daughter are both fine!"

A celebration erupts in the street outside Willow's home. It's a glowing moment when grudges, pains, and sorrows of the community are forgotten and those who've gathered here don't just *hear* the glad news, they allow themselves to enter fully into it. Homeplace *has a daughter!* Someone begins singing an old song and everyone joins in.

Jariel watches them and listens with a mixture of relief and delight. *Among families of rank in Aegea, the news of a birth in someone else's house or family is answered with tepid congratulations. What do the fortunes of another family matter? Here, the same annoying closeness of everything is also a means of experiencing shared joy.*

The song comes to a part where only the men sing, then another where only the women sing . . . then both together in an intertwined harmony. She's never heard anything like this before. *It must be a song of the sacred self.*

The midwife appears in the doorway of the living room, wiping her arms on a cloth while she speaks to Willow and Nathan. "Give me a few more minutes to finish washing them up before you come in."

Willow sees an old friend nearby in the window and draws close to clasp hands and share the joyous moment.

Outside, when Francis recognizes the face of the old widow in the window, he stops singing and retreats down the street.

###

Now that the uncertainty is over, Jariel is eager to see Shaye and the baby. Eventually, the midwife appears again and beckons those standing in the living room to come and see. As they squeeze into the hot little room, she tells them, "Shaye is alright, but she's weak. I want her to stay abed tonight. I trust the two of you," she says, putting one hand on Willow and the other on Jariel, "to help care for her and the baby for a few days."

While Iris translates for her, Jariel looks around. A basket filled with fresh moss sits beside the bed. Large bundles of cloth are waded up in buckets. *So much blood!* The wooden floor is wet because the midwife poured water over it to cleanse it.

The midwife blows out all but two lights in the room and Jariel's attention turns to Nathan when he leans over to tell her in Command Dialect, "I hope you remember it was you sister here who save you life. She stand watch over you and care for you when you so sick in the forest. I hope the difficulties between you are all past. You sister and this little girl need a good strong household to care for them."

Jariel solemnly nods before she moves to the front of the little crowd in the room. The new mother sits, propped up on the bed with her long hair in a thick braid draped over the pillow behind her. Her skin and her lips are pale, but there is a look of fierce determination on her face as she holds her precious gift, tightly wrapped in strips of cloth. The baby's little, round face is framed by black hair, and she's silently gazing at her mother.

Willow leans in for a closer look. "Oh look at those eyes! They are as blue as the sky! How beautiful she is!"

After Jariel bends down to look, she suddenly wobbles and Iris steadies her.

A chorus of "*Eh eh!* Are you okay?" echoes the concern of all the visitors in the room.

"I . . . I'm fine," Jariel replies. She kneels down with her focus riveted on the baby, but it finally shifts when she realizes that the child's mother is squeezing her hand.

"We can talk," Shaye says in a weak voice. "Perhaps tomorrow."

Homeplace's newest citizen yawns before the midwife points to the door and speaks with quiet authority. "You have seen them and can share the good news, but mother and daughter need their rest now, so out with you all."

The visitors all file out of the room and Nathan goes to stand in the entrance to the home and give a brief report. "We are indeed blessed! We have a new child in homeplace. I have seen her and she is healthy and very beautiful."

When he is finished talking the crowd disperses, and many hurry to share the latest bit of news with the rest of the village.

Benjamin is at home when he hears the commotion and the voice of a runner—one of those whose duty is to factually convey information throughout the community on a regular basis. Earlier in the day he'd heard that Shaye was in labor, so he assumes that all the current noise is about the birth. He waits until the crowd has disbursed, but his curiosity won't let him go without hearing the latest update. He opens the shutters on one of his windows and leans out as a young man trots by.

"What news have you?"

"Shaye had her baby! It's a girl, and they are both well!"

Without comment, Benjamin leans back into his house and closes the shutters.

Back in Willow's home, the midwife has appointed herself to take the first watch over Shaye to be sure there are no complications. In six hours, it will be Willow's turn. Although her turn to watch over mother and daughter isn't for another twelve hours, Jariel's mind continues to swirl with excitement and with questions.

The crowd has departed to share the news across the village, so she steps out onto the porch for some air.

She hears a familiar voice speaking in simple words. "You feel okay? You have no color."

It's Samuel. He's been waiting for quite some time.

She's more than relieved to see him. More than encouraged. In fact, she can't describe how good it is to have him there. She exhales loudly and answers as best she can with her limited vocabulary, "I am well. I am scared, but now okay."

"You not see a baby born before?"

Her eyes widen and she shakes her head. "No. In Aegea much different. People don't come like this for a baby. Only family. Life for many people is . . . " She doesn't know the word for "private." *Do the Genon even have such a word? Nothing seems private here!* She tries to describe the concept. "I don't know word for this. Only family knows . . . what happen in house don't tell outside."

His chin moves up as he takes in this thought. "Ah. So you don't know of babies. Older women don't speak of this to young women? You don't see animals give birth?"

Her face flushes. "I . . . no. Not me."

He searches her eyes. "How hard it was, to be kept like that. Alone."

It's as if he's looked into her very heart and seen the years of loneliness. She suddenly feels vulnerable and afraid she might reveal more than she should. She looks down at her feet.

It's obvious she's uncomfortable, so in a cheerful voice he says, "Oh, but you are in the fellowship and community of homeplace now. You will learn *everything* you need to know about life." He chuckles as he adds, "Maybe more than you *want* to know."

She looks up and laughs before she answers in her own language. "Of that I have no doubt."

He moves an open hand out toward the street. "Would you like to walk?"

"Yes. But I must ask Willow first."

CHAPTER 16
First Friendship

"Like sun, good soil, and water are to a seed, so the love of others is to the human heart."—*An ancient proverb of His people*

Today is a sort of holiday for all the women at Willow's house. With all the birthing and watching and extra work throughout the night, everyone needs a rest.

All the shutters are open in Shaye's room this bright morning and a gentle cross-breeze wafts through, making it a perfect balance of warm sun and cool air. As the baby in her arms drifts off to sleep she's tempted to do the same. Her eyelids have just closed when she hears Jariel in the doorway.

"May I put her in the cradle for you?"

Shaye nods and gently passes the sleeping child over saying, "Keep your arm or your hand under her head."

With an odd mixture of terror and joy, Jariel accepts the little bundle. She's never held a newborn before. It's heavier than she imagined, and limp—a bit like holding a sack of sand. As she bends down to place the girl in the cradle, bright blue eyes flutter open momentarily to look at her then close. The thrill of recognition sweeps over her again. She gently brushes a finger across the little face and studies the tiny fingers complete with fingernails. She's thinking aloud when she says, "This is the biggest thing that's ever happened to me."

"What?"

Jariel sits on a stool near the bed, and after cautiously glancing at the windows and the doorway, she whispers, "I almost couldn't sleep last night. This is the biggest thing that's ever happened to me. She has his eyes."

Shaye exhales slowly, and the color in her cheeks deepens. "I was hoping . . . I was hoping it would always be my secret." Her focus darts to the windows and the door as well. "There's really no point in anyone here knowing."

"I will honor your wishes, but I'm glad that I know. I realize we've been adversaries for many years, but our feud seems so . . . unimportant now . . ." She glances back at the cradle. "Now that we have *her*. This makes the three of us," she leans in closer, "as you would say, 'kin' now. I can't describe what this feels like. It's as if a piece of my family has been given back to me. She is beautiful."

"Yes. She is." There's a look of sweet satisfaction on Shaye's face that Jariel hasn't seen in a long time.

"Have you decided on a name?"

"Elle. After my mother."

"Ah. That's a good name. . . . You know, a memory just came to me." She closes her eyes. "Ty and you and I, riding in a wagon carrying plants. We traveled through an orchard filled with white, sweet-smelling blossoms on a sunny day. I sat on the front seat, next to your mother while she drove the wagon." Jariel pictures the slender woman with long, black hair and golden-amber eyes. "I remember her smiling at me."

Although Shaye might not recall the specific moment, the thought of it must give her a sense of the happiness her mother felt that day, for the smile that lights her face is a mirror reflection of it.

Jariel's expression becomes serious and she takes Shaye's hand. "I promise you that I will guard little Elle with my life."

"Thank you."

"I take it that Ty doesn't know."

Her face turns sad and she looks out the window when she hears the question.

"I had no way to tell him. The day your *mmm* . . . " she stops, then rephrases her thoughts. "The day I ran away, the day you were taken . . . I saw a box in a wagon on the perimeter road and it had your father's mark on it, so I thought it would be taken to town. In desperation I crawled into it, hoping it would be taken there and I would be able to find Ty."

Jariel pulls on a loose thread sticking out from the thin mattress on the bed. She's feeling it again. A conviction that's been steadily growing in recent weeks. She swallows hard and says, "The day you were traded, I knew things had gone too far. I knew it was my fault. I knew what my mother planned to do was wrong, but once she got in such a fury I was afraid to tell the truth. I'm sorry for what I allowed to befall you without speaking up." She doesn't dare to look into her old enemy's face. "I will regret to the day I die that I didn't stand up for you.

Had I been downstairs, doing that . . . perhaps *neither* of us would have ended up in that box."

At first, Shaye is startled by the confession. "Why are you saying this now?"

"Because . . . when I look at my life—I realize how selfish and heartless I have been. Samuel says if we want to walk in the truth, we must be willing to own the truth—even the truth about ourselves. I had so much, but I was ungrateful. I wanted to believe I was better, but in my heart I was jealous and afraid." She closes her eyes. "I'm so sorry for the spiteful things I've done to you, the hurtful things I've said to you. I'm sorry for the lies I told. I'm sorry, all the way to the bottom of my feet. Please forgive me."

After a long silence, she opens her eyes and sees tears streaming down Shaye's face. "If we are owning truth, I did many spiteful things to you, too." She wipes tears away as she shrugs. "I don't even remember how all of the hating started."

Jariel sits on the edge of the bed and they briefly embrace.

A short laugh escapes Shaye's mouth as she uses her sheet to dab her eyes. "The joke of it is that everyone here is probably right. The Maker put us in that box together and here we are. No one else could have planned all this—or seen how it would change our lives. The situations aren't ones we chose . . . but we have an opportunity for a new life. And you're right. We're kin now. We can be friends like we were when we were little, can't we?"

"Yes. I would like that very much."

The sound of children's voices outside the far window draws their attention before a woman's head and upper torso are framed in its light. It's Joony, who lives just two houses down from them. She is very much an oddity—whom Jariel has come to think of as the village "character." During the first days after their arrival, Shaye discovered that Joony was of the same linage as Old Menoh—the line of Tosh, and it gave her more of a heart for a comical-yet-sad woman whom Menoh would most certainly would have attempted to fold into Genon community life if she lived in Aegea.

Joony is never seen without her toddler on her hip and three other children in tow. She and her little troop roam from place to place during the day, trading whatever they have on hand for other things. She generally starts the day by bartering something she's made or found for a generous portion of food. They partially consume the food before she attempts to trade what's left over for something else, trading smaller and smaller bits of one thing for another until there is nothing left. By the end of the day, they've kept busy and managed to eat enough to get by. Each morning, they start the process over again.

The two women wave at Joony and her toddler, who is sucking on three fingers. To his right they can see the top half of the oldest boy's head, whose eyes are just above the sill, taking in every detail of a room he's never seen before. One hand appears over the sill and meekly waves back.

"Good day," his mother says to the women inside.

"Good day," they both answer.

She looks down at one of the children who is out of their view and says, "Give it here."

A little hand holding a green object appears above the window sill. It's a little bird, made from strips of palm fronds, complete with a long tail and sticks for legs and feet. The woman sets it on the sill for them to admire for a moment before she passes it in to Jariel. "I made a gift. For the baby."

Jariel hands it to Shaye, who turns it around several times admiring the craftsmanship from different angles. "What a lovely gift! Her first gift. You honor her."

Joony nods before one of the smaller children tries to hoist himself up. She ignores him and asks, "Is Willow home? Malachi said she was taking the day off."

"Yes," Jariel tells her. "Come around to the front door and I'll tell her you are here."

She disappears from the window with the chatter of children following in her wake.

Inside the house, Willow exits her bedroom just in time to see that one of their regular visitors has arrived.

While a trade for a generous portion of dried fruit for a hand of fresh bananas takes place, Jariel notices that the little girl in the entourage is growing taller, and that her dirty dress is nearly too small. When the visitors are gone, she formulates the words in Genon so she can ask Willow, "Does Joony have a husband?"

"Yes. But he is out on the boats either fishing or exploring most of the time."

Jariel understands all the words but one. "'Exploring?' What is this?"

"Uh, going new places to look around and see what is there."

"Oh."

"I think he only comes home long enough to make more children," the old woman whispers, making a round motion in front of her own stomach.

"*Oh.*"

Willow's eyes take on a soft look. "Joony is. . . ." she says in a hushed voice. "Well, everyone needs something. We must all try to take care of each other. You understand?"

Jariel nods before they hear a little squeak from Shaye's room. It's a prelude to a cry.

Jariel hustles through the door and asks, "May I pick her up for you?"

"Yes."

Gently lifting the baby, she stands, holding the soft bundle close against her body. Within moments, however, she feels a warm sensation . . . and then clammy wetness spreading downward before she realizes the reason for it. "Oh my. I think we will need to . . . fix something here. Uh . . . I've never done this before."

Willow enters the room holding a bowl and sees the odd expression on Jariel's face, then the growing wet spot on her dress. "Oh, so you've been initiated by the baby, have you?" She chuckles. "Get used to it since it will happen frequently now. It's a common part of life for households with a baby."

Shaye starts to scoot toward the edge of her bed. "I can clean her up."

The old woman wags a scolding finger at her. "*Eh eh!* We promised to help look after you *and* this girl. You'll have *plenty* of opportunities coming up soon." Handing her the bowl she brought into the room, she says, "Here. Malachi from next door brought soup for us. It's very good—made with *sooshi* hen and special vegetables." She gives Jariel a knowing wink. "I think he knows that *sooshi* is Shaye's favorite. Now, as for you," she addresses the new mother again. "You just stay where you are right now and eat your soup. I will show Jariel how it's done."

CHAPTER 17
Hissing Machines and Radios

It's a wheeled vehicle the likes of which has never been seen in all of Aegea. At the front, a shiny copper-clad boiler and steam engine. Attached to the engine is a cab where the driver sits with a steering wheel, two levers, and a dashboard with gauges and valves. Behind the cab is a long compartment, made mostly of wood, with an upper and lower floor.

Two men wearing goggles and elbow-length leather gloves walk around the contraption. One of them, Aegea's master inventor Sage Dooley seats himself in the cab while the other, his assistant, Dell, stands by the engine.

"Clear?" Sage asks loudly.

Dell holds up both hands. "Clear!" At the first *chugs* of the machine he leans forward to check a valve.

Inside the cab, his boss adjusts the valves on the dashboard and the number of chugs increases. Once there is a steady throb, Sage gives a loud "*Whoop!*" and jumps out to slap his assistant on the back.

It's at that moment that two visitors step into the large, secluded warehouse where so many wonders have been produced. The inventor tries to rub a smudge off his left goggle lens before he realizes his leather glove won't do the job. He pulls off the goggles and squints to focus on the men, wondering who would have permission to get past security. After the kidnappings that took place on the day of the general's appointment, the number of armed guards around anyone or anything considered essential to the government doubled. That meant Sage, his wife, his assistant, his warehouse, and his home were nearly on lockdown.

As soon as he recognizes the guests, he tells Dell to shut down the engine, and walks over to greet them, speaking with a loud voice so he can be heard over the steam that is *shooshing* out of the engine.

"General McClaren. It's good to see you and Ty."

"I realize we were going to come tomorrow," the general tells him, "but my schedule worked out better for today." He looks over at the hulking object, "Is this the 'bus' you told me about? When will it be ready for a test on the road?"

The sound of escaping steam stops just as Ty yells, "What's a bus?"

Sage smiles, then answers in a normal volume. "It was called a 'bus' in ancient times . . . and that," he says pointing to the machine, "is a steam engine that will pull it. Come and look at it," he says walking back toward it. Pointing to the enclosure at the rear of the vehicle, he continues, "As many as two dozen people can sit on benches on the upper and lower decks. The driver sits in the cab there, and the engine pulls the vehicle down the road without horses—perhaps as fast as 15 miles an hour on straight stretches! You can send two dozen workers or soldiers to Westland in a little more than two hours. Other adaptations would be to use engines for plows, or haulers for produce. It can push or pull virtually *anything* that needs to move."

Ty walks over to the vehicle and steps up through the doorway of the passenger section. "Wow. Just wow. How do you think of all this stuff?"

The inventor shrugs. "I don't. I can't really take credit for it." He pauses to address the general with a question. "He knows about the archives?"

The older McClaren's eyebrows arch up. "You mean about our history? Yes. He knows."

Sage resumes his explanation. "My father and my uncle—they were real geniuses. And many of the things that people think I 'invent' . . . well actually, I more rediscover and adapt. This steam engine, the tramway down the mountain . . . the aqueduct system and so many other things came about due to the diligence of some of the Firstlanders who were engineers, mechanics, and builders. They meticulously drew and described all this stuff when they realized that everyone was stuck here and the people would soon have *none* of the technology that got them here. They wrote it all down for us. I'm just a guy who found the drawings and explanations and made them real again. This bus has been in the works—on and off—for nearly ten years. It took that long to find some of the materials and then make parts to the right specifications." He places a hand on the vehicle the way one would place a hand on the shoulder of his child. "Very soon we'll be ready to start testing her."

Jubal is anxious to hear about a different development. "How's the radio project coming along?"

"I have several that are ready to test. If you'll come with me," he says, turning to walk toward his office in another part of the building, "I can give you a small demonstration."

"What do you think the range will be?"

"Well, you could have one at either end of Aegea and transmit and receive with no problem, but I have no way of knowing what the longest range is. We'll just have to keep trying over greater distances and see. It's my understanding that distance is somewhat dependent upon atmospheric conditions and terrain, and we have no control over those—but I suppose we'll learn all the intricacies over time."

Ty jogs a few steps to catch up to Sage. "What is radios?"

"A radio is a device that can transmit sound—voices or other audio signals—across a great distance to another radio."

Ty stops walking. "How great a distance? Like making the sound louder so everyone could hear it?"

Sage turns to the young man before he answers. "That's a good guess, but, amazingly, the signal travels—invisible and unheard—through the air and can only be received by another radio that captures the signal and turns it back into words or sounds for you to hear."

"How is that *possible*?"

His father interjects, "Perhaps Mr. Dooley would be willing to allow you to tag along for some lessons at another time. Right now, he's busy and so are we."

They walk to the back of the building where a fifteen-foot cube with a wide door and no windows serves as Sage's "office." When he lets them in, Ty's eyes quickly scan the space. This is the inner sanctum where so many things have been invented or resurrected out of long-dead memories and re-engineered for life here.

Books and odd objects are stacked everywhere in the well-lit space. The top of his small desk, however, is noticeably clean with piles coming just level with the surface on either side.

The inventor stands completely still for a moment while he recalls where he left the things he currently wants.

"Now where . . . ? Oh, right," he says to himself as he steps around a pile of different kinds of wood cut into planks. On a shelf behind his desk he picks up a rectangular object a little longer than his hand. He locates a button on the top of it, then pulls on it to extract a telescoping antenna that's a foot and a half tall. At the other end, he flips out a small crank then quickly turns it several times, before flipping it back into its slot. Finally, he turns the whole device so they can see the face of it. "This round, grill-looking thing is the microphone—you speak into it." He points to another raised circle above it. "This is where the voices come out for you to hear. This button here," he tells them as he points to a rectangular piece on one of the thin sides, "is what you push in order to talk—to transmit to the other device." After all that, he demonstrates how it's done.

"This is base to pretty lady. Base to pretty lady, over." After he repeats these sentences several times, a woman's voice comes back over the device. As soon as he hears it, he holds the device away from his face so that the other two can hear it as well.

"Sage," she says, "I'm still here and this thing still seems to be working, and I have other things to do today."

Both of the guests look amazed. He looks at them and shrugs before talking into the device again. "The general and his son are here and they're listening. Over."

"Oh. Well I don't know what I'm supposed to say, other than this is the radio and I can hear you. Over."

Before continuing, Dooley looks at the general and says, "Just so you know this is in real time, ask a question for her to answer."

Jubal thinks for a moment. "What was her—"

"Wait. Here, you hold it." Sage says to him. "Like this. Talk into it after you press this button."

Ty watches his father follow the instructions, then ask the question. "What was your name before you married?"

Sage points to the device. "Now take your finger off the button so you can hear."

As soon as he does, the woman's voice crackles through the earpiece. "—was Tressa Harris."

The general's eyes widen for a moment before he looks at his son and mouths the word, *wow.*

His son nods in agreement.

"Where is she right now?" Jubal wants to know.

"At our house. Just up the hill. But Dell and I tried it from Oldtown to here yesterday. Still worked."

"And you think it will work between the forest and the plateau?"

"*If* what I read is correct and *if* we have made the devices correctly, we should be able to bounce a signal off the planet's atmosphere for hundreds of miles. We won't really know till we try it. If it meets with your approval, we'll try it from Westland to here next."

Ty's mind is exploding with ideas. "How long have you known how to do this?"

He shrugs. "Years."

"Could you use this to transmit information to multiple people in different locations all at once?"

"Yes."

"To listen to someone far away who doesn't know you're listening?"

"Yes."

"Why didn't you make radios before?"

Sage looks at Jubal and Jubal nods.

"I want you to think about it, Ty." Sage holds up the radio. "Technology is a powerful thing. It can help or harm people. It can be used to lift a society up . . . or hold it under the influence of a tyrant. Would you give power to a man, such as General Fairmont, who didn't have long to live? Would you do it if you could see that his successor might be a man like Col. Mosely?"

"Oh."

"It has to be about more than making things just to make them. Just like your father is teaching you . . . my father and my uncle taught me about the responsibility we carry for the things we set loose in the world."

The young man nods. "Now I understand."

Sage realizes it's time to get back to the task at hand. "So, General, do you want to have a test between Westland and town?"

"I'll arrange for a trip there."

CHAPTER 18
Plans Gone Awry

Although the old décor in the mansion has the appeal of military tradition, this refurbished room is just the beginning of a planned make-over for the entire compound. The new general was glad to see his wife take an interest in something besides sitting alone in her dark bedroom. He told her to do as she wished with the place.

In recent weeks, Duana McClaren allowed a couple of her old friends to visit, and today marks the first time she's invited someone who isn't a close confidante into the home.

" . . . Of course," Duana tells her, "This room is just the beginning of the work indoors. I'm not sure what the former general was *thinking* when he had the outside of the house painted white, but that will definitely have to change." She leans forward and her slender hand hovers over the delicate china pot on the tray. "More tea?"

The young woman smooths the skirt of her olive green dress. "Yes, Ma'am. Thank you."

The girl knows better than to mention certain topics. They've already discussed her parents, her new hairstyle, the intricate embroidery on the bodice of her frock, the weather, her own plans for the upcoming months, and the comfortable chairs in the room—which then expanded to Duana's plans to redecorate the home. Is there anything else to talk about? She waits for her hostess to steer the conversation.

A wisp of steam rises as the last of the hot liquid trickles into the fragile cup. Before looking at her guest, Duana chances another glance at the shadow on the floor. Although important buildings and the homes of officers now have clocks and the attempt to synchronize the life of the people of Aegea by these devices has met with some success, shadows are the way many people in Aegea have measured time for generations. Old habits are powerful things.

The young lady notes her hostesses' fleeting look at the shadow. Her parents do the same thing—and her mother did warn her not to wear out her welcome. She clears her throat and says, "It's been so good to see you, but I should be going soon. I promised to help my mother select the flowers for her window boxes today."

One of the doors swings open and a young man strides into the room.

"*Ahhhhhhhhh.* There you are," Duana says. "Look who's here."

Upon seeing him, the young woman coughs on a sip of tea.

He stops near his mother and she takes his hand before he says, "I'm sorry. I didn't know you had company or I wouldn't have barged in like this."

"Oh, nonsense. Linsey and I were just having tea. Have a seat and I'll send for another pot."

When he turns to see her, she says, "Hello, Ty. It's good to see you."

He nods. "It's good to see you, too. How are your parents?"

"They are well, thank you. Are you staying in town?"

"Just tonight. I came for a quick visit with my parents and I'll be heading out again in the morning."

"Oh. It's a shame you couldn't stop in and say hello to my parents. They were just inquiring after you the other day."

"Sorry. Not this trip. Perhaps on another trip, though."

"Well, since you're here right now," his mother chides, "take a chair and sit with us."

After he hesitates Linsey rises from her chair. "Well, as I told you, Mrs. McClaren, I promised my mother I'd be back in a couple of hours." She carefully folds her napkin and places it on the corner of the tea table. "I really should be going."

Ty's mother gives him a look that says she expects him to do something.

He offers his arm to Linsey. "I'll walk you out."

The strain of having a visitor is over. Duana leans back in her chair. "It was so good of you to come, dear. I'd like to do this again."

Linsey bows her head slightly and says, "Thank you. I had a lovely time. It was kind of you to ask me."

She loops her arm in Ty's, the way she used to when they would go on long walks in days gone by, and they stroll out of the house together. When they reach the front porch of the home, some of the awkwardness of the encounter has dissipated. She stops walking so he disengages his arm from hers and pauses as well.

As they linger in the shade of the covered porch, she tells him, "I must say I didn't really expect to see you today."

"Imagine that. My mother *accidentally* had you come over for tea when she knew I'd be arriving."

Her mouth lifts into a gentle smile. "Yes. Imagine that."

He doesn't offer any other comment.

Perhaps in an effort to distract herself from the unease of the silence, she retrieves cream colored gloves out of a small purse and pulls them on. She's still methodically pushing the cloth between each finger when she says, "I must admit I was hoping to see you." She chances a glance at his face. "Other than that time we said hello on the street a month ago, we haven't spoken since . . ."

"I know. I haven't been in town much. I would have been poor company, anyway. I haven't felt like socializing."

The color in her face deepens and she allows herself to peer deeply into his eyes. "I thought we were more than just social acquaintances." There's tension in her voice. "I mean, I know we aren't bound by the wishes of our parents, but I thought we actually liked each other at some point, didn't we? You've disappeared from *everything* . . . including my life. . . .

And you've changed." He's staring at the stones in the porch floor so she blunders on. "I see you're still not wearing your uniform. Are the rumors true? Did you quit the Academy? Are you resigning your commission?"

He lets out a sarcastic laugh before he looks up and answers. "So glad that everyone in town thinks they've figured out my life."

"I'm sorry. I didn't mean to upset you. I shouldn't have—"

He shakes his head. "No. I'm not upset. You haven't upset me. It's just that the rumors are . . . just rumors. Granted, I'm not currently attending classes at the Academy, but I haven't resigned my commission—I'm *on leave* from the Academy. I'm still actively working on assignments for my father."

"So . . . you're not in town because you're still trying to find out what happened?"

A servant walks through the garden nearby. As they watch him pass, Ty notices there is also a guard standing near the fence of the property.

He lowers his voice and chooses his words carefully. "Yes, I keep an eye out for any new evidence, but as much as that, I make sure the lands out west are tended and I have oversight of a few projects in Westland. Since my father became general, they've been staying in town. Someone needs to keep watch on things in the west."

"But your sister was taken so many months ago."

"*Two* women were taken, Linsey. Two women."

When it happened he made no secret of the fact that he believed the other girl was also a victim of the kidnapping, not a perpetrator. "Well, yes, and the servant girl, too. But, surely, there are no more leads to follow. Surely, you can't be holding onto any sort of hope that . . . you must realize finding them is impossible."

"Mostly, things are impossible because we *give up*." He stops a moment before he continues. "That came out harsher than I meant it to." He tries to explain himself. "It seems a lifetime ago that we would sit and talk or go for long walks . . . but I remember we would talk about believing that there was something bigger than all of us. We both felt life had purpose, that we were being guided in that purpose. I still believe that we can be guided by someone who . . . can make the impossible . . . possible."

She takes a step back from him. "Now you're scaring me, Ty. Those things we said back then . . . they were just the foolish talk of young people who had too much time on their hands and no responsibilities in life."

"I've said a *lot* of foolish things . . . but this isn't one of them. If anything, faith gives my life meaning in the midst of all this. Believing the One who made me knows me and cares about me has given me hope."

Her eyes widen as if she were a small creature, cornered by a fearsome beast.

"I haven't lost my mind, Linsey," he says in a soft voice. "I've found the courage to hold on and to believe there is more to life than what we see."

She searches his face. Is this really Ty McClaren, the one she first met when she was six, the one she grew up knowing she would marry. "But won't there come a time for you to . . . won't there be a time for you to take your place in society again? To resume your life? Even your mother has begun to move on."

A sad expression settles upon his face before he tells her, "I know our parents had expectations for us." He gently takes both of her hands. "You're an exceptional woman and I wish nothing but happiness for your future. . . ."

Her eyes well up. "I know you're hurting. You're not yourself right now, but I can wait."

"Linsey. What lies before me is a different path from the one our parents planned for us. My heart and my will are already set upon this path. You *deserve* someone who will be fully present for you, who will take his place in society *with* you, who will love you and grow old with you. I'm not that man."

She slaps his face, then steps back, horrified by what she's done. "I . . . I shouldn't have done that."

"You only did it because I hurt you. I am sorry for that, and I hope that someday you can forgive me."

Inside the home, Duana sees Linsey rushing by the window. Alone.

Outside, Ty watches as the woman his parents always planned for him to wed pushes through a gate and quickly steps into a waiting carriage.

CHAPTER 19
Bush Tea and Bullets

The small storeroom only has a window, but lamps are needed to provide more light. In the background, the never-ending din of cascading water and the grinding pulse of the turning waterwheel hamper his concentration.

When he continues to look indecisive, Canaan the Exile points again to a handful of dried leaves and asks, "How about these?"

Ty looks at his old friend, Basil.

"Don't look at him for the answer," Canaan chides. "You're separated from everyone else, you're alone in the forest and you can't keep down any food. Is this the bush for a tea?"

Picking up one of the leaves, he rubs it between two fingers and sniffs it. It has a nasty, sour smell. "No," Ty finally answers. He looks around the leaves, sticks, and roots displayed on the table before pointing to one with leaves similar to the one he's holding. "That's the plant I would want," he says, then picks it up and sniffs it. "It grows on a spindly bush in the shade, usually near water. I would separate each leaf from the stem, boil them and drink the tea."

Everyone in Aegea knows that the Genon have great knowledge of the medicinal value of plants. According to the Genon, it is knowledge that's been passed down from generation to generation since the first man and woman of creation. Often, a particular part of a plant must be boiled for what they call a tea. They refer to the practice, in general, as making "bush teas." Learning the different bushes is just one of many survival skills that all the men going on the mission must master. By keeping the knowledge of the most valued medicines a secret known only to blood kin, some families have managed to elevate their status in Aegea by working as apothecaries, dispensing tonics and cures to others.

"And what's this?" his instructor asks.

Ty starts to answer in Command Dialect, but Canaan interrupts him. "*Eh eh!* In this room, we are in the Great Forest. Only Genon is spoken here. Not the *clink clank* sound of your language." He throws up his hands. "Your language, it has no *music* in it!" Done with his rant, he picks up one of the stems in a pile. "Tell me what this is."

This time, he answers in Genon. "It looks like the bush for fever, but it is poison."

"Good! Now, tell me what you would use on a wound."

"Depends. If it's a fresh wound, I'd soak some of this," Ty points to a plant on the far corner of the table. "I'd bruise the leaf and place it directly on the injury. If the wound is going bad," he adds, reaching over to touch a fruit, "I cut some of this and wrap it right on the skin. If there is rotting flesh, I'd let flies land on the wound and lay eggs. The larvae will eat the dead flesh and leave the living tissue alone."

Canaan allows his student to wait for a moment before he nods. "Very good. That's enough for today."

Ty tries not to show obvious relief, but this is the first time he's gotten every question right. Perhaps he and Basil will laugh about it later, but before there is any free time, it's his friend's turn to be quizzed.

When the test is over, Canaan hands them each a cup of "tea" that's been steeping while they answered questions. He hoists his own cup to give the traditional toast of forest gatherers, "So we are strong in the forest." They all drink the bitter liquid together.

Ty squints, then shudders after he downs the last swallow.

Basil laughs and slaps him on the back. "We'll make a Genon out of you yet."

In the first generation, the Genon gatherers observed that many who went into the forest had severe reactions. Because of this, fewer and fewer soldiers went into the jungle and began calling it "the Poison Forest." Eventually, the hunter/gatherers discovered the main cause of the problem was a particular tree that was abundant throughout the known forest. Once the Genon isolated the problem, they tried making "teas" of the various parts of the tree. They discovered the roots and bark were toxic but the leaves produced a bitter tea that, taken in small amounts over time, gave them immunity.

Sgt. Shocky has to stand next to Ethan rather than behind him, to observe the shot. Ethan is unusually tall for a Genon and Shocky is on the short side of normal. The bullet hits the outer rim of the target.

"Better," the sergeant tells him.

Ethan lowers the rifle. "I know I can do better. I'm still having trouble adjusting. A crossbow pulls away," he says moving his arms outward. "The rifle," he declares while simulating the recoil of the weapon, "kicks back at me." He rubs his right cheek and jaw. "It's making my face and shoulder hurt."

Shocky nods. "Go ahead and reload."

Ethan, whom the soldiers on the plateau call "Stack," is a cousin of Basil's, and started working for General McClaren's father when he was a teen. Now nearly forty, he has more than a decade of valuable experience in what Aegean's call the "far region" of the forest—which is the greatest distance anyone from the Aegean Plateau has traveled to and returned from safely.

While Ethan reloads, it's the other man's turn to shoot.

As Asher fires the rifle, the sergeant checks his stance. When the bullet clips the side of the bullseye, there's a grunt of approval before he says, "Again."

Until a few weeks ago, neither Asher nor Ethan had ever fired a rifle. Like the vast majority of the people on the plateau, they'd never even *held* one. For the past four decades, only soldiers carried the limited number of handguns and rifles on the plateau—brought out mostly for show at ceremonies.

It was these two hunter/gatherers "Stack" (Ethan) and Asher, who found the first clues that helped unravel the mystery surrounding the disappearances of Shaye and the general's daughter. When looking for more clues, they found Canaan, near death in the forest. It was Asher who went at top speed back to the plateau to tell Ty's father they'd found an Exile who was gravely ill. The man was delirious with a fever and would soon die without skilled care. Ty's father arranged to bring the Exile up to the plateau in secret and be taken to the mill where Menoh could care for him.

Hours after their quiz on bush teas, Basil and Ty sit on top of a boulder. The room-sized rock, along with several smaller ones, probably rolled to this spot in a landslide centuries ago. When they were boys, they came here to eat or dream up stories about the giant creatures that used to roam the plateau.

Dark clouds skiff by overhead and the cool wind threatens to roll away the small cloth sack containing their food. Basil grabs it before can disappear over the edge of the rock.

"Think it'll rain?" Ty asks.

His friend pulls a sandwich out of the bag, peeks between the slices of bread, then hands it to him before retrieving another sandwich for himself. "Maybe, later."

They watch the birds and listen to the wind in the trees until they can see a couple of wagons moving along a road in the distance.

As if he's thinking aloud, Ty says, "We'll be on our journey soon."

"Do you think they have any more inventions for us to try?"

Ty's eyes widen at the thought of it. "I don't know. I'm not sure how much more information my head can hold . . . or how many other inventions I want to test. I'm still sore from when that last one threw me onto the ground."

Basil laughs as he pictures the look on Ty's face as he flew backwards when he pulled the trigger on a sonic weapon for the first time. "It was pretty amusing to watch though. Who would think that a *sound* could blow someone over like that? It's much worse than the rebound of a rifle."

"I never would have imagined that *anything* could change the path of the water coming down the waterfall like that."

"Now I know why they picked that location for testing though. At least the loud crash of the water covered most of the sound of the gun."

The two fall silent again and work on their sandwiches before Basil asks, "How long do you think, until we leave? Days? Weeks?"

"I can't imagine it would be more than two weeks. Your grandfather thinks Canaan is strong enough. All we need now is for him, Dooley, and Shocky to tell my father we're prepared enough to survive the trip."

Basil dusts the crumbs from his sandwich off his clothes and leans back on his hands while his eyes sweep over the panorama. "I will miss it. I shall be happy to return to the woods and the land here."

"Do you mean to settle down when you get back?"

He focuses on the outpost in the distance before he shrugs and nods.

Ty smiles. He knows that his friend has kept track of the innkeeper's youngest daughter for more than a year now. "Does she know?"

"She knows that I have noticed her, that she pleases my eyes. Her eyes say she would consent to court me."

"So you haven't asked her?"

"Women are creatures of curiosity. Why would I ask her to court and then make her curious—or angry—about my absence?"

"Good point."

"What about you and Shaye? Somehow it doesn't seem possible."

Ty just shakes his head. "One impossibility at a time, my friend. One at a time. For now, I'm still working on getting down into the forest and then through it. Even if we succeed, we don't know what will happen here on the plateau after that. My father, no doubt has some long-range plans. Who knows?"

He shrugs. "What I do know for certain is that he offered land to anyone who helps find Jariel. If nothing else, I'll claim my right to a bit of land and live on it. That suits me fine. I have no ambitions to rule over all of this," he says sweeping his hand across the view before them.

"Maybe that's what makes you more fit to do it than most."

He ignores the remark. "What about you and Ethan and Asher? Will you claim land and tend it?"

"If we come back, I will. I think Ethan would try it, too. Asher? Well. I don't know. I think he likes hunting in the Great Forest too much to stop and become a farmer. He and Canaan discovered that they're distant cousins, you know."

"Really?"

"Asher always said that the Great Forest gets in your blood and you don't want to leave it. Aegea may be too tame for him. Perhaps he and Canaan can continue to hunt there."

"You don't see Canaan living in Aegea either?"

"*Eh eh.* I've never seen a man so uncomfortable with his surroundings. I know part of it is that he is lonely, but we dare not let him be seen here before this is over. Even if we told people he was mute, it would still be mere minutes before the cousin quiz started."

Ty tucks the last wad of bread in his cheek. "Ha. You got that right. Every Genon woman with eligible daughters or nieces or granddaughters would be poking us to find out who he is related to, finding out what line, what family he came from, who his brothers and sisters are, what work the family does."

"He'd be discovered in no time."

"And the whole plateau would know within days."

"I'm thinking, once he gets back into the Land of Cloud and Leaf, he won't want to return here. Perhaps your father could help him find a situation in the forest . . . one that wasn't so bleak."

"Like what?"

"Perhaps he could start some sort of outpost in the forest. If we succeed, the whole world will know that the Exiles exist and that they have a settlement. If both sides agree to trade and communicate, there will be travel. Outposts along the way make travel easier and safer." He nods to a spot in the distance. "Like that one. A good place to stop, to rest, to eat, to make repairs."

"Actually, that's a good idea. Perhaps something like that *could* be offered to Canaan."

They hear a "Hello," from below and Ty leans his head over the front of the boulder to see who it is before calling out, "Up here, Shocky. Come around the back. There's a way up."

Within moments the sergeant, wearing civilian clothes, appears behind them. His straight stance looks oddly stiff without his uniform to give it context.

"It's nearly time to report in," he tells them.

"*Yyyyeah.* But it's not time yet." Ty points to the bag, "And we have an extra sandwich here. Would you care to join us?"

He looks back and forth between the general's son and his friend. Such a friendship between the races is rare. He sits down on the boulder and takes in the view for a few moments before he replies. "I would like the sandwich."

Basil hands the bag to him. "You know, you'll have to tell us what your first name is. We can't call you *Shocky* for the whole trip and *Sergeant* definitely won't do in the forest."

"Perhaps," he says before biting into his sandwich. They wait while he chews. "Perhaps I will tell you when we are in the forest."

Ty chuckles. "We were just talking about the giant secret network of Genon mothers in Aegea. We could probably find out your name with relative ease by asking Basil's mother."

He shrugs and nods, but just keeps eating.

CHAPTER 20
The Lost One

As is the custom after giving birth, Shaye spent the first weeks at home, getting stronger, caring for her child. It is also the custom that whenever a baby is born that family, friends, neighbors, and well-wishers give gifts of food and other supplies to ensure a safe beginning for the new life—and this they did in great measure.

Today is her first time out of the house. For more than a month, she's never been more than a few feet from little Elle, so it feels very odd to be in the market without her. Willow's friend, Iris, offered to help her to shop while Jariel stayed home, watching the baby.

It's a perfect day, with a cool breeze blowing, white puffs of clouds in a bright blue sky, and the sound of the surf nearby. When they first enter the market they hear singing and see that two old women, glad to be out and about today, are dancing. Each has one hand holding her friend's hand, the other holding the hem of her long dress and swishing it back and forth as they step in a circle and sing. Many of the shoppers have paused to clap to the rhythm of the song and cheer on the women. Everyone laughs and applauds when the women stop, breathless and happy.

As people go back to buying and selling, many of them note that Shaye is out and about, each of them stopping to congratulate her and inquire about the baby—which greatly extends the time it would normally take to do a little shopping. The only thing that will take longer, she supposes, is the first time she takes Elle out of the house and everyone wants to *see* her.

Although it's been good to be outside in the sun and fresh air, she's tired by the time they're nearly done shopping. They only have one more vendor to see, and they'll head home.

"May I have some of that cheese?" she asks, indicating the kind she wants. While he's wrapping it up, she turns to Iris and says, "It's taken me a while to get used to cheese made from goat's milk. In the house where I worked, only the finest cheeses from cow's milk were served. The *ishi* allowed no goat products in the house. She thought they smelled bad."

"*Mmmmmm.*" her companion says, momentarily closing her eyes as she recalls it. "I must admit I still miss cow's milk, cheese, and the occasional piece of beef."

Shaye nods. "Yes, I especially miss milk . . ." she says, pinching her thumb and forefinger together as if she's holding a fancy cup, then extending her little finger, ". . . in my tea."

They both laugh before a loud conversation draws their attention—along with that of nearly everyone in the vicinity. It's Flint the hunter, haggling loudly with a poultry vendor. After a back-and-forth uproar that lasts another minute, a bargain is struck and Flint strides out of the market. Business resumes.

The two women leave the hubbub of the selling booths before Shaye broaches a topic that's troubled her. She leans closer to Iris before asking in a confidential tone, "What's the puzzle with Flint or Francis or whatever you call him?"

Iris stops walking and takes hold of Shaye's arm. "You haven't mentioned him to Willow, have you?"

"No. Why?"

She shakes her head and sets down her large cloth bag. Obviously, the answer will take a bit of time in the telling. "It's such a tragedy. On all sides, a tragedy."

Shaye sets down her bag as well. "What is?"

"It started many years ago. Francis' father was an independent sort of man. More so than most. As you know, our people are of an independent nature. But we also know the value of *inter*dependence—we allow ourselves to rely upon one another in times of need. Well, Amos—that was the name of Francis' father—was a *very* self-sufficient man, some would call him prideful. He married a nice woman by the name of Tulip. Her mother and Willow's mother were second cousins. Anyway, Tulip and Amos lived just outside of the village and they did well for themselves. Right off, they had Francis, then one after another, three more boys who were all learning to hunt—just like their father. You wouldn't know it now, but Francis was a *good* boy when he was younger and very kind to his mother. My friend Maple told me that at least once a week she'd see him walking home from the woods with a handful of flowers for his mother." She stops and sighs. "Anyway, when he was around twelve, Tulip became pregnant a fifth time. When she tried to give birth, the baby was breech but Amos wouldn't send for a midwife. After seeing four healthy sons delivered, he thought he could deliver a baby as well as anyone here." Willow sighs again. "A midwife could have saved her, but he refused to call one. She died, and the baby—a handsome boy," she stops to tap herself on the head, "was damaged."

Shaye's eyes widen. "*Oh, lah,* I am so stupid. I met him and I just thought he didn't speak because he was shy."

"Oh, he can speak, he just doesn't do so very often. He's slow. His brothers watch out for him mostly."

Shaye's brow scrunches up. "Come to think of it, I've only seen Francis and *three* brothers. Where's the fourth? And what does any of this have to do with Willow?"

Her friend moves closer and speaks just above a whisper, "On that terrible day, the day of the flood, the second son of Tulip was supposed to be watching out. No one goes there now, but there's a nice pool of water up the hillside on a stream west of the village. It was where many of the village women went once a week to wash clothing on the rocks while their children splashed in the shallow water. As was the custom, a hunter would go along, to make sure no fierce creatures came near and no one harmed the women or the children. But on the terrible day, the young man who was supposed to be watching decided to wander off. He heard the roar of the rushing water while he was a good distance away, and when he realized what it was, he ran as fast as he could . . . but by the time he got there, they'd all been swept away. He ran along the riverbank finding some of them dashed upon the rocks among the wet clothing. He went all the way to where the river empties into the ocean and even swam out to look for them. But he was too late."

Shaye can barely speak. "How horrible."

"For two weeks, severe arguments raged through all of homeplace. I dare say the flood and the days following could be rightly described as the worst days of our people here. Some wanted the young man put to death. It was Benjamin—one of the men who walked through the forest with you—who argued the most forcefully for death. Nathan and some of the elders interceded, saying our people couldn't do such a thing, especially since it was a case of carelessness, not malice. But most of the families who lost women and children said he deserved death since his neglect brought such terrible destruction upon so many. His father, Amos, disowned him and said he would agree to whatever punishment was decided. Francis argued vigorously on his brother's behalf—as much so as if his own life was in the balance. But it was the argument of Jared the potter that brought a compromise of sorts. After much deliberation, the elders agreed to do something the first settlers here said they would *never* do: exile one of our own people. The families who lost the women and children agreed the young man could live on, but only if it was as if he was *dead to all of us*."

"What did they do with him? Where did they take him?"

"Some of the fathers and husbands of those who died went with Nathan and two other elders to take him up the river, deep into the Great Forest—and from that day, no one would be allowed to even speak his name. A decree stated that as long as he was 'dead' to all of us, he could exist in the forest but if anyone of his kin said his name or spoke of him like he was alive, those who lost family had the right to go and kill him. And, if he ever came past the big bend in the river into our lands again, he could be killed—with no punishment to the one who took his life. So far as I know, no one has seen him since they left him in the forest and no one knows if he survived. I think Francis would have gone into exile with him if it wasn't for Seth. His father and one of the brothers, Boaz, tended to beat on the boy if others weren't there to stand up for him. After that was when he took to calling himself 'Flint.' Says his heart is 'made of stone' now. He's never been the same, and, as you can see, he rarely misses an opportunity to go against the grain of the people here. Amos died from a fever last year and Francis refused to mourn him."

###

It's later that night that Shaye suddenly realizes *who* the man banished from homeplace is. When she does, she knows she must tell his brother what she knows.

CHAPTER 21
Telling Flint

Shaye walks down the road with Elle wrapped in a sling, close to her chest. She started out more than half an hour ago but has made little progress. Every few steps someone comes up to greet her and asks to see the baby. Surprisingly the little one seems oblivious to all the noise of the village, all the new voices, and the peeks of light on her face each time someone wants to look at her. And, of course, along with the "*Ooooos*" and "*Awwws*," over the baby, most want a bit of an update on the household.

"How is Willow?"

"She's well."

"Give her my greeting."

"I shall."

"How is the girl you brought here?"

"Jariel?"

"Yes. Jariel. I heard she was working for Caleb the weaver and that she was doing good things for him."

"She is."

"Praise the Maker. Things are working out nicely for all of you."

"Yes."

Who would have thought a trip through one small corner of the village would take so long?

Closely stacked houses give way to homes with gardens, then to open land, then to rising forest. Finally, she finds the well-worn path she's looking for and begins the climb up a gentle, curving slope. The trees here have a certain smell and she can't make up her mind whether or not she likes it.

The long walk upward turns out to be more than she planned and she finds herself needing to slow down and rest along the way. Although she's never been here before, so far as she knows, there is only one family who lives up this trail.

Perhaps it's just around the corner from that stand of larger trees ahead.

But as she rounds the corner, she realizes that the next stretch of path is even steeper and she stops to consider it.

Oh my! No end in sight.

Her cheeks expand as she slowly blows out a long breath and pivots to look back down the way she came.

Maybe this is a bad idea.

Just as she turns back, she hears shouts echoing through the trees farther up the hill, followed by the sound of something crashing down the hill and ending with a bare-footed man rolling out onto the path about ten feet in front of her. When he sits up, she realizes it's Flint—and he's as stunned to see her as she is to see him.

Standing up, he brushes dirt and leaves off his patched clothing. She's never seen him look so . . . destitute.

Perhaps it's washing day for the men at his house and his other clothes are on a line somewhere.

After pulling a few twigs from his wild mane of hair he gives up on the cleanup effort and steps closer, but when he attempts to speak, he realizes his lip is bleeding. He pulls the lip into his mouth to clean it off, then says, "Good day," like nothing is wrong, as if he always rolls down the hill to greet visitors. His elbow and the knuckles on his right hand are scuffed and bleeding as well.

"Good day," she responds.

He continues to approach. "I see you are walking about with the child."

Since he gives no excuse for his appearance she decides to ignore it as well. "Yes. . . . It's a fine day for a walk."

Everyone else has asked to see the baby so, more out of habit than anything else, she moves the cloth on the sling so he can see Elle's face. Serenely lost in the sound of her mother's heartbeat, the little one's eyes open for a moment then close again.

Flint's expression softens into a smile. She can tell it's probably a genuine smile because even his eyes are smiling. During the effort, though, his lip splits open again. He wipes it on a ragged sleeve, then says. "Nathan is right. She's a beauty."

"You honor her."

They can hear the sound of someone chopping wood echoing down the hill from a distance while he waits for several moments for her to say something else, but she doesn't.

"So . . ." he finally asks. "What are you doing here?"

"I was hoping to see you."

"Really? What for?"

"I wanted to see you alone, and please," she says, holding up one hand, "don't make any rude remarks about that."

There's a smirk, but no comment.

She takes a deep breath and tries to explain. "It's just . . . well, if the situation were the other way around, I'd want someone to tell *me* about my brother."

"I thought you were an only child."

She groans in frustration.

"Sorry," he says, shrugging. "Are you talking about one of *my* brothers?"

She nods, but before she can answer he says, "Seth? Of a truth he would never hurt . . ."

"No. Not Seth."

"Boaz?" He points to his own face. "As you can see, Bo has quite the temper, so it's quite possible he offended—"

"No."

"Not Boaz . . . so it's Reuben?"

"*No!*" she says with a little stomp of her foot.

It's several seconds before he finally apprehends her meaning. She can see in his eyes the moment that he understands.

Putting his hands on his hips he leans forward, and with more than a hint of concern in his voice asks, "Then *what* are we talking about?"

"Someone told me more about what happened two years ago . . ." her voice trails off as his countenance hardens into a frown. She takes a breath and tries again. "But, after they told me, I suddenly realized something." She looks around before adding, "I saw him—I saw the one who is lost to you—when we traveled through the land of cloud and leaf. Once I realized who it was, I knew I must find a way to tell you what happened."

He's breathing faster now and when he speaks she can barely hear his question. "They didn't kill him did they?"

"No. He was very thin, but other than that he looked well the first time I saw him."

His eyes glisten but he maintains control. "What happened?"

"The first time was when the others weren't nearby. I had just awakened and realized I was somehow in the Great Forest.

That's when he came to me and asked me to speak to him. It made no sense at the time. Jariel was still unconscious—in fact, she never saw him for he disappeared just before the others arrived. Later that night, as I sat with the men in the camp of the widow tree, I asked where he was, and they all stopped talking. Nathan said I must have *imagined* I saw someone. This puzzled me greatly, but I realize now that his intention was to state that the one condition by which your brother could live *hadn't* been broken—that he wouldn't *allow* it to be broken. As an elder, he was giving an example for the others to heed. And they did. Even later, when everyone would have been able to hear his voice in the distance, they acted as if they heard nothing—so I began to think I really did imagine him. But then I saw him again, following us, and I knew he was real."

Francis bends forward as if he's in pain. He nods but he doesn't look up.

She speaks softly. "Iris said the sorrow over what happened with your brother is what changed you. So I wanted to tell you that he saved Jariel and me. He did. He interceded for Jariel when she was helpless and stopped me from a terrible mistake that would have cost her life. . . . He sang over me when I was so full of sorrow I thought I might die. He kept watch over us from a distance until we got to the river—that's when he stayed behind to make sure no one followed us. If he hadn't been there, Jariel and I both might have died in the forest. I don't even know his name, but I'm so grateful he helped us. I wanted you to know this. . . . I understand what it means to carry deep sorrow over the ones you'll never see again . . . and I know what it's like to feel you have no place in this world."

He straightens his stance, but he still looks shaken. He starts to say something but he's interrupted by a sharp sound coming through the trees above. It's a whistle—the kind that Genon often use to signal each other over distances.

His gaze becomes steady, and his statement sounds like a command. "You should go now, before anyone sees you here." He moves off the path so she can pass him.

She nods and starts walking. As she moves by him he speaks again, this time with a softer tone.

"I beg of you, don't speak of this to anyone else."

She stops and makes the sign of a vow. "I won't. I give you my word." She's several steps away before she hears him in the distance.

"You belong with our people. I'm glad you were saved. May you always prosper, Shaye from the line of Zim."

The encounter with Flint gives her much to think about, but she must hurry home before Elle awakens, wants to eat, and needs to be changed. Even though she's pretty dragged out by the time she arrives home, as soon as her girl is all cleaned up and fed, it's time to start cooking supper.

She kisses Elle on the cheek and puts her back in the carrying sling. "No time to rest," she says with a tired smile. "We must feed the adults now."

Just as she lights the fire on the stove, she hears a knock at the door. She turns to see a neighbor, standing just outside the open door of the home. She has often seen him walking by, always greeting Willow. A quiet, hard-working man—he's probably in his late thirties with dark gray eyes and a few gray strands in his dark brown hair. He's holding a brown clay cooking pot wrapped in a cloth, and a looped strand of cord is slung over one of his shoulders.

She smiles. "Good afternoon, Malachi."

"Good afternoon, Shaye. Willow asked me to look at the bed in your room. She said it needed repair."

"Yes. A strap broke away from the top left corner. Do you think you can fix it?"

"It should be no problem. My brother would be able to make a new strap, but I can use this cord. It should work as well in keeping the mattress level. May I take a look?"

She nods. "It would be much appreciated."

He holds up the clay pot. "Willow said you liked the soup I made. . . . Just after the baby was born . . ."

"Yes. I remember. It was delicious."

"Well, I was making it again for my family and I thought I might as well bring some to you—to all of you . . . you know, since I was coming to look at the repair."

"You honor us." She steps back, and allows him to come into the home and place the pot on the stove before she asks, "Do you do all the cooking at home?"

"Well, um, yes. Now I do."

Shaye realizes her blunder, but she can't take the question back. His wife died in the tragedy, leaving him with four children—the youngest only two years old at the time. Embarrassed, she looks away from him. *So much sorrow for one community to absorb.*

He sees her discomfort and adds, "My oldest—Isaac is learning how, but," he smiles, "that's a thing that will need more practice. Much more practice."

"Ah. . . . Willow tells me you made the cradle that Elle sleeps in. It's beautiful. I can't tell you how much I've admired it."

"Thank you. My family has worked with wood for as far back as anyone knows. Isaac doesn't seem to have the patience for it, but I think my younger son may, and my older daughter, it seems, has some skill at fine detail work, so I hope at least two of my children will follow after me."

"My mother's family," she tells him, "worked with plants and became gatherers in the Great Forest. She taught me a good bit, but she died when I was young, so my education is incomplete. I'm hoping that Nathan will—*ouch!*" When Elle grabs a loose lock of her hair and starts pulling the conversation stops.

Malachi understands. "Does she scratch as well? One of mine was terrible about that."

"Well, not yet," she says while trying to pry little fingers loose from the long strands. "*Ow*, please let go!"

He clears his throat, "I'll just have a look at the bed, then."

"Oh, certainly," she points her chin in the direction of her room. "In there."

Soon she can hear the bed being scooted around, so she gets busy setting the table and stirring the soup while she softly sings to Elle.

Within twenty minutes he's removed a rotted leather strap from under the mattress and replaced it with several well-knotted cords. When he returns to the main part of the house to tell her it's fixed, he sees that Willow is home and playing with Elle while Shaye fetches water outside.

"Good afternoon. The bed is fixed," he tells her. "I put the mattress back, but she'll have to put her covers on it. Let me know if the cords need adjusting. My brother could make a new strap, but this will probably work just as well."

The old woman looks up, still smiling from her interaction with the baby. "We are grateful for your help. And I see you brought us some of your soup! Truly, you honor us. What can we do for *you* in return?"

He looks away. "Uh. Well, I have smelled some of her baking. Perhaps she could bake something for us one day . . ."

"I'm sure that could be arranged."

He turns to leave and nearly bumps into Shaye, who is balancing two full buckets.

"Here," he says as he swiftly lifts the buckets out of her hands. "Tell me where you want them."

"One in the kitchen, the other one, well . . . just outside the bathroom door would be fine.

He quickly sets the pails where she indicated, then moves to the door. "Have a good evening."

"We appreciate all that you've done for us," she says with a nod of her head. "Good evening to you as well."

Shaye takes her seat near Willow and holds out her hands for the baby, but the old woman isn't ready to surrender her prize. "Take your time, mama. Rest a moment. Elle and I are doing just fine without you." She smiles down at the child and says, "You're my little sunshine, aren't you?" Her expression turns serious when she looks up at the young mother and says, "I hope you will never go far from me . . . but I do hope you will find someone and make a good life here."

"*You* never remarried," is the quick response.

"You keep saying that, but . . . but raising a little one alone is so much harder, isn't it?"

She sighs. "I have you and Jariel. Maybe that's blessing enough for me."

The old woman leans forward and places a hand on top of Shaye's then looks out the window to be assured no one is listening. "First of all, you're assuming that Jariel won't marry and leave our home. And . . . there is so much left of your life. I hope you'll find room in your heart for more. It's not just you, I'm thinking of. It's Elle. How much did you miss having a father in your own life?"

"I know," she says, looking down. "It's just that . . ."

"Goodness knows, there are plenty of candidates to choose from." She squints at the young mother before she says, "*Eh eh!* I saw you roll your eyes. Yes, there are some scoundrels among them, but there are plenty of good men here who would treasure you and Elle. Some are already good fathers, struggling to raise children alone . . . like the one who lives next door for instance."

"*Willow!*"

"You may think it's not my business," she says before peeking out the window again "but I see the way he looks at you. I have known Malachi since he was a babe, and I can tell you he's truly a *good* man. . . . I'm just saying you should give these things more consideration."

CHAPTER 22
An Elegant Gift

"**W**hen you can see joy in the
eyes of the one who gives
a gift, it's a reflection of a
generous heart.—*A saying
in the Sacred Tell*

The monsoon season
has passed and the people
of homeplace are looking
forward to a feast. Most of
the year, common meals
shared among the people
in small neighborhoods are a weekly treat but in monsoon
seasons, the constant heavy downpours make outdoor
gatherings impossible. By the time the rains depart, everyone
is aching to stand under an open sky and celebrate. Tonight,
nearly everyone from the village will gather at the beach to
feast, and a full moon will light the night for them.

As evening settles in, people make last-minute
preparations for the meal. Men and women aren't out on their
porches talking to neighbors. Children, who would usually be
running up and down the street, are busy doing extra chores.
It's quiet in the neighborhood.

"You will come tonight, won't you?" Jariel asks.

Sitting in the small living room, Shaye is doing her best to
get Elle to smile. Since the little girl first smiled two days ago,
getting her to do it over and over has become the pre-
occupation of everyone in the house.

She gets the smile and enjoys the glee of it for a moment
before looking up. "You and Willow can take the food we're
supposed to bring and then she will stay for the singing and
most of the meal. I know she gets tired early, and it's only fair
she should go first. When the meal time is winding down, she'll
come home. As long as the girl here is asleep Willow can just

go to bed and keep an ear open for her. So . . . what were you thinking you'd wear?"

It's hard for either of them to imagine that only months ago they'd decided to become friends. Once they did, animosity from years of mutual torment began to melt away, and they spent many hours learning to understand one another, playing games together, and sharing secrets. Both of them began to view the time they'd spent in the same home yet hating each other with regret.

Without hesitation, Jariel says, "The dark pink dress in the cupboard. And in my hair I'll wear the comb I decorated with the little pink shell-bones I got on the beach and that beautiful feather David gave me on our trip down the river."

They've both been informed that, contrary to what Shaye's aunt told her, the name is just "shells." Of course, thinking of them as *bones* was logical, since the creatures who originally lived inside had no bones and shells served as a type of skeleton on the outside. Over time, as the shells were passed down through Shaye's family, the description got mixed in with the name. Now Shaye, Jariel, and Willow all say "shell bones" as their own little joke.

"The pink dress looks well on you. And the comb will be lovely, but how will you get it to stay in your hair?"

"I'm going to make a little braid for it to rest in. What will *you* wear?"

"The blue dress."

"That tired old thing? It's too big on you now."

Shaye considers the distress she's felt over all the changes to her body that are the result of having a baby and remembers something a fellow servant in the Great House, Beth, said at lunch one day while the women spoke of the ravages of pregnancy.

"Yes. I sag here and there. Yes, I bear the marks of all that growth on a body that used to be so smooth and tight . . . but I have children. The Maker gives us the ability to grow children inside our bodies! Children who will live beyond us—who will be testimonies to our lives. My husband doesn't mind the marks—he says they are evidence of the good fruit that comes from our vows."

She can't help thinking, *Even if I wanted to take vows with someone, here I am, all marked up in advance. . . . Stop it! There is no point in this. It doesn't help. It's not as if you plan to take vows with anyone anyway.* Finally, she shrugs and says, "I know. But, it's comfortable, and I love the color. I will just be happy to go to the feast, I don't really care how it looks on me. Speaking of dresses, did Joony's girl get the dresses you made for her?"

"Yes, and Joony traded me some wonderful creatures for it," Jariel says, hopping up from her seat to go back to her room and return with a small cloth bag. In it are more than a dozen little animals, skillfully woven from strips of palm tree fronds. There are birds, fish, crabs, starfish, and lizards of different sizes.

"Do you remember," Jariel asks, "how, in Aegea, people would make a little wooden hoop, then use string to hang colorful objects from it and put it above babies' beds?

Shaye nods.

"These would be so cute hanging by Elle's cradle, in the window where the wind would blow them around, don't you think?"

"What a great idea."

"So I had Joony make these and traded her for the simple dresses for Bella. And I was thinking if people saw the idea and liked it, maybe I could show Joony how to do it and she could trade them with other people for other things she needs."

"*Ahh!*" Says Willow as she enters the room. "Now you're thinking like one of His own people. Good for you."

#

Hours later, Shaye's room is dark and quiet. Just as on other days, after cooking lunch for workers at the shipyard with a baby on her back, she's exhausted, but despite her fatigue, she is determined to go to the feast. It seems like a lifetime ago that she went to a "gathered meeting" on a rooftop with her great aunt. That last time, everyone blew out their lamps and listened to the story of the stars while they stared up at the sky.

She sits on her bed for a moment. *Oh, how I miss Aunt Pearl . . . and Mosha . . .*

"Hurry, Shaye," Jariel whispers from the doorway.

After one last look at her sleeping angel, she rises.

"*Come on,*" is the hushed urge.

"Wait," she whispers back. "I need a shawl."

Jariel leans in to grab her hand and pull her into the living area. "Leave it, I need to show you something." Two of the chairs from the table are stationed near Willow's chair, where the old woman sits, waiting for them.

"Sit down."

"I thought you were in a hurry to get back to the feast."

"Sit."

She sits while her friend rushes off to retrieve something from the other bedroom.

There's a look on Willow's face that Shaye hasn't seen before. *What is it?* Perhaps that of a child waiting for a surprise.

Jariel soon returns, hugging some folded cloth. She also has this look of . . . glee? She seats herself before she holds the bundle up by two corners. The folds in the cloth fall open to reveal the most beautiful shawl Shaye has ever seen. The center of the intricately woven garment is her favorite shade of blue, fading in both directions to purple, then to red, finished on both ends with beautiful beadwork and shells, ending with tassels.

She slowly reaches out to touch it. "Oh my. I get to wear this?"

"Of course you can. It's *yours.*"

She stands and Jariel puts it around her shoulders. She caresses the garment for a few moments before saying, "It's so beautiful . . . and so soft!" As she moves, the shells among the beads make a delightful *tinkle-ty-clink* sound. She waves her arms in and out to listen to it. "How did you *think* of this? How did you *do* it?"

"I didn't do the shells and beads, Joony did."

"What? *Joony* did this?"

Willow nods. "Her mother used to do some of the finest beadwork many years ago. Joony learned from her . . . she just didn't have much in the way of materials or the opportunity until now." She winks before she says, "There's a lesson in it: Everyone has surprises hidden inside them."

A few women coming home from the feast have gathered at the window and feel free to comment as if they were invited guests in the living room.

"Look what Jariel made on the looms! And Joony did the shells with beads!"

"It's for Shaye!"

"Have you ever seen such a thing?"

"What do you think? Is it not the most beautiful thing?"

Never in all of her life has she been given such an elegant gift. "Just so. I have never seen anything so wonderful before. Not even in Aegea."

"It was my joy to make it for you."

Willow gently takes one of the tassels in her hand and lets the soft threads slip out of her grasp before saying, "She wanted to make it from the start, but she had to work for a while to pay Caleb for all the dyes and threads to make this— and then get the beads for Joony." She looks at Jariel and adds, "Caleb should have *paid* you to make it. I should think his business will gush with orders for shawls—beginning tomorrow." She takes hold of one of the tassels again. "But I would dare to guess that none will be quite like this one!"

The women in the window agree. *Who wouldn't want something like this?*

"Hurry now," Willow says. "You'll miss out on the best food if you tarry any longer. Don't worry about our girl, I'll be right here for her."

Before they go another step, Shaye takes Jariel's hands and simply says, "Thank you."

CHAPTER 23
The Feast

The surf will be a little higher tonight due to the full moon, but even the tallest waves are only knee high and they break many yards from the shoreline. The time of singing was longer this evening than in feasts of recent memory. Perhaps it's a reflection of a growing sense of gratitude among the people of homeplace. After the singing and thankful prayers, a meal—prepared in part by every household—is served.

Once the families have eaten their fill, it's time for music while everyone moves around tables to linger for a while in small groups, then move onto other conversations. The sound of flutes, timbrels, small drums, and stringed instruments ebbs and flows through the gathering much like the surf moving over the sand, then receding.

At the near end of the crowd, a waist-high enclosure made of bamboo and palm fronds is staked into the beach. Inside, toddlers and infants are tended without the worry of them wandering into the nearby water. The women in the enclosure can let them nurse or run and play in sand that's still radiating warmth from a day of full sun. As Shaye and Jariel walk by, several of the women want a closer look at the shawl. One of them is their neighbor Malachi's sister, Rose, a woman with a generous figure and a contagious laugh. She's in the pen with her brother's youngest child, Opal, and two of her own.

As soon as little Opal sees Shaye, she runs to the fence and puts her arms up, hoping to be hoisted out of the enclosure. She cannot pronounce the name of her favorite neighbor correctly, but that doesn't stop her from trying. "*Say! Say!* I go with you!"

"*Ohhh,*" she answers in a sad voice. "Not tonight, Opal. Miss Jariel and I are going to eat dinner and then I must go home to my own little jewel. I will see you tomorrow, though, right?"

Rose bends down and holds the little girl's chin in her hand. "You know we need your big girl help here, don't you?" She motions to the far corner of the enclosure with her chin.

"Look over there, your cousin needs your help digging a hole in the sand."

The little girl sprints away before Shaye says, "Opal. That was Willow's daughter's name."

"Yes," Rose sighs. "Willow's Opal and Anna were best friends from the time they were old enough to walk. Anna and Malachi named their first daughter after Mal's mother. When this one was born, Anna insisted on naming her Opal."

"Oh."

One of the other women in the pen comes closer. "It won't be long now before Shaye and Elle join us here with the little ones, eh?"

Jariel's grasp of Genon and her esteem among the people here are growing every day. "True," she chimes in. "*If* Willow is ever willing to part with Elle's company."

They all nod and smile. It's no secret that Willow is completely taken with Elle.

A mother with a sleeping babe in her arms joins the conversation at the fence. "It is a wonder to see how having the two of you and a new baby in her house has brought Willow back from the shadow. No one would have believed such a thing was possible a year ago."

Rose nods. "It's true. Malachi says it's like the Maker saw her locked in the darkness of her sorrow and entered right into her house like a sunrise. You have brought such joy to her and many of us are grateful to see her doing so well." She looks directly at Shaye. "And I think some of that sunshine has gone right out through your window into my brother's house next door. . . . Oh, I see you're embarrassed—don't be. The other day, I heard him humming for the first time in more than two years. I can't tell you how glad it made my heart to hear it."

"Oh my, and he has such a great voice," the woman nearest to Rose adds. "I remember the days when he and Anna would sing . . . it could give you chills to hear their voices together."

An outburst of laughter from the larger gathering down the beach momentarily pulls everyone's focus in that direction.

Jariel looks at her friend, "Is it time to move on? Before all the food is gone and the conversation is done?"

They say their goodbyes before walking down the beach to join the gathering.

As they pad through the damp sand, Jariel leans over and asks, "Is there *anything* here that goes unnoticed? Is there any such thing as a secret?"

"Ha! There's a reason they call it 'shared life'."

They approach the feast, with a large table in the center where the food is served. Many torches brightly flicker atop poles stuck into the sand around the table and throughout the area which is a jumble of tables and chairs. Shaye walks to one end of the buffet and grabs a section of a wide banana leaf for a plate before moving slowly down one side, selecting the things she wants (and noting with satisfaction that all of the food that she prepared is gone). Meanwhile, a steady stream of women approach her or lean across the table to admire the shawl, wanting to touch the soft texture, to examine the fine beadwork, to handle the tassels, and to inquire where she got it. Each time, she smiles and pokes her chin in the direction of her housemate, who isn't far away.

"Jariel made it, in Caleb's shop. And Joony did this part with the shells and beads."

When she gets to the far end of the banquet table, she looks up and sees two of the women she still remembers from the day she first entered the village: It's Naomi and her cousin, Beryl. Just as they did then, they stand like stone sentinels glaring at her, arms folded, nostrils flared as if they were smelling a bad smell. Iris told her they considered themselves to be the most eligible women in the village . . . until the two newcomers arrived. In the past, Naomi had made it known that she wanted Benjamin to court her but then held him off while she savored the pleasure of a multitude of suitors circling around her for just a while longer. But when he returned from the trip to the Great Forest, his interest in her had cooled. Her cousin Beryl, on the other hand, had set her sights set on Samuel, so the girl's displeasure with Jariel was growing by the day.

An amusing thought occurs to her. *Huh. They don't frighten me the way they used to. I wonder if they realize how unattractive they look when they scowl like that. Mosha would warn them that their features could permanently stick in that pose.* She takes in a full view of Naomi. *You can have Benjamin, girl. I would almost feel sorry for you if you took vows with him.* She smiles and dips her head slightly, as if to say, *Good evening, ladies*, then turns around to find a place to sit while the grim statues glare at her retreat.

"Over here, Shaye!" Jariel calls out.

Before she takes three steps her entire dinner is knocked off the leaf by a man pressing through the crowd. He stares down at the plop of food at his feet.

"*Eh eh!* That was my fault. I'm sorry . . ." he says before looking up at her. "Oh. Good evening Shaye." He pulls the leaf from her hand and in one swift move, scoops the sand encrusted food under the table. "May I get you another?"

"Good evening Malachi. No, it's fine," she reassures him. "I can get it."

She allows herself to notice that he's looking at her as if he's both scared and delighted all at once. Unlike all the other attention she's gotten, this isn't annoying.

"No," he tells her. "I insist." Glancing down, he realizes he still has some of her dinner on his shirt and takes a swipe of it with his finger, then tastes it. "*Mmm.* Coconut sauce." He looks down the table. "You must have had some of Elizabeth's coconut tart."

She grins and nods.

"What else did you have?"

"A couple of those spicy little fried fish that Clay makes."

"I heard that you hated fish."

"When I was pregnant, I admit the smell was awful to me. But it doesn't bother me now. And since I started working with Clay making food, I like some of it the way he makes it."

He eyes the small pile under the table. "I see some rice as well. What else? Did I notice a crab claw in with all the other food?"

"Yes. Just one. That's all."

"Are you sitting with Jariel? I can bring it to you."

She nods and smiles.

When she arrives at the round table where her housemate is sitting with several others, she needs to pull an empty stool up to get its legs out of the sand, before repositioning it and taking her place. Samuel and Iris are seated across from her on either side of Jariel.

"Good evening!" she tells them.

"Good evening," everyone echoes back before Samuel resumes a conversation with a man at the next table.

"I love the shawl Jariel made for you!" another woman at the table says to her. "The beads are marvelous! Who would have thought to put them like this on a shawl?"

"You honor me, Esther" she responds and then laughs. "Or, should I say, you honor Jariel and Joony!"

Esther looks at the artisan, "It is a great work, my friend," she says, then leans back toward Shaye, "but also you look radiant in it. The colors suit you."

Iris studies her for a moment. "You *do* look fine in that shawl tonight. And you look different somehow. Content. I'm glad to see it." She glances down at the spot on table where a plate of food should be. "Aren't you going to eat? Where's your food?"

"Someone offered to bring it to me."

Jariel turns and sees Malachi approaching with two banana leafs of food, and notes he seems to be headed straight for Shaye. She nudges her friend's foot under the table. "*Eh, eh!*"

Shaye looks up and sees him as well. "Stop it."

She grins. "Who, me?"

"Stop."

As the two playfully banter, Iris watches them with a questioning look, then turns to see Malachi. "Oh. Now I see it."

Shaye looks across the table at her. "You, as well. Stop."

"You know," the older woman suddenly says, "I've eaten too much and I think I should walk for a while. *Oh, good evening, Malachi!* You can have my seat, I was just leaving."

Jariel nudges her housemate's foot again and gets a wide-eyed stare in return.

"Good evening, Iris," Mal says. "Don't leave on my account."

"Oh no," she insists as she spins around on the stool and puts on her sandals. "I was already getting up—I need to walk off some of this food."

When she departs, Mal stands by the vacated stool and reaches across the table to set one leaf in front of Shaye. "May I join you?"

She nods. "Of course you may."

"Is that the same food you had before?" he inquires.

She surveys the plate. "Yes, and it was nice of you to bring it to me."

"Yes. How *nice* of you to think of Shaye," Jariel says.

He looks down and sees she doesn't have a plate. "I could get one for you as well," he says, starting to rise from his seat again.

"No, that's fine. I may get more later, but I've already had some."

Shaye feels a need to clarify. "He brought this because I dropped my food—"

"Actually," Mal says, "I was trying to squeeze through all the people near the food table and I knocked it out of her hand." He points to his shirt. "I'm a specialist in spilled food— I have children."

He's rewarded when both women laugh.

Someone starts singing at another table and the song gains momentum as more and more people join in. Most of the musical instruments fall silent as a chorus of voices intertwine in a melody that's both sad and sweet. Neither of the newcomers knows the words so they simply listen to it. When the men at her table start singing, Shaye realizes that her neighbor, indeed, has a superb singing voice. As the song ends the gathered people rest in its afterglow for a few moments before they resume conversations.

Jariel's eyes are closed when she says, "I hope I never get over the feeling I get when I hear everyone singing. I never heard anything like this before I came here. It will forever be the sound of homeplace to me."

"It's the sound of His own people," Samuel tells her. "He gifted us with music and with song but we take that for granted sometimes. All of us should let it speak to our hearts the way it speaks to yours."

Shaye nudges Jariel's foot.

Before long, multiple greetings are heard as Nathan and Peony arrive at the gathering. Shaye notes that Nathan has woven a crown of flowers for his wife—something he does often—and the two of them are radiant with delight.

"What a glad night this is," the old man says to Shaye and Jariel. "How happy we are to be in it with everyone here." He points across the water. "And look what a beautiful moon we have. I don't think I could have hoped for a better night than this to celebrate."

Many people voice agreement with what he says.

It's then that a movement behind the couple catches Samuel's eye. He watches as a man turns and walks out of the gathering.

Excusing himself from the table, Sam attempts to follow the man, but isn't able to draw closer because of the crowd. Once he's outside the gathering, he realizes he needs to speed up if he hopes to catch up. Once he's out of the range of torchlight he has to depend on the moon to light his way along a beach that looks like a silver road threading the gap between shadowy trees and dark blue water.

"Ben!" he calls out as he tries to close the distance. "I've been looking for you."

The man knows this voice so he slows down, then looks back over his shoulder. "Hey, Mule."

"Can we talk?" Sam points to a fallen palm tree nearby and the two men walk up to where sand gives way to plant life. The tide is coming in, but the tree trunk is still on dry ground. Behind it, the leaves on sea grape trees and palms continuously flutter in the cool night breeze. Ben arrives at the dead tree trunk first and roosts on it. With the sounds of music and laughter still pulsing in the distance, he watches his friend and fellow traveler take a seat.

He takes a drink from a bamboo cup and asks, "What is it you want to talk about?"

"I haven't seen you in weeks."

He shrugs. "I've been busy."

"You've never been too busy to come to gatherings before."

He pulls in his lips as if he's trying *not* to say something, then finally spreads his hands wide. "Well, I'm here now. Say whatever it is you want to say."

"Ever since we came back from the Great Forest, you've become increasingly distant. . . . Why are you so angry? Can't we talk about it? Why are you avoiding everyone? "

"*Everyone?*" he scoffs. "What makes you think that you and the rabble that attends meetings with you are *everyone*?"

"So it's true? You're gathering a group for yourself?"

"Let's just say there are some of us who hold the purity of our blood and our ways in higher regard than you."

Sam scratches his beard as he tries to think. "Can you explain that for me?"

"You used to know what I mean."

"Did I?"

Ben looks away. "Of a truth, maybe you didn't." He tries to take another sip and realizes his cup is empty. Frowning as he stares into it, he says, "Perhaps you were just waiting for outcasts to show up and teach us *their* ways."

"Are you saying that only people with pure Genon blood can know the Maker?" When there's no answer, he asks, "You know that's not true. If it were, who among us would have any hope? Which one of us knows with certainty that he has an unbroken family line? And, who among us can say they are perfect?"

A large wave breaks onto the shore and fans across the sand. It splashes over one of Ben's sandals and he quickly rises from his seat. "Your fondness for that strange woman," he says with growing irritation in his voice, "has made you blind. You can tell yourself the Maker planned all this—and with the new females to attend gatherings, you certainly have no shortage of men willing to come and sing with you. But where were all of them before the women got here? I tell you no good will come of it."

Sam looks pleadingly at his old friend. "You're telling yourself that you know what is best for our people, but neither of us knows the whole of it. Can't we reason together like we used to?"

"I have no wish to reason with someone who has lost his sanity."

"My brother . . . what grievance is leading you to say these things? Would you have us go back to the hopelessness that so many have felt in the past two years? Would you have us all just plod through our days, mourning and childless until we fell into our graves? You seem only to want us to share your bitterness and your hate—is there no longer room for anything else in you? How does this honor our people or our faith?" He stands to plead his case. He can't see his friend's eyes, but he focuses where they would be. "Our faith is one that is carried along in our shared *life*. We have been reminded of hope. If you would just allow yourself to—"

"I will not join you in this . . . this abomination. Soon there will be nothing left of our faith!"

Another wave shoots across the sand, but this time they both must take several steps away from each other to avoid it as it touches the fallen tree.

"You're wrong, brother."

Ben throws down his cup and the receding wave catches it, pulling it down toward the ocean, but he makes no attempt to retrieve it. He turns and walks away, while Sam watches the successive waves wash away the footprints between them.

Shaye couldn't stay too long at the feast. Not only was she tired, but her breasts got so swollen with milk that she had to get home and feed Elle. It's perfect timing too, since the baby has just awakened when she arrives.

Willow walks with the little one to keep her quiet while her mother quickly washes up and changes her clothing.

"There's my girl," Shaye says, opening her arms to receive her daughter. Once she's there, Elle's only interest is to get to the milk. She starts to nurse the child before she says, "Thank you for watching her. You are good to me."

"Did you enjoy the feast?"

"I did. It was nice to sit with the others and have conversations," she says with a wistful smile. "And you were right. So many women loved the shawl. And I saw Nathan and Peony. And we sat with Iris. . . ." To avoid any comments, she omits the details about Malachi. "And those sour-faced girls, Naomi and Beryl were there giving Jariel and me the stinky look."

"*Hmph.*"

"And there was singing. Jariel is still there enjoying it—although I don't know where Samuel got off to. Usually, he's not far from her."

"I wouldn't be surprised if that ended in a good match."

Shaye stops her reverie and sighs. "I would be happy for her . . . but a little sad for us. We just started being friends . . . and now she's so dear to me. I know it's selfish, but I've come to appreciate our situation here."

"Just so. But I do want the best for all three of my girls." She slowly rises from her chair. "Before I see all of that accomplished, though . . . we need a good rest." She softly squeezes Elle's foot. "Good night."

Soon, the lights are out, leaving mother and daughter to go and snuggle up on a comfy bed. Shaye goes over the evening in her mind while her little one drinks her fill and falls into a deep slumber.

It isn't long before she hears Malachi coming home next door and getting all of his children settled for the night. The last thing she remembers before sleep is hearing him, humming a sweet lullaby for his little Opal, and thinking, *Oh Maker of all things, you are the one who heals our hearts. I am grateful.*

CHAPTER 24
Unexpected Vows

"The one who makes a hasty promise usually has a long time to regret it."—*A proverb of His people.*

The midday meal is over and only a couple of men sit at a table in the back of the eating area. In the past few days, the little restaurant has served record numbers of customers. Not only are three large boats in the harbor, but Ren the boat builder has just finished a new ship and tomorrow, they will launch it. The dock and the area near the new vessel are filled with workers who are hauling, loading, and unloading. Nathan was right—the village is buzzing with hope.

Shaye wipes off the full-length counter that separates the kitchen from the rest of the open-air dining space. She'll be able to go home in a few minutes, feed Elle and maybe sneak in a nap of her own while the girl sleeps.

Since Willow repairs nets, she's had a lot of work, but she can do most of it in her home, so she watches Elle in the middle of the day and then Shaye helps her with the nets in the late afternoon. If there is a deadline that needs to be met, Jariel and Shaye light all the lamps and help with the nets after supper, talking and laughing into the late evening. If the day's work is done, they may sit out on the porch and talk to neighbors, while children with boundless energy run up and down the street in the breezy night air. The women of Willow's house are in a season with a pleasant rhythm.

Today it's unusually warm, so the walk home takes a little longer. When she steps through the door, she's surprised to see Willow in the kitchen with Elle on her hip, working at something.

"I'm home!" she announces.

"Oh good. Come and get Elle while I finish this.

The little one sees her mommy and she holds out her arms while saying "*Ahhhhhhhhhhhh!*"

Shaye moves into the kitchen and lifts her daughter into her arms before asking, "What are you doing?"

"Wrapping up rice, beans, and some of our dried peppers. It's an unexpected turn of events, isn't it?"

"What is?"

"Oh. Since you work at the harbor, I thought you'd have *heard* by now."

"Heard what?"

"Ren the boat builder's daughter, Beryl. Ha! One of the girls who gives you and Jariel the bad faces all the time. She took vows this morning. I'm packing up the customary contributions for the bride and groom's household." She stops to wipe a sleeve across her sweating brow. "Do our people in Aegea do that? Give foods and other items to stock up the newlywed couple's first home?"

"We rarely had food or goods to share. Who did Beryl take vows with?"

"*That's* the unexpected part: Benjamin."

Shaye steps back. "No!"

"Yes!"

"But this is so sudden. And I thought Beryl was the one who wanted to take vows with Samuel and it was *Naomi* who wanted Benjamin. Those two didn't even court, did they?"

"Yes, yes, and, no, they didn't."

"Why would she marry the man her cousin wanted? Surely she can't love him! And why would he pick her?"

"All good questions." She ties a knot on the bundle of rice then turns to look at Shaye. "If two people were angry with Samuel, might there be a way to cooperate in it?"

"Take vows with someone . . . to get some sort of revenge? What a stupid idea."

"Revenge is never smart in the long run, Shaye . . . but there is another factor to consider. Beryl's father has done *very* well for himself in building boats, and Naomi's father is a shoe maker who barely makes ends meet—so long-term security may also have played some part in this. Plus, Benjamin does have the respect of some in the community. He's worked hard to put himself in contention to become an elder someday. He's studied under Jared since the flood, and Ren's family mostly sits under Jared—who presided over the taking of the vows. He has a large garden behind his house and I hear it was there."

Shaye squints as she thinks about it, then shrugs. "Well, many in Aegea take vows to secure a better future . . . but to step over her own cousin to take vows with *Ben*," she shudders.

"I know, I know. The two of them have sour dispositions, so maybe it's a better match than we'd think."

The baby has had enough of the inattention. She tries to grab a loose lock of her mother's hair and immediately has her full focus. "No no *no*. Mommy's hair, Miss Grabby Hands. Here." She puts the grasping hand on her daughter's head. "Pull your own hair and tell me if you like it."

As if she understood her mother's wishes and wanted to comply, Elle pulls some of her own hair, then starts to wail.

"Ohhhh! I'm sorry . . . but you see how it hurts?" She pats the girl's back while bouncing her up and down a bit and the crying subsides.

Willow continues with the conversation. "Well, love or not, brokenhearted cousin or not—they took vows." She moves the bundle with the rice before she spreads out another piece of cloth inside a bowl, then scoops out three measures of beans into it and ties it up. "And I heard that Ren is giving one of his boats to Ben and Beryl as a wedding gift. Benjamin doesn't know the first thing about sailing on the ocean but I suppose he's going to learn now."

"Oh my."

CHAPTER 25
The Journey Begins

"How far can love travel? It is as limitless as the Maker who first gave it flight." *An ancient proverb of His people.*

Father and son sit together, going over the details. Dawn is nearly two hours away, and it will be time to leave soon. All their unspoken words cannot fit into the few minutes they have left and neither of them knows how to have a conversation that could be their last, so they've talked about the mission. Now their time is nearly up.

"I wish I could go in your place," Jubal McClaren says.

"I know."

"You have my gun and ammo in your bag?"

Ty touches the satchel. He's practiced shooting the weapon, and he understands it can end a life in a blink. "Yes—and I will only use it to defend life."

Jubal starts to say something, but there's a knock on the door. His aide, Seph, opens it and leans in.

"The signal's been sighted."

Jubal says "Acknowledged," and Seph exits. Father and son both rise before he says, "It's time for you to go. Basil and Shocky will meet you at the tram with the gear." He places a hand on his son's shoulder. "We'll be waiting every evening an hour after sunset for messages."

Ty meets his gaze, and says, "I'll do my utmost, sir." He's surprised when he's drawn in for a hug. It's only the second time he's been held in his father's arms since he was a child, and he expects the embrace to last for only a second or two, but his father's head remains on his shoulder and he hears something even more unexpected.

"Whatever happens, son, I want you to know . . . how much you mean to me. Please come back to us." The general lets go and clears his throat before saying, "Find Jariel. Bring her back."

###

A group of twenty soldiers on horseback exits the military stables, taking the longer route around Midtown on their way west. As soon as they pass out of sight of Midtown, they will break into a gallop. This will, no doubt, attract the interest of anyone watching the roads.

Shortly after the soldiers leave the stables, a wagon loaded with refuse departs from Oldtown on its normal journey through the trash gate. The wagon slowly rumbles along the perimeter road—an unpaved access way used by workers and laborers that runs along the wall bordering the plateau. The aging wheels on the wagon wobble as it slowly passes fields and orchards. Hidden in a pile of rags in the back of the wagon, Ty moves his head back and forth until a small gap opens up and he can see the starry night above him.

A fingernail moon and myriad stars shine in a clear sky. Gazing up at them the thoughts he's tried to keep at bay for the past few months spring into the forefront. *I am a father!* It still takes his breath away every time he thinks of it. *My child is alive somewhere beyond the forest. And Shaye has no reason to believe that she'll ever see me again. Could she already have taken vows with someone?*

When the wagon passes the tram station, the driver knocks on the wooden seat. The station is situated halfway along the long wall that extends along the cliff at the edge of the plateau.

The previous general had grand visions for Aegea. One of them was a road to another plateau with more land for farms and orchards, and room for a new settlement for future generations. The road project was poorly executed and had continual obstacles—ending in a large avalanche of boulders that not only wiped out months of hard labor, it took the life of Shaye's father and seventeen other men. General Fairmont's last attempt at a grand project prior to his death was this tram. He wanted it to be used for passengers and cargo, a means of bypassing the long trail between the plateau and the forest. The rapid transit would save ninety minutes walking down, and up to three hours on the return up the trails. He changed his mind when challenges to the security of the tram and its cost arose, settling for a less than optimum build. The result was a ride that was too steep (and possibly too hazardous) for humans. In the end, the aging general decided the tram shouldn't be used at all. Had he lived on, the project would have fallen into disrepair, never having fulfilled its purpose. Yet, on the day he died, the tram was used—to transport kidnapped women in a box down into the jungle. Today, it will be employed, possibly for the last time.

Ty wriggles out of the rags, rolls out of the back of the wagon, then quickly sprints to the elevator that will take him up to the station, then works the pulley system that lifts the elevator to the top of the wall. Once there, he enters the loading dock for the tram where Sage Dooley, Aegea's foremost inventor, waits with Basil and Sgt. Shocky. They can barely see each other in the pre-dawn light, but they will not risk using any sort of torch or lamp that might be visible for miles in the darkness.

Dooley wants to get him up to speed. "We've already gone over the checklist of equipment. The other team is already waiting in the forest with the provisions, medical supplies, and other necessary equipment. Now, gentlemen . . . are you ready for the ride of your life?"

Ty swallows hard. Basil has a grim expression on his face. It's Shocky who answers with a stone-faced, "Yes."

None of them wants to go on the tram, but they are reconciled with the fact that they must. Walking the trails down the mountain, the trio would encounter officials, workers, and hunter/gatherers along the way—all of whom would know they weren't supposed to be in the forest. The tram was the most expedient way to get all three of them off the plateau unnoticed.

Ty remembers standing in this very spot with his father on one of the days when the tram was tested. *What a thrill it was to watch the suspended car shoot down the cable toward the jungle. I never considered the prospect that Shaye and Jariel would be sent down on it. I never thought I'd be following them.* He steps near the edge of the platform and his eyes follow the cable. He can't see more than 30 feet of the line dropping into blackness below. *It's probably good you can't see any further. . . .* He looks at his own hands and realizes he's got a white-knuckled grip on the railing.

Quiet until now, Basil puts a hand on Ty's shoulder. "The women went first, and we know they survived," he says. "We can do it."

When they hear Mr. Dooley clear his throat, they both turn to receive any final instructions.

He surveys the three grim faces. "Just remember to breathe," he finally says in an upbeat tone. His comment doesn't appear to have made things any better, so he rubs his hands together and adds, "Right. Let's get to it then!" He escorts them into the car and shows them where to lie down on the floor, then starts pulling straps over their legs and torsos."

"Not sure what's more likely to kill us," Ty states matter-of-factly, "riding this thing or being restrained in it and not able to escape if it crashes."

Sage ignores the comment and yanks the chest strap tighter after cinching it to a metal loop in the floor. "It's best if you stay as flat as you can, here in the middle of the car. These straps will hold you securely, but you'll *definitely* feel like you're falling. Try to remember it's a *controlled* fall." His words remind him of something and he trots out of the car for a moment, returning with three small bags stuffed with padding. He places one under each man's head saying, "You'll want to thank me for this later," then resumes his final instructions. "As you approach each cable support, you'll feel the vehicle lean forward and slow down," he says tilting his hand as if it's the car. "That's the braking system. *After* each cable support, you'll pick up speed again, then slow down at the next support and so on. The good news is it'll be over in about five minutes. It'll not only save you the walk down the trail, you'll bypass the charcoal pits and be thirty minutes further west in the forest. Just don't try to get out until the car has come to a full stop." He rechecks all the straps before telling them, "Believe it or not, I wish I could go with you."

"Ah," Ty replies, "but then you'd have had to learn to swim."

The Exile, Canaan, insisted that if they wanted to ensure their own survival, they'd all have to learn to swim. None of the Aegean men going on the mission knew how, and for Ty it was a harrowing experience in the beginning.

Sage gives him a wry smile, then continues with his instructions. "No matter what, try to keep those radios dry. Try calling when you've reached the bottom. After that, we'll be listening for your messages." He exits the car and takes his position near the control panel before he pulls a lever and waves. "Good luck to all of you."

The wheels above the car begin rolling along the cable and it soon starts to pick up speed.

After experiencing the longest five minutes of his life, Ty remains on the floor of the tram car, shaken, and thankful that it finally stopped moving. Several times after slowing, when the car dropped and picked up speed, he was certain the cable must have snapped and the car was in a freefall. Each time, his rigid body went weightless for several seconds. As the cable sprang back into play, his head slammed against Sage's improvised pillow. At least twice during the ride, he heard terrified shouts joining his own.

He looks up at the growing light on the clouds and tries to normalize his breathing. As panic leaves his body, his vision expands and his other senses begin to exert themselves on his conscious thought again. It's then that he realizes he can smell smoke from the charcoal pits a few miles upwind of their location. He remains still for a few more seconds, thinking, *Man! I chose to get on this thing. Shaye and Jariel were in a box and thrown onto it.*

No one has moved yet. Finally, Basil's voice cracks as he says, "Hey kid. You alive? That. Was. Terrible."

Ty takes another long breath before he tries to laugh but only manages to huff out some air before he says, "I'll make a soldier out of you yet."

They unbuckle themselves and slowly sit up. Even the stoic Sgt. Shocky looks pale.

A few months ago, when Ty asked where the unflappable sergeant got the permanent nickname "Sgt. Shocky," Basil told him, *"There are two stories: One says it was a kind of joke— like when you call a big fellow 'Tiny'. The man's face never seems to change, so, of course, they called him 'Shocky.' The other story is that he was so good in any sort of competition, so good in the games, and so good at being a soldier that he continually shocked the military and everyone else. Maybe it's both things."*

Once they're able to stand, Basil unties one of the large duffle bags and reaches in to extract a case. He sets it down and flips up the latches. The seal peeling open makes a sticking noise before he flips the lid back and lifts the radio out of the case. Precisely the way he was taught, he flips up the antenna, then quickly turns a crank several times. Once he slides the crank back in its slot, he hands the device over to Ty.

Although all three of them have practiced using the apparatus, it still seems like a magical device to them whenever it makes a sound. Basil and Shocky would rather that Ty use it. If it somehow gets damaged or broken, they figure that the general's son is less likely to face severe consequences.

Ty holds the radio close to his head but turns it so the earpiece is facing his companions as well. Somehow, it seems rude to be standing with people, yet having a conversation with someone they cannot hear. He presses the talk button. "Down safe. Repeat, down safe."

"Over," Shocky reminds him. "Say 'over.'"

"Over." Ty says into the radio.

They all hear Sage's voice crackle in the earpiece: "Good luck. Over." He stares at the device as he hands it back to Basil saying, "Sage told me people used to talk to each other with radios all the time." He points up, "even when they were in the sky—up among the stars, but it's hard for me to believe."

The other two nod.

Once the radio is safely stored again, they set about unloading all the gear from the cable car. Unless they're on the radio, from this moment on, Genon will be the official language of the expedition.

All of their gear is off the tram and on the ground when they see three Genon men approaching. One of them is Canaan, one is Basil's cousin Ethan, and the last is Asher.

All of the men have studied under Canaan for many weeks, learning how to survive beyond the bounds of the "known" forest and he's expanded their vocabularies to speak the more fluid Genon language of the Exiles. In addition, Basil, Ty, and Shocky had to learn basic cautions for life in the forest—what not to drink, eat, or touch, places not to walk or sleep.

Three decades ago, many in the leadership of Aegea decided the forest was endless and that continued exploration was a waste of resources. Time and effort, they said, were better spent on works directly tied with the ongoing survival of the people on the plateau. Canaan's knowledge of what lies in the regions beyond what is known to them may make the difference between life and death in the weeks to come.

A week ago, Ethan and Asher went through the front gate of Aegea with Canaan inside a loaded cart, pulled by two mules down into the forest. Meanwhile, Ty, Basil, and Shocky spent dedicated time learning how to use special equipment that Sage Dooley developed: Radios, solar sheets, flashlights, composite crossbows, a sonic gun, and tranquilizing darts that could be shot from a gun or blown through a tube. Although the Firstlanders of Aegea had many similar items, no one has seen or used such things in three generations.

Still a little shaken from the ride, Basil keeps one hand on the stair railing while he clasps hands with his counterparts.

"How did it go with placing the supplies?"

"We saw some other gatherers the first day, so we waited to move out," his cousin tells them, "but then we were able to stash the supplies several days north of here. After that, Asher left the mules at the depot over by the charcoal pits. From the point of the final stash, Canaan will lead us into the shroud."

Ty's eyes widen. "The shroud?"

"Yes. As you know, gatherers tried to explore there, but stopped going into it about twenty years ago. It's an area known for thick mists and dense shadow where large spiders and other deadly creatures lurk. There is also a swamp in there where insects that carry the fever thrive."

"Then why chance it?"

Canaan speaks up. "If anyone was attempting to follow us, they would likely turn back rather than go in there. Also, it will shorten our journey to the river. We'll only cut through a corner of it for a long day, then come out and camp in a safe place. That's what many of the Exiles used to do."

"I know of no one who would follow us into the shroud," Asher says, then looks at Ty and adds, "I've heard that your own father was nearly taken by a massive snake there many years ago, That's one of the reasons it was taken out of our range."

Ty's attention drifts a moment while he considers it. . . . Capt. Frank Penway, who travelled with Jubal whenever he went into the forest, rescued him that day. It was Penway who fell in love with a beautiful Genon gatherer and created a scandal by marrying her, resulting in his dismissal from the military. The Penways had only one child, a daughter they named Shaye, before Frank died doing manual labor on the road project. When Ty asked his father if the story about the snake was true, the senior McClaren looked grim and only replied, "Yes. He saved me."

Basil's cousin is still talking and Ty tries to concentrate on what's being said.

". . . and if all of us are able to make good time, within a week we'll be beyond where any Aegean gatherers have ever gone and returned safely."

"But heading mostly north," Ty adds.

The Exile nods. "North, until we reach the river. We'll find some of the old camps from my people." he tells them. "But we'll be a good way down the river before we find any *fresh* signs of Exiles. Since they had such a close encounter with soldiers last time, they won't have ventured this far up river for fear of discovery. Plus, they just had a monsoon season there. Travel is dangerous and difficult in the monsoon season.

"*Monsoon season?*" Ty asks.

"Rain. Every day. More rain than any Aegean ever sees. It goes on for weeks—and it happens twice a year. Even without the monsoons, traveling back up the river, against the flow of the water, is hard work. When the monsoons flood the river it's nearly impossible to travel back this way." He thinks for a moment before he adds, "It would *almost* be like you trying to climb the mountain by going up the waterfall by the mill."

Ty lets out a whistle before Canaan puts a hand on his shoulder and says, "You're in the land of cloud and leaf now. It's a different world than you know."

When he walks away, Basil leans over to Ty and says, "This is the most alive we've seen him yet."

"Yes. He's a man nearly home."

CHAPTER 26
The Box

It's past midday when they come across the wooden crate that was used to transport Jariel and Shaye into the forest. A skull, missing its lower jaw and picked clean by insects, is still lying near the box—just where Asher and Ethan found it so many months ago. The wooden lid, now just rotten planks, is on the ground a little further from the box. When they first come upon it, Ty just stares at it for a long while before he puts his hands on the rim and looks inside. Mold, rot, and termites have eaten away much of the wood at the bottom of the box, and a small fern has taken up residence in one corner. A few metal objects, abandoned by men who died within minutes of opening the box are still there, rusted and covered with rotting leaves.

A voice breaks into his thoughts.

"This is where I first saw them. I was here before the other men of my people came."

Ty turns to see Canaan, who has a look on his face that's as haunted as his own.

"The soldiers lifted the pale girl out of the box." He points to a spot on the ground. "And they set her here."

Everyone stops to listen.

"The men from my people were tracking a *k'mosh* on the day we found the women. I picked up the trail first, then stopped and watched when I saw the soldiers with the box. I was in that tree," he points above and to their left, "as the beast came upon the soldiers. They shot it several times—which stirred its anger greatly. It struck the first man and killed him and the others ran so it chased them." He points through the trees, "They went in that direction, but I saw your sister was helpless, so I stayed behind to defend her if it doubled back, and I shouted to the others which way it traveled." He walks around to the other side of the box and faces Ty. "That's when Shaye crawled out of the box on this side. The sound of the screams from the beast must have awakened her. She was dazed because of the bad smell in the box."

They all know he's talking about the fumes from the chemical-soaked rag they used to sedate Jariel and placed in the box. They listen as Canaan continues his account of the encounter.

"She quickly realized where she was, and she understood I must be an Exile. I spoke to her and told her that the others were coming."

While he's listening, Ty's right hand gravitates to the center of his chest. Through the cloth of his shirt, he can feel the small bulge of the little pouch containing the strands of Shaye's hair and his fingers close around it.

"I told her," Canaan continues, "the Maker was watching and she must speak for the other girl. She wanted to know *'what other girl?'* so I showed her."

Ty has heard all of this before, but now, standing in the place where it unfolded, the sorrow and anger are more tangible than ever. He can't help interjecting. "I always knew she had nothing to do with this." He looks at the Exile. "Sorry. Go on with what you were saying."

"I had to move off after that. The men killed the *k'mosh,* and when they returned they questioned Shaye. She convinced them not to kill or leave Jariel, but to rescue her. That is when they had the idea to leave everything as it was—except to bury the beast so that anyone looking would think the *k'mosh* still lived. They hoped it would make anyone searching afraid to explore very far."

Asher shrugs. "It was a good plan. If we hadn't found the arrow they accidentally left behind, that's exactly what we would have thought."

Ethan nods and points in the same direction that the Exile indicated. "That's where we found the other bodies of several soldiers. And just beyond there, the arrow, high in a tree."

"The man whose arrow you found," Canaan tells them, "his name is Benjamin and he will be among those who give the most opposition to you."

They move on and travel throughout the day, pushing north, where fewer and fewer Aegeans have traveled. The ground beneath their feet slopes ever downward, and as they descend, it's as if they are traveling into a warm and timeless place. Ancient trees, with giant, looping roots and smooth bark tower to heights Ty has never seen, spreading a green canopy more than seventy feet above the ground. Just as there is a food chain among animals, there is a chain among plants—and these trees are the kings of their domain. Late in the afternoon, the men come upon a place that Canaan tells them is an old camp of his people.

They've stopped several times during the day to apply mud from small streams on their faces and other exposed skin in order to fend off the bites of mosquitoes and other insects. At one point Ty looks up to see a bird with brilliant feathers flying between the trees.

"Basil, look, he's just like Topper out in Westland."

His friend nods and they watch the bird fly out of sight before Canaan reminds them, "No Command Dialect here. We are in the land of cloud and leaf and we speak the language of the One who made all things."

Ty nods. "Just so."

At times, the canopy of leaves above is so thick that the world around them is dim. The air doesn't move at all, making the heat oppressive. At one point, they change course to detour around a part of the forest where spiders bigger than a man's hand live in abundance. "They make a rattling noise," the Exile tells them, "that you never want to hear."

It's an hour before they're once again on course, usually traveling single file, as is the custom of experienced gatherers.

When daylight begins to fade, they're still under a thick canopy, but this place doesn't smell as dank as some of the places they walked through earlier in the day. Canaan tells them they will stop here and make camp for the night so Basil and his cousin clear the ground and make a small fire.

"Does the whole forest smell musty like this?" Ty wonders aloud.

Canaan shakes his head. "The ground keeps descending, the soil, trees and plants change. Different animals as well, so the smell changes somewhat, too."

"Are there no singing birds?"

"Not here. Frogs sing at night though."

"They sing?"

"Well, it's just two sounds. Like this," he says, then whistles two short notes, several times. "You will hear it soon."

Ethan and Asher nod in agreement.

Once they're all near the fire, Basil opens one of the packs they've carried all day. "Sage gave me things that some of you haven't seen yet." He pulls out the items. "These," he says, extracting some rope and pulleys, "we can use to pull a man up or lower him down from trees or rocks. It's special rope."

Ethan picks up a length of the rope and stretches it. Good rope. How did he make this?"

Basil shrugs before he continues. "These," he says pulling out four long arrows with paper tubes attached, "can be used to signal each other when other means aren't possible. We can light them and shoot them up into the sky. Sage says they are visible for a mile in the day, many miles at night." Everyone nods while Basil puts the flares aside so he can get more things out of his pack. "These," he says with a bit of wonder, "are something new that he made for us to test on our trip. No one on the plateau has them. They're called fl—fl—fl," he says, with a growing irritation at not being able to say the word, "they're *f-f-f-lashlights*." He extracts six, sealed tubes that have a crank at one end and a glass lens at the other. "Watch this!" He holds the tube in his left hand and there's a soft *whirr* as he gives the crank a few fast turns. To everyone's surprise, when he slides a small switch on the side of the tube, the lens lights up.

Ethan takes one and gives it a crank. He peers at the steady light in the lens, then shines it up into the trees nearby. They're all fascinated by the circle of light that moves wherever he points it. Soon all of them are shining their flashlights around the camp.

Asher shakes his flashlight and stares into the lens. "Is that a spark of fire inside?" He touches the lens on the front of the light. "Does it get hot?"

"No. Sage told me what the light is made from, but I forgot. He says we should try not to drop them, though, and we shouldn't put them in water." After spending several minutes fiddling with the lights and looking over the other gear, Shocky and Ethan distribute some of the food rations they brought from Aegea. They won't take time to hunt or to gather much from the forest for the first few days, since they wanted to get out of the range of other hunters and trackers as quickly as possible.

When they figure it's about an hour past sunset Ty moves away from the group to use the radio. When he's done he gives the group a thumbs-up signal before joining the discussion on hunting while they all watch the fire and heat up their rations.

Asher throws handfuls of green leaves into the fire, creating billows of smoke that fill the air, fanning out below the thick canopy of trees to create a gauzy haze all around them.

During a lull in the conversation, Sgt. Shocky speaks for the first time since they started walking through the forest. "My given name is Garamasala."

Ty's eyebrows shoot up, "*Gar*-am-mas-*sah*-la?"

"Yes. Like the hot spice."

No one dares to make any sort of joke about it.

After clearing his throat, Ty says, "So . . . was it your mother or your father who liked the spice?"

"My mother. Mostly they just call me Garam. You can call me that."

"*Gar*-am," Ty repeats.

Shocky's head bobs—his usual, single nod to indicate a correct answer.

Just then, Asher holds up a hand to get their attention. "You hear it?"

They sit still for a few moments before they hear two little notes.

"The frog?"

Canaan, Ethan, and Asher all agree. Within minutes, the trees around them are echoing with the sound of many frogs, each sounding his two little notes, filling the air with a chorus. Throughout the night, whoever is on watch will keep a small fire going and occasionally throw more leaves in—since the smoke will help to keep mosquitoes and other insects away.

That night, Ty uses his flashlight for a few minutes to write in a journal, a leather-bound book his father gave him to chronicle the discoveries they make and his observations.

> End of Day One
>
> I suppose it's appropriate that I am the father of a child who is the most recent descendent of Aegea's first record keeper. I hope to faithfully record an account of our journey through the Great Forest. I'm traveling with Basil of the line of Tosh, Ethan of the same line as Basil, Asher of the line of Imm, Canaan, an Exile of the same line as Asher, and Shocky (who told us tonight that his first name is Garam!) of the tribe of Manash.
>
> It was a hard day for me. In many ways. We found the box that was stolen for the purpose of kidnapping Jariel, and also carried Shaye into the forest. I thought I had already gone through all the emotions I could feel about this, but looking into the box made it more real for me than I could have thought.
>
> We were able to make contact with Home Base using our radio tonight.
>
> The forest is hotter than I imagined, worse than the middle of a day of hard work in Aegea. The atmosphere here is so thick with moisture, it's almost as if you could grab the air with your hand. We can hear the

whistles of many frogs in the darkness. How must the women have felt that first night in the forest?

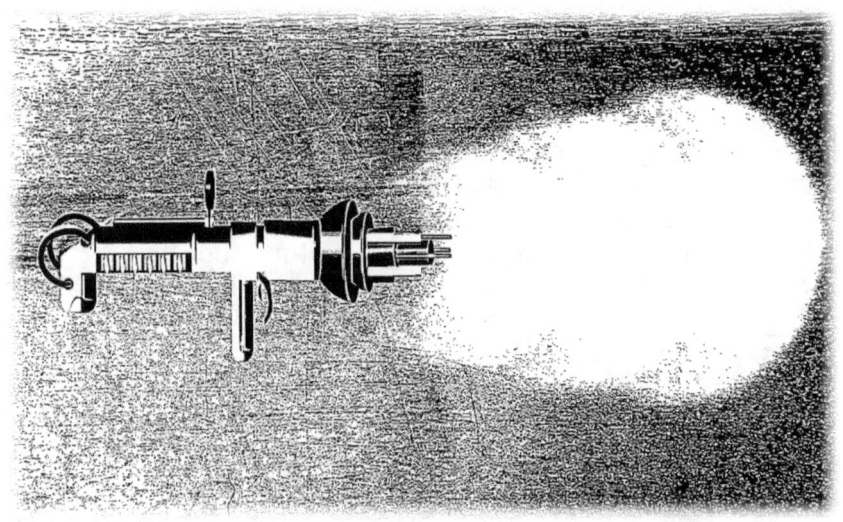

CHAPTER 27
The Sonic Gun

Day 11

Today we had our first real-life use for the sonic gun. It was so hot today, that after our afternoon meal, we decided to take a short rest. Garam went off through some trees to relieve himself and came back running. Seeing him bolting back toward us at full speed, holding up his pants would have been funny if a *k'mosh* hadn't been right behind him. Asher was the one who had the presence of mind to grab the bag with the sonic gun in it. I hate to admit it, but the rest of us (myself included) scurried up into trees before we tried to shoot at it. Asher stood his ground while he got the weapon out, shouldered it, and then shouted for

Garam to get out of the way. Gram dropped to the ground and Asher pulled the trigger.

Just like what happened the first time I shot it, Asher wasn't braced for the kick, so it sent him backwards when it went off. But to our great amazement and relief, the creature stopped. It crouched down with its ears back, snarling. It might have tried to advance again, but Asher got up, turned up the setting and fired again. The creature fled! Of course, all our ears were ringing for hours afterwards.

Canaan says it was smaller than the *k'mosh* that killed the kidnappers, that it was an adolescent. Still, it could have easily killed any of us. I guess this is one topic where I can see a division of opinion among us. Garam, Basil, and I would have been content to kill such a deadly creature, but Asher, Ethan, and Canaan—the men who love the forest—were glad that it could live on. *All* of us, however, agree in the hope that it was rattled enough by its encounter with us to leave us alone.

When I spoke with father tonight, he was really glad that Sage had made the gun. So was I.

CHAPTER 28
Old Friend

After more than two weeks of hard travel, the men are walking through a part of the forest that only Canaan knows. While they're on the move, they rarely talk, but when they stop for food and rest they share stories of their lives. Even Garam has added to the conversations at times. Looking at the stoic sergeant, Ty wonders who started out as more of an outsider in the group, himself or the inimitable Shocky?

Over time, the men become increasingly intuitive, aware of signals, protective of the group. Canaan taught them some of the whistle signals they can use to communicate imminent danger or a call to assemble together.

It's not yet midday but they've stopped for a rest. Everyone could have gone further, but Canaan said he wanted to stop in this area so that he might look for a creature that befriended him when he lived here. No one has any idea what the creature might be, and even Canaan doesn't know if it is still alive, but he wants to look for it.

The men are eating some of the fruit they picked that morning when the Exile returns with something dark on his shoulder.

Ty hops up from his seat and asks, "What is that thing?" More thinking aloud than anything else, he hears himself saying, "It looks like a hairy little man! With a tail! *What is it?*"

Basil rises to his feet and it appears that he's prepared to run if need be. Even the normally placid sergeant looks puzzled . . . and possibly concerned. Asher and Ethan must have seen creatures like this before, since they don't appear as shocked or as worried as the other men.

"It's a monkey," Canaan says. He leans over and takes a piece of fruit out of Ty's hand and then offers it to the creature. "For more than a year, he was my only friend."

The monkey takes the fruit and cautiously eats it.

Not wanting to step any closer, Ty leans forward to watch it devour the food. "It's got arms and hands. And legs and feet. It even has fingernails and toenails! And look at that little face! Does it bite? Is it poisonous?" He steps back a little when the monkey's tail loosely wraps around the Exile's neck.

"He would only bite if he thought he was defending his life. I don't think his bite is any more dangerous than that of a human. And he fellowshipped with me for many days when I was alone."

The branches of trees around them begin to rustle, and when they look up, they can see more creatures like this one, staring down at them.

"We have seen ones like this before," Asher says, "but never this close. We never tried to capture or tame them. They looked too much like children."

Ethan nods. "Just so. When our people saw how sad it was to bring animals from the forest up to the plateau to die or to live in cages, we stopped the practice of catching anything that wasn't for food. And in the forest, we only kill creatures that we eat or that pose an immediate threat. We didn't want to eat the . . . *monkeys?* . . . and they didn't harm us, so we always left them alone."

"I didn't capture this one," Canaan tells them. "He is braver than the others and he came near because he wanted to share my food. I let him come and go as he pleased." The Exile turns to look at the little monkey and smiles. To everyone's amazement, the creature smiles back!

"Does he talk? Like a parrot?" Garam asks.

"He can make sounds, but he doesn't speak like us." The monkey turns on Canaan's shoulder, and begins sorting through the hair above his ear. "He is looking for bugs. He will take the bugs out of your hair if you have any."

The men chuckle.

"He can do tricks that will make you laugh, too. . . ." He looks up through the trees. "Yes, the Maker took pity on me and sent me a friend. This one spent time with his family but he would come and spend time with me, too."

"We should move along soon," Asher reminds them.

Canaan agrees. "Just so. We still have a long way to go today." He walks to a low-hanging branch and lifts the monkey off his shoulder. It grabs the branch and runs along it with amazing speed.

"Good bye, my friend," the Exile says and waves.

The little creature waves back, then disappears into the greenery.

All of the men repack bits of gear, then heft the heavy packs onto their backs. Canaan tells them they must make their way through the jungle and down several large embankments before they stop for the night. The embankments will pose the first test of the rope and tackle they carry. The Exile tells them that without good rope and fellow travelers, climbing and ascending these steep walls is impossible.

END OF DAY 17

Today Basil and I tried to use the two radios we have to speak to each other and we were able to communicate. The radios may still prove handy for all of us later if we can keep them in working order.

Also, Canaan showed us a creature that he calls his friend. He says it's called a monkey (mun'-key). It looks like a tiny man with dark fur all over except on its face and the palms of its hands and feet. It has facial expressions that mirror the countenance of humans, but Canaan says it isn't able to talk in a language. It also has a tail that it can move like a flexible arm. It was very strange to look at.

It took us four hours, with the ropes and tackle we brought to descend several embankments with all the gear. Tonight we are all very sore and tired, but Canaan says that this will take several days off the journey and that we should reach the river day after tomorrow. If we could travel in a straight line, unencumbered by the jungle and terrain, the whole trip would probably take a couple of weeks. Perhaps in the future, if we set up trade with the Exiles, a road or dependable pathway could be made, with outposts along the route, making the trip easier, safer, and shorter. Perhaps one day Sage Dooley will send a bus to the river.

We tried two new varieties of fruit today. I liked them. Asher and Ethan killed a snake and cooked it for dinner. It wasn't bad.

We're still travelling mostly north northwest. Canaan says straight north would reach the river days sooner, but that the water turns to a waterfall in several places, so it cannot be traveled from there.

I must admit that each day that we draw closer to where Shaye and Jariel are, I become more impatient to get there.

CHAPTER 29
The River

"Wake up, Basil! Wake up!"

His eyes slowly open, then track across the five faces looking down at him with concern. Finally, he focuses on the one with a dark red moustache and the fringe of a beard along his jawline and says, "Hey kid."

Ty huffs out a large breath before asking, "Are you alright?"

Sgt. Shocky moves in closer. "Do you know where you are? Can you remember my name?"

The patient's eyes close for a moment. "We are in the Great Forest. By the river. You are . . . Garam."

A single nod, and was that a brief smile? "Yes. Can you move? Can you sit up? "

Basil touches the screaming pain on the left side of his head then looks at his hand. "I'm bleeding. What happened?"

"Don't you remember?" Canaan asks. "We were chopping the tree and it spun around as it fell. A branch grazed your head."

"I don't remember that."

"It's a good thing you were able to get mostly out of the way as the tree fell. If you hadn't, we would be digging your grave. We will have to sew up the gash so it will stop bleeding and heal well."

Basil sits up. "That doesn't sound very enjoyable."

"Can you stand? We need to get you to an area where there is more light."

Ty gives him a hand to help him stand before he says, "And people were worried that *I* was the one who would end up slowing up progress on the mission."

With blood running down the side of his face and onto his clothes, the injured man tries to laugh. "Well, the mission isn't over yet, is it? You still have time."

Soon, the cut on his head is cleansed, then sewn shut with a slim needle made from bone and some clean thread. Canaan and Garam both agree that he shouldn't exert himself for the remainder of the day while the rest of them begin carving two "boats" from the tree they felled.

As the others walk toward the water to give another look at the small, crude boat that Canaan made for himself two years ago, Ty wants to be sure his friend is safely situated.

"You need anything?"

Basil tries to find a way to hold his head that makes it throb less. Once he's satisfied that it hurts no matter how he holds it, he closes his eyes. "Nah."

"You're not supposed to fall asleep."

His eyes open. "It's like someone is *pounding* on my skull. I don't think it would be *possible* to fall asleep." He looks around the area. This is only the second place they've made camp where there are signs of previous use. Perhaps the further they got from Aegea, the Exiles had less concern about being discovered. From here, less than a hundred feet from the river, he can see where others cut through the underbrush and then it grew back. The new branches are thinner and a lighter green than the rest of the bush. His friend interrupts his thoughts.

"Canaan says it'll take the rest of today and tomorrow, maybe longer, to carve two boats out of the tree. He says it took him nearly a week to make that little boat of his—because he didn't have the tools that we have, or the help."

"Why are we making two boats instead of one?"

"He says it would be too heavy to drag into the river once it was made, and a longer boat would be harder to steer. Plus he said that if we had only one boat and it tipped, we'd all be in danger—as opposed to half of us still dry and able to help."

He starts to nod, but the effort is too painful. "Just so."

"I still can't figure out how all of it stays on top of the water. And how does one 'steer' them?"

"I don't know either, but Sage Dooley could probably tell you."

Ty chuckles. "Probably. I wonder how it feels to be the smartest person in the world."

"I don't think this is something you will need to worry about."

"*Eh eh*. Nor you."

Garam comes back up the path toward them. "We need the other ax and a hammer."

He's still not used to seeing the former sergeant with a scruffy beard and tousled hair. Even stranger is the fact that Garam and Canaan the Exile have become friends. *Who would have thought that possible?* Ty wonders before saying, "I know where the ax and hammer are. I'll bring them."

###

DAY 26 OF THE MISSION

The men have already finalized their plans for the coming days and weeks. Canaan cannot go with them past what the Exiles call "the big bend" in the river, so Asher will stay behind with him. These two are the most familiar with the forest and while they wait for the return of the others, they will paddle back up the river, scouting along the banks for the most suitable location to build an outpost in the future. At sunset every day they will listen to the radio for news from the other travelers. None of them knows if the radios will transmit that far, so if there is no word from Ty and the others and they don't return within a month, Asher and Canaan are to go back to Aegea with only tools or supplies they need and Ty's journal. At the fire that night the men fall silent, most of them staring into the flames.

The Exile, like his stoic sergeant friend Garam, rarely starts a conversation, but tonight is one of those occasions.

"Tomorrow, we start the last leg of our journey. It will be easier in some ways because it will require less physical exertion, but it will also be more dangerous. You are unfamiliar with boats and with the river. There will be many distractions—new sights, sounds, and smells, but don't let down your guard. It is a proverb of our people, 'Wherever you find great beauty in the world, danger is seldom far away.'"

Asher and Ethan nod.

For a while they strategize for the days ahead, but the conversation slowly turns to their thoughts about the journey so far, and the things they'll remember most when they get home.

When they've all settled down for the night, the general's son takes out his flashlight and opens his journal to write about the progress thus far.

END OF DAY 26

Basil was able to work today and join us in trying out the boats. After spending two days making them we took a couple hours this evening to practice how to paddle, steer, and secure them so they won't drift away from us whenever we park them.

Now we only need to wait for the sun to rise before setting off down the river. Canaan will tether his own small boat to the rear canoe to use once we leave him behind. For the first few hours, he will steer the lead canoe and Garam will steer the other, but we will all take turns—this is necessary because for the final two days and nights of the journey, Canaan must remain behind. As planned, Asher will stay behind with him and they'll keep some of the gear and one of the radios, in case something goes wrong.

Even though I must start wearing the silly clothes tomorrow, I'm looking forward to seeing the sky again, to being out in the sunlight and feeling the movement of air. I have also missed seeing the moon and the stars at night.

After all these months of waiting and weeks of travel, in a matter of days, we could be at our destination. I don't know what I will find, but my anticipation and longing to finally be there will make it difficult to get any sleep tonight.

The Exile stands on the bank of the river to give them their final instructions before they step into the boats and let the river take them toward his home.

"The water is high right now and in the center it is running swiftly, so we can make good time. Remember, there are snakes, fish, and other creatures in the water and along the banks that will kill and eat you if they get the chance, so unless I say so, don't get into the water or wander along the shore."

Ty recalls the warning about swarms of little fish with razor-sharp teeth that could overtake a man and pick his carcass clean in a matter of minutes. He shudders.

Their guide is still talking. ". . . and if you fall out of the boat, what should you do?" he asks, looking at Asher.

"Swim back to it if I can and the others will help me get back in, otherwise they will paddle to me and pull me in."

"Yes."

On their journey to the river, he had the men collect specific plants he said the people of homeplace would find valuable. All of these things are either in a basket or in a cloth sack and both of them are already stowed in the boats with the gear. As a last edition, Canaan puts several handfuls of mud under a cloth in the back of the boat—for men to smear on their skin later in the day when the sun is high in the sky.

Only one thing remains before they climb aboard.

"It's time," Garam tells them, "to put on our shades."

Before they left on this trip, Canaan told them that some of them would have trouble with insects and the sun on their softer skin, and that Ty's fair skin in particular would not only provide a feast for biting insects but also get badly burned once they were on the water out in the open. Although mud smeared on the skin would provide protection, it might be better if they could think of something that would stay in place and block both insects and the sun's rays. Sage Dooley came up with the idea of using a wide-brimmed hat with shade cloth draped over it, much like what Aegea's beekeepers used to keep from getting stung. While allowing them to see out, the shade cloth would provide excellent protection from most insects and protection against sunburns.

Despite the fact that the hats look like ladies' bonnets to him, Ty puts his on first. In addition to the hat, he's wearing long sleeves to protect his arms from the tropical sun and has mud smeared on his hands.

"You could scare children looking like that," Basil says.

"Well, if you ever have any, I'll give it a try. Come on, we're wasting daylight. Get in the boat and let's go."

Although the shade screen blocks some of the wind, Ty find's the trade-off tolerable. He's also found that keeping his shirt wet helps to cool his skin in the merciless heat. Three of the men, Canaan, Asher, and Ethan start out without their hats, but by mid-day they put them on.

The general's son is amazed at how quickly he feels at home on the water. *Being able to glide along and watch the scenery go by is such a pleasant experience . . . but the return trip, against the flowing water will be long and arduous. . . . If she is with me, though, nothing will seem difficult.*

There's a tap on his shoulder and he turns to see Basil pointing toward the western shore. "Look at that one."

"Where?"

"In that tree. See the black bird?"

Once his vision zeroes in on it, he is amazed by its huge, rainbow colored beak that's nearly as long as he is tall!

"How do you suppose he stays upright or flies with such a large nose?"

"Perhaps even Mr. Dooley couldn't figure that one out."

"I hope as long as I live, I will not forget this sight."

Nearly every hour, the men from Aegea marvel at animals or plants they've never seen before. Basil and Ty continually tell each other to look at something unexpected.

###

That night, when Canaan finds a good place to make camp, they drive stakes into the ground and tie up the boats. Although they haven't worked as hard as on other days, the sun has taken a toll on everyone's energy.

"We made good time today. Tomorrow afternoon, you'll make the big bend in the river," the Exile tells them, "so it's likely that hunters or gatherers from my people will see you traveling on the water or see your fire in the night and take word back to the others."

"Perhaps we shouldn't have a fire after tonight."

He frowns with the weight of the thought before responding. "No. It would be unnatural. A good hunter will spot you before you see him anyway. If he wants to do you harm, you would never see him. If anything, you should be more deliberate and open in what you do to make it clear you aren't trying to sneak up and bring harm to them. Speak only Genon, speak only of peace in case they are close enough to hear you. Our people are not raised to be warriors, we have no soldiers—but nearly all can hunt and even the women will fight fiercely to protect their families."

That night they feast on a large bird and tell stories of when they were young boys, stalking small prey and imagining themselves as brave heroes.

CHAPTER 30
First Sighting

Basil calls out from the front of the lead boat. "I see boats coming! They have men with bows."

The warning of Canaan is ringing in Ty's head.

> "Don't stop on the right side of the river. That is Genon territory, they may think of you as invaders. Pull up on the left and wait for them to come to you."

"Steer to the left shore!" he answers.

They drift to the left as far as they can but trees growing along the bank keep them from actually grounding the boats. They tie up to the branches and wait as the stern of each boat drifts around with the current. The men move slowly and keep their hands visible as they sit down.

When everyone is within hearing distance, one of the Exiles calls to them. "Who are you?"

Basil calls back to them, "Good day. I am Basil of the line of Tosh and these are my companions. We have traveled for many weeks hoping to find you. We wish to bring a message from Aegea to your elders." Only Ty still has his hat and shade cloth on. The Exiles continue their approach, with several bowmen at the ready. One of them, he notes with curiosity, has a shaved face.

Men in the Exiles' larger boats continue to paddle against the current and close the distance. Soon, they are only forty feet apart.

"You speak our language well for men of Aegea."

"Yes," Ty answers them, "We wish to honor the language and customs of the Genon."

One of the Exiles who appears to be in his forties stands in the front of the lead boat. He asks, "Why do you wear that strange costume? Why can't we see your face?"

Now they are close enough to see each other's eyes.

"It is because my skin is very fair," Ty answers, "and I am not used to such a strong sun."

After he slowly lifts the shade cloth over the brim of his hat and removes it, there is an audible gasp. One of the bowmen takes direct aim at the foreigner, but the man in the front of the boat tells him, "Steady! If there is blood spilled today, we won't be the ones who started it."

The boats are only ten feet apart.

"As you can see," Ty tells them, "I am not Genon by birth, but I know your language and your ways. The leader of Aegea has known of your existence for many years but has maintained the distance between us until now. He has sent me to consult with your elders on matters of great importance to all of us."

She finishes cleaning off the large spoon and sets it aside before wiping her hands on her apron and looking up at the sky. It's well past midday now—time to go home and feed Elle. Since the child was teething and fussy, Willow agreed to stay home with her. Shaye gathers up the spoon, a fork, and a large clay cooking pot and carries them back into the kitchen at the rear of the building. Just as she closes the back door, a runner enters the open dining area.

"I have news! I have news for everyone!"

Shaye moves to the counter hoping to be close enough to hear. Last night, the elders of the people were called together for an urgent consultation, but until this moment, nothing has been made public. Willow told Shaye and Jariel such things don't happen often, and they never involve good news, so many of the people of homeplace are already on edge.

"Last night, a hunter spotted strange men traveling on the river in dugout canoes—"

Before he can go on, a round of comments springs out at him.

"I knew it. I knew something big was up last night . . ."

"How many men?"

"How many canoes?"

"Are you sure?"

"Were they soldiers?"

The runner moves his hands up and down to quiet the listeners. "Jared, Nathan, Tanna, and all of the other Elders sent out a small group of hunters together last night to go out and reconfirm the report of four men in two canoes."

"Who are they?"

"Are they soldiers?"

"What do they want?"

The runner holds up his hands once again. "If you will let me, I will tell you all that I was told. Two of our hunters have returned saying that all of the men were speaking in Genon, but some are wearing odd hats and clothing. Since the Elders do not know how these men found their way to the river or what their intentions are, they're asking that the markets and the shops all close and those with children to go home. All of those who are strong or skilled with bows or spears are asked to gather with some of the elders at the top of the hill on the shortway."

Shaye feels tremors running all through her body. *What does this mean? What will happen to all of us?*

The owner of the eatery, Clay, asks everyone to leave and tells Shaye that he will close up the place. She hurries home, taking the main road from the beach to the little street where she lives. Along the way, worried women pull reluctant children along, men trot toward wherever they stored their bows. In all of her life, she's never been in such a situation.

Willow has already heard the news by the time she gets home. Jariel arrives just moments later, looking frightened, and asks, "Have you heard?"

She and Shaye clasp hands. They both seem to understand this new trouble may bring revelations that pose a danger to them both.

"Yes, we heard," Willow tells her, "But I heard them say that these men were all speaking Genon. Surely that can't be so terrible. I know that, since our people first came here, no gatherer or hunter has found their way to the river . . . but that was bound to happen someday, wasn't it? Let's try not to speculate or borrow worries. We'll stay here together and wait for news." She looks at Jariel and says, "You can help me make some food while Shaye feeds Elle. Keeping busy will help pass the time."

###

On the River

After a brief consult, the Exiles put one man with an oar in each of the newcomer's boats before heading downstream for several miles. They pull in again along the left hand bank where there is dry ground and an opening in the trees.

Although no one is actively pointing a weapon at the newcomers, the statement that they need to disembark is not a request. Once they're ashore, half of the Exiles stand around them like a barricade. Ty slowly turns and scans their faces until he gets to the clean-shaven one. They stare at one another for a few moments while the Exile tilts his head to one side as if he's contemplating something. Ty almost expects a challenge of some sort, but it doesn't materialize. When he finishes looking at each one of the captors, he addresses the only one who has spoken to them thus far.

"I am Tyrone."

"I am Jacob," the man answers back.

"If you will allow me to get it, I have a letter I brought, written by one of the elders in Aegea to the elders here. He is Menoh of the line of Tosh, the grandfather of Basil," he says, poking his chin at his friend, "and he writes to introduce us and give your elders an outline of what we hope to discuss with them. Along with other gifts, we bring a copy of the Sacred Tell that came to Aegea with one of the Firstlanders of the family of Anab. His line has ended in Aegea, but if any of his kin still survive here, it would belong to them."

The men of homeplace look at each other before Jacob says, "Go and fetch those things."

Two men walk with Ty back to the canoe and he can almost feel the eyes of others who may be hidden among the trees, arrows at the ready. When he returns he hands both the pouch with the letter and the book wrapped in oil cloth to Jacob before he says, "We hope the elders will consider what is said in the letter."

Several of the men huddle together with Jacob before he and two others head back to one of their boats and head downstream. Ty and company aren't surprised when several men with spears take up positions near the remaining boats and their canoes.

Homeplace

Elle is napping so the house is quiet. As unnerving as the news they've gotten is, the odd quiet out on the street only heightens the tension. Never have they seen so little activity during daylight hours.

It's only two hours till sunset when runners arrive to deliver an update. Willow, Shaye, and Jariel stand outside their home along with all the other residents on this street as the runner's voice loudly rings out:

"The newcomers are men who have traveled from Aegea, and they're asking to speak to the elders. Half of the elders and some of the strongest men from homeplace took the shortway over the hill to the river. They will meet with the men there and decide what shall happen next. They intend to camp near the river tonight, so no one should expect further messages before tomorrow."

"What do you think?" one of the women near the runner asks loudly. "Why would they keep the newcomers at a distance if these were kinfolk seeking refuge as all the others have been? Why did they take strong men and hunters with bows with them?"

He shakes his head. "I am a runner. I would lose the honor of this task if I spoke anything but what I was told. I can only carry to you the message that was given to me."

Shaye hears Elle crying inside the house, so she steps away from the crowd. Just as she reaches the door, Jariel catches up with her and follows her to her room.

"What should we do? What if these are partners with," she lowers her voice to a whisper, "the ones who took us?"

Shaye busies herself cleaning up the baby before she answers. "I don't know. It seems to me we can only wait."

In Aegea

The sun set nearly thirty minutes ago. Sage Dooley sits with General McClaren on the roof of his office building, waiting for a radio call from Ty and the other travelers. The general looks tense, but Aegea's resident genius isn't very good at small talk, so for the most part they sit in silence.

"I've been meaning to talk to you," Sage finally says, "about something my wife's been wanting to do for a long time."

"What is it?"

"She'd like to start schools. For *all* children. Basic education, perhaps in the afternoons, or early mornings. As it is," Sage looks out over the town below, "it doesn't look like Tessa and I will be able to have any children of our own. It got us to thinking how this next generation will need builders, and engineers, and planners. We'll need to identify who those people are and channel them beyond the basics into the training they'll need for the future if Aegea grows and goes on."

"Have her write up a proposal and I'll consider it."

In the Great Forest

Asher and Canaan wait with the radio in their camp, back in the forest. It isn't long before they hear Ty's voice speaking in Command Dialect.

"Base, this is traveler one, over."

Although hearing a human voice coming through a man-made thing still feels unnatural to them, they both lean closer to hear the conversation.

"Traveler one, we hear you, over."

"We made contact. We handed over the letter and I believe it will be delivered. At least for tonight we must stay by the river. Still hoping for a meeting. Not much else to say, over."

Canaan looks at Asher. "They aren't letting them into homeplace. That could be bad."

The radio crackles before they hear General McClaren's voice. "Conditions?"

This is Ty's opportunity to say whether or not he feels they're in danger.

"T.L.," the general's son answers. The letters stand for *They're Listening.* "That's tango lima. We are doing well."

"Give them my greetings."

"Will do, sir. Over and out."

By the River near homeplace

Ty pushes down the antenna on the radio while his Exile guardians stare with a mixture of awe and fear. When he first asked if he could get something out of a case that was in his boat they were suspicious. After some negotiation and his assurances that there was no weapon inside "the leather box," he allowed one of them to retrieve it from the boat. He slowly extracted the radio from the case, and then told them what it was and what it would do. When he first spoke into it, they all laughed. But when a voice sprang out from the device, the laughter stopped.

"What did you call it again?" the man named Jacob asks.

"It is a radio. The men and women who first came to this world had them, and someone wrote down the knowledge of them. Someone in Aegea rediscovered the instructions and found a way to make them again. When I first saw and heard one working, I felt as you probably do now."

"I suppose you have other devices and weapons."

"As you well know, the Great Forest has large beasts and many other dangers. Our main concern was to defend ourselves against the beasts in the forest."

One of the men from homeplace steps closer and asks, "The same forest where your people left our ancestors with no weapons?"

"Boaz," Jacob tells him, "You weren't brought here to speak for us. Don't make me sorry that I didn't leave you in homeplace with Ben. You were called here only to defend, if necessary."

Ty ignores Boaz and addresses his comments to Jacob. "We can understand your caution, but we intend your people no harm. We came openly and we have complied with your requests, hoping only to speak with the elders regarding the contents of the letter."

"What if they tell you to leave and not come back?"

CHAPTER 31
The Next Day

After only a couple of hours of sleep, Shaye is awake and it isn't yet dawn. Waiting is a torture. It's tiny increments of time, each moment dissolving away with excruciating slowness.

Someone lights a lamp in the other room and she sits up. *Is there news? No. There would be noise and lights out on the streets if a runner showed up with any sort of word from the river.*

She gets up and walks into the main room of the house before closing her door.

"Could you not sleep, either?" Willow asks.

"No."

The door to the other bedroom opens and Jariel emerges.

"Well," the old woman observes, "that is something to behold. Jariel is awake, too."

"How long have the two of you been up?"

"We both came out just now."

"Oh," she says, making her way to a chair at the table. "When do you think we will hear something?"

"Nathan wasn't one of the men who went to the river, but runners would have brought news to him and the other elders even if it isn't told to everyone. It's probably a good thing we've heard nothing so far. There have been no calls to come and fight. I figure the first news will get here about an hour or two after dawn."

At first light, people begin gathering in small groups in front of homes, but it will be many hours before any word concerning the travelers arrives.

###

Nathan and Samuel

It's nearly noon when the women of the house hear someone on the porch. They simultaneously turn to see who is at the door. It's Nathan . . . and Samuel.

"Come in, come in!" Willow tells them.

Once her brother steps through the door, he turns and nods to Samuel who seems to know exactly what that means. The younger man takes a stance in front of the home as Nathan motions for the women to gather with him at the table.

"You look so grim. This cannot be good," his sister says.

"We aren't sure what it is," he replies. "But no matter what happens, *all* of our lives are about to change. The whole world is about to change."

Shaye feels lightheaded. "Are they from the evil men who took us into the forest?"

Nathan puts one hand on hers and the other on Jariel's. "I don't think so, but we cannot be certain."

"All of them will be escorted to the village and they should be here within another hour or so. It was decided last night that there was no point in keeping them away since they knew so much already. There will be a hearing in front of all the elders to decide the full truth of the matter."

"Have they done something wrong?" Jariel asks.

He frowns as he concentrates on the question. "No. But one of them is a soldier and he bears news that will affect all of us."

They can hear Samuel talking to people outside—keeping them away from the windows.

Shaye's body is swimming with adrenalin. "Who is the soldier? What news did he bring? What did he want?"

"I was told his name, but it's a foreign name, so I don't remember it. The man said his father is the leader of Aegea. He says he was sent to inquire about both of you and to make offers of peaceful relations between Aegea and the Exiles in the future."

The young women exchange a terrified look before Jariel says, "General Fairmont had no son."

"It was said Fairmont was very ill, though," Shaye chimes in, then looks at her housemate and asks, "So who would be general if he died? You would know him."

The old woman looks at her. "*You* would know him?"

Jariel's mind is racing through any information that might apply to the situation, so she doesn't even hear the last question. "It would have to be one of the four colonels: Paul Kraton, William Wexler, Grason Mosley . . ." she looks across the table, "or Jubal McClaren. Kraton had no sons. If the man who came here is telling the truth, he would have to be the son of one of the other three." She looks at Shaye again and lets the possibilities sink in before she speaks to Nathan. "What does this man look like? If I said the names of who it might be, would you recognize his name?"

"I have not seen him yet, but Francis told me that the man has hair the color of hot peppers. That should help, shouldn't it?"

Jariel covers her face and starts to weep loudly before Samuel appears outside the window, looking alarmed. When Nathan turns and waves him off, he moves away from the window. Tears simmer in Shaye's eyes and she quickly wipes them away as they start to spill down her face.

"So this is an evil man?" the old man asks.

"No," Jariel finally manages to say. "His name is Tyrone."

"Yes. That sounds like the name."

"I am not in anguish," Jariel tells him, "I am overcome with so much all at once."

Jariel pokes her chin toward her friend and says, "Perhaps it's time."

"Nathan," Shaye begins in a shaky voice, "I must now tell you and Willow, some things that I have both greatly desired and greatly feared to say to you. In Aegea, I lived and worked in the house of a high-ranking man for most of my life. His daughter was my sore enemy for many years and we gave each other much distress." She looks at the old woman. "You know, you nearly guessed it once—that Jariel and I had a common life. She was the daughter of that man and I was a servant in his house."

"Does this mean," Willow looks at their housemate, "that *her* family traded you off?"

Jariel looks at everyone with sorrow, then answers the question. "My mother did do this . . . but it was my fault."

"Oh my," Willow breathes out.

Shaye continues the story. "The man and his wife also had a son—whom I believed that I loved."

Nathan begins to think aloud. "And their son . . . he is . . ."

She nods. "He is Elle's father . . . but he doesn't know he has a child." She's shaking so much that the elderly brother and sister join Jariel in holding her hands.

"Everything else I told you," she continues, "about how we got into the forest is true. I ran away, not knowing that evil men had stolen Jariel—and then we both ended up in that box. I woke up in the forest, and there she was, lying on the ground. The legends among our people in Aegea say that the Exiles will take the life of any non-Genon who sees them and Benjamin acted as if he was going to kill her. So I lied." She tightens her grip on her friends' hands. "And I would rather have the weight of that lie on my heart than the responsibility of her death. . . . I never wanted to lie . . . I just didn't know what else to say. The lie has confined me to a solitary existence among you—the very people I spent a childhood longing to know as my own."

"I'm so sorry," Jariel says quietly.

The elder leans back in his chair, stunned.

"Can I talk to you in the kitchen for a moment, brother?" Willow asks.

The two of them move to the kitchen and stand by the large bowl that serves as a sink, keeping their backs to the table where the two young women sit.

"I can see you're upset," she whispers to him.

"What have I gotten us all into? What have I done?"

"What *could* you have done? Left them in the forest to die? Let the beast kill them? Walk them back up the trails into Aegea? Let Benjamin slit their throats? You know he might be capable of it. I, for one, *rejoice* that you found them and saved them—they are as dear as my own daughter to me. Don't you *dare* regret it for even so much as a blink of time!"

"Yes," he says with a sigh. "Now that you say it, I see it. But I must think about what to do."

He returns to the table and remains quiet while he tries to formulate a plan. Finally, he leans forward, looking first at Shaye, then at Jariel before telling them, "I'm not asking for either of you to tell any untruth, but don't tell *anyone* else what you've said here unless you are required to speak before the council. If the elders ask, you should answer whatever questions they have with truth. But until then, hold your peace, since this might endanger Jariel. Benjamin and Jared the potter are already stirring up David, Philip, and others about the arrival of these men so there are likely to be fiery discussions starting everywhere. No matter what you hear, stay silent on these matters."

"What will happen when Ty and the others get to the village?" Jariel asks. "Do you think people will try to harm them?"

At this, Shaye grasps the edge of the table to steady herself.

"They haven't committed any crime that I know of," the old man assures them, "but they aren't like any other visitors in our history. They *found* their way here. Do you remember the day that you came, how people ran ahead to spread the news of your arrival? Nearly the entire village came out to see you. As soon as word gets out, you can imagine everyone will run to see the one with 'the bright hair.' He isn't one of us—he's a soldier. That alone makes him guilty or at least a threat in the eyes of Benjamin and others."

Jariel looks nearly as shaken as Shaye.

"Before you panic," he says, "I'll tell you that the elders who met them at the river gave the offer of hospitality. All the men who were there would know and runners are already being sent out to make a general declaration of it. Anyone who attempts to harm those under the protection of the elders will be held accountable."

"Can we go out and see them?" Jariel asks.

He pauses before he responds. "It would be better if you didn't. At the entrance to the village, every ear will be listening to what is said between you, and things might be revealed that make their arrival even more complicated. Let the people of homeplace get a look first. Let the rush of excitement cool down."

He studies Shaye's ashen face before he says, "I will do all I can to see there is a private reunion as soon as possible. There has been much tension over the past day and too little sleep. The elders who were at the river are traveling back to homeplace with them. Some of the bowmen will stay behind to see no one else is coming down the river. The elders will come home and rest, then we will confer with each other privately." He tries to look both of the young women in the eye before he adds. "Let us take courage, have faith, and pour our hearts out to the Maker. It is said that secret, humble prayers are the ones that have the shortest path to His ear."

Shaye can hear Elle cooing in her crib, so she scoots away from the table, but then lingers in her seat. She's unsure if she can process any more upheaval, but also not certain she can walk without wobbling.

Jariel sees how unwell she looks. "Stay right there. Let me go get Elle for you."

"I suppose I've created enough curiosity with your neighbors already," Nathan says, rising from the table. He nods to them. "I will go now, but I'll send Samuel with word as soon as I can."

As soon as he exits the home, Samuel appears in the doorway, eyes searching the interior of the house while other people approach the windows. When Jariel emerges into the living space with Elle, he's visibly relieved.

"Inside." he says.

Jariel is just as happy to see him. "Good day, Samuel. Come in."

He glances at all the people stepping up to peer through windows, then at Nathan before responding. "I cannot . . . we need to go. Are you well?"

She gives him a fleeting smile and nods. "It is well, for the Maker watches over us all, does he not?"

Another look of relief. "Yes."

She can hear Nathan's voice. "Mule, we must go. Now please."

"I will come back when I can."

She nods.

As soon as he's gone, Willow stands up, moves to the front door and closes it.

Their friend Joony is already at one of the windows and says, "Good afternoon."

"Good afternoon," the old woman answers back. Then, as a proactive apology, she says, "There are so many people on the street today, and Shaye needs to feed the baby," just before closing the shutters on the bottom half of one window. "If you need anything, I'll be available in half an hour or so . . ."

Joony steps back and says, "Okay," as Willow leans out to grab the shutters on the next window.

"I'll see you soon then?"

"Yes."

Willow gives her one last smile before closing the shutters between them, then motions to her housemates that she wants to move into the back room of the home. "Shaye, you can sit on my bed and I'll bring you some water to drink."

When they're settled in the back bedroom, Willow puts a wedge of wood in front of the door to block it open a few inches to allow for a cross-breeze to flow through the house, then opens the shutters on the top half of the windows in her room.

As soon as it's quiet, she bows her head. "Oh Maker of all things . . . it's been a while since I prayed with others, but the situation is urgent and we need your help. Through these girls, you've opened my heart to believe in your goodness again, you've opened my heart to believe that you care about the sorrows and hardships of this world. We are in distress now, so please hear our prayers."

On their way back to his home, Nathan waits till no one is nearby to say, "Mule, this isn't to be said elsewhere until the proper time."

"What isn't?"

"Ty is Jariel's brother. And Elle is her niece."

He stops walking as the revelations work their way through his understanding. A sad expression comes to his face before he says, "Then he has come to retrieve his family."

"Yes."

CHAPTER 32
The Arrival

The old man moves forward through the gathered crowd as politely but as urgently as he can with Samuel close behind. "Excuse . . . Excuse . . . Excuse," he says as a request for each person in his path to step aside. If he were not an elder, several of them wouldn't have given way. There is such a sight to be seen, and no one wants to lose a vantage point.

Even after the elder and his pupil emerge at the front of the onlookers, they continue to move forward along the road that snakes its way up through fields and orchards then continues over the hills. Just above them on the right, they see a man on top of a retaining wall with quiver of arrows on his back, holding his bow, scowling as he stares up the road.

"Good day, Benjamin."

It would be the height of rudeness to not reply to an elder. "Good day, Nathan."

Sam doesn't speak and they pass him by. When they're another fifty feet up the road they see several people rounding the corner above them, on the last stretch of the road to the village.

The old man stops. "My eyes are not as good as they used to be. Tell me when you see the one with the bright hair."

"Not yet. Francis must have traveled back up to meet the group this morning. I see him with Boaz, and . . . I see Adam the bowman and John the fisherman . . ." Samuel continues naming more men, then finally says what Nathan is waiting to hear. "And three men I can't recognize . . . and another, *eh eh*, that really *is* bright hair."

"So you see them."

"Undoubtedly."

The old man begins walking forward again. "You walk back a bit so everyone else doesn't think they can run up the road."

Samuel watches as the old man joins the group then walks with them back down the road. When they are nearly there, someone in the crowd behind breaks out and starts to run up the road. With that, all restraint disappears as more join him and the throng closes the distance to the newcomers.

As they approach the village, Ty's eyes keep scanning the crowd.

Just as the villagers did when Shaye and Jariel arrived, they form a parade of witnesses that walk by, examining the new arrivals who must now stand still, unable to move forward against the steady flow of people. As each one catches sight of Ty, there is an exclamation—and many of them lean forward to look at his eyes or reach out to pet his hair. About halfway into the inspection, a woman beholding him says, "*Eh eh!* Peppertop!"

People start laughing and parroting the same label. "*Peppertop! Peppertop!*"

One of the elders traveling with the newcomers raises his hands and loudly proclaims, "People of homeplace! *Have you no manners?* This is not a proper way to greet men to whom we have offered *hospitality!* These are not like so many who have traveled here in this generation. They speak our language right well."

Nathan stands beside him, "Just so. Calm yourselves! They will be staying in our village and, should you wish, you can introduce yourselves to them soon enough. Get your looks in now and then get back to your work."

As the stream continues to press by them, Ty's eyes continue searching.

Nathan leans close to his ear and speaks in Command Dialect. "You won't see the women here. Later."

The young man nods once and says, "Thank you," before he looks up and sees a frowning man standing on top of a nearby wall with a bow in one hand and the other resting on the handle of a knife and he wonders, *Is he a defender or an adversary?*

When the new arrivals are finally able to move forward along the road again, Nathan and Samuel stay close.

The man on the wall calls out to Sam as they pass. "I hope my words remain with you. We shall all regret this day."

"Benjamin," Nathan says, "No one needs to defend homeplace today. Come down from the wall."

When they hear the name of the man above them, Basil and Ty exchange a look.

###

At Nathan's House

After a discussion as to whether it would be better to divide up the newcomers or keep them together, it was decided that was easier to keep a watch on them if they were all together. Nathan offered his home as the place where the "guests" could stay. It's the average size of a dwelling in homeplace, like his sister Willow's home, only his is situated at the edge of the village, up a short incline, with a garden in the back that's enclosed by a short retaining wall. He tells the travelers they can roll out mats in the extra bedroom or camp in his garden.

"I have to warn you," their host says, "if you choose the garden, there are *sooshi* hens in a pen in the back. They can make quite a noise if they are disturbed. And if it rains, you'll get wet."

"I think I would like to be under the stars," Ethan answers. "I have missed seeing them. I will take my chances with the hens and the rain."

"And the breeze out here is very nice," Garam adds. "I should like to be out in it as well."

Basil can't resist. "Well, I don't know about Peppertop, but I shall enjoy the garden as well."

Ty smiles sheepishly and shakes his head while some of his fellow travelers have a laugh at his expense. "Seriously, though," he wonders aloud, "was my hair such a source of amusement at home"?

"*Ha.* Who would dare?" Ethan asks.

Garam shrugs and nods over this assessment.

"Well, once," Basil says, trying to maintain a serious look, "I did hear someone compare it to a sunrise."

Even Garam joins in the laughter.

Nathan watches them for a few moments before he approaches them. "Excuse the interruption," he says, putting a hand on Ty's arm. "There are two things I must speak to you about . . ." he looks at his bright-haired guest questioningly, "will you say your name again for me?"

"Tyrone. Everyone calls me Ty . . . well, until today they did," he says with a smile.

"Ty. Ty. Ty," their host says, trying to set it in his memory. "Well, Ty, if I may, I would like to speak with you in private." He leans closer and speaks softly. "It is about the women."

"Where would you like to go?"

The old man looks around the group. "Surely everyone is hot and hungry after the long walk over the hill. There is a meal for everyone inside. Perhaps the others could begin the meal while Ty and I speak for a few minutes out here."

When the guests move inside, Nathan points to two chairs under the shade of a large tree. Once they're seated, Ty wastes no time.

"Where are they? Are they well?"

He nods. "They are very well and they live with my sister. I was leading the group that found them in the Great Forest. May I ask? What gave us away?"

"You hid your tracks very well, but we found two things that led us to *hope* that you had rescued the women, and one thing that let us *know* you were there."

Nathan's eyebrows arch upward. "What told you we were there?"

"It was this . . ." he says as he straightens his leg to reach into his pocket. He pulls out the arrowhead and hands it over to his host. "It was way up in a tree and wouldn't have been found—but one of the trackers, Ethan actually," he says poking his chin toward the house, "climbed the tree to get a wider view of the scene and he met it there."

The old man holds the arrow at arm's length and squints at the markings on it.

"Please tell me about Shaye and Jariel."

"I spoke with them just hours ago. One of the reasons I wanted to talk with you alone is to tell you that my sister, Samuel, and I are the only ones who know who Jariel is—and we just found that out this morning."

Ty keeps a straight face. "What do you know about Jariel?"

"She is your sister . . . which makes her the daughter of Aegea's leader, yes?"

"Yes."

"Which puzzles me. If your father is the leader of all of Aegea, surely he had men to send on such a trip. Why would he risk sending *you* here?"

"I insisted on coming. There are many reasons for this. My parents were deprived of a daughter and I would see her restored to them. My father wanted a peaceful negotiation with you—and I told him I could best represent his wishes. . . . But, of a truth, the reason I *had* to come was for Shaye. I had to find her. She's worth all of Aegea and more to me." He holds his breath and asks, "Has she taken vows with anyone here?"

The old man looks as if he is on the verge of saying something, then appears to change his mind. After what seems an eternity to Ty, he eventually says, "No, she hasn't, although there *have* been many offers of courtship." The old man frowns with the weight of some of the questions elders will undoubtedly ask. "Your skill in our language surpasses anyone who has come here in decades. How is it you know Genon so well?"

"I knew a good bit of the language through one of the men who traveled here with me, Basil. He's been a companion and friend to me since we were children—and his father is a respected elder over the Genon in the west of Aegea. Once we discovered evidence that your people may have found the women, I devoted myself to learning as much as I could."

"And *how,* exactly, did you find us?"

"When they first went missing—before we knew what had happened, I began to pray that the Maker would help me find them. I believe that we were *led* to everything that helped us get here."

"Does your father believe this, too?"

He shakes his head. "Although anyone who has worked with or for my father knows he has great respect for the Genon, I cannot say with certainty that he believes in the Maker. But both of us know that if you hadn't found the women, they would have died in the forest. As for myself, I believe that the Maker also *led you to them.*"

"Just so."

Ty continues, but omits the part about Canaan. "My father had long known the Exiles survived and that they'd settled somewhere beyond the known forest. After we realized the women were probably with you, we tried to figure out where you might be. The ancient records were searched until we found something written in the first generation that described a large river running through the forest to an ocean. That became the focus of our study."

"I must ask. Why would *soldiers* take the women in the first place?"

"It happened the very day my father was made the leader of Aegea—something neither Jariel nor Shaye know yet. Rivals of my father took Jariel in a failed bid for power. I don't think they intended to take Shaye, but her disappearance helped them to cast suspicion on all the Genon in Aegea."

"Have those rivals been caught? What has been done to them?"

"Their judgement has already been settled. You saw that some of them died in the forest. Two others died before they could stand trial, but the remainder of those who planned and carried out the crimes were brought before a judge who saw and heard the evidence, and decided they were guilty. The three men of high rank who planned it were hanged. The other two are in . . . I don't know the word in Genon. They are no longer free. They are captives for many years. My father knows the difference between justice and vengeance—he let justice have its way."

Nathan leans back in his chair and strokes his beard while he thinks. "And you, what do you want?"

"First, I want to be able to safely take Shaye and Jariel home." He opens his hands toward Nathan. "Only time will tell if I will be allowed to do so. Second, if your people would like to have peaceful trade with us, I am prepared to make offers."

"Nathan," Peony, says from the doorway of the house. They both look at her before she tells him, "Samuel brought the people you sent for."

They can see Sam standing beside a lovely woman with honey colored hair.

"Why don't you come inside," Peony says to her husband, "and eat while they talk alone."

"Yes. That would be good," he answers, slowly rising from his chair. After he's inside, Samuel remains in the doorway but the young woman steps out into the garden. Basil and Ethan join Sam in the doorway, and they're staring wide-eyed at the woman.

"Ty," she says.

The voice is familiar. She steps closer.

"Ty. It's me."

His mouth drops open as he blinks several times. "*Jariel?*"

She runs to him as he gets to his feet and she nearly knocks him back into the chair when she flies into his arms, sobbing, "I never thought I'd see you again!"

Samuel moves away from the doorway, but the other two keep watching.

Ty sets her down and holds her at arm's length as he looks at her. "Jariel. I can't believe it's *you*. The last time I saw you, you had no," he struggles to communicate, "you had no . . . shape. And you were so pale. . . . And your hair was darker."

She smiles and says, "I know," but then her expression becomes serious. "How are mother and father?"

"We were all devastated by your disappearance, but Mother took it *very* badly. She was doing a little better when I left, but she still doesn't know that you are alive. . . . She doesn't know I left Aegea . . . or anything about this place. Father is the one who sent me to get you."

"And he is the *general* now?"

"Yes."

"There are a million things I want to ask you. Did you marry Linsey? How is Mosha?"

"No, I didn't marry Linsey. Mosha," he says with a sigh, "was shattered by what happened, but she yet lives. There is so much more to tell you, but for now . . . where is Shaye?"

Jariel slowly puts a hand on his chest and it confuses him because it feels as if she is trying to console him.

"Is something wrong? What's wrong?"

"Shaye is here, but she wanted me to come out first, and she wants me to stay while you speak with her. Is that okay?"

He looks back to the doorway and feels a shockwave pulse all the way through his body when he sees her. She's looking straight at him until they make eye contact, and then she looks down. With a flushed face, she steps out into the garden and slowly walks to where he and Jariel stand. The child is nowhere in sight.

She keeps looking at the ground, and moving almost as if she's being shoved there by an unseen hand rather than by her own will. Taking his cue from her reluctance, he stands entirely still, heart pounding. She stops when she's more than a foot away.

"Shaye," he says in a barely audible voice.

She doesn't look up.

Jariel starts to retreat, but Shaye quickly tells her. "Don't go. Whatever he has to say to me, he can say in front of you."

"Will you at least sit down?" he asks.

"No," is the quick response.

He takes a small step closer. "I've prayed night and day that I would see you again." He tries to take her hand, but she pulls it away.

Still looking down, she responds in a monotone voice, "It is good that all of you survived the forest and are well."

He's thought about this moment for months, but most of the words he planned to say seem to have fallen into some dark recess in his brain and he cannot find them. "I can't blame you for being angry with me. You must think I abandoned you."

She looks up for the first time, her anger no longer containable. "You *did* abandon me, didn't you? You said you'd find a way for us, but you never came back and your mother traded me off. You said you loved—" she stops and looks down at the ground again, but now she's shaking.

He kneels down so he can look into her face. Embarrassed by the scene, Basil and Ethan stop watching and leave the doorway.

"I cannot remember a day in my life when I didn't love you, but I was reckless with that love. You've paid a price that I haven't shared." Ty tells her. "I foolishly thought I'd have plenty of tomorrows to make plans. With all my heart I beg you to forgive—"

She steps backward. "Stop it! I don't want your apologies."

"Shaye, just look at me. Even if you can't forgive me, I've come to take you home."

Her voice is trembling. "That was *your* home. *This* is my home."

Before he can utter another syllable, she spins around and bolts from the garden, disappearing into the house. Stunned, he stares blankly at the doorway for a few seconds before he jumps to his feet and sprints after her, leaving his sister behind.

When Jariel hears something crashing through the brush along the retaining wall on one side of the garden, she looks over to see Flint bounding down the hill toward the front of the house. He has a quiver of arrows on his back and a bow in one hand.

"*No!*" she shouts, before she runs to warn her brother.

When she reaches the doorway, Samuel intercepts her.

In a panic, she cries out, "Go and stop him! Flint is after my brother!"

Ty's fellow travelers rise up ready to run to his aid.

"Wait!" Nathan tells everyone. "I asked the man to keep watch over Ty. He is the best bowman in all of homeplace. He's only trying to keep up."

Once he got through the front door of the house, Ty could see a throng of onlookers who'd gathered outside, all staring after the departing Shaye. When they turn back and see him, they close ranks, forming a wall to keep him from pursuing her. He tries to push his way between two of the smaller men, but as the group crowds in around him; they start shoving him and pulling on his shirt to stop his forward progress. At this point, Flint squeezes into the commotion and pulls him out while Nathan shouts from the doorway.

"All of you! Leave our guest and get about your own business," he admonishes. "Don't you have work to be done? Don't you have homes? Were you not told that this man and his companions are under the protection of our hospitality?"

The sounds of tooth sucking and disgruntled mumbling can be heard as the people begin to retreat.

Ty looks at Flint and recognizes him. "You're one of the first ones I saw on the river, aren't you?"

The man grins as he strokes his beardless chin. "You recognize me, do you?"

"Yes. Thank you for helping me."

The old man steps out of his doorway. "Better come back onto my property. Until everyone calms down, you are better off here. And you come, too, Francis. I am grateful for your help."

When they walk back through the house, Ty's sees that his friends are all on alert.

"It's fine," he tells them. "I'm fine. Everyone, go ahead and eat."

Nathan opts to stay in the house when Flint follows him back into the garden. Once he's there, he plops into one of the chairs and slumps forward, shaking his head.

"Didn't go as well as you hoped, eh?" Flint asks.

More to himself than to anyone else, he says, "She hates me!"

Flint laughs. "Brother, I know what hate looks like, and I know women. I saw the way she looked at you before you realized she was there. Believe me, hate isn't what she feels for you."

Ty sizes him up. "You know Shaye that well, do you?"

"Oh, *I'm* not your competition, I just understand her." He sits in the other chair. "You traveled this far—and it's impressive, I'll give you that. But she's had to close the door on *a lot* of grief in order to go on. You weren't here to see some of the people distain her and think lowly of her as a pregnant woman with no husband. You didn't see her—eight months heavy with child—struggling to carry a large basket of fruit on her back after a full day working in the orchards. You weren't there when she was having trouble in the birth." He watches the full impact of these ideas register on Ty's face before he goes on. "When I first saw you, I realized how much of her sorrow has to do with you."

"How did you know that?"

"Your daughter has your eyes."

He sucks in a breath and his eyes burn. "A daughter."

"Her name is Elle."

"So she never spoke of the baby's father?"

"Until today, I think that was her secret." He shrugs. "But this is homeplace. I'd give it two days at most before others look at you and figure it out . . . and then the whole village will know it." He lightly smacks Ty on the shoulder, then stands. "You have a lot of work ahead of you if you want to win her back. Before you set about doing that, though," he says, walking to the wall at the side of the garden, "you'd better let her cool off. She's been storing all that anger for a long while." He must find his next thought amusing because he's grinning when he says, "If you'd have caught up with her, I'm thinking she would have left some *marks* on you. Given all the witnesses, I'm also thinking it would have been worthy of a *lot* of talk in the village. For your sake—and hers," he says holding up one hand, "stay here tonight." He sits on the wall in preparation to swing his legs over to the other side and exit into the trees.

"Wait," Ty says, walking over to him. "Did Nathan say your name was Francis?"

He rolls his eyes and sighs. "Yes."

"Do you have four brothers? Is yours the family of hunters?"

"Yes."

"We need to talk about something."

Inside the home, Jariel watches as her brother and Flint appear to be having a serious discussion. At least, it seems so, given that Flint has lost his smirky expression.

"What could that man possibly say that would be of *any* use?" she says aloud.

Nathan momentarily joins her and glances out the door. "There is more to Francis than you know."

"Do you want to wait and talk to Ty again before I walk you home?" Samuel asks her.

"Yes."

He starts to say something, then stops himself. After another start and stop, he finally says, "I fear you will leave homeplace."

"If I go, it will be with sorrow."

She turns when she hears a voice behind her.

"Miss Jariel. I wouldn't have recognized you."

There's a sad smile on her face when she says, "Basil. I'm glad to see you. How are you?"

It may be the first time she's actually looked him in the eye or spoken to him since they were children.

"I am well. I'm happy to see how you have prospered here among His people."

"Thank you. How are your parents? And how are Menoh and Fiona?"

"They are all well. They will be very glad to see you again."

\#\#\#

Willow's House

The lower shutters on the windows in Shaye's room are closed, but just in case there are listening ears outside the house, Jariel whispers to Shaye in Command Dialect. "He knows about the baby."

"*How?*"

"He says he found out three months ago. That girl, Chessie, told him. How did *she* know?"

Shaye turns her face to the wall. "It's a long story."

"I know you'll just think I'm defending him . . . but he's been in agony since the day we were taken. He told Father and Mother that he loved you that he would always love you no matter what happened. He told them that he'd never stop searching for you. He was so insistent that Father actually let him leave the Academy to continue the search for us, and when they found out where we were, he insisted on coming to find you."

Shaye pulls a sheet over her head and Jariel can hear her voice quaver when she says, "Well, that was a waste of his time, wasn't it? He isn't taking me or my daughter anywhere."

There's a knock and she turns to look at the open doorway where Willow stands, holding Elle. "Is everything all right?"

Jariel studies the outline of her friend under the sheet. "Not at the moment. She needs some time alone." She puts her hand on Shaye's shoulder and says, "We can talk later."

\#\#\#

Nathan's Garden

He holds the radio close to his face and speaks in Command Dialect. "Traveler one to base, traveler to base, over."

It's been an excruciating 48 hours for Jubal. His voice comes back over Ty's radio almost immediately. "This is base. Go ahead."

"We made it. We're in the village of the Exiles. Most conditions are better than expected. I've seen Jariel and Shaye, and, believe it or not, I didn't recognize Jariel when I first saw her. She's . . . all filled out like a woman now and quite beautiful. She has a job in a weaver's shop and she's amazing everyone with the things she does. I never would have believed it, but she has flourished here. Over."

There's a short silence before a response. His father's voice sounds thick with emotion. "I'm so relieved to hear it."

"For now, we are staying in the home of one of the elders. His name is Nathan. He's probably about the same age as Menoh, and he seems very reasonable. Tomorrow all of us will stand before the whole council for the first time and they will decide if they believe me or not. Don't worry. They seem like good people on the whole and Jariel says they've been *very* good to her. The village has a few hotheads and probably a few like Lemon . . . but they've treated us decently. As long as the radio is still working, I'll call you again tomorrow and tell you how it went."

"We'll be waiting, son. I've missed you."

Ty taps his forehead with the radio for a few moments before he says, "I haven't seen her yet, but your granddaughter's name is Elle. Someone told me today that she has our blue eyes."

There's a prolonged silence before he hears Jubal's voice again. "Good to know. I'll be waiting to hear from you. Over."

"Over and out."

CHAPTER 33
Open Council

"A true villain assumes that everyone else would be like him—if they had the opportunity."—*A proverb of His own people.*

The newcomers spent their first night in Nathan's custody. They won't be allowed to move about in homeplace until they speak before the council and a preliminary decision is made regarding their presence—around midday.

Ty has already told the others that they can freely answer any question posed to them as long as they withhold any information about Canaan and Asher. Any revelation about the former Exile might cost both of them their lives.

The day is already warm but a steady breeze makes the heat tolerable. The men wash up and prepare to travel to the meeting with Nathan.

In case they faced deadly beasts or an all-out attack from the Exiles, Ty has been wearing his father's handgun strapped onto his calf, under his pant leg. His captors never knew it was there. Today he's decided not to wear it. He removes the bullets from the weapon and puts them in his pocket, then puts the gun in a wooden case.

"Are you sure you want to do that?" Basil asks.

He thinks about it for a moment then slides the box in the bottom of one of their gear bags. "Well . . . the trust has to start somewhere. I feel peace about this. If a man like Nathan has remained so high in the council throughout the years, doesn't that say something about the kind of people they are in general?"

His friend slowly nods. "I think my grandfather would agree."

As he's placing other items in the bag, Nathan appears in the doorway. "It's nearly time to go."

"Is it alright if we leave our things in this room?"

"You can leave your things here," the old man tells them. "An occasional item goes missing here in homeplace, but that is rare and usually the mischief of young people. I know the men searched your bags yesterday, but that was a precaution. I hear they found a number of strange things, but nothing they considered dangerous once you showed them what the devices were. For the most part, this is a peaceful place where people respect the belongings of others."

Ty smiles when he recalls how everyone jumped back when he showed them how a flashlight and the radio worked. There was also a good deal of wonder over the rope they brought. He was glad they'd left the sonic gun, the darts, the crossbows, and other gear with Asher and Canaan.

Soon they're on their way, collecting a gaggle of onlookers who follow from a safe distance—safe from being scolded by Nathan. As the guests approach the shoreline, they again express wonder at the water that they could only see from a distance yesterday.

"I thought nothing could rival the many beauties of the forest . . . but I have never seen such a color of water in all my life," Ethan says.

"I have never seen such a color at all," Ty adds.

"Just so," Basil chimes in. "I wonder what makes it that color."

Nathan beams. "Everyone says that when they see it for the first time. It isn't muddy like the river. It's clear. You know, if you were to go out on one of the boats we have, you could still see down many feet to the bottom. But you cannot drink from the ocean for it is very salty. I hear that the water in Aegea is extremely cold, colder than I can imagine, but this water is warm. You can spend some time in it later, if you'd like."

"What makes it move like that?" Ty wonders aloud.

"You know," the old man tells him, "Shaye wondered the very same thing. Jariel loves the ocean—she has even learned to swim."

"No."

"Yes!" he says with a chuckle. "She is much braver than anyone thought when she first came. She helps to teach some of the children how to swim now."

The general's son smiles and looks at his friend, Basil. "Who would have thought of Jariel as brave?"

"Not I. It seems this place has made her an entirely different person."

"And Shaye," their host continues, "loves to look at the water, but she won't get in it. She says she feels like it is licking at her feet and fears that it wants to consume her."

Basil frowns. "That's a disturbing thought."

"And what is *this*?" They all turn to see Garam, gazing curiously at a tree.

"Oh, that is a palm tree."

"*Hmph*. This shouldn't be called a tree. It isn't right somehow."

Ethan is amused. "What do you think it looks like, then?"

"I don't know," he tells them. "It looks more like a *creature* than a tree. Perhaps a large spider. Lurking on a tall pole perhaps. . . . Look at how it moves with the wind," he says, "waving its legs around. No. I say it isn't a proper tree."

Nathan laughs and starts walking. "Well you should be kinder to those trees. They bear coconuts. Very good to eat, very good in many ways."

When they step into the sand for the first time all of them look down at their feet while they walk.

"Where does this strange, white dirt come from?" Ty asks. "It looks almost like salt . . . and it's so . . . " he looks at the others and uses Command Dialect, since he knows of no suitable descriptions in Genon, "yielding?"

The others all comment.

"It's squishy."

"No, this is not squishy. It's dry."

"Maybe the word is 'soft' . . ."

"No, it's not just soft. Look, it is filling my sandals."

"Yes, and then draining out like . . . dry water."

"Ah, yes." Nathan says. "This is *sand*. It comes from the ocean and it is a type of dirt all on its own. The oddest thing about it is that—believe it or not—it becomes firm when it is wet. People spend many hours playing with it, shaping it, digging in it. Just for enjoyment. You'll see. Later."

When they arrive at the shelter where the meeting will be held, a group of men and women have already gathered under the shade of a thatched roof to meet them. Most of the people on the council are past middle age, a few are middle-aged, and two—Samuel and Benjamin—appear to be in their late twenties. If this is the same way the Genon do it in Aegea, Ty knows how it works. The most respected "elders" (those who are widely recognized among the people as wise) are commissioned to take on students—younger people who are likely to become respected elders in the years to come.

Ty says, "*Eh eh*," to Basil then pokes his chin out at Ben. His friend nods, then drops back to quietly say, "The enemy of our friend is here," to the other two.

Once they've all stepped up onto the sandy wooden floor under the roof, Nathan introduces the newcomers to the rest of the gathering—which, owing to the politeness of the Genon, takes more than ten minutes. When they are all ready to be seated, Ty looks out on the beach and sees a great number of people have congregated all around the shelter, just outside the roof, to watch and listen. Even Francis is standing among them.

There is a short delay while the elders quietly confer, then everyone under the roof sits in wooden chairs. Despite the fact that there are five runners present who will be sent with the solemn task of accurately relaying the outcome of the meeting to the general public, it's obvious that a good number of people in homeplace want to witness what happens for themselves.

A woman on the council by the name of Elizabeth, rises and says, "We received the book and other gifts you sent and we have all read the letter that was written to us. Which one of you is the grandson of the writer?"

"I am. I am Basil of the line of Tosh," he says, raising his hand. "My grandfather, Menoh, has been a respected elder of the Genon of Aegea for my entire life."

The woman nods at him before she continues. "We would like more time to consider our response to the letter. Perhaps in a few days we can speak to you about it again. In the meantime, we have decided that you don't pose an immediate threat to our community, so we extend to you the freedom to move about in homeplace, asking only that you respect our ways as you walk among us."

CHAPTER 34
Lunch and a Walk on the Beach

"Each person in each generation must choose to accept the real love of the Maker and to be an example of it . . . or to be held in the clutches of a kingdom that knows only what it wants." *The Great Aunt of Shaye, Pearl Penway Curtis*

Having been released to walk about on their own, the four newcomers enter the small, open-air eatery on the beach that caters mostly to men who work on the ships. It's the place, Nathan told Ty, where Shaye works cooking lunch most days. Within moments of their arrival, the place falls silent and everyone turns to look at them. Some of the people look curious, some apprehensive, and a few have eyes filled with animosity. Ethan is the only one in the group who is unaccustomed to being at the center of so much attention. The other three have years of practice.

Seeing the line of men walking by a long counter, Basil says, "Must be like at home." He walks up to stand in line and beckons Ty, Garam, and Ethan to join him.

"Smells good," Ethan says quietly as they take their places behind Basil. "I like these fish animals."

The whole line moves forward a step before Ty can see her standing behind the counter, with her back to the room, stirring a large clay pot filled with some kind of hot stew and ladling it into bowls. He can see that one lock of her long black hair has fallen out of her bun and is trailing all the way down her back. When she turns to see what all the silence is about, her eyes meet his before she quickly turns back to the pot.

Basil is the first to reach the counter. "Good day."

"How will you pay for the food?" the owner of the establishment asks without any other sort of greeting.

Everyone is listening.

"What is this worth?" Ty asks, taking a small, shiny knife out of a sheath and placing it on the counter.

A buzz goes through the room as those in front tell others behind them what Ty offered.

The owner's eyes nearly pop at the sight of a new metal knife. "Well, uh, let me think . . ."

Shaye glances around just long enough to see the knife before she quietly says, "It's worth at least two weeks of lunches for all of them."

Obviously it's worth more than that to him, for he has trouble hiding his glee long enough to shrug and say, "Well, I'm feeling generous today, and the elders said to show hospitality . . . so I will give all of you two weeks' worth of lunches."

Ty only takes his eyes off of Shaye long enough to nod at the owner and say, "Done."

"A lunch," Clay tells them, "is a bowl of the stew, a portion of fish cooked as you like it, and a scoop of rice. How do you want your fish?"

Basil shrugs. "What's your recommendation?"

"You like it baked, extra spicy, fried crispy, or a combination?"

"Give him the spicy crispy" Shaye says, without turning around.

Basil nods again.

The owner quickly puts a scoop of rice and two small fried fish on a banana leaf, then places the leaf, a bowl of stew, and a wooden spoon on an old wooden tray before sliding it over to him.

"I'll have the same," Ethan says, after eyeing Basil's tray.

"Same," Garam says.

"I'll have that as well," Ty tells him, "and do you have any sliced peppers to go with it?"

"*Eh eh!* Peppertop wants more peppers! Maybe he needs to replenish his hair!" someone seated behind him says. A few of the other patrons chuckle.

When they walk to a table in the back, the man already seated there gets up and moves to another table before they sit down. Ty sits facing the counter and they eat their food while three of them discuss the taste of the fish, the heat of the peppers, and this stuff called "rice" as they watch patrons come and go . . . and the patrons watch them back.

Once several of the tables are vacated, Shaye comes from behind the counter with a wet cloth to wipe them down. Ty watches her the entire time.

Even though she never looks up at him, he can tell she's aware of him. Her face begins to flush and she turns so her back is to him while she swipes the crumbs off the last table, then returns to her work behind the counter.

On the Beach

As per Nathan's advice, the newcomers are trying to take it slow, to not go anywhere alone, and to gradually ease out into the community so that people can get all the gawking at Ty and the questions about Aegea over and done with. Late that afternoon when the sun's heat is diminishing, Ethan and Garam ask a couple of fishermen if they can watch them cast nets off a dock.

Ty and Basil decide to walk along the beach—mostly because Nathan told Ty that, sometimes, Shaye walks there in the late afternoon. They're amazed by the large birds that glide through the air overhead, then dive into the water, then surface and swim!

"Truly, it's a marvel to realize the vast variety of creatures and beauties in nature that we never dreamed were possible," Basil says.

His friend can only nod.

There are less than three dozen other people along the strand of beach, but as they pass groups and families, sitting on the sand or splashing in the water, children stare with mouths agape at the sight of Ty's bright hair and fair skin. When the newcomers find a place to sit, a handful of youngsters run up and touch his hair, one at a time, as if it's a feat of great bravery they were dared to undertake.

"Go ahead," he says to one who seems to lack the courage. "You can touch my hair."

"He almost never bites people," Basil adds with a straight face.

The children's eyes grow wide and they run away laughing when Ty makes a silly face at them. He stretches out on the sand with his hands behind his head. "Nice stuff, this sand. I like it." When he closes his eyes, a little girl comes and stares down at him.

"Did you get it from eating too much peppers?" she asks.

His eyes open. "Uh, no," he tells her, "I got it from my daddy. His hair is even brighter than mine."

She sits down. "Truly?"

"Yes. Truly." He shields his eyes from the sun and looks over at the child's parents. "Just like you have your . . . mommy's hair . . . color."

Beyond the girl's parents, he sees her slowly walking along the damp sand in her bare feet. There's a bundle slung over her left shoulder, across her body, and down across her right hip—like a little hammock—and she's cradling it with her left arm. A baby's leg is dangling from the low side of the hammock and above that, a little forearm is stretched out with a hand resting on her chest. As she pads along, she's looking out over the water, lost in thought.

Basil sees her, too. "You know, I think I'm going to try to swim in this ocean."

Ty doesn't respond.

"Sure, I'll be careful," Basil says.

"Who are you talking to?" the little girl asks.

"Apparently, no one," he answers, before he springs up and wades out into the water.

She's only ten feet away when she looks back onto the beach and sees him. Her foot hover's a moment in midstride before she continues. It's too late to turn around. Doing so would only stir further rounds of speculation regarding yet another departure from this man.

He stands up but doesn't approach her. His eyes are darting back and forth between her face and the bundle. "May I . . . walk with you?"

Now he understands why Nathan worked at making their first meeting private. He can see all the attention they're getting is painful to her.

There's a tug on her dress and she looks down to see the little girl who was talking to Ty. "You shouldn't be scared. He says his hair isn't really hot peppers, and his friend says he doesn't bite people."

Shaye lets out a nervous laugh. "Oh. In that case maybe I will let him walk with me."

When she continues walking, he turns to face the direction she's moving, then matches her pace.

After several steps she breaks the silence first. "You've grown a little taller."

"Have I?"

"And your face has more hair."

"Yes."

When they are out of everyone's earshot, she sighs before slowing her pace and saying, "I know this is a terrible way to meet your daughter for the first time. I didn't intend it this way. Would you like to see her?"

He can't speak, so he nods his head.

"This is Elle."

She pulls the sling away from the baby's face and he peers into eyes as blue as his own. When he finds his voice he asks, "Can I hold her?"

They've reached a vacant spot on the beach, so she stops walking. "Let's sit here first."

Basil watches them from a distance. When the couple sits

down on the sand he smiles. When he sees her hold out the baby to his friend, he can't help himself. "Yes!" he whispers, while he splashes the water, "Yes, *Yes!*"

Ty's hands brush over hers as he grasps the baby and she realizes that they are no longer the soft hands of a wealthy man's idle son. They are callused and sinewed with real work. He takes hold of Elle under her arms and draws her in to his chest, holding her close. He closes his eyes as he kisses the top of her head and says, "Hello, Elle. Your mommy picked a good name." He shifts her to the crook of his elbow so he can study her. "What a beautiful girl you are." He chances a look at her mother, "You know, I think my heart is going to pound its way out of my body."

Shaye pulls her knees up close to her chest under her long dress and tucks the hem around her ankles to keep it still in the steady breeze, then turns her face away. He can hear the voices of people carried on the wind and the cries of strange seabirds as they glide overhead but the greater noise is the ocean. Each wave of water creates a rolling boom as it folds over and crashes along the length of the beach, followed by a sizzling noise as the water fans onto the shore, ending with the rattle of a thousand tiny shells in the foam.

His daughter is staring at his hair, trying to reach it with one of her hands, and he's smiling at her, but keeping her mother in his peripheral vision—and taking solace in the fact that she hasn't grabbed the baby and run off.

Shaye finally turns her face back toward him and shades her eyes with one hand as she watches the way he's holding her daughter.

"Ask me anything, Shaye, and I will tell you."

"Jariel told me that Mosha still lives, but that you also said there was more to the story. I would very much like to know what has happened to her."

His hand is shaking when he takes hold of the baby's hand and kisses it. "Yes. I have news of her. There is no other way to describe it but that she was completely shattered by losing you. Much has changed but she is holding her own now." In the corner of his eye, he sees her wipe away tears before he continues. "The fact that you and Jariel went missing together led some people to speculate that you had something to do with her disappearance. But from the moment you first went missing, Mosha stood up for you. I wasn't in Westland when it happened, but I heard that she even stood up against my mother." He pulls Elle closer. "Within a week of that, Great House was emptied out. Although my father visited for a couple of days while he and Menoh wrote the letter for us to bring here, no one has really lived in the house since the days just after you were taken. You know that my father has always loved Mosha like she was family. For her sake, he got her a position with General Fairmont's daughter in town. She's still grieving for you, but she is in good health and Fairmont's daughter treats her *very* well." He faces Shaye when he says, "I went to visit her just two weeks before I left, but I didn't tell her where I was going. It would have meant months of turmoil for her . . . and if we didn't find you alive, it would be like losing you twice."

She turns her face away again.

"I also have news of your aunt," he tells her.

She wipes her cheeks on her sleeve and looks at him again.

"She is very well. Just after Ethan discovered the box in the forest, Basil and I sought her out and talked to her in secret. Like us, she was very glad to think you might yet be alive. She helped us with mapping and finding old records. No one admitted to her we were coming here, but she knows. She gave us the copy of the Sacred Tell we brought here. Also, when I told my father of the harsh conditions where she lived, he offered her a better home. Of course, she didn't want to leave all the people she loves in Oldtown." He's gratified when Shaye nods and a tiny smile lights her face. "So he found her a better apartment there and made sure she was well situated in—" His shoulders suddenly flinch upwards. *"Ow!"*

Elle's little fingernails scratched his chest as she latched onto the cord of a necklace and pulled it outside his shirt.

"You're wearing jewelry now? So what's in the little pouch?"

He closes it in his right hand. "Strands of my beloved's hair."

Her expression sours. "You brought some of Linsey's hair with you?"

"I never loved Linsey, and I never told her or anyone else that I did. The last time I spoke to her I told her plainly that I wouldn't marry her." He can see she's listening so he has the courage to go on. "You have no idea how much has happened since the day you were taken. In the early weeks, it was all I could do to hope you were still alive. It was Chessie who finally gave us a clue that helped solve the whole thing."

"I suppose she couldn't *wait* to tell everyone that I was pregnant, too."

"I know you weren't friends, but she has changed—and I owe her much because she helped me find you. She didn't tell *anyone* about you at first. It was months later, when she realized how deeply I cared for you that she told me. In secret. She didn't do it with any look of triumph, either. Right now, the only ones in Aegea who know about our child are Menoh and my father."

When he says "our child," he sees a blush of color come to her face, but she doesn't look angry so he forges ahead. "She was the one who told me about Lemon bringing back the wagon with a cargo box that morning."

She almost spits out his name. "*Lemon.* I hope he comes to a bitter end."

"He did."

"He's *dead?*"

"Yes."

She looks out over the water. "That was a bad thing to say. I shouldn't have said it."

"I understand. I was so angry with him when we first found him, I would have harmed him greatly if I had been alone with him that night. When Basil and I found him he was in bad shape because he'd been drinking *meechi* non-stop for months. Menoh and Fiona took care of him—and they convinced him to confess to his part in the crime before he died. It was a horrible thing to watch and in the end I just felt sorry for him. He'd wrecked his whole life . . . and ended with nothing. It's been harder for me to forgive the others."

"Others?"

"It was Col. Mosely who planned Jariel's kidnapping and had the box sent down into the jungle. He was trying to overthrow my father by every means—and he came very close to succeeding."

"So, did anything happen to *him?* Did anyone dare to touch him? Will he ever be punished for doing this?"

"He and two other officers stood before an open tribunal. Anyone who wished to come could attend—so all of the elders of the Genon and many other people were there to see it take place. Mosely and the others were found guilty of kidnapping you and Jariel, of the murder of the soldier in the tower at Westland, and the murder of another man involved in the plot. They were publicly hanged in the courtyard outside the fort more than two months ago. Two soldiers of lower rank were also tried and will be imprisoned in the fort for twenty years. The judge said that all soldiers were being put on notice that they couldn't think they would escape unpunished if they harmed people."

"That is the truth?"

"Yes, it is." He realizes he's still holding the little pouch in his hand when he says, "But you asked me about the hair didn't you? Ethan was the one who found some of your hair snagged on the wood inside that cargo box in the forest. Those few strands were the only evidence that you were taken down to the forest and might still be alive. I've carried them with me ever since."

He tucks the pouch back into his shirt before he tells her, "After that night on the roof when I realized you loved me, too, my plan was to make a way for you to be extracted from your life and brought into mine. What I told myself was that I could somehow ensure what happened with your father and mother didn't happen to us . . . but I see now that what I was looking for was a way that didn't involve any real cost for me. In fact, the day my father became general, for those first few hours, my heart was soaring with the idea that things had swung in my favor. Then I was told you and Jariel had vanished and it was like I couldn't breathe. I've been holding my breath ever since that moment, praying and hoping to find you, praying and hoping for another chance to come up for air in a world where I could start over with you. I'm *still* holding my breath, Shaye. I'm still praying that you will let me start again, that you will allow me to see the world through your eyes. You have *always* deserved that. I'm not just someone who *wants* you, I'm a man who loves you. And, this time," he says, touching his heart, then his lips, then pointing up, "I will trust the Maker to determine our course."

She doesn't speak, but she's looking directly into his eyes. He knows her well enough to know that she is weighing what he said. Although it gives him more hope than he's dared to feel in a long time, he knows not to press her for an immediate answer. She needs time to process all of this.

When Elle plops a hand on his cheek, it's the perfect opportunity to change the focus of the conversation. He turns his attention to his daughter and smiles at her. When she works her little fingers into his mouth, he opens his eyes wide and puffs out his cheeks as he blows her fingers out with a loud *Pffffttttt!*

Without warning, a bouncy, gurgle-y vocal sound followed by a big squeak comes out of the baby's mouth.

Shaye leans in, "*Did she just laugh? Did you just make her laugh?*"

His face lights up. "I think so! Hasn't she ever laughed before?"

"No. Do it again."

He puts the baby's hand in his mouth and does it again . . . and she laughs! It's such a funny collection of little noises, they both laugh as well. Ty suddenly starts cackling even harder as he says, "Oh, wait, I think she just peed on me." He lifts her up and it's evident that she has. He pulls her back in so her face is near his face, then puffs out his cheeks and makes the same noise through his lips and she laughs again.

Shaye laughs harder as well. "You know," she says, trying to catch her breath, "she wet on Jariel the first time she picked her up, too."

He's still chuckling when he says, "I need to go rinse off so my clothes are at least *evenly* wet. Can I take her with me? I'll just walk her out and back."

Shaye's expression becomes sober again. "*Um.* Jariel is the only one who's ever taken her into the ocean before."

He hands off the baby and rotates to a kneeling position before he holds out his hands to get her back. "It's okay. I learned how to swim in order to come on this trip." He looks out and can see several people who are only waist deep in the light surf. "I won't go past where those people are and I'll be careful."

She slowly hands over her child then points a few feet away. "Only out to there, where she can sit in it."

"So . . . just above my ankles. That doesn't help me much."

"Trust me. Just sit with her. I guarantee you'll get wet all over."

He shrugs. "Okay."

Baby in his arms, he puts one foot in the water, then looks back at Shaye. "I can't believe how warm this is."

She shades her eyes as she looks at him. "Yes. It feels odd, doesn't it? But nice."

When he gets just where the waves flatten and shoot up the sand, he stops and reclines on one elbow with his back blocking the action of the waves and he seats Elle in front of him. She surveys the water in front of her for a few moments before she begins to frantically splash it.

He blinks and sputters as it gets in his eyes. "Hey. You're splashing me. And this water really IS salty."

The baby starts shrieking as she continues slapping on the water, so he squints over at her mother. "Is that okay? Is she okay?"

"Oh, that's happy yelling."

"Oh."

He's still holding onto Elle and getting a salt water shower when a little girl in a billowing dress, comes running down the beach shouting, "Say! Say! We are here!"

"Hello, Opal!" she calls back to the girl.

"I brought my sister and my daddy!" the girl shouts.

About twenty feet behind the running child, Ty can see an older girl and a man. He picks up Elle and wades back in as they approach. The girl reaches Shaye first and throws her arms around her. "I miss you," she says before she looks up to see Ty. Her mouth falls open for several moments before she asks, "Is that man's hair on fire?"

"No. It's just a bright color," Shaye tells her.

Opal's father and sister arrive just as Ty does. The man and his older daughter are more polite, but both are clearly intrigued by his hair.

"Malachi," Shaye says, "this is one of the men from Aegea you've heard about. His name is Ty. Ty, this is Malachi, my neighbor. He is a fine carpenter—he made Elle's cradle."

Mal looks at Elle then Ty several times as if he's analyzing the entire picture, including the fact that Ty is holding her. Perhaps he's even noticing the eye color thing. "Good evening," he finally says. "My daughters wanted to come to the beach before dinner . . . and Isaac wanted me to leave the house while he tried to *not* burn the dinner."

"Isaac," she informs the Aegean newcomer, "is Mal's oldest."

Ty nods, but he isn't certain how to make conversation. Salty water is still dripping down his hair and into his eyes. He pushes back the hair then uses a finger to squeegee all the moisture from around his eyes. "This is my first time . . . in the ocean." When he looks at Elle again, he forgets his awkwardness. "And this girl here was showing me how much she likes it."

The baby holds out her arms for her mom so Shaye quickly stows the girl back in the shade of the sling. As soon as the baby is there, she starts rooting around and squeaking in hopes of a meal, and Shaye realizes she needs to get back home. If she doesn't start to nurse soon, milk will soak through her clothes and Elle will fire up for a big cry. With a few adjustments, she can start to feed the girl but she'll have to hurry home before the baby soils the sling. She rotates to put her back to everyone for a moment. Once Elle latches on and begins to drink, the sling is adjusted to cover the whole process. When she turns back around, she tells them, "I need to get her home and rinse her off."

"May I walk with you?" Ty asks. Her face flushes again. Is she upset? Embarrassed? Surprised?

She glances at Malachi before she looks back at him and answers, "*Um*. I think I'd just like to hurry back home alone."

When Ty hears the contented sounds Elle is making each time she swallows, it dawns on him. "Oh. Sure."

She takes a step before he holds up an index finger and says, "Just one question: May I come to visit you later?"

She considers it for a moment before she nods, then turns and walks away.

Malachi's daughters have begun collecting shells so they don't notice Shaye's departure, but their father watches her for several seconds before he looks back at the bright haired man. "So . . . are you something to Shaye?"

Basil arrives just after the question is asked and his presence is a welcome diversion.

"Malachi," Ty says, "this is my friend Basil. Basil, this is Shaye's neighbor. He's a carpenter."

They nod at each other before Mal looks at Ty and follows up on his question. "Well?"

Ty's brow furrows with a few questions of his own while he looks at the man and his daughters, but he settles for saying, "Basil and I have both known Shaye since she was three."

The man persists. "But are you something more than a childhood friend to her?"

His eyes drift over to her departing figure. "Only Shaye can answer that."

"It's nearly sunset," Basil says. "We need to head back to Nathan's for supper."

The Visit

That evening, by the light of a three-quarter moon and a small oil lamp, Samuel leads Ty through the streets of the village that lead to Shaye's house. Sam promised Nathan that he would escort the visitor to and from the destination, so Basil reluctantly stayed behind.

As they walk by a garden, Ty spies a bush full of fragrant white flowers. He stops and asks, "Do you think it's okay if I pick one of these?"

"Everyone here knows a flowering plant on the border of a property is fair game."

"Good to know," he says as he plucks one off the bush and sniffs it.

"You know, among the people here in homeplace, white flowers mean—"

"I know. They mean that in Aegea, too." He looks directly at Sam. "Have you offered one of these to Shaye or Jariel?"

The question catches him off guard. "No. But, of a truth, I do have feelings for Jariel. It's just that . . . now that you are here . . . I'm not sure where that leaves me." They walk along in silence for a few moments before he asks, "I'm not asking for your specific plans . . . but do you plan to be here long?"

"I realize people here want time to consider everything. We'll wait."

"What will you do if the women don't want to return with you?"

Ty looks up at the stars as he listens to the ceaseless surf in the distance. "I can see why. This place is . . . magnificent." They walk a few more steps before he adds, "But it's really not up to me."

His chaperon nods. "I understand."

"So, tell me about yourself. Tell me about your family. What do you do?"

"My father is of the family lines of Hoste, my mother from the line of Imm. I am the middle of six children with an older brother and sister and a younger brother and two younger sisters—all still living. My father went home to the Maker nine years ago, my mother three years ago. The traditional skill of the family is stone working. My family built most of the walls you see along the roads and we built all of the buildings in homeplace that are made of stone. . . . Of course, we all know about your father. Does your mother still live? How many siblings do you have?"

"My mother is alive. And," he glances around, "I only have one sister."

When they turn a corner, Sam says, "Here it is," and steps up onto the small porch. "*Inside,*" he calls through the open doorway.

Ivy, the old woman who lives across the street, sees them and beckons to her husband with an urgent whisper. "Abel, come look, it's Peppertop."

The new name for Ty has already swept through the entire village like a hurricane. The man and his wife stand in their window and watch his arrival with great interest.

From inside the home, the visitor can hear an unfamiliar voice say, "Mule. How nice to see you," as his escort steps into the light of the doorway. Once Ty enters, he sees a small, gray-haired woman rising from a chair in the front corner of the living area and walking toward them. "Well. Good evening. You must be Ty."

"How did you guess?" he asks with a smile. "You must be Nathan's sister, Willow. I'm honored to meet you."

"Both of you, come in."

His guide blows out his little lamp and rests it on the top of a waist-high shelf near the door before proceeding. Ty follows in his footsteps and quickly scans the entire space. It's probably about twelve feet wide and twenty feet long with seating near the front windows. There is a big pile of some sort of net on the floor around the chair where Willow was sitting. The home has a small dining area with a table, and a cooking area that's separated from the rest of the space by a counter. Shaye and the baby are nowhere in sight, but he can see Jariel standing near the sink, wearing an apron and wiping a dish before putting it away. The incongruity of this isn't lost on him. In Aegea, this entire space would probably fit in Jariel's craft room . . . and he's never seen her clean a dish before in his entire life.

She takes off her apron and hangs it on a peg as she greets them, her eyes reflecting genuine joy. They are under the watchful eyes of neighbors and she knows she shouldn't seem too familiar with Ty. "I'm so glad you're here."

"May we stay and visit for a while?" Sam asks.

"Certainly! Come. Sit at the table with us. Would you like some water?"

The men assure her they don't need anything to drink.

While her brother is looking at her, she pokes her chin in the direction of a doorway, "She's just putting Elle down to sleep. Shouldn't be too much longer."

When they're seated, Willow places a hand on Ty's shoulder, "Are you sure we can't get you anything?"

"I'm sure, thank you."

"I'll only sit here with all of you for a moment," the old woman tells them. "And then, you won't take offense if I go back to repairing my net, will you? I promised to have it ready tomorrow."

Inside her bedroom, Shaye rocks with the baby who is well on her way to dreamland. She was close to nodding off herself when she heard Willow greeting visitors . . . and she heard *his* voice. Suddenly, she's wide awake.

Outside the home, several people appear at the windows and remain there, as if they were invited. Mostly, they're staring at the bright hair. Willow, Sam, and Jariel seem oblivious to the total lack of privacy.

Ty watches his sibling with amazement. *Who would ever have guessed that she could be so pretty . . . or so at home in a culture with surroundings that are completely contrary to everything she's ever known? Mother would faint.*

"How long was your journey to get here?" Willow asks.

"You know, it's hard to keep track of time in the jungle, but I believe it was just short of a month."

"How did you get down the river?"

The people outside lean closer to the window.

"We felled a large tree. It took us several days, but we carved it into boats. My friend, Basil, got an injury to his head when the falling tree nearly hit him."

"Really?" Jariel asks with concern.

He nods. "Well, obviously, he's fine now, but we had to stitch him up."

"What do you find the most surprising so far?" the old woman asks.

"*Hmm.* It's hard to say. There are so many sights that I've never seen before. I suppose it's the ocean. The color of it. The vast size of it and the way it moves."

"Just so," Jariel says. I don't think it could be described to anyone who hasn't seen it."

He smiles at her effortless Genon and the use of "Just so." *Father would be grudgingly proud. Mother really would faint.*

"Is it a fair night out tonight?" she suddenly asks.

"The sky is clear and there's a fine moon out." Sam tells her.

It's evident that Shaye must have entered the room when Ty's attention suddenly shifts.

"Well," the old woman says, "here's mom. Is our girl sleeping?"

Her eyes dart around the whole scene—the windows, the people, the table, Sam, Ty. She nods nervously. "I let her play for a while in the bath tonight, so I think she'll sleep well."

"Did she tell you that Elle laughed today?" Ty asks.

"*What?*" Jariel and Willow say together before the old woman continues with, "She *laughed*?"

"Yes!" the girl's mother tells them. "I was in such a hurry to get her out of the sling before it was soiled . . . and then it was dinner time, and then it was bath time, and then her bedtime. I just forgot."

Jariel pulls another chair to the table for her friend and places it next to her own. "How did you make her laugh? What did you do?"

"Actually," she says looking at Ty, "he did it."

"Yes," he says, swelling out his chest as if he'd just won a prize, "I did. I made her laugh." He notices the nearly imperceptible smile Shaye gets when she's truly pleased. It makes him forget what he was going to say next.

Willow pats his arm. "Well you'll have to demonstrate it tomorrow when the girl is awake!" It's then that she notices someone outside the front window and she says, "Joony! I haven't seen you for two days. Are you well?" She looks at Ty and Sam before telling them, "Excuse me," and scooting from the table. She walks to the window to chat and soon, despite the lure of the view of the bright hair inside the house, the witnesses at the window get caught up in finding out what is going on with Joony.

They can hear Joony saying, "I came home two days ago and my husband was there."

"Oh? And how is he . . ."

Back at the table, Jariel nods toward the window and tells her brother, "You know, Joony is a cousin to Basil."

"Seriously?"

She nods.

"Menoh will be happy to hear it. He wants so much to know about any family here."

His sister gives him a look that says there is much more to the Joony story, then mouths the word, "Later."

He watches Shaye pull in her lips to keep from smiling and nudge Jariel. It's a simple gesture, but it communicates a friendship that seems unimaginable.

"I didn't hear when he told us earlier," Sam says. "What clan are Basil and his grandfather from?"

"Tosh. Menoh was a small child during the exile when his oldest brother, was taken away. I'd have to ask Basil again, but I believe the brother's name was David."

Sam thinks for a minute. "Yes. I think I know of him. He went to the Maker when I was a boy. More than twenty years ago. He married and had a good number of children and grandchildren before he passed."

"Maybe Basil can meet some of the cousins before we leave."

Jariel suddenly turns to Sam. "Didn't you say that it was a pretty night out tonight, Sam?" She pokes her chin toward the door.

"Ah. Yes." he answers, "The moon is nearly full and there are no clouds so the sky is filled with stars. Could I take you for a walk?"

Shaye gives her a pleading look but she ignores it. "I would love a nice walk. You honor me."

Within moments, Samuel quietly secures a promise from her brother that he won't attempt to go anywhere alone, and then leaves with Jariel.

It's obvious that this will be the most privacy they'll be allowed tonight. Ty waits till the audience is absorbed with the exit of Sam and Jariel. Polite, "good evening" greetings are being exchanged outside before he takes the white flower out of his shirt pocket and slowly sets it on the table, midway between himself and Shaye.

She stares at it and then her focus zooms to each of the windows, to see who may already have taken note of it. Her shoulders give an involuntary jerk when she sees someone in the corner window behind, Ty's right shoulder. He turns around to look.

It's Benjamin.

Almost as if by some herd survival instinct, when the other window gazers see Ben, they cluster together and shrink away from his presence while they look back and forth between him and the bright-haired fellow inside the home.

"You think this woman *belongs* to you?" Ben asks with a hostile tone. "You think you can take her back with you as a *slave*? Her daughter is a child of homeplace. You cannot take one of our children from us."

They all watch Ty slowly rise from his chair and stand directly between Ben and Shaye. His voice is measured and calm. "No. Shaye doesn't *belong* to me. She owes me nothing and she can live wherever she wishes. She has the power to choose where she and her daughter live. I say she has the power to choose her friends . . . and whom she can court."

All eyes dart back to Ben, who seems stymied for a moment. Score one point for Peppertop.

The focus shifts to the newcomer again when he dares to turn his back on his challenger to face her. "Shaye Penway, you are a free woman. You are free to choose what happens next in your life," he says softly. "I've come all this way to *ask* for the opportunity to win your heart."

No one makes a sound while she considers the blossom for several seconds, then picks it up.

If they were alone, Ty would have jumped and shouted with all his might, then taken a deep breath and exhaled the longest exhale of his life. But they aren't alone. She watches his shoulders rise, then fall as his whole body relaxes. He peers into her eyes and whispers, "You have blessed me greatly."

Two of the women at the window start to nudge each other as if to say *Awww*, but all the witnesses jolt when Ben yells at full volume, "You can't do this! You're a devil! This is against our ways!"

To everyone's surprise, Willow walks over to where he stands, "Oh, go home and wilt some flowers. This is our house, he is our guest. You are being rude, so apologize or leave."

A chorus of *"Eh eh!"* resounds from the huddle as they all jostle to get a good look at Ben's face.

###

Although they haven't been gone long, Sam realizes it's probably time to get back to Willow's house. Since he promised Nathan to be a shepherd for the evening, he's not entirely comfortable leaving Ty unattended. They start walking in that direction before he can't bear the uncertainty any longer. He stops and asks, "Are you going to leave with them?"

The sorrow in her eyes tells it without a word. She lets out a deep sigh. "It's as if my whole life has been turned upside down. Again. I want you to know I have loved nearly every day that I've been here. I've found *life* and more joy than I ever knew existed. I feel a gratitude I cannot begin to express. But I must go back. My parents have suffered greatly and need to see that I am alive, that I have prospered in the care of His own People. Perhaps hearing my story can end the speculations and the turmoil in Aegea about what really happened that day. The people there should hear it from my own lips . . . so they will know that they have nothing to fear from the people of homeplace." She steps close to him. "I want to protect people here that I—" She stops when she sees someone she knows, Ivy, swiftly approaching with an obvious mission.

"*There* you are." her neighbor declares. "You didn't get to see it."

"See what?"

"Peppertop offered Shaye a white flower . . ."

Jariel tries not to flinch when she hears the name "Peppertop" applied to her brother.

"Then Benjamin—the one who was with you in the forest— started shouting that Peppertop was a devil and this was against our ways."

"We need to go back to your house," Sam says. "Right now."

Ivy ignores him " . . . and Shaye accepted the flower."

Jariel grabs Sam's arm as she looks at the woman. *"What did you say?"*

"Shaye took it!" She giggles. "I thought Benjamin's face was going to split in half! And Willow told him to take his rudeness away."

"Oh *my.*"

Since Jariel's response doesn't add any spice to the story, the woman rushes off to repeat the tale elsewhere.

Sam and Jariel hurry back to the house but to their surprise, when they arrive, everything appears as it was when they left. Ty and Shaye are seated across from one another at the table. Willow is still attempting to engage Joony in a conversation that will occupy the attention of the last two women who remain by the window.

Jariel seats herself at the table and leans in as if she has a secret to tell. "I hear that we missed all the excitement," she whispers.

Shaye rolls her eyes. "*Oh lah.* Sometimes I actually miss the isolation of Westland."

Later that night, Jariel and her brother stand together in the garden behind Nathan's house.

He initiates the transmission. "Traveler one to base, traveler one to base, over'"

"This is base, go ahead."

As soon as she hears her father's voice, she tears up.

Ty presses the button on the device and responds. "It went well today, but I'll talk to you about it later. Jariel is here and I'll let her talk to you first."

He hands the radio to her saying, "Just like I showed you. You push the button to talk, then take your finger off the button to listen. It helps to say 'over' before you let go of the button so they know you're ready to listen."

She puts her finger on the button, then lifts the device to her face. "Hello . . . over."

After a short silence, she hears her father's trembling voice say, "Jari. I never thought I'd hear your voice again . . . are you alright?"

Once he sees she can work the radio, her brother steps away to give her some privacy. As he's leaving, he hears her say, "Daddy? I never thought I'd hear your voice again, either."

When she's done, she waves at Ty and he comes back.

"Hold on for a moment," he says into the radio.

She embraces him tightly and says, "I love you, so much."

"I know we didn't say it often back home but, I love you, too. When you feel up to walking home, Samuel is waiting inside to take you."

After she's gone from the garden, he speaks into the radio. "This is traveler again, over."

"Go ahead."

"The council has agreed to consider the letter and they gave us freedom to move around the village today. You wouldn't believe the ocean. It's a color none of us has seen before—sort of a light, greenish blue, and it continually moves in a rhythm. Words' can't do it justice. And Jariel has learned to swim in it!"

"Really? I'm impressed."

Ty takes a deep breath before he says. "I saw her today, father. I saw Elle. She is so beautiful." He tries to swallow down the emotion. "I made her laugh. It was her first laugh. And she loves the water. Did you feel this awed and thrilled and afraid when Jariel and I were babies?"

"Yes. . . . I did."

"Seeing Shaye with Elle makes me almost burst with joy and sorrow all at once. . . . Shaye is forgiving me, Dad, but she says she won't go back to Aegea. After all she went through, I can't blame her. I don't know how to tell you this, but if the elders will allow it, I will stay here."

"You would do that?"

"Yes. Gladly. Can't you think of a way to help us?"

There is a pause before his father says, "I do have one more offer to make . . ."

CHAPTER 35
Second Council

"**T**here is a difference between inspiring people to change and inciting them to hatred."—*A proverb of His own people.*

Just after everyone takes a seat, a group of nearly a dozen people approach the shelter. Most of them appear to be young men in their twenties, all of them look angry. One man in the front nods at Benjamin, who is seated inside the shelter.

Benjamin stands and says, "Before this council begins, I claim the right to voice grievances."

Jared the potter rises and asks, "Do these grievances pertain to the decisions we are here to consider?"

"They do."

"Then you may speak."

Ben walks across the rough floor beneath the roof to where Shaye, Jariel, Ty and the other newcomers are seated. Everything about him says he's edgy. For a few moments, he just stands there staring at Ty and the others, bouncing on the balls of his feet as if he's marshalling energy, like a cat about to spring upon a prey. But first, he looks back and flashes a smile at his mentor.

"You honor me, teacher. You are always gracious and let the people be heard," he says with a little bow of his head toward Jared. Then, he refocuses on Ty and says, "We wish to protest the presence of these uninvited newcomers, and this man in particular. We fear that he's brought evil to our doorstep! It isn't enough that soldiers think they own everything in Aegea. Now he has come to take the two women and a child *who was born here* from us. What we must wonder though, what else is he here to do? Is he here to spy on our prosperity? To find our weaknesses? You should all take note of what I say! Eventually they will attempt to enslave us! If he is allowed to return to his homeland alive with news of us, soldiers will return to steal all that is ours!"

A chorus of, "Just so," comes from the disgruntled group.

Nathan and Samuel are visibly agitated but say nothing.

Jared puts up a hand and says, "We've heard your words. I see you're filled with the zeal of a young man. Be assured, we were already considering some of these concerns, and will continue to do so as we take counsel together."

After a short pause in the proceedings, the General's son is asked to speak.

"Men and women of the council, I am grateful that you would allow me, an Aegean, to address you. I know that from the beginning, the Genon people have honored the Maker by weighing information and seeking wisdom before making judgements.

"From the first meeting I had with some of you on the river, I was open about who I was and why I traveled here. Yes, my main hope was to find the two women—Shaye and Jariel— who were stolen from Aegea by evil men. Even before my father sent me here, he already knew that some of your people found the women. He also knew that they would have died in the Great Forest if you hadn't rescued them. So he—and I— want you to know that we are *truly* grateful." He raises both of his hands slightly before continuing. "Contrary to this man's charge, I didn't come here to force either of the women to return with me, though I did have hopes that they would, since there are many who would rejoice to see them return alive."

"How did your father know our people rescued them?" Jared asks.

Ty starts patting his pockets to locate the object. "Trackers he sent into the forest looking for the women discovered the box that was used to transport them there. Along with the box, they found the bones and other remains of the men who carried it there. It was obvious that the men were killed by a *k'mosh*. But no bones of the women were found—which led to a wider search of the area around the box, and that's when they found an arrow, stuck high up in a tree. Sap flowing from the gash the arrowhead made was newly dried, so it was a fresh shot." He removes the arrowhead from his pocket and hands it to Jared.

The elder inspects it, then glances at Benjamin before he hands it over to be examined by the other elders. While they pass it among themselves, he motions for Ty to continue.

"Neither the arrowhead, nor the wood of the shaft, nor the feathers in the fletching came from Aegea or even from the forest near it. The only other conclusion was that it was made by an Exile, who came from outside the parts of the forest known to us. Since my father knew of the legends of the Exiles and had always believed they were living beyond the lands we had explored, this was no surprise. As he examined the written testimonies from Firstlanders, he discovered several accounts that spoke of a river north of us that emptied into an ocean. It was then that we began to formulate a plan to travel the river and then to the ocean in hopes of finding you. *If* we found you, my first priority was to inquire about the women."

While Ty is talking, the arrowhead continues to be passed between members of the council. When the last one to look at the arrow sets it on a small table near the side of the shelter, Flint slowly moves around to that side, inching closer to the table, then slowly leaning in to look at it.

"Ha!" he says in a loud voice. "This arrow belongs to *you*, Benja-*mean*! You always were a useless shot under pressure! Good thing you've been given a new line of work, eh? I hope you're a better ocean fisher than you are a hunter."

Surprised, Ben seems to shrink, while a buzz goes through the citizens who've gathered to listen to the proceedings.

Nathan lets out an exasperated groan before he says, "Francis, do you . . ." he pauses to peer out at Ben's crew of friends and nearly two dozen other listeners, "and I would ask, the others—do you not see that we have runners who will carry the news of what is decided to all of homeplace? You could go about your business and you'll still find out what happens here."

"Oh, I see the runners," Flint responds, "but this is getting really exciting, and I'm cancelling any other plans for the day." He walks back to the area in front of the shelter and sits down in the sand with a big smile on his face. Benjamin's people and some of the other curiosity seekers sit down as well.

Although Ben is obviously shaken by the news of the arrow, he's unwilling to let go of his argument. "This soldier from Aegea is a *liar!* He will bring back more soldiers to come and trample homeplace."

"Ha!" Flint yells. "Seeing as how it was *your* arrow that gave them the idea to find us, shouldn't *you* be the one to blame if this happens?"

"The soldier isn't one of us!" Ben shouts, "He's trampling our laws and our beliefs! The Aegeans will take what is ours and defile it!"

Jared raises his hands. "Both of you, *stop!* This is an open meeting. You are allowed to *listen*, or to speak if called upon, but not to argue with each other. If you disrupt the meeting again, you will have to leave."

Ty waits until it's quiet, then asks, "May I continue?"

"Yes. We apologize for the rudeness."

Ty looks at his accusers then the elders. "I think most of the dispute actually centers on the women." He pauses to look at Ben. "Shaye in particular. . . . Perhaps this man is uninformed. She has already declared that she doesn't want to return to Aegea, and as far as I am concerned, she and her daughter are free to go or to stay. Do the elders give her that freedom as well?"

"What about Jariel?" one of the elders asks, looking at her. "Do you wish to leave or stay?"

Jariel clears her throat. "I will go back to Aegea."

Sounds of surprise echo around the space before other questions are asked.

"Why? You have become a beloved sister to many here. You have satisfying work that has added something to the beauty of life here. Since you have no family in Aegea, why would you return there?"

She looks at each of them before responding. "I *have* been greatly blessed here. I have found so much life and joy here. But now I must share a truth with you. I *do* have a family in Aegea . . . and none of them are Genon." She pauses while several of the listeners make comments, and Ben mutters, "I knew it. I knew it."

When she sees the affectionate gaze of Samuel, she finds her resolve. "The only reason this was told to the men who found us was to save my life—for Shaye and the other Genon in Aegea all believe that if anyone who is not one of His own people sees an Exile, that person will be killed."

Before her accuser can open his mouth to speak again, Nathan rises and asks, "Benjamin, if we call David and Loash to come and give a truthful account of your first encounter with the women, will they tell us that you threatened—by action or words—the life of Jariel if she wasn't Genon?"

All eyes focus on him as he sputters for a few moments, then says, "This was the way of the first Exiles. I only have the good of our people in my heart!"

Nathan says it slowly. "Did . . . you . . . threaten . . . her life?"

"I might have asked about her. I might have touched my knife."

"And didn't you, just minutes ago, stand before everyone here to say that we shouldn't let our guests return home alive? It seems to me that your solution to any number of problems is death."

He ignores Nathan's remarks. "We can all see that Shaye is an impure woman—and now we know that she is a liar—why is anyone surprised by what she's done? Think about the peril we may all be in as a result of her lies."

Basil slowly grasps his friend's right elbow. Ty could easily pull away from the grip, but it's a timely reminder. There are more important issues than responding to Ben's insults.

"Shaye," Jared the potter asks, "did you lie to the men who rescued you?"

She feels as if a huge weight is falling off of her when she says, "Yes. I did. Perhaps to some of you here there is no excuse that could justify it, but I'd heard all of my life that no one from the line of soldiers could look upon an Exile and live. During that first encounter, I was certain this would be the case with Jariel. I will tell you plainly, it scalded me to tell the lie, doubly so because Jariel and I were enemies in Aegea. But even if they had merely left Jariel in the forest, it would certainly have resulted in her death. When weighed against her life, I hoped the Maker would forgive me. I will stand and take a mark for the untruth if you decide to give it to me."

Her accuser interjects, *"Her dishonesty may kill us all—"*

"Benjamin," Jared interjects, "did I not warn you that you couldn't disrupt?"

It's a surprise when Nathan rises. "If I may . . . Benjamin seems to have much to say. Perhaps we should let him say it. I wouldn't want it to seem as if we suppressed the truth. As long as he can do it calmly, I'm not opposed to letting him speak."

There is nodding among the council.

Jared seems surprised by Nathan's concession. "Very well," he says. He turns to his student and admonishes, *"Calmly."*

Ben dusts off his shirt and takes in a sniff before he continues. "It is clear to me that Shaye's untruths—not to mention her uncleanness—are leading to the pollution of homeplace altogether. The only reason all of this has happened, the only reason they," he says, actually pointing a finger at Ty and Jariel, "are here is because Shaye lied to us. They represent all that we hate and all that we have suffered at the hands of Aegea. We can have no compromises with soldiers." Having said that, he sits down to another round of "Just so" from his companions.

"What Shaye did," Ty rebuts, "was to save a life when this man left her no choice. Are the commands of the Tell taught here? Isn't all life still *sacred?* My position before the council isn't about your *law.* I haven't broken any laws. It isn't about belief either—I accepted the Maker years ago. Many of you here can testify that Jariel has made that same decision and is walking in it before your very eyes. Viewed over the course of time, her presence here has resulted in someone who now walks with the Maker and serves as an example among you."

Just loud enough to be heard, Ben speaks under his breath. "Neither of you will ever be Genon."

Ty turns to the elders. "Do you have a copy of the *Sacred Tell*? One of your own or the one I brought here as a gift?"

Iris, responds, "Yes. I have it here."

"I confess," he tells her, "although I can speak Genon, I cannot read it. I have, however, learned some of the *Sacred Tell* by heart. Would you do me all the honor of reading something specific from the book for me?"

The other people of the council all nod, as Iris says, "Yes."

"Thank you. There are some words on faith I would like you to read for me." He walks over to her to tell her where to find the passage.

She clears her throat as she finds, then scans the passage. Her brow slowly lifts and she nods before reading it aloud. "'Whenever we attempt to marry faith to tradition or race, it is a match that will not result in virtue. The substance of faith isn't in our collective habits or our common flesh, it exists in our *shared hope*.'"

"Just so," Samuel and several others add while an, "*Ohhhhhhhhhhhh*," drifts through some who've congregated outside the shelter to listen.

One man at the rear of the spectators shouts, "*Eh eh! Peppertop knows it better than Benjamin!*"

While some chuckle, Benjamin tries to identify the anonymous heckler.

Several council members ask to see the passage for themselves so the book is carefully passed between them, each one pointing to the place where the passage can be found.

Nathan rises again and Jared nods as a sign that he can speak.

"This is a reminder that the Sacred Tell always proves true. I have watched Jariel blossom, not just as a woman, but as a woman of faith. I don't think her devotion is any less pure than that of any daughter here."

Another round of agreement is heard.

Everyone is surprised when Garam, a man who has barely spoken since arriving in homeplace, stands. "I have something to say on this issue. May I speak?"

The elders lean in to briefly consider it before Jared shrugs and says, "Yes. But, please tell everyone your name first."

"My name is Garamasala of the line of Manash. In Aegea, I am called Sgt. Manash, because I am also a soldier in the Signal Corps of Aegea."

There's a collective gasp among all who've gathered here.

Flint shakes his head and quietly laughs before he says, "This just gets better every moment!"

"Yes," Garam tells them all, "I am one of His own people, of pure bloodline, but I am also a soldier." He turns to look at Benjamin and his crew. "Do you think you can only have freedom in this place—isolated from anyone offends your sensibilities? Do you think it's your seclusion that will preserve your faith? The blood in your veins? Do you *think* you are free? Free from what? What hardships have the people living in Aegea worked upon you in this generation? I have endured much from soldiers *and* from my own people, but I was taught that a life built around injuries is no life. I *choose* to walk in this world a free son of my Maker, a man of the linage of Manash. I choose to be that man no matter *what* I wear, no matter who I am with, no matter where my feet are standing." He taps on his chest. "Being a son of my Creator is who I am in here. It's not up to you to give it or take it. It's between me and the Maker." Turning to face the elders, he adds, "I would *hope* that the men and women who guide this community are walking in that same freedom."

Benjamin leans over and spits at Garam's feet, but the sergeant doesn't even blink.

"That's enough," Jared says in a disappointed tone.

"Oh," Flint says, "that's all he's got. He's quick with the threats or the spit when he's standing in the safety of a public place. Like a little boy throwing stones—while he's standing near his mama's skirt."

Two of Ben's minions hold onto him while the meeting devolves into shouts of indignation and arguing. After a brief huddle between the elders, Nathan calls for silence and makes an announcement.

"We have decided that the rest of the meeting will be private. Emotions are running too hot, and we won't be able to get through all of the ideas for consideration if we must continually stop because of outbursts and rude behavior. Shortly, we will send out some of the runners with what is *known* and what has been decided so far. I beseech all of you *not* to embellish what has been said here or to add to it or you will stand before the council. There are black marks and several unsavory jobs to do—reserved for gossips and mischief-makers." He waits until Ben's crew is standing before he continues. "The newcomers will stay for talks. Anyone else who is not on the council or one of the designated runners is asked to leave."

As people start to walk away, Samuel catches up with Jariel and Shaye. "It's probably better if the two of you went home for the rest of the day. May I walk you there?"

Jariel nods at him and says, "Would you? But don't you have to stay for the meeting?"

"No. The meeting is for the men from Aegea and elders only. I study under Nathan—just as Benjamin studies under Jared, but we are students, we're not on the council."

He quickly guides them out of the crowd of those departing the meeting. Even when the three of them can speak freely, no one says a word. As they quietly walk together, Samuel takes her hand and she holds on tightly.

All the fire that Ben and his followers brought with them has dwindled and the group disburses. While he's walking along the beach alone, he can hear Flint's voice behind him.

"Well, Benja*mean*, how sad for you that three lives have again been rescued from the threat of your knife. Time to go home to your adoring wife and console yourself, eh? Hopefully, she won't come to the conclusion that she rushed to take vows with you too soon."

Back in the council meeting Ty is asked to continue.

"You have the letter I brought with me. When I spoke with him last night, my father had one more idea to offer: That you would choose from among you at least one person, but several if you'd like, who could go on the return trip to Aegea under the same gracious offer of hospitality that you have extended to us. They would be free to come and go from a dwelling set aside for them. They could serve as your representatives and collect first-hand reports about what life is like in Aegea now—sort of like the runners you have here. Let them meet with my father, the elders, and others who govern there. Their reports to you may express some complaints or even some concerns—but we believe that words from your own people will give you more confidence that my father doesn't intend to threaten you or your way of life. You will hear and see that he is actively working to build a system that will advance the quality of life for everyone there. It's not without challenges, it's a work he's just begun but I believe mutual respect and communication between us can grow."

"What about the items for trade that were mentioned in the letter?" one of the elders asks.

"When and *if* you are ready, Aegea is willing to trade. I could help you to compose a list of things that would be of interest to people there. We are also open to a limited migration between here and there. Each of our lands has opportunities that might appeal to people in the other place, but neither country would do well with a sudden, large shift in population. If you approve, we could discuss a process that allows travel between us to *slowly* develop."

When Ty is finished speaking, many of the elders have questions or points they want clarified. After two more hours of talks, the consensus is that they know enough to give General McClaren's proposals more consideration. They make no promise as to how long their deliberations will take, but they tell him they hope to meet with him again in less than a week.

As the council meeting is winding down, a group of more than twenty people approach the shelter from the beach. It's nearly dark so they are carrying lamps and torches. There is an eerie intensity about the group. Garam stands and speaks quietly to Basil and Ethan before they stand as well. Ty looks up and recognizes the one in the front of the group.

It's Benjamin.

Jared moves to the front of the shelter saying, "Let me speak to him."

Elders and newcomers watch as the group comes to a halt just outside the shelter and Benjamin steps up onto the floor.

"What are you doing here?" Jared asks him.

"We've talked it over, and we demand that you don't make any sort of agreement with them."

"Demand? What if you don't get your way? Are you threatening us?" Jared turns to address at the group. "David? Loash? Adam? Boaz? Are you in such a hurry to have your way that you would throw away wisdom? What has he told you?"

One of the youngest men, David, responds. "We don't want you to allow Aegeans to corrupt our faith and our home. There will be no agreement with them."

Jared's shoulders sag as he looks at his student. "Why have you done this?"

When Ben offers no answer, the elder speaks to David and the others again. "Have you not listened to what we or the Runners reported today? We believe these are men of sincerity who brought a peaceful offer to us. Jariel—whom you all know—believes them to be good men and she can return with them if she wishes. At this time we have not accepted or declined their other offers. We will reason together over these things and then *we* will make a decision."

Nathan stands and says, "Benjamin was duly warned. I recommend that, once this other matter is settled, he should stand before the council for stirring so much trouble."

"You should no longer be honored as an elder," Ben fires back. He then turns toward the crowd who followed him and declares, "He's grown soft toward compromise and he lacks the strength of will and body to keep our people strong. We need leaders who still have zeal for the ways of our people, who will keep us safe! If we stand fast in these things, the Maker will provide for us!"

"Just so!" shout several among the crowd.

While most of the attention is riveted on Ben and his followers, a man emerges from the seagrape trees near the shelter and walks forward.

Garam notices him first and moves to stand between the figure and Ty. Ethan and Basil quickly move into defense mode as well.

It's Flint. He steps up onto the floor and is about six feet away from Ben before he speaks to one of the group in particular. "Boaz!" he shouts to his brother. "What are you doing with this rabble? Surely, you must know there is no profit in it for you." He looks at some of the others in the group. "David, Loash, and Eli—why have you let yourselves be enticed by this foolishness? What sort of men are you that you would let this coward exalt himself over you? Do you actually think that if you kill the people Aegea sent here that there will be no retaliation? Who among you is trained for war? Do you think the Maker will suddenly be so pleased with you that He will blow out the rest of the soldiers in the world like candles? Do you think He will reward you by fashioning some new women up among the coconuts and dropping them into your midst? This man is a fool, and if you follow him, you are fools as well."

"I would expect someone like *you*," Ben says, "to take the side of this demon and his whore!"

"Oh *that's* it!" Ty shouts as he moves toward Ben. "It's *ON!*"

Basil and Ethan together can barely contain him.

Ben draws his knife as he runs toward Ty. Flint tries to grab him but the man slips out of his grasp. In a flash of movement, Garam grabs the hand with the knife and twists it while he drops the attacker to his knees, then kicks him flat onto the floor. He's still holding Ben's wrist and has his foot on Ben's shoulder blade when he points to the knife that fell during the takedown. "Ethan, would you take that up?"

Once he's sure that Ty is contained, Ethan picks up the weapon then deftly tosses it in the air to catch it by the blade and hand it to Jared.

Flint gives an impressed whistle. "Not bad," he says to Garam. "Not bad."

When Garam allows Ben to stand, the man suddenly bolts into the trees.

"Let him go," Jared says. We could waste all night searching the bushes for him. In the morning, we will send some men to find him and bring him to the council." He turns and looks at the newcomers. "Meanwhile, stay together and stay on guard. We'll ask some of the men here to help keep you safe."

"Traveler one to home base, traveler to base, over."

"This is base."

"I only have a few moments. All is well so far, but a lot has happened. There has been some opposition, but I think it's getting sorted out. You wouldn't believe it. One of the turning points today was when Shocky addressed the whole council."

"Say again?"

"You mean the part about Shocky or all of it?"

"Shocky."

"He spoke before the whole council. Who would have ever guessed? He was great."

"Wow."

"Exactly. There was a bit of a skirmish with one man at the end, but we're all okay. The council said they hope to have an answer in the next week. I have the impression that it's not a question of if they will agree, but how they want to start the process."

"Excellent."

"We're headed to Shaye and Jariel's house now so I really need to go, but I wanted you to know. . . . And, Dad? Thank you."

While they're waiting for Ty to finish his radio call, Sam approaches Garam.

"I want to thank you for what you said this evening. I want you to know that your words inspired me. Sometimes, I get discouraged and I need to remember; being well-liked isn't what we are called to, it's recognizing Him, living out our faith."

Garam gives him one nod and a hint of a smile.

Samuel places a hand on his shoulder. "If you ever want to return to homeplace, I would welcome you as a brother."

CHAPTER 36
The Vigil

"**W**hen you are a babe, the world consists of the span between your
mother's elbow and her face. From childhood into adulthood, the
world grows larger as you learn to walk about in it. But when you
grow old, the world grows small again.—*A proverb of His people*

She has no idea how long she's been asleep, but she can
hear a soft rapping on the door. She grabs her shawl and
drapes it over her shoulders as she rushes to the door. She has
her hand on the latch, but she doesn't move it. Instead, she
asks, "Who is it?"

"It's Garam."   There's a short pause and then a
clarification. "It's Sargent Shocky . . . and Samuel . . . and the
others."

She unlatches the door and opens it. "Is everything all
right?"

In the dim light, she can see a group of men with Sam and Garam in the front, then Ty . . . *And is that Flint in the back of the group?*

"We wanted to make sure all of you were safe."

She opens the door and beckons them all to come in. "Why? What happened?"

As he walks by her, Sam says, "Ben tried to attack Ty."

"WHAT?"

Shaye flies into his arms. "Are you unharmed?"

He smiles at his friends. "It's fine. I'm fine."

Willow's door opens and she comes into the room followed by Jariel. "What's happened? Why are you here so late?"

"Everyone is okay. But Ben and about two dozen others came to the council and there was a short fight. Ben tried to harm Ty but he never even got close to him. Garam," he says, poking his chin in the sergeant's direction, "had him down in no time, but as soon as he was allowed to stand, Loash and David helped him get away and the three of them ran off into the night. They will be found tomorrow and the council will sit to decide a punishment for them. We don't think any of you are in danger, but—just in case—we thought it best if we made sure all of you were watched over till then. A couple of us will be staying outside the house and we wanted to let you know we were there."

Garam turns and looks out the door before he tells them, "I think you should look."

As the men gather in the doorway, they see people coming from both sides of the street and along the sidewalk, carrying torches or lamps. As they get to the front of the home, they stop. All the neighbors on the street including Malachi, Ivy, Abel, and Joony are among them.

"What do all of you want?" Samuel asks.

By now, Willow has opened one of the shutters so the women of the house are also peering out at the growing throng.

Joony speaks right up. "We came to tell Willow, Shaye and Jariel that we are for them. We care about them and we will watch over them."

"There are a small number of people, "Malachi adds, "who are making fools of themselves over all of this, but many in this village have come to know Jariel and Shaye. We see you as those who have tried to walk uprightly among us." He looks at Shaye specifically. "Whether you stay or go, we are for you, we pray for your welfare, and we will stand to defend you."

A woman urgently pushes to the front of the crowd. As soon as she sees Willow in the window, she heads straight for her.

"Jasmine," the old woman says, "you look upset, is something wrong?"

Ty looks at Shaye and Jariel for some guidance as to who Jasmine is.

"She's Nathan's daughter." Shaye whispers.

"Mother sent me to fetch you and Samuel," she says. "Something has happened to Father. You should come right now."

Samuel squeezes next to Willow. "What has happened to him?" he asks.

They can hear the strain in Willow's voice when she asks Jasmine, "Is he alright? Is your brother there? I'll get my shawl and come with you."

"He felt dizzy and then he fell down. They got him onto the bed but he's very weak. Yes, Peter is with him now." The fear in her eyes communicates what she's not saying. "He asked for you and Sam."

The report immediately works its way through the gathering. Within moments, several of them are rushing off to wake the village with calls to a "vigil."

"We'll get dressed and join you," Jariel says.

The old woman stops and says to them. "I will go right now. You and Shaye come as soon as you can." She looks at Ty. "You and the others will keep them safe, won't you?"

"Yes."

When Willow and Sam depart, some of the crowd fall in behind them as they walk to Nathan's house, some say they will stay behind until Shaye and Jariel are ready to walk to Nathan's.

Shaye's eyes fill with tears. "Nathan is so very dear to me. I don't know if I could bear it if he died from all this," she tells Ty. "I want so much to go with everyone to pray for him."

"Nathan saved us." Jariel adds. "He has been like a father to us and watched over us."

They both look so shaken that Ty can't help but fold them in his arms. "It will be all right."

The small gathering is waiting behind closed doors pondering their next move, when there is an urgent knock on the door. Benjamin tells his wife to see who it is and they all can hear an excited voice before a young man bursts into the room.

"Benjamin! Nathan may have had a stroke! Everyone is gathering at his house to pray. If he dies, the people might blame . . ." He stops speaking for a moment as Ben stares him down, then continues. "Do you think people will believe it's *our* fault? Do you think we should all go and make amends?"

When Sam and Willow arrive at the house, Nathan's son Peter opens the door. He looks grim as he leads the way to Nathan's bed. "I've mixed up some medicine" he tells them, "and given him some tea. He was able to swallow it. . . . Now we must keep him still and wait."

Peony is on the far side of the bed with her hand on his shoulder. Willow hugs her and then they both peer down upon a man who means so much to both of them.

Samuel kneels down on the near side of the bed and takes Nathan's limp hand.

After a few minutes, the old man speaks without opening his eyes and his words are slightly slurred. "When I was a baby, my world was small. I knew only that within arm's reach. Now that I am full of days, my world grows small once more. I don't think I will ever walk in the Great Forest again or travel along the great river. I'm not sad about this, though. If I am not here, that means I will be with my Maker in a garden far grander than anyone has ever seen."

Within an hour, more than a thousand people have filled the street and woods around Nathan's house, holding candles or lamps, praying and singing without ceasing. Throughout the night more and more gather with Shaye, Elle, Ty, Basil, Garam and Ethan adding their voices to the songs and the prayer for a beloved elder of homeplace.

When the sun is nearly up, Nathan's son comes out of the house. Shaye notes he looks tired, but not grieved.

"My dear brothers and sisters," he says loudly. "I think the worst has passed. My father still lives and I think he will recover."

Inside the home, Nathan can hear a song of thanksgiving being sung outside and he opens his eyes.

"Stay still, my love," Peony tells him with tears of joy. "The Maker has granted us all more time with you. Don't be in a hurry to leave us. Just rest now."

CHAPTER 37
The Sudden Exit

"Like a beast bearing a great burden or a ship heavy-laden, stubbornness carries its own punishment.—*A proverb of His People.*

Many of the people who held the vigil are walking back home or heading off to work. Shaye is on her way home to change and feed Elle, then put her down for a nap. Only about a hundred people remain outside Nathan's home, talking amongst themselves when a man runs up the street and speaks to several people. In turn, they pass the word along, then start running down the hill toward the beach.

As more people show up on the beach, the entire strand fills with people staring out over the water. Ty and the others ran to the beach when they saw everyone else running, but they don't know why everyone has gathered here.

"What happened?" Ethan asks a fellow bystander.

The man next to him doesn't take his eyes off the ship in the distance while he says, "Benjamin and some of the others took it and left."

Someone on the other side of the man chimes in. "Isn't that the ship he was given as a gift?"

"Yes."

"Is that bad?" Ty asks.

The man looks at him, then nods as if he realizes why Ty doesn't get it. "He's not going fishing. He loaded up his wife and his goods—and some of those who follow him loaded up their wives and goods, if they had any . . . and they all *left*."

A woman points toward the dock. "And they disabled the two ships that were tied up there. The rest of the boats are in for repairs. No one will be able to follow him."

They all stare at the retreating speck of a ship on the horizon before the first man says, "Ren's not going to be happy about this. Not at all."

"Poor man. He's lost his daughter, one of his boats, *and* his ability to fish all at once," the woman chimes in. "When a man lets his son-in-law in on his business, he expects to keep his family together *and* get some profit in it. What a day this has been."

CHAPTER 38
The Question

Eight days later

Nathan has recovered well. He's still a little weak but getting stronger by the day. He complains about the near-constant surveillance of Peony, Willow and his daughter Jasmine, yet they know he doesn't hate all of the attention entirely.

This morning, there was another council meeting with Ty. Although Nathan wasn't in attendance, he was kept informed and agreed with their consensus. After the meeting, Ty spoke with Samuel and then he found Francis (Flint) to speak with him.

###

Late in the afternoon, Ty strolls up to Willow's house alone. He stops in front of one of the open windows, then places both his elbows on the sill before resting his chin on one of his hands.

"Good afternoon, ladies," he says.

Shaye's face lights up. "Good afternoon."

Jariel looks up from her task in the kitchen and greets him as well. "Oh Ty! Come in! Come in! We made supper for us and for Nathan's household early and I was just setting ours aside to heat up later. Do you want to eat with us?"

He walks around to the door and enters. "I do."

Since there are no other witnesses at the moment, she gives him a quick hug. Her focus, however, stays on the door. "Is . . . anyone else coming?"

Ty glances at Shaye, who pulls in her lips.

"Well, Basil, Ethan, and Garam agreed to help some of the men who catch fish off the dock in exchange for a meal of that fried fish. Is that who you're talking about?"

There's a hint of disappointment in her voice when she says, "I suppose so."

"Oh, and Samuel might come over later."

She smiles. "Thanks."

"Who are they with? Surely not Ren's people." Shaye asks.

"Uh, no. The man's wife is a cousin of Ren's wife, but he is a cousin to Samuel and he has a boat of his own."

"Micah?"

"Yes. That's his name."

Jariel laughs. "How well we are learning to play the cousin game."

"Ha! Basil keeps saying he'll make a Genon of me yet."

His sister's expression becomes serious again. "Any news on our return?"

He gives her one nod. "Soon. Two weeks."

Two weeks for her to say goodbye to Shaye, to Elle, to Willow . . . to homeplace. Two weeks to bid farewell to many dear friends. She'd breathed new life into Caleb's shop and taught much to his son, so when he got the news the old weaver wept and told her that he would miss her. And how will she part with Samuel? She told Shaye privately that the only way she can to bear the thought of leaving homeplace, is to believe that she will return someday.

Shaye stays put in Willow's comfy chair, allowing her friend a few moments with her brother. Soon enough, he approaches and briefly takes her hand while he steadily gazes into her eyes. "I'm sorry I didn't get to see you at lunch. How are you today? How is Elle?"

"She's sleeping—but I figure she'll be awake any minute."

He sits in the chair closest to hers and leans back before he says, "I suppose this is how you know when the village has become entirely saturated with excitement."

"How?" Shaye asks.

"Just look. All the shutters on your windows are open, and I'm here . . . and no one but Jariel is here to watch us."

His sister looks at them from the kitchen, then takes off her apron. "I'm going to my room for a while," she tells them as she exits.

Shaye's hand is now resting on the armrest, so he gently lifts it again, but this time, he holds on. "It's a perfect time to tell you again just how much I love you and Elle. You know, we've been officially courting for—what—more than a week now . . . and when you add it up with all the years we've known each other and all the years I've loved you . . . it seems like *forever* to me. So," he says, pulling a pink flower from his shirt pocket, "I want to ask you: Will you let me be your husband?"

Even her neck flushes with color before her eyes begin to glisten with tears.

He needs a better clue. "Is that a yes or a no?"

She squeezes his hand. "I love you with all my heart."

"So . . . that's a yes?"

"I just," she wipes the tears away. "I just don't know how I can go back to Aegea. How could I take a *baby* through that horrible jungle . . . to live in a place where I've known so much shame and sorrow?" She searches his eyes. "Despite Benjamin and a few others like him, this is the first time in my life I haven't felt like an orphan. I feel like I *belong* here."

"What if I told you that we could live here?"

She blinks. "Did you just say we could live here?"

"Yes. But it would be a pity if you *never* went to visit our plot of land and our house in Aegea—the place where we would live whenever we were visiting."

"What land? What house?"

"My father promised land—two acres actually—and a house, a barn, a goat, and *sooshi* hens to anyone who helped find you and Jariel. I fully intend to collect on that promise."

She's still just blinking at him.

"Oh, the house would be *grand* . . ." he tells her as he looks around Willow's home, "almost as big as this one. But I'm not sure you'd like the neighbors."

"What neighbors?"

"Basil . . . and the woman he's going to court and then ask to take vows with him when he gets back. They will have the place next to ours." He squints as he thinks. "I think you may know her. Her name is Joy."

He can see an excitement light up in her eyes. "Wait. *My Joy? My* cousin Joy? Basil is going to ask her to take vows?"

He lets out a fake sigh. "Yes. But you probably wouldn't want our children playing with their children anyway, right?"

She's just blinking again.

He leans toward her. "I'm not going anywhere. I plan to make a home *here*."

"You can't do that, can you? What would your father say? What would you *do* here? How would we live?"

Just hearing her say the word "we" makes his heart leap but he marshals all his patience and tells her, "Yes, I can do that. My father would tell you he's sorry for the things that happened to you. He's given me the task of being Aegea's first representative here. We will have to wait for the first trade items to begin arriving in order to provide for our needs—but the elders say I can find work here in the meantime. I will do whatever it takes. Then, in a year or two when Elle is older and they've established the safest route through the forest, perhaps we could travel back to Aegea to visit family. Wouldn't you like to see Mosha and Joy and your Aunt? Can you imagine how thrilled they would be to see you and Elle?" He can tell that she's caught up in the happy prospect of seeing her family, so he continues. "And isn't it proper that my parents would *eventually* get the opportunity to meet their first grandchild?"

The gleam in her eye disappears when he mentions his parents. He gazes at her for a moment before he adds. "My father was never unkind to you, was he? And all of this has softened his heart in a way that surprises even me. I believe he will do more than treat you with respect, and I know he will love Elle. I can't make promises concerning my mother. All of us want the opportunity to start fresh, though, don't we? Seeing our little girl *might* change her forever. Do we not owe the Maker for His mercy toward us? Didn't He give me a chance to apologize to you? Didn't He give us another chance to be together? If Mother decides to turn down the mercy offered to her, then she will miss us at her table and it will be her loss. Whatever happens, we have our own lives to live, and this village will be Elle's home, *our* home."

"This all sounds so . . . impossible."

He stands and pulls her up into his arms. "Impossible? I've been brought through I don't know how many impossibilites to get here, my love. I can speak this truth: *Nothing* is impossible for the Maker." He twirls the pink flower close to her face. "He brought both of us this far. Please, let's trust Him with our future. Take vows with me."

She takes the flower and he leans in to kiss her, but Elle starts to cry.

A door flies open and Jariel springs out, saying, *"I'll get her!"* as she sprints toward Shaye's room.

"*Hmmm.* Do you suppose she was listening?" Ty asks.

Shaye laughs. "I think she's learned more about 'shared life' in this village than merely eating the food."

Keeping his arms around her, he turns his head toward Shaye's bedroom door and speaks loudly. "So. Do *you* approve, Jariel?"

"Absolutely!"

He faces his love again, then pulls out the two wooden pins that hold up her hair before it tumbles down over her shoulders and her back. He leans in and rests his head on her shoulder for a moment before he inhales deeply. "Can I tell you now that you smell," he says with a delighted sigh, "wonderful?"

She can barely speak. "It's a mix of coconut and other oils."

His face moves up toward hers and he manages to mumble, "I could happily drown in your scent," before he kisses her.

Ivy from across the street and another old woman show up in the window just in time to catch sight of a passionate kiss and see the pink flower dropping out of Shaye's hand. The word is out in no time: *Shaye has agreed to take vows with Peppertop!*

That evening, Shaye, Ty, and Jariel take turns holding little Miss Elle so each one of them can eat their dinner while she is entertained. Once the meal is over, Shaye gives the baby her final cleanup of the day, then takes her to her room to nurse her and put her to bed.

When she emerges, from her room, Jariel and her brother are sitting in the little living room of the house. She no sooner joins them before Basil, Garam, and Ethan appear in the nearest window.

After greeting the women, Basil addresses Ty. "We have an opportunity. Micah's boat is fixed. He says he is taking a short ride on it to make sure all the repairs are good—just inside the bay here—and he invited us to go. Do you want to come?"

Ty's face brightens and looks at Shaye. "Do you want to try it?"

Her eyes widen. "Do all of you know that there are creatures out in the dark waters that could swallow a man whole? I've heard the fishermen talk of them."

"He's just going around in that little bay, not into the deep," Basil says. "Besides," he adds with a hint of a smile, "you're not a man, so you'd probably be safe."

Ty takes both her hands. "Come with us."

His sister chimes in, "I'll stay with Elle."

Shaye gives the apparent collusion a frown before Ty puts his face in her view. "*Come with us,*" he repeats in a playful tone.

"They have a vest you can wear to make you float," Basil tells her.

"Really?" Jariel can't help asking.

"Yes. Micah told us about it. It has this fiber from a tree in it that makes anyone who wears it float on the water—even if they don't swim. Of course, the men on the boats only wear them in a storm, but I'm sure you could wear one."

Ty leans in so his nose is touching Shaye's. "There's a full moon tonight—let's go and see what it looks like from the water." He can see she's weakening, so he adds, "Would you pass up an opportunity to steal a star for me?"

After another minute of cajoling, Shaye reluctantly agrees to go. When she gets to the boat, not only is the vest tied tightly about her, but both Ty and Basil promise never to leave her by herself for the entire cruise.

The transfer from a little boat to the bigger ship goes smoothly, but when the men haul up the sailboat's large, stone anchor, the vessel begins to drift and she starts feeling a little panicked.

Ty moves behind her and puts his arms around her waist, just below the vest. "You're okay. You'll be fine. I'm right here. In fact," he says looking at the man who's standing at the wheel of the ship, "can we sit back there on the roof over that little door there?"

The fellow nods.

Ty seats himself first, then lifts her up before he wraps his arms around her again and pulls her close. The boat is just slowly drifting and she's *almost* relaxed when the command is given to open some of the sails. As the cloth catches the wind, the vessel lurches forward and begins to list to one side while some of its wooden parts make creaking noises.

She sucks in a breath and closes her eyes for a moment.

"This is all normal." Micah tells his guests. "The wind fills the sails and pushes us along—and that makes the boat lean over. It's built to do that."

To the amazement of the passengers, the ship surges forward at a good speed—with no one paddling. Soon, the only sound they can hear is the prow slicing through the waves.

When Ty feels her relax in his arms, he leans close to her ear. "Better?"

She turns to look at him briefly. "Yes."

"Oh," he says when he looks to their right. "I could get to love this. Look. It's more beautiful than ever."

A giant moon is rising above the water with myriad stars winking all around and above it.

"You think you could grab one of those stars for me?" he whispers. "I'd keep it for the rest of my life as a reminder of this night."

Basil glances back at the couple to see if Shaye looks still looks terrified. He watches his friend say something to her before she smiles and reaches up toward the sky.

In less than an hour, the ship is ready to drop anchor.

Ty rests his chin on her shoulder. "I think this has been the best day of my whole life."

"For me, too," she answers.

"Traveler one to home base, this is traveler one to home base."

"This is home base."

Ty takes a deep breath. "Plans are taking shape now for Jariel's return. Everything should be set for a departure in two weeks."

"Are they sending people?"

"Yes. At least one representative, maybe more, and I hired a skilled hunter to make sure Jariel has added protection on the way back."

"Is he good?"

"He's the finest bowman they have. He knows this end of the forest well."

"This is all good news, son."

"And, tonight, all four of us and Shaye got to ride on an ocean ship that's powered by the wind. It was so amazing."

"By the wind?"

"Almost like a kite attached to the ship. It makes the boat just glide over the top of the water. Basil will have to tell Sage all about it."

"That does sound amazing."

He takes a deep breath before saying, "I saved the best for last. Shaye and I are taking vows next week."

"I wish I could be there. And I wish you great happiness, son."

CHAPTER 39
Red is the color

"White is the color of courtship—purity hoping to meet destiny.

Pink is for betrothal, the blush of anticipation.

Red is the color of marriage—for it is the color of love, conflict, passion, and the bond of blood you will share in your children—*From the Traditions of His People*.

Nathan and Peony stand facing Shaye and Ty. Behind the young couple nearly a hundred people have gathered on the beach at the dawn of a new day to witness the taking of the vows. Upon their heads, the bride and groom wear garlands woven with red flowers. Willow is in the front row of witnesses, holding Elle. Next to them are Jariel, Samuel, Basil, Ethan, and Garam.

The wind is calm, but the slow cadence of the surf along the sand lends a perceptible pulse of life to the gathering. Orange and yellow rays of a corona burst around clouds while the sun slowly lifts through the heavens—as if to add a "just so" over this day.

"How far can love travel?" Nathan asks. "In the beginning, in love's first garden, the man and woman were given to each other as a blessing. And so it is that we gather at the beginning of this new day, as a recognition of a sacred call to a union of love that has travelled from before time and will continue until time ceases to be measured. Remembrance of this call is part of the vows you take today for it's only when you recognize and stand in the love the Maker has for you that you can also fully love. So I will ask, do you both recognize the One who made all things, the One who made you?"

"I do."

"I do."

"Do you recognize that your Maker has worked, is now working, and will continue to work in you?"

"I do."

"I do."

"Do you declare that you will share your lives, your bodies, your possessions, the fruit of your works, your time, your fidelity—one with another—as a living picture of the Maker who gives all for the love of His own?"

"I do."

"I do."

Peony places a small flatbread and a cup on the rough wooden altar in front of Ty and Shaye. "Do you agree to share with one another the bread of life in abundance *and* humility?"

They answer together, "We do."

Ty takes the tiny loaf and breaks it before he gives her half. She feeds him the piece in her hand, he feeds her with the piece he's holding.

"Do you agree to share the cup which contains both joy and sorrow?"

"We do."

Shaye takes the cup and gives him a drink, he takes the cup and gives her a drink before they face Nathan, holding hands.

"Do you declare before our Maker and before His people that you will do this in mutuality—being one *for* the other— throughout your lives, through losses, and gains, as long as you still draw breath?"

"We do."

"Then it is witnessed by your Creator and your brothers and sisters gathered here, that you are husband and wife."

As the couple embraces, Basil and several others within the witnesses shout, "Just so!"

CHAPTER 40
Packing up a life

It seems appropriate to Jariel that the day begins with rain. Today is the day that she will part from everything that is precious to her. Early this morning, she had to say goodbye to Shaye—now her dear sister. To Elle—the first baby she ever held in her arms, her beautiful niece, knowing that even if she can return, she will miss so many milestones in the little girl's life.

"You will teach her the song about the bird and the mouse that Mosha taught us when we were little, won't you?" She asked Shaye. "I would so much like for all of us to sing it together the next time we see each other." Shaye agreed and they wept.

She said goodbye to her only brother.

"I feel like we are just now to the place in life when we could enjoy each other's company again," she told him.

"True. But we'll have the radios if they keep working, and next year, who knows?" He seemed to be lost in thought for a few moments before he added. "Listen. I know Mother can be . . . hard. And, now that you look like a woman, she'll redouble her efforts to make you into a cold and distant *thing* to be acquired in the never-ending game of Aegea. Don't let her wear you down." He hugged her. "Show her what warmth and *real* beauty are."

She said goodbye to Nathan—who saved her life, rescued her from the forest, and lovingly guided her throughout her days at homeplace. Will she ever see him again?

She bid farewell to friends—something she never knew in Aegea.

Goodbye to the beach and to the village where she wandered daily in her bare feet.

Lastly, she must part from Samuel, who might be the first person who actually recognized her sacred self. She's not sure when she came to love him so much. Her feelings for him—a man she might never have noticed in Aegea—rose slowly, like a sunrise that got brighter until it was full day.

She told Shaye, "Now I know some of the terrible heartache you must have felt as we were led away through the forest. Every mile you walked was a mile farther from the one you loved. Every day, the distance between you and Ty was greater, and there was no knowing that you'd see him again. This is how I will feel about leaving Sam."

Although she has the hope of seeing him again, that day isn't a certainty. For now, he will remain in homeplace. Given all the events and upheavals in recent weeks, the village needs as much stability as possible. If Ben and the others who left with him should return, the people here need voices, young and old, that speak wisdom.

Last night, she sat with him on the shore of the great ocean. She took deep breaths of the salt air while she sifted the warm sand through her fingers and dug her toes into it, knowing it would be a long time, if ever, before she might do any of this again. She suddenly had an idea and grabbed two handfuls of sand and emptied them into her pocket.

Sam gave her a puzzled grin. "What are you doing?"

"I will put all this in a pouch at home so I can show people what sand is like. I already have a collection of shells."

He waited till he had her attention again before he said, "I must tell you something and ask you something, and I want you to speak truly to me," he said.

Her heart rate sped up. "I will."

"I love you, Jariel, are your feelings for me the same?"

She studied his slender face and peered into his warm brown eyes—wanting to commit them, his voice, and his words to memory. "Yes. I love you."

"Tomorrow I will let you leave me," he said, "but my deepest hope is that you will come back, or that next year you will beckon me to come to you." He draws the crude outline of a house in the sand, then places her hand in the center of it and covers it with his own hand. "Were it not for the open path that now lies between here and Aegea, I would ask something else of you."

She wanted to hear him to say it. "What else would you ask me?"

"I would offer to take vows with you."

"You could ask me right now. I would say yes."

He closed his eyes for a moment. "Although this delights me, the timing is not right, and you have unfinished matters in Aegea. You must let your parents see you and tell the people in Aegea how you came to live among the Exiles. I have things to accomplish here as well, but I'll complete the first part of my apprenticeship under Nathan within the year."

"I don't care about Aegea anymore. I'd rather be here."

He nodded. "I would rather you were here as well. But those unsettled matters would remain between us. Your brother came all this way, well aware of all the sacrifices and risks—willing to lose all that Aegean's hold dear. He was as prepared as one can be for whatever might lie ahead with Shaye. When you came here, the whole of Aegea was shut to you. You never thought you'd see it or your family again. But now, all of it stands open to you and a prosperous life there is possible for you."

"The existence I had there was empty of companionship, of fellowship . . . of joy. I want to be with you."

He grins as he brushes his hand over the side of her face. "The people of Aegea didn't see in you the woman who first captured my heart, that day when she beheld the marvel of the humming birds among the flowers. The woman I saw then is the woman you are now. You aren't a starving stray we found on the forest floor, you are full of life and beauty that shines through to every part of you now. Everyone who knew you before should see the woman you've become and know what the Maker has done for you. Like Nathan and the soldier Garam I have come to realize that we all need to be certain of *whose* we are no matter *where* we are. The beauty of our faith wasn't intended to be hidden away or hoarded. So it's with sorrow—but also with hope—I will watch you leave. Go home and show yourself to them. See what the Maker might do with that. Truly consider what is there for you—what you might stand to lose if we took vows. If that joyous day comes for us, I want it to be with no blindness, no regret."

"Aegea is changing already."

"Yes. As can homeplace. But our life together cannot be predicated on changing other people's hearts. Go back. Give yourself time to weigh it all. Then, if you come back to me or call me to you . . . I can ask and you can answer from a full heart."

After their time on the beach, he slowly walked her home. Once they arrived at the house, they had a last meal together with Willow, Ty, and Shaye.

Later that night, she said her private goodbyes to Willow—a woman who had showered her with a mother's love and care. After she gave her a shawl she'd made, there was a secret to share with the old woman.

"In a year, either I will try to return here, or Samuel will try to come to me. And then, the event you've predicted might take place."

"Then this will be my comfort and my hope, dear one."

Now, she's standing just feet away from the boat that will bear her away from nearly everyone dear to her. Six extra men from the village will help to row her, and her fellow travelers upstream, past the big bend in the river to the spot where she and Shaye first saw the river and boats—what seems like a lifetime ago.

All the men mill around while she says her final goodbyes to Sam. Her eyes well up.

His anguish is obvious. "Please don't cry. I don't think I can bear it."

She quickly wipes her eyes. "Then I won't."

He steps closer, so there is no more space between them. "Remember what I said to you."

She lifts her face to his. "You remember what I said as well."

He pushes the hair off her shoulders and gently slides his hands behind her neck before he pulls her in for a kiss.

Embarrassed by such a show of affection in public, some of the men who know Sam either laugh or make smooching noises. When the kiss lasts longer than a few seconds, most of them look away or resume loading the boats. Garam, Ethan, and two of the oarsmen step into the first boat.

Basil, a pair of oarsmen, and the two men who will represent Homeplace in Aegea step into the second boat. He and Ty said their goodbyes in the village, early this morning.

> Both men placed their hands on each other's shoulders.
>
> "Stay away from falling trees, brother," Ty told him.
>
> "Don't let Shaye make you fat with all of her food."
>
> "Invite us when you plan to take vows. We may not make it there, but maybe we can send gifts."
>
> They embraced briefly, before Basil started walking up the shortway to the river.

Now, he stows his packs and takes a seat in the boat, facing away from Jariel's affectionate farewell to Sam.

Before Sam lets go of Jariel, he whispers in her ear. "May the Maker watch over you every day. Part of my heart will be travelling with you."

She can't speak or she'll burst into tears, so she just nods. She turns toward the boat and two men take her hands so she can step into it. Once she's in, she steps over one seat then sits on the next one, facing the stern so she can watch what she's leaving behind. She puts on one of the hats that Sage Dooley made for the men who journeyed here and pulls down the veil, grateful for a little privacy.

Flint is the last one into Jariel's boat and he steps around everyone till he gets to the seat in the bow. He set's down his gear, then turns to face the stern before seating himself.

"You keep her safe," Samuel says to him.

He nods and waves. After a push away from the shore, the oars go into the water and the men start singing a song with a rhythm that keeps them all on the same pace. Through her tears, Jariel fixes her vision on Sam until he is just a dot above the surface of the river and then cannot be seen at all.

Three days from now, when Asher radios to say that Jariel is upriver, General Jubal McClaren will tell his wife he's sending a contingent of troops and hunters down into the forest. Then he'll tell her that her daughter is alive and returning to Aegea. After that will follow the revelations about her son and his wife . . . and a granddaughter. In several weeks, all of Aegea will know.

CHAPTER 41
On the Roof

"**W**hat is faith? Our forefathers believed they could soar above the sky in complete safety. Were they fools? Faith is choosing to trust the One who sees the beginning and the end of the journey."—*A saying of Kya, a Firstlander*

In homeplace, three months later

It's their first night in their new home. With the help of others, Ty and Shaye worked evenings and every spare moment to repair and upgrade the tiny house at the edge of the village. It's smaller than Willow's home, but like hers, it has two bedrooms, a bathroom, and a small common area with a kitchen, dining room, and sitting room all combined. It has one difference from the other homes in the village, however. Accessible only via a ladder the inside of the home, a small porch extends out from the roof on one the side of the home. Under this porch is shade from the midday sun and above it is a view of the entire sky.

As is tradition, the people of homeplace brought gifts of food and household goods to the newlyweds and they spent the afternoon putting most of it away.

The day is over, the evening meal is done, the lights are out, and now there is a little time to relax on their rooftop porch—something that will become an evening ritual unless there is rain. Ty places a large pillow on the floor, against a railing and leans back on it. Shaye leans back on Ty, and Elle is in her mother's arms as they all listen to tree frogs and the distant sound of the surf.

Ty wraps his arms around Shaye and takes hold of Elle's hand before he says, "I hope I will never forget how full my heart is tonight."

His wife turns and lifts her face to his to give him a kiss. "Same for me."

Leaning over his wife's shoulder, he can see his daughter's bright eyes in the dim light and he speaks to her in a gentle voice, "Have I told you yet that I used to call your mommy 'Stargazer Shaye'? She didn't laugh as much as you do," he says, playfully wiggling a finger on the baby's tummy. Elle gives one short giggle and pushes his hand away before he continues. "She was of a more serious nature." He points at the open sky. "But she did love to look out at the stars at night, just like we are right now. I used to think she could pluck one of them out of the sky and put it in her pocket. Perhaps, one night, she will show us how."

The End
Book 3 of the *Scions of the Aegean C*

EPILOG

"The Maker has continued to connect our people since He first set us on this planet. We cannot seem to truly escape each other. Although each can survive without the other, the lives of those separated are incomplete outside of the whole. We should all remember whose we are . . . and always long for the fellowship that abides in the whole."—*Nathan, after he blessed Jariel and all the travelers going back to Aegea.*

Aegea

After her first journey back to Aegea, filled with faith and sweet memories of fellowship in homeplace, Jariel was reunited with her parents. She would sit before an official inquiry and give testimony that would be part of the permanent record of Aegea. Within six months of her arrival, she would help Sage Dooley's wife, Tessa, establish the first formal school system for all children on the plateau.

Basil, Garam, Ethan, and the young woman Chessie all took up the offer of land promised by Jubal McClaren. Basil courted and took vows with Shaye's cousin, Joy.

Garam "Shocky" Manash was the first Genon to become an officer in the military. Others would follow in his wake, but he would forever remain in the people's minds as unique.

The Exiles' first representatives to Aegea would establish communication between the government of Aegea and homeplace and reconnect the broken network of Genon families in the two places.

The Great Forest

Francis (Flint) the hunter traveled with Jariel and the others on her return to Aegea was reunited with his brother, Canaan.

Canaan never climbed the road back up into Aegea. He spent the rest of his life in the Great Forest with his brother Francis and their brother Seth. They established the first outpost for travelers along the trade route established between Aegea and homeplace.

A second outpost was built and managed by the hunter/gatherer Asher and his family.

Homeplace

Benjamin, and some of those who sailed away from homeplace wouldn't be seen again for six months. Their return brought both reconciliation and hardship to the people of homeplace.

Nathan the elder lived another three years but never again traveled through the Great Forest.

Willow lived on for more than a decade, enjoying shared life with many adopted daughters, sons, and grandchildren.

Samuel stayed in homeplace for a year and then became the representative of his people in Aegea for another year before he returned home.

As for Shaye and Ty—their story and those of their children and grandchildren would be recorded in the Histories of the Aegeans and of the Exiles. Their union would mark the beginning of an era of enlightenment and innovation for *all* the scions of the *Aegean C.*

If you have enjoyed this book/series, kindly take the time to post a review online.

A note from the author

I began Book 1 in this series with a note to readers and, although I intend to continue the series in the future, I thought I'd restate my purpose here.

While the ultimate theme of the series is unashamedly from God's redemptive perspective, I wanted to shine a light on the role our relationships play in shaping both our mental and spiritual lives.

It's my hope that no matter who you are, no matter how old you are, and no matter what you've done thus far in your life, God says you are *worth* redeeming and he is right there with you even as you are reading these words, wanting you to turn to him and receive a life-transforming relationship with him. If you do so, you can walk in the freedom Jesus Christ has *already* purchased for you.

You need to know that a walk with God isn't just an inward "spiritual" thing, it's something that should bring about an *observable* transformation in your life. The change in you can be greatly enriched by a growing connection to others who know Jesus, who will support, encourage, and exhort you in faith—in shared life.

In Him,

Terry L. Craig

"For this is how God loved the world: He gave his one and only Son, so that everyone who believes in him will not perish but have eternal life. God sent his Son into the world not to judge the world, but to save the world through him."—Jesus Christ, John 3:16-17—NLT

Peter's words pierced their hearts, and they said to him and to the other apostles, "Brothers, what should we do?"
Peter replied, "Each of you must repent of your sins and turn to God, and be baptized in the name of Jesus Christ for the forgiveness of your sins. Then you will receive the gift of the Holy Spirit. This promise is to you, to your children, and to those far away—all who have been called by the Lord our God."—Acts 2:37-39—NLT

By his death, Jesus opened a new and life-giving way through the curtain into the Most Holy Place. And since we have a great High Priest who rules over God's house, let us go right into the presence of God with sincere hearts fully trusting him. For our guilty consciences have been sprinkled with Christ's blood to make us clean, and our bodies have been washed with pure water. Let us hold tightly without wavering to the hope we affirm, for God can be trusted to keep his promise. Let us think of ways to motivate one another to acts of love and good works. And let us not neglect our meeting together, as some people do, but encourage one another, especially now that the day of his return is drawing near.—Hebrews 10:20-25—NLT

About the Author
Terry L. Craig

Born in the Southwest, Terry has lived all over the US and spent many years living in the Caribbean. She is a people-watcher and a comparative thinker who is fascinated with words, art, and ideas. She has a passion to share spiritual life in a way that allows the reader to weigh the values of different ideologies from a non-threatening perspective.

Terry is a follower of Jesus, a wife, mom, and grandma who currently resides in North Carolina with her retired professional pilot husband (her lifetime love) Bill. The development of true friendships and healthy community life are high on her list of life's essentials.

You can learn more about/connect with Terry L. Craig at:

www.terrylcraig.com

Or, you can check out her author pages at:

Wild Flower Press, Inc. (**www.wildflowerpress.biz),**
Amazon.com
Smashwords.com
Terry L. Craig on Facebook

Other Books by Terry L. Craig

- *Scions of the Aegean C Descent into the Wilds,* Book 1 of this series

- *Through the Land of Cloud & Leaf,* Book 2 of this series

- Apocalyptic Scifi novels, *The Fellowship of the Mystery* trilogy,
    1. *GATEKEEPER*
    2. *SOJOURNER*
    3. *SWORDSMAN*

- An Apologetic study on Universalism entitled, *What Mama Never Told You about the Afterlife*

All of Terry's books are available as paperbacks and/or eBooks through Amazon.com, Smashwords, Apple iStore, Barnes & Noble and many fine retailers.

Check in at Wild Flower Press, Inc.
https://www.wildflowerpress.biz
Or, at Terry's website at https://terrylcraig.com for updates on future projects.

Other Books Published by Wild Flower Press, Inc.

Fiction

- The *Within the Walls* trilogy by Stephanie Bennett is a series of futuristic novels chronicling the life of Emilya, a virtual travel agent in 2070.

  1. *Within the Walls,*
  2. *Breaking the Silence*
  3. *The Poet's Treasure*

- The *Fellowship of the Mystery* trilogy by Terry L. Craig is apocalyptic fiction from an uncommon perspective.

  1. *GATEKEEPER*
  2. *SOJOURNER*
  3. *SWORDSMAN*

- *Scions of the Aegean C, Descent into the Wilds* by Terry L. Craig is Book 1 in the *Scions of the Aegean C* series.

- *Through the Land of Cloud & Leaf*, Book 2 in the Scions of the Aegean C series.

Non Fiction

- *Passport for the Journey, 21 Day Challenge* by Tonya J. Brown is a Devotional / Journal for use by individuals or groups.

- *What Mama Never Told You about the Afterlife,* by Terry L. Craig is a discussion of the differences between the teachings of Jesus and Universalism on the topics of faith, salvation, discipleship, heaven, and hell.

All of our books are available as paperbacks and as eBooks through fine booksellers globally.

www.wildflowerpress.biz

www.ingramcontent.com/pod-product-compliance
Lightning Source LLC
Chambersburg PA
CBHW051525260626
47170CB00003B/781